DIARY
OF
KNIVES
A KNIVES OF ENGEN NOVEL

MATTHEW DANIELS

Published in Canada by Engen Books, St. John's, NL.

Library and Archives Canada Cataloguing in Publication

Title: Diary of knives / Matthew Daniels.
Names: Daniels, Matthew, 1984- author.
Identifiers: Canadiana (print) 20210126949 | Canadiana (ebook) 20210127279 |
ISBN 9781774780206
   (softcover) | ISBN 9781774780213 (PDF)
Classification: LCC PS8607.A55685 D53 2021 | DDC C813/.6—dc23

Distributed by:
Engen Books
www.engenbooks.com
submissions@engenbooks.com

First mass market paperback printing: February 2021

Cover Image: Ellen Curtis

DIARY
OF
KNIVES

A KNIVES OF ENGEN NOVEL

MATTHEW DANIELS

ENGEN
BOOKS

To all those who are struggling
to cut their way through.

`

PROLOGUE

Aboard the *Huginn*, International Waters

"Do you even use the machines?"

Jacinta was well into her fourth incision. Silas, the one who spoke, was not really looking for the answers to the questions he was asking. He imagined this whole process – the surgical auditorium, the surgical team, the subjects, the students (for lack of a better word), the researchers, the scientists, the operatives and Section Heads, all of it – to be like ancient Greek theatre. There were performances, lessons, rhetoric, and dialogue. A sense of community. Allegory, in a manner of speaking. Silas was asking his questions for the benefit of both the live audience and the recordings.

Everything was recorded. Not only the obvious data, like which anatomization room (AR) was used, which staff were participating, and what were the subject's physical and mental states, but anything else the researchers might need for posterity: who attended in the gallery; shipboard time; people of note who were absent; weather and other conditions outside the facility; location at sea to a thou-

sandth of a second; subjects before and after this procedure; what other work everyone in the AR had done that
day; equipment used; and so on.

"I use everything," Jacinta eventually replied. "Note
the bone responses in the left ulna, right radius, ribs, and
tibia." A myriad of cameras had been set up at a wide
variety of angles. She pointed as she spoke. "When one
works at a calibre such as my own, and indeed at the scale
we seek here," she continued, waving her scalpel about
to take in everyone present, "one must be sufficiently
adept so as to proceed without halting to consult every
measure. Imagine writing a journal entry in which you
stop to consult a dictionary for the spelling of every word.
That would do more than slow you. You wouldn't follow
through on a mood, you would miss big-picture elements,
and you might even make mistakes in your grammar.
Forests and trees. Pay particular attention to the thermal
scanners while I explore the nerve clusters surrounding
the left infraspinatus."

Many of the audience blinked or sat straighter as Jacinta hopped between musing aloud, holding conversation, and directing her team. "Noted," Silas said, the moment she'd finished speaking. He was grinning behind his
mask. He knew she'd know that, most likely from the tone
of his voice. But he wondered about the things she could
know. And how she knew them.

Jacinta was an event in herself. In the years he'd
worked with her on Engen's ship-borne labs, Silas had
found that getting to know her wasn't about watching her
grow. Most people, as you got to know them, developed
as you watched. You saw them cut people or things out

of their lives. Dating, shifts in friendships or marriages, having children, the empty nest, education, changing jobs. Ambitions, goals, book clubs, sweaters. Yet Silas was starting to wonder if Jacinta had a kinship with the subjects of the *Huginn*.

Learning about Jacinta was an exercise in cross-sections.

"Why Baroque?" Silas asked suddenly. While the surgeon kept her gaze on her work, he could afford the odd glance, and he saw the ripple and sparkle of attention in the audience. While there were some muffled whines or muzzle-snuffed screams from the subject, most of the sound in the AR proper had two sources: the life supports, vital surveillance, and surgical implements on the one hand; and music from the speakers on the other. It was low volume. Background: intended to encourage concentration and creativity. In contrast to the majority of the people working in both Sections of the operation, Jacinta's music always came from a record player.

Knowing that there was a needle carving a path was important to her.

"While I love the ideology of the Renaissance," Jacinta answered, laying a hand on the patient at the edge of her incision as she explored, "I do not pursue world change just for the upheaval. I want what's built after. They carved stone more than anything else in those days, but you can learn many things from where the surface splits. From the blade and where it parts things." Her tone wandered from a clinical answer to a slower, more hushed distraction.

They were listening to *Tonos Humanos*, a collection of secular classical work composed by the Spaniard José

Marín in the late 17th century. Some of his history had sparked Jacinta's interest as well, but she left the discussion at the Baroque.

Silas glanced at whispers, furious notes, and gleaming gazes. "You're never really talking about what you're talking about, are you?"

Most of the others in the Section felt they had two missions: fulfilling their role and learning from Jacinta. They never used honorifics, nicknames, or other such things. The only other person named Jacinta used her middle name because the Sections reserved that name, set aside like a social monolith.

The surgeon rolled her eyes. "I'm proud of what I've accomplished, and of what I'm continuing to do with my life," she said. Silas got the impression she wasn't talking to him. "But what we're doing is far more important than status." It was her teaching tone of voice: imperious, but oddly coaxing. Like a monarch nudging his most promising general into an unprecedented battle. "This subject is not an individual, but an organ in a bigger system. We don't get uncomfortable cutting out bad organs for transplant, or studying the tissues. We work toward greater healing, something bigger and more alive."

"I'll take that as a no."

By now, Jacinta had completed the preliminary stages. This would be a lengthy, elaborate exploratory procedure. With proper equipment and such an exemplary team, the subject should be sustained for many hours. He may even survive, which would have value for future studies. But it wasn't necessary.

As she delved further, both into tissues and into her

ideas and the vast network of knowledge she was bringing to bear, she found that her surroundings became like the music. It was present, and she'd notice it if she really concentrated, but doing so would derail her work. Even her own commands were background: "Prepare ultrasound implants. Here. Here. Here."

Others said things that she automatically acknowledged but which were instantly melded into her mind map of the whole process. In a way, she'd cut herself out of the room. All of this blended with a thought experiment she'd been playing in the back of her mind for a long time, though often in a blurred way. It had needed years to percolate as she played with the world and tried to make it blink.

Even with a shallow, straight cut. Even without a scar, and no need for stitches. Even with nothing removed. Once you've parted the surface, you've cut something away. None of the removal was the point, however; what mattered to her was how this changed what remained. A chunk of wood carved away loses weight, size, strength, and any trace of ever having been a tree. Nevertheless, all that cutting away turned it into a wheel, an ornament, a weapon, furniture, pieces of houses, or bridges.

What could you fashion by cutting away bits of the world? Life? Society? A person?

Yourself?

This was what she called the Diary of Knives.

"Machina deus est," she said.

CHAPTER 01
THE EXECUTION OF EVERYDAY THINGS

Mill Bay Beach Park, Kodiak, Alaska

The ocean wrote its shadows on the beach. Feet cut their play into it. Laughter and the songs of sunlight strayed from the scripts of calendars and pay stubs.

A volleyball filled Iseult's face.

"I'm not even playing!" she huffed as she picked herself up.

"Oh, have some fun!" Nick chided. "The world is our oyster!"

"What if I don't like oysters?" demanded Iseult as she gathered herself up. She was the only one not exposing her legs. Nick wore shorts. Kelly had a two-piece bathing suit and Tash, the group's de facto mother, wore a one-piece, a towel, sunblock, and sunglasses.

"You love oysters!" Kelly declared, grabbing up two fistfuls of sand and whipping them upwards while spreading out her arms. The result was an (attempted) arc of sprayed earth, like the human answer to fairy dust.

"You're not the boss of me!" Iseult did her best to deliver the childish line with bravado, but then dropped the volleyball in order to kick it at Nick.

"That's not h-" started Nick.

A child swept between them, grabbing the ball in a running bear hug and continuing, without losing stride, to go beyond their unmarked boundaries.

As Iseult and Nick stood blinking, Kelly called out a half-laughing, "Hey!" and was the first to give chase. The other two followed suit, with Tash calling out, "Go, little guy! You got this!"

"Traitor!" called Nick and Kelly at once.

Shaking her head and chuckling, wondering how the others managed to sweep her up in this, Iseult began gaining ground on Kelly. Neither of the three were running full tilt; the child couldn't have been a day past seven years old. Iseult called out, "Quack! Quack! Quack!"

"NOT THE DUCKS!" cried the child, swinging the ball side-to-side to keep his balance with each stride.

A pair of adults with a picnic setup called out the child's name, but the trio didn't relent in their mock chase. Slowing with fatigue, the little one suddenly turned and called out, "Parley!"

Unable to resist, the trio all stopped and doubled over with laughter. "That's not…" Nick got out.

"…not what that…" Kelly added.

"…means!" Iseult finished.

"Three to one! Not fair!" said the kid, holding the ball. His father stood with hands on hips while the mother, smiling, just shook her head. Tash, a grin on her face, returned to her book.

Nick turned to the ladies. "I guess we'll need a spokesperson to parley." He began to step forward.

Swiftly, Iseult inserted herself at the fore. "I'm Captain…" she thought for a moment, reflecting on something she used to enjoy when she was the boy's age. "…Innkey! Of the *Pierian Spring*," she declared proudly. "And I won't stand for your pirate ways!"

The child drew himself up. "Respect, Cap'n Inky! I'm General Wallop from the Starship…" here he touched his lip, awkwardly adjusting the ball. "…*Spongepants*!"

Nick went red, struggling not to laugh at the child. Kelly put on a serious face with better success. Tash looked up at Iseult when she heard the reference to the Pierian Spring. She felt obscurely proud. The parents caught her gaze and they exchanged smiles.

"Well, General," Iseult strove for straight-faced diplomacy, "I must ask why you've secured our property upon the…" her lips wrestled "…*Spongepants*."

"Volleyballs are for everyone!" the child proudly declared.

As they watched this exchange, Nick and Kelly stole glances at each other. Both resisted the temptation to speak out of turn. After all, their captain was parleying. Nick registered that a crowd far to his left, some distance past a cluster of splashing rocks, included seven children moving in an ungainly way. They held their arms straight in front of them, wrists limply suspended, and slowly chased one youngster wielding a foam bat and a toy gun that fired little hollow balls.

"We're vacationing in these waters," Iseult replied, "and we brought that ball for our adventure. You wouldn't want to interrupt our adventure?"

"Can I be a pirate?" asked the boy.

"You must be," she reasoned, "because why else would you take the ball? But you said you're a general, and they don't take things."

"They do if it's for everyone! It's a pirate's honour!" This "General Wallop" stood so proudly that Nick burst out laughing at the sheer brazen confidence.

"To the brig with you!" Iseult commanded with a half-smile. "This is parley!"

Doing his best to look dejected, Nick obediently walked down to the water's edge and promptly sat on the moist sand. With each lap of Alaskan sea water, he gasped. "How do people swim in this?" he murmured under the sounds of surfers and swimmers behind him. He faced the other youths and did his best to only watch Kelly. Out of the corner of his eye he could still clearly make out the eight children playing at a zombie chase.

Kelly looked over her shoulder at Tash, who was frowning and consulting a notebook. *I'll have to call her out on that. We're not the only ones who need a break.*

When Nick accepted his punishment, Iseult had immediately turned her attention on the interloper. She hadn't yet noticed the eight. "Are you a general turned pirate, then?"

"Yes'm!" he said, and thumped his chest with a closed fist in the fashion of centurions. He was playing fast and loose with all manner of historical or fictional references. "I became a pirate to save Ruby Gloom!"

"That's…" Iseult's voice shivered with suppressed humour "…that's just so admiral of you! I mean, admirable," and she broke down giggling. "I'm sorry," she said as she recovered herself.

The child also laughed. "It's okay! Even people with big ships make mistakes!"

Kelly noticed something about Nick, even from the fifteen feet or so to the shore, that tugged on her. He put on a brave face, and looked like he was watching them, but she knew. She knew when he wasn't blinking quite often enough, or that little difference in tension between one side of the face and the other. He was looking at (or thinking about) something specific. Her thoughts about this distracted her from the conversation.

"Well?" Iseult demanded. "Lieutenant Kelly?" *I need this. I hope his parents are nice.*

"Hm?" she looked at Iseult blankly.

"Here!" the little one said suddenly as he threw the ball to her. She caught it, blinking her eyes and tucking in her chin.

"Whoa!" Kelly said.

Iseult put her hands on her hips and pretended to be offended. "General Wallop!" she declared.

"It's for everyone!" he said, as though this were the most obvious thing in the world. Then: "She could use it. Wanna help me find pirate treasure?"

"All right," the boy's mother called. "Let the nice people be, now."

"Oh, it's okay! We were just having fun," Iseult said with a friendly wave.

"Your friend all right?" the father asked, arms folded and lifting his chin in Nick's direction.

The two girls turned his way and saw that he'd shifted. His expression was a rictus of silence. Kelly and Iseult looked at each other with a frown and started walking toward him, looking in the direction of his attention.

A girl with a Russian accent was running from the other seven. She'd most likely been talking already, but this was the first time anyone in the trio heard her words. "Down with ze undead!" she cried, shooting a boy in the leg with a toy ball. He fell to the sand and started crawling at her, making exaggerated groans and calls for brains.

Nick sat. He watched the children and did not feel the surf on his behind. He heard no waves, no birds. The scents that dove into his waking moments came not from the beach but from a house in Atlanta. Even as the Russian girl fired her gun, he heard glass shattering. Red stenches filled his nostrils and wooden songs of people fighting in a house shattered his-

"Nicolas!"

It was like the lifting of the stomach as a person slips at the top of a flight of stairs. Held in the desperate gravity of a hard moment, he needed a second to be himself again. His contacts were steel grey today. They were focused on Tash, who stood in front of him. She still held her pen. Kelly's hands ran through his hair. He forced a smile. "Mill Bay Beach Park," he said.

"Sometimes it tastes bitter," Iseult said.

Everyone looked at her.

"The beach?" Nick's quip was pale.

Iseult stuck out her tongue. "Medicine, dork."

Tash knelt in front of Nick. Iseult dug her nails into her palms. Every time she spoke up, it seemed she was doing something awkward or telling jokes that didn't translate. But these people made her want to try, anyway. She watched them try to help Nick. If she knew exactly how he felt, why couldn't she help him?

"Ah, c'mon!" He started. As he shuffled his legs to stand, Tash pressed him down with a hand on the shoulder. "You're embarrassing me in front of the war hero!"

"Am I a war hero?" Kelly asked.

Nick blushed. "Well, yes, but…that is, I meant…" and he pointed a helpless finger at the children. Even as he glanced at the kids going off in another direction, a defeated "zombie" tearing open a packet of mini-cookies, the parents of the youths were lounging in Nick's peripheral vision, oblivious to the women and their sitting friend.

"I told you before about the eyes," Tash admonished. "Pick a colour."

"I did!"

"I mean the same one."

"They're both grey!"

Tash sighed and stepped away. "Maybe we should go home…"

"No!" Iseult protested.

They all looked at her again.

She stood her ground. "We've already done therapy. We said we'd try a vacation. Take it easy. Step back. No pressure. No remembering."

"I'm fine," Nick began.

Iseult pressed on: "None of us are fine. That's why we came to a place that's four places." Tash furrowed her brow and opened her mouth, but Iseult continued: "A mill, a bay, a beach, and a park. We're now at the beach called Mill Bay Beach Park," and now she attempted a grin. "But I don't think we actually need to go to a mill." Iseult usually felt like the adult, but when her jokes fell flat, she was suddenly the most teenaged of the teenagers under Tash's care.

Kelly helped Nick stand. "So you're saying walk it off?"

The twinge was brief, and she thought it should have been anger. It was sadness. Iseult breathed out of her nose. "Well, sort of. We knew this sort of stuff would happen. You all heard me talking in my sleep, or so you said this morning."

"What do you think?" Tash asked Kelly.

"I think we should just swim right now," Kelly replied after a moment of tapping her chin. "We can talk and unpack and study and stuff when we get back to the hotel."

"I'm game," Iseult said. She was their best swimmer.

"I'm sure you are, dear," Tash said. She did her best to suppress a smile.

Even as Iseult blinked, Nick and Kelly set about carrying her to the shoreline. "I have extra lives!" she declared and tried to get out of Kelly's grip. Nick had her legs and wasn't going to lose to her. Not like this. "I'll respawn! I'll…I'll CAMP!" but by this point she'd found her way into the air.

Then came the water.

Nick and Kelly high-fived, then Nick whumped under the water. Tash and Kelly started laughing. "I'll be your knight in shining armour!" Kelly declared. "I'll save y-" she slid backwards as her feet were pulled out from under her. She recognized Iseult's grip.

Iseult popped up. "Naaataaashaaa! It's two against-"

The sound of a blast, if you're at the right distance, grows in the ears and the bones like a kind of mould. You think it's coming from inside you. At the very least, it covers the surfaces of things. Water ripples, glass clinks, even the teeth can hum. You feel it, you see the evidence of it. Only then do you hear it.

Nick and Kelly re-emerged even as Iseult was looking around. "What was-" Kelly started.

Tash was already on her phone.

All activity on the beach had ceased as everyone turned about, looking for the source of the blast. The child claiming to be Captain Wallop called out, "There!"

Kelly, Iseult, and Nick were marching toward Tash as best they could in the water. It was colder than they'd all expected, but no one wanted to admit to it. Even in spring, it was the kind of cold that tensed muscles to the point that moving was a blocky and wooden experience. Everything seemed sharper, even the shuddering of the earth and sky as the blast reached the vacationers.

"What's goi-" Nick started, but Iseult and Kelly each put a hand on his shoulder. Kelly scanned the youths to be sure they were okay. Iseult's attention was on Kelly and Nick. South, past all the hilly mounds of rock and shrubbery, smoke rose from down the road they'd taken to get to the beach.

Tash put a hand over her mouth as she continued talking. "...don't be. You couldn't have known. I'll be there soon. Thanks for telling me personally. Yes, thank you. You too. Good luck!"

She hung up, continued to stare at the rising torrent of smoke, and took a breath to gather herself.

"I thought this was a private trip?" asked Iseult.

Tash blinked. "Hm? Oh! It is. My contacts told me

Alaska was all clear. Until I just called them, wondering what was going on."

"Cops," Nick said. Before anyone could say anything, he added: "Fire department. Paramedics. Hell, they probably have neighbo-"

"It was Providence," Tash interjected. When Kelly raised a brow, she clarified: "The Kodiak Island hospital." Her mouth was a firm line. "And you know I'm no amateur, young man."

"Sorry," he said, feeling a little lame.

Iseult frowned. "Should you be? I mean, why not emergency services?"

"I chose this place because I had it scouted," Tash repeated. "You wanted to be far away from Gavin, didn't you?" Kelly shuddered. Tash gave her a look like chocolate still warm from the hand. "I know, sweetie, but you need to at least hear his name without getting wigged out."

"Who were you talking to?" Kelly asked.

"Make-up," she replied.

"Huh?" Nick said.

Iseult caught on: "Less is more."

"You don't wear make-up," Nick said.

"Glad to see you still have that talent for observation," Iseult said dryly.

"Why are you letting us banter?" Kelly asked.

"Because I'm thinking about what we should do. Get your things," Tash said as she folded her portable chair and collected her notes and her book.

They continued to talk as they obliged. "How will I know more by not knowing who you were talking to?"

asked Nick.

"You'll catch on," Iseult said when Tash didn't reply. Then: "So, let's hear it."

Silence. They reached the car, loaded up, and were in even as Nick said, "Let's hear it, Mom."

Tash looked at Nick through the rearview mirror, a smile poking through even as she wrestled with getting them involved. This was a vacation, they might get mixed up in something now, and Nick just called her Mom. He probably meant nothing by it. She rubbed her mouth with one hand as the other turned the ignition. "When I called my contacts, they were already investigating. We don't have a lot yet. There's so much chaos. I'm so sorry."

"For what?" asked Kelly.

"We came here to heal," Iseult said, "not to be safe."

The couple looked at her. Tash drove. She opened her mouth a few times but didn't know how to respond to that. Instead she focused on the issue: "Suicide bomber. They didn't think it would go this far. They were keeping tabs on him." Then she answered the question she knew was coming: "My contacts thought the bomber might be… of interest to us."

Nick was watching out the window now. Kelly was in front with Tash. Iseult was thinking, but Tash could see in the rearview that Iseult's thinking looked a lot like staring forward intently. Tash took a breath through her nose. Kelly asked, "Like us?"

There was a different kind of heat in the car.

Tash drummed her fingers on the wheel. "You know you kids mean more to me than your gifts." It wasn't a question. Kelly squeezed her hand. Nick nodded, looking

Tash in the eye through the rearview, wearing an expression suggesting that that was obvious. Iseult showed no sign she'd registered the conversation.

"I just meant the gift thing," Kelly said. "Like, having them." She blushed.

Tash swallowed. The hospital, a crowd, and emergency lights glittered into being around them like daytime starlight. "I'll get the shirts and stuff in the trunk," Nick said.

"Thank you," Tash said as she stepped out of the car.

Iseult got out too but did not join Nick because she was more covered than the others. Not too covered to be out of place sitting on a beach. Reaching her elbows and knees, her spandex seemed a little odd to be out of the water. She'd pulled on sneakers, not bothering with socks, when they got to the car.

In front of them, people were a faceless cloud mirroring the ashes that rose from the hospital.

Police were already on the scene, struggling to push back the ever-growing crowd.

"There aren't enough," Iseult said to no one.

But the crowd changed. Nurses came waddling out of the hospital wearing a pouched shirt/dress that made them look like flying squirrels. In each pouch was a baby. This was how they got the newborns out of the nursery. Some people were wheeled out. Others were using crutches. The crowd parted ways when the fire truck approached. It stopped being about spectators and curiosity. The police maintained a barrier and focused on a head count, conferring with nurses.

The doctors seemed nearly as much at a loss for what

to do as the general public. Iseult watched them and understood: they helped the victims of this kind of situation. They weren't supposed to be the ones displaced, and such a remote community probably didn't do much to train them for it. She watched as someone gathered them all together and led away the ones who struggled to recover or hadn't already joined the relief efforts. Tables were being set up. Beverages, food, blankets, and other sundries began growing out of the milling throng. Cars came and went. Firefighters went to work.

"Seeing anything I'm not?" Tash asked Nick.

"Not really," he said. "Nothing that helps."

Kelly put a hand on his belly and the other on his far shoulder, resting her chin on the nearer one. "Let us be the judge of that, handsome." She pecked his neck.

He leaned his head on hers a moment, conferring more gratitude to her than most of the others might have noticed. Iseult folded her arms and closed her eyes. Nick began: "The woman helping the doctors is with the public library. She gave someone a card with the library's info. They're helping coordinate the town, I think. But there are more service people, like cops and stuff, than what we've got here in front."

Tash made a small, quick turn to face Nick a little more closely. "Go on."

"They're using the community in front as a distraction so they can do most of their investigation in the back. Number of assailants, building sweep, victims still inside, making plans, that sort of stuff."

"How can you know that?" Kelly asked with surprise.

"Lines of sight, plainclothesmen with a certain walk, clipboards, a lot of little things," Nick answered. "They wait for moments in the crowd, like when some of the injured children came out carrying each other? Yeah, that's when they do their moving. They dodge through cover, like with trees and whatever."

Tash nodded. "Anything else?"

"A bunch of medic alert bracelets, some of the firefighters are angry, the cops on this side are struggling to keep their hands off their holsters. I think they're afraid there's more in the crowd like whoever did that," he said, lifting his chin at the swath of the hospital that had been cut out of the world. "Reporters are already hard at work, but they're getting some harassment. See? There and there."

He pointed at different ends of the crowd. A person on each end was wearing a less distressed expression than the others. One a tall woman, still in her gym clothes. The other a man whose blocky build made him look shorter than he actually was. "But how do you know they're reporters?" Kelly asked.

Nick shuffled his feet a little. "I've…uh…been practicing lip reading."

Tash did not look at all surprised. Then she very much did, and she whirled around. "Where's Iseult?"

Nick whipped his head back and forth. "Over with th-"

A bristling wooden crash snapped from within the hole in the building. Several people cried out. A scream, like a surgery of sound, left everyone teetering on the edge of silence. Nick tried to step forward, but Kelly held on tight and Tash grabbed him too, for good measure. "Someone's still in there!" he shot at them with distress.

"You have a good eye," Tash said, "but you can't let that cut your brain out of the equation. See what you're looking at!"

Kelly looked at Tash with new admiration. Nick could be stopped with walls, fists, and the like. But bringing his attitude, his will, to a halt? That took something else. "Two firefighters and some random dude," Kelly started, referring to the ones dashing into the hospital. There were still gurneys and the like being wheeled out. People had brought makeshift stretchers, running the gamut from broken doors to surf boards, to help move patients who didn't have beds out of the building.

"Park ranger," Nick said. "He's buddies with one of the firefighters. They fist-bumped before they ran in." Nick had relaxed enough to accept that the hero's work wasn't for him today. Beyond the fire trucks, ambulances and other vehicles such as vans and — ominously — a hearse had been lined up to take in the badly wounded. Nick continued: "...and Iseult is doing her thing."

Before, when she stood behind Tash and the couple, Iseult had been concentrating. Now, Kelly saw, Iseult was amongst the worst of the wounded. As she'd waded through the crowd, Iseult had been searching for a certain flow in things. Not just blood flow, which was her gift, but also things she might recognize: suspicious people, the laisser-faire attitude she'd seen too much of in Atlanta, care takers who weren't taking care. So far as she could tell, though, it was just a community frightened and fighting in the face of an explosion. Compassion versus Death. Everyone's blood was fast and carried the sparkle of adrenaline. She waded through weaknesses, like murmuring hearts and mouths running without the brain's attention:

"How could this happen?"

"But we're safe here."

"Town's small…"

"All these things happen to noisy places."

"This isn't right."

"Where's Mom?"

"Where's Kevin?"

"Where's Stacey?"

Where, where, where.

Tash ran a hand through her hair and answered her phone. "Got anything for me?" she said without preamble.

Nick watched it all and felt guilty for the gift of his eyes. What good was having the power to watch others struggle?

Kelly took a breath and stepped back from him. "Anything's better than nothing," she said to him. He held her gaze and they shared a thought.

Iseult shuddered. Two individuals in the area gave her an icky feeling, like grease that had burned, been left to cool, and then got in the hair. She didn't have much opportunity to seek them out, though, because there was one person just as she was approaching the ambulances who had something in his blood flow she recognized. She moved in to catch him a flash before he started to fall.

"I'm a first aider!" she said as the cluster surrounding her looked on. "This man is having a stroke!"

CHAPTER 02
BLOOD SAMPLES

Kodiak, Alaska

"Who the f-" a young woman started.

But the man, one side of his face slackening, had already begun crumpling into Iseult's arms.

"He's never…" started an older woman who was part of the group, but Iseult was already in action.

"You!" Iseult said, pointing at the youth who'd gone from hostile to helpless. "Get one of the paramedics!" As she began adjusting the man's body for rescue position, she pointed to two more people in the throng. "You and you! Push everyone back! Give us some room!" Then she tuned everything out and concentrated on the man. It was like her brain had a heartbeat separate from anything in her chest. She knew the spot afflicting him and did what she could to stymie the cluster of broken vessels and crowded blood cells. Much like telling the people what to do as a first aider, this was crowd control. But he was a TV with poor reception, so it was crowd control with one hand and no words.

This was limiting damage, not healing. It might not

even have been enough for hope.

Tash, meanwhile, had abandoned her phone for now. She had first aid training as well, so she was in the thick of things. "You'll be all right, gentlemen," she crooned as she deftly tied an improvised elevation sling on a man sitting with his back propped against the side of an outdoor bench. It was the sort with wooden slats between concrete sides.

Another man, dressed in a postal uniform, was properly seated on the bench. The one Tash was helping was right beside him. While he was being treated for a leg injury by a paramedic with gauze, he watched Tash work. He said, "Arms and legs, sure. But that's not what's really hurtin' here, ma'am, meanin' no disrespect."

"None taken," she said as she met his gaze. She couldn't bring herself to smile, but the warmth in her eyes was unmistakable.

More service workers arrived. A news van showed up, though the group was only tangentially aware of it. Iseult couldn't get much more than the raw fear of people, raging under their skin like a river under a frozen surface. Tash noticed people shouting, crying, gathering, arguing, giving and taking orders, using phones, struggling to make sense of what they were seeing.

Nick saw police trying to get statements, answers, or even some sense of who was who. No one wanted to stop for that. Everyone had something else to contribute, and the ones most eager to talk had the least to say. It was the little things he saw in the cops — micro-expressions, twitches, blinks. Much of the building was blocked off now so the firefighters could do their work, but there was detritus all around them. He kept glancing at a pile of rubble. Something was niggling at him, but he couldn't quite sort out what he was seeing, or almost seeing. He tapped one of the officers, who turned a weary eye at him. "I'm Nick. I'm following Kelly's lead," — he pointed her out — "and we're talking while we work. We'll update you."

He glanced again at the rubble. There wasn't enough light coming from its spaces to be a twinkle or a sparkle. But there was a moving half-glitter he couldn't quite get from this angle. The officer replied, "We've gotta find the attacker, sir, and get things under control. I know we're short on hands-"

"That's not what I mean," Nick said. "You keep on keeping on." He stopped himself from telling the officer that Tash was the one to update; the cop wouldn't recognize that ladder of authority. Instead, he just added, "One of us will fill you in about what everyone's saying, get a picture. You're obviously shorthanded. We're rooting for you to stop the scumbags who attacked a hospital!"

Nick was too focused on returning to the rubble to see it, but Kelly saw the warrior spirit spark back to life in the officer's hardened eyes. Pride in him lined a side of her heart like sunlight limning metal. She'd been running this way and that, moving water bottles, distributing volunteer-provided blankets and foodstuffs, carrying messages, and helping to move debris out of the way of paths, people, and vehicles. Everywhere she went, she spoke to the people. What's your name? I'm Kelly. Did you see who did it? I'm Kelly. How can I help? I'm Kelly. Did anything lead up to this? Were there arguments or announcements? People moving unusual stuff? I'm Kelly,

Diary of Knives

I'm Kelly, I'm Kelly.

"SOMEONE'S IN THE RUBBLE!" Nick shouted.

Most of the doctors, seeing that the explosion was attended by rescue workers and the law, had been shaking off their dismay (for now) and getting into the fray. Supplies, supplies, supplies. Some of them looked up at Nick's cry, but they were busy restoring order to medical services as best they could in the upheaval. A lifeguard, three fishers (one of them a stocky woman), a man in a business suit, and a woman in a skirt she'd cut so she could run, all came to Nick's aid.

The almost-light he'd seen was an eye, looking out from between a rocky chunk of stone wall and a contorted metal spider of what once was a hospital bed. Nick's hands were dirty and trembling as he strove to turn over rock-like bunches of destruction. Everyone's efforts were admirable, if only for the spirit and the attempt. Twice any two of the others, the fisherwoman hauled and turned and guided others through lifts. Nick worked harder, inspired by her drive, and half of him wondered if she could arm-wrestle Poseidon after slamming a flask of whiskey.

By the time they reached the buried woman, her eyes had seen their last.

Kelly was in a bind. She'd lost sight of Iseult. Tash popped in and out of view, navigating the crowd and soon slipping into a leadership role. She was proud to have Tash at the helm, never mind the arguments and the chores and "taking responsibility for healing." Kelly briefly caught sight of Nick, now inexplicably far from the pile of rubble where before there was so much commotion. He was helping Tash reconfigure an oxygen unit for a woman in a wheelchair, tears streaming down his eyes.

And here was Kelly, holding up a recovered IV line and hoping no one would notice her hand hidden by a machine. She didn't know what it did, but its battery was failing. She'd promptly placed her hand at its side, nothing but the side of the building able to bear witness. Feeling the charge like static leaving her body was a sensation she wished she could describe to someone. It was like hunger, but moveable.

She felt for the charge as she stood there, and the machine made a variety of sounds. Some low and slow, others louder or sharper. She was afraid to overload it, but adding electricity was not like pouring water for a potted plant. So far, she hadn't broken the machine, but this was a tenuous situation at best.

A nurse ran over to help; the patient was attached to the machine but had been carried out in a stretcher, the machine haphazardly shoved into a suitcase and rolled with him by a retractable handle. Before the nurse could kneel, Kelly thought fast and said, "A doctor was just here. He said the battery's failing. He couldn't stay, but told me to find one, and I don't know what it takes. I…" and she trailed off.

"I do," said the nurse. "Let's have a look."

Kelly pointed at the news van. "Maybe they'd-"

The machine screeched.

Running off in a direction entirely different from the van, the nurse called over her shoulder. "I'll be back! Stay with the patient!"

Almost as soon as the failing battery made itself known, Kelly returned the hand that she'd used to point at the van. It was a risk, but what would happen if the nurse touched her hand now? And she couldn't do this forever. The arm holding up the IV was already beginning to quake. It only weighed as much as one or two bottles of soda, but holding up even that much for so long took its toll.

A doctor had taken over with Iseult's stroke patient. She was impressed with Iseult's efforts, despite the fact that first aid could do little for a stroke. The patient was completely stabilized. Iseult, however, was not. She was so covered in blood from other people that her grip on a tourniquet slipped twice. One more patient — a young woman Iseult's age who'd lost a hand — had stabilized as well, but three more patients bled out or faded away from shock because of the shrapnel from the explosion.

The young woman's eyes had a frightening clarity. The absence of her hand would mark so much in her life going forward, but right now Iseult could tell something else was consuming the teen. The blast, perhaps, or the loss of all innocence. "It can't happen to me" is a powerful shield, but when the immortality of that belief is stripped away, one is faced with a raw, naked fear. This young woman was beyond Iseult's help.

Standing, Iseult made another futile effort to wipe her hands on her knee-length spandex. She'd want to throw out or donate everything when she got home; if not the red, the memory was there to stay. A nurse ran from an ambulance carrying medical-grade batteries. Three fire-fighters emerged from the building. Two of them each carried a person over his shoulders in the fireman's carry. The third carried a child in each arm, neither aged to double digits, and tears streamed down the man's face.

The children were still.

Nick had run up, along with several others, to help the firefighters with their burdens. "What did he mean?" said one of the people. The firefighter set her down, nodded at Nick as he secured the woman, and went right back in. Nick waved his hand in front of the woman. "Hey," he said, his voice parched by tears but steady. "Look at me."

The woman looked at him. Middle-aged, she had a purple streak dyed into her hair and wore a custodian's uniform. On her left wristband was a collection of key-chains, all of child-oriented properties like Hello Kitty, Mickey Mouse, and what Nick thought was a dinosaur. "I'm Nick," he said, feeling a little foolish. "What's your name?"

"What did he mean?" she said again.

Nick took that for shock. "You seem to be breathing okay," he started. The woman looked him in the eye.

"I'm okay," she said. He opened his mouth but held his tongue. She continued, "But he wasn't."

"Who wasn't? Is someone else inside?" Nick looked around nervously. Two people had taken the other survivor from the other firefighter, but that person was having trouble breathing so they took up a lot more attention.

Everyone else had surrounded the third firefighter. Many wept openly. Nick was fairly certain no one was related to the children, and he wasn't sure if that was better or not. Regaining his attention, the woman said, "The bomber."

Suddenly Nick couldn't hear anything else. Every ray of light that he took in came from her. He was acutely aware of every micro-muscle, every stray hair, and only saw the flecks of raining ash when they immediately fell before her face. "Let's get that off your chest, then you can get some water and rest, okay?" he said as gently as he could.

"I was passing the waiting room for Gastro," she started. Nick wasn't sure what that meant but didn't interrupt. "This weirdo was in there with a big heavy coat, yammering about vets and his lizard. I tried to call security, but he pushed me away and ran down the hall. Tall guy, seemed too thin to wear a coat like that."

Nick took her hand. She wasn't looking at him but stared ahead. Sometimes she furrowed her brow, other times she made quick turns and shakes of her head. It was like she was arguing with her own memories. "He kept saying, 'Bring me back!'"

There was a lot to unpack here, but Nick had to keep things moving. "Tell me about him. Do you know his name?"

She shook her head. "Couldn't get him to talk much sense. This was the first time he came in so covered up. Not sure when it started exactly, but I heard about him a week ago. I know he was here a bunch before that. Never that covered, though. Everyone called him Band Camp because he was super awkward and always wore band shirts."

"What kinds of bands?" He felt stupid as soon as he said it. Nick had never before identified with the phrase "I need an adult" like he did today.

The woman ignored the question. "I have kids, you know," she said, holding up the bracelet. "Never got them a pet, though. Pets are supposed to help…"

Taking a breath, Nick tried again. "Tell me what he looked like."

"Tall," she said. "Looked wrong in that coat, too lanky. And pale, too. He was like one of those toys, you know, the bobble-heads? Except everything bobbled. Kept talking about his lizard."

"Did he have an accent or anything?"

"'Bring me back!' he kept saying," she replied absently. "What did he mean? Bring me back, bring me back…" she trailed off, muttering.

He saw Tash moving about with water bottles and granola bars. Desperate with relief, he dashed to her. "This woman saw the guy, sounds like there was only one, um, perp." He avoided "bomber" as though the word would bring out the action. "I think she knows more, but…"

Tash nodded. Iseult once remarked that Tash seemed to have a gift for completing a puzzle when she didn't even have all the pieces. Nick couldn't have agreed more. "You should go to Kelly," she said. "I'll take care of that poor soul," Tash lifted her chin in the direction of the custodian. "And find Iseult. Make sure you all take a break. That's an order," she added. "There's a pavilion set up with motorbikes as a barrier. The bikers are helping people find their families and making sure rescuers take breaks."

Glad for the opportunity to not think for a moment, he sought out his girlfriend.

A bomb technician came through and entered the building once the firefighters were all accounted for. Iseult watched from where she knelt. At her knees was a little girl with a shattered length of metal pole embedded in her abdomen. It was one of those IV walkers, a torn IV line still attached at the other end. There were bits of gyprock in the wound. The piece of metal must have gone through a wall before reaching the girl. She'd been brought out by four people who'd been nearby, one to each limb. Her mother had been with the group but was currently sitting on the edge of an ambulance. A paramedic and a nurse were wrestling with her hysteria.

Iseult barely registered the distressed mother any-more. "I think this one's stabilizing," she said to the doctor who'd joined the group. He nodded agreement. "Is that just one bomb tech?" she asked, pointing a bloody finger at a heavily armoured person carrying a special kit.

"I'm surprised they found one at all," the doctor re-plied. "This isn't exactly Los Angeles, and we don't get bombs here. Impressive work with the child," he added.

Iseult just shrugged. She almost wanted to feel sick, covered as she was in blood and noise.

One of the people who'd carried the girl asked, "Can we move her now?"

The doctor looked at the other man in stupefaction, his opened mouth a silent rebuke for staggering igno-rance. Iseult spoke up before anyone could make an issue of the doctor's contempt. "I'm afraid not, sir. You're all gonna have to take turns keeping on the pressure." At the moment, an elderly woman was pressing a blood-soaked cloth on the girl's wound, around the piece of metal. De-spite her age, she'd been the carrier at one of the wounded girl's legs and had had no trouble keeping up with the others — except for slowing down on the stairs once be-cause of her hip. No one had complained.

"I can keep this up a while yet," the senior said. She had sweet, brown eyes. Those eyes held Iseult's gaze. This was a woman who'd seen some things in her time. Iseult could sense the robust warmth and strength of the elder's blood.

"I believe you," Iseult started.

"She can't stay like this forever!" chimed in another man. His Hawaiian shirt was a stark contrast to, well, everything. The background was interspersed with prayers, weeping, people shouting for answers or rage or supplies.

"Once the bomb tech comes back out," Iseult said, levelling a glare at each of the men beside her, "the girl's-"

"Abigail," interrupted the first man.

The doctor put in, "The nurse is right." Iseult flushed; she wasn't a nurse. But she wasn't about to correct him. He went on: "Little Abigail here is going to need immediate surgery. She's stable for now, but we can't be positive about the extent of the damage until we have access to proper equipment. The longer she's here, the harder our conversation will have to be."

Iseult restrained herself from saying something like, "It's about time!" It was a relief to finally see the doctor assert some authority. She was so very much out of her depth here. Instead, she looked at the one in the Hawaiian shirt. "Does she have family here?"

"I'm her father," he replied. "He's her uncle," the father continued, pointing at the one who'd asked if Abigail could be moved.

Iseult nodded. She was doing her best to look like she was resting, but it was more her effort than the elderly woman's that was keeping the bleeding in check. It wasn't enough. Even if the surgery room were intact and immediately prepped, there could be no hope of sterilization after a bombing. She didn't know what to do. Tears flowed freely, though she managed to remain stable. Not one sob.

"Will there be help from neighbouring communities?" she asked no one in particular.

No one answered.

Iseult looked around. She clenched her left fist and concentrated her efforts on it so that it was like she was holding an invisible rope to Abigail's bloodstream. Nonsense, of course, but she did what she could with what she had. Particularly endangered patients had been loaded into the ambulances, the doors closed, to provide as close to a controlled environment as possible. Sometimes one would be opened long enough to carry a conspicuously human-sized bag to the clusters of tent-covered sleepers on the other side of the crowd. The people maintained a clear path to it and helped when they could.

"Shouldn't we have a second group over here?" Iseult asked the doctor, pointing behind the ambulances beside them.

He sighed and rubbed one eye with a knuckle. "I think they like only having one way they don't want to look, young lady."

Iseult looked again.

The bomb tech was one person and had an entire medical centre to examine. The fire had been put out, but that was the easy part for the firefighters. They threw off their protective gear. Some of them joined the police in investigating the perimeter. It had been secured against people trying to get in, and the building had been cleared, but they were giving the officers opportunities to rest or isolate evidence.

Several men and women had tried to get in, ranging from screeching to furious, in order to find friends or family. More than once, those people were directed to the tents. Just to be sure.

More than once, they found who they were looking for.

Iseult saw Nick and Kelly among the people collected with the bikers. Their heads leaned together and their hearts weighed them down. Nick looked up and, before Iseult realized she'd been noticed, he gave a small wave. Iseult lifted a hand to wave back, looked at it covered in blood, and lowered it. Kelly held a hand to her own chest, and held it out toward Iseult. Kelly had a way like that. A kind of static that drew them together.

Iseult's eyes widened.

"Why'd you stop?" demanded the father. But the elderly woman just sat back and wept.

Iseult had felt it in her hand. Like a rope of starlight gone slack. "I'm sorry," she said to the two men.

"There's nothing vital there! Do CPR!" The uncle had stood up, nostrils flaring.

The father, tears in his eyes, got up and put both his hands on his brother's shoulders. "We have t-"

"No!" It was surreal, to see the uncle more outraged than the father. Was it just grief moving at different speeds? Was there a greater story here?

An officer stood behind the uncle and coughed.

The uncle, unwavering, shoved his brother away. "Save my niece!" He pointed a finger at the father, the Hawaiian shirt somehow taking on a new light now. "What's wrong with you!? Get in the ring, man!"

As the doctor stood, Iseult's eyes met those of the officer, a woman with a scar at the left edge of her jaw. A tacit agreement grew between them as the doctor said, "I'm sorry, sir, but the match is over."

It was a brief flash of motion: weeping uncontrollably, the father stepped back and helped the senior. The uncle lunged for the doctor, whose spine erected a defence of stillness. The officer slipped her arms over and around the man's arms, pulling him back at both elbows, and Iseult pushed hard at his chest so that it looked like she stopped him from stepping on the girl or getting too close to the doctor in his mad fit of denial. What she really did was the equivalent of tossing a hunter's net over the uncle's blood pressure. He slumped against the officer, who was well-trained but half his size, suddenly outweighed by his own inexplicable fatigue.

Then Tash was washing Iseult's hands with bottled water and what looked like a torn-up shirt. "What?" Iseult blinked dumbly. The father, the uncle, and the officer were carrying away the girl. Someone was offering a tensed arm for the elderly woman to hold onto while she made her way to the resting area. "But they were jus-"

"Hush, now," Tash said. She, too, had mastered the art of lightweight tears. They flowed freely, but she was not too tense to do what needed doing. She breathed steadily and spoke with a heavy but controlled voice. "You need rest. We've been here for seven hours already. Come along. And eat this. We haven't even had lunch."

Mechanically, Iseult ate what she was given. She stopped repeatedly, as if lost, and Tash would wash her face or stroke her hair, gently encouraging her. She knew she'd eaten, and sometimes brought an empty hand to her mouth, but couldn't remember what it had been or when she'd finished it.

"I could have helped more of them," she said. She was sitting now. *When did I sit? Where's Tash? Oh, on the phone.*

Nick and Kelly were holding hands behind Iseult and sat on either side of her. They rested their heads on her shoulders and braced her back together. They weren't sitting on something with a back. Iseult moved to rub her eyes with the sleeve of her shirt, but stopped within an inch. Blood was smeared tightly and in streaks. Someone must have rubbed her down a bit.

"There's only one of you," Nick said, "and too many of them. Well, and us."

"You did great," Kelly said. "We've got a lot to do yet, though, I think."

Iseult shifted and shuffled until the couple were forced to sit aside a bit. Iseult pulled herself back together and drank from the - "When did I get tea?" she asked.

"Bunch of folks from the local markets and stuff," Nick said.

"I hear the librarians got them together," Kelly said. "They've been working with the bikers to give everyone a cup of something to relax them. It's not a lot, but what can you do?"

Iseult absorbed this and nodded. She sipped absently and struggled to pull herself back together. "It's like a big family," she remarked.

Nick and Kelly looked at each other with concern, but they looked around them, at the people running or resting or working with the children to calm them down or help them understand. It was like a camping trip when someone realized that no one remembered to bring the necessaries for fire. It somehow felt smaller here, calmer, like the calamity was not as big as it felt. Across the way, someone was making a speech. There were more cameras, speakers, and milling people who hadn't been there for the...cleanup.

The bomb tech stood with the person who might have been a mayor. An officer, with a chief-of-police air of authority, stood at the makeshift podium as well. The town was rallying. Countless patches of family dotted the crowd. People holding each other, offering food, words, blankets, hands, and all manner of love under fire. The bomb tech carried a box of samples. It was an armoured briefcase, more or less, and reminded Iseult of the movie scene containers for vials of viral weapons or plasma gun cells or just good old-fashioned blood.

CHAPTER 03
DROP POINT

Kodiak, Alaska

Hotels could put everyone on the same level. It's not just having a door with a number; it's the kind of anonymity people pretend really hard to have when they're at a hospital with a curtain pulled closed. The next room could be housing a convening jury, a criminal on the run, a tourist, a cheating spouse, a loyal spouse on the way home, a businessperson...anyone at all.

"Cut it out," Nick said. He was lounging in a chair by the window. "I just wanna read. It's been exhausting."

"You spent all yesterday napping and reading!" Kelly declared. This was Nick and Iseult's room. Tash and Kelly had the one across the hall.

Tash was sitting on the bed, staring at the TV but not seeing it. Notebooks and a computer tablet were lying on the bed on either side of her like pets. Iseult wasn't in the room. Tash registered that the young couple were talking but didn't process their words. She was running through everything in her head. The explosion at the hospital had all the hallmarks of a case her team should be investigating, but there was nothing conclusive yet. She'd dimly felt the comings and goings of room service the last two days; she and the kids weren't the only ones who kept to their rooms.

Nick sighed. He was holding a copy of *The Complete Collection of Sherlock Holmes*. "Why don't you ask Iseult? She was knee-deep in it, too."

"She doesn't have magic camera eyes."

"Please don't call them that. It makes me feel like a video game character," Nick said. Then a thought hit him: "Do you think Doyle was a...was like us?"

Tash worried about Iseult. She knew the gifted young woman was probably just staying in the other room today to process things in her own way, but it was hard to be supportive by not burdening the troubled youth with well-intended support. This was a nagging corner in Tash's mind, and had been since--

"I found my mortal man," Kelly started with over-played sensual enthusiasm, "in the land of Atlanta where the shadows lie."

Nick set down the book and, without looking at the container filled with fresh lens fluid, picked it up to deposit his contacts. Once they were set aside, he linked his hands while resting his elbows on the arms of the faux mahogany chair. His eyes were like boiled eggs, de-shelled but otherwise whole. No pupils, no iris, and — because he was calm — no visible blood vessels. But while the white was pure, it wasn't surgical. He regarded Kelly coolly. "Doyle gets what it feels like, you know."

She was about to ask, but realized he meant the author. Kelly thought back to watching shows of Sherlock

Holmes. She didn't know if she should be hurt or sympathetic. "Do you want to do cocaine?" she asked.

This broke through Tash's reverie: "Wait, what?"

The couple broke into laughter.

Tash narrowed her eyes.

"We were talking about Sherlock Holmes," Nick said, rubbing his face with both hands. Laughter brought the tension of Atlanta to the surface, and the freedom of not wearing the contacts like small masks made it easier to wipe that tension away.

"No, you weren't," Tash said sternly. "You're not the first to talk about the paint instead of knocking on the walls."

Kelly and Nick looked at each other. "Huh?" Kelly responded. "Should we get Iseult? Is this Family Talk Time?"

Tash shook her head. "Sorry. I was really hoping to take you all to a vacation where you — you know — vacation." She studied the layout of her bed: phone, tablet, notes. And the other bed: empty except for Kelly, who did her best not to disturb the pillows. "You know one of the reasons I picked this place was because we're north of most of Canada?"

"I remember you looking at a jacket with the Kodiak brand and saying, 'That'll do,'" Kelly corrected.

"Don't talk back," Tash said, and she almost grinned. She squelched the urge to add "...to your mother," because she didn't quite know yet where Kelly stood on that. Even Nick's slip of the word was something she had to cherish carefully. They had to come to the idea of family in their own way, on their own time.

"Things happen everywhere," Nick said. The women regarded him with something between amusement and… seriousness? Disappointment? "What I mean is," and he shifted awkwardly, "Atlanta didn't really change — except to us. They got a couple of news stories and some of the neighbours moved, but we're the ones who'll never be the same."

"Is that why you won't talk about the hospital?" Kelly asked. She was one of the only people who regularly and comfortably looked him in the eyes when he was (so to speak) being himself. Even Tash would do it as a sign of respect or an effort to be inclusive or something, but it was an effort. Not much of one, because she was more comfortable with such things than most. But everyone else looked at his eyes. She alone looked into them.

It was one of the many things he loved about her.

"Kind of?" he answered. "It's just: you were all there, too. I think Sir Arthur Conan Doyle would get me, but I don't think I'm Sherlock Holmes. I feel like him sometimes, especially when I try to watch movies, but I'm not super smart like him. We got — well, not lucky in Atlanta. But luck got us — or me? — out of it, and I did what I could. I just don't want to think this is our fight. Does it have to be part of our…thing?" Subtle shifts in the muscles of his face and neck gave Kelly cues few others could catch; she knew when he was looking around, even when he didn't have contacts to give away his line of sight.

When his hair grew back after Atlanta, he left it tousled and unkempt and deliberately cut it himself — poorly, so that it was short but always looked like he'd just gotten out of bed. When she teased him about his "clean-freak" ways, he resolved to this because he thought it was funny. And though he'd spoken with hesitation, he was learning to believe in her faith in him.

That spirit was one of the many things she loved about him.

"Well," Tash started, "I've gotten what I can out of my contacts. I've told Victor and some friends about what happened, and that we're shaken but mostly okay." Nick picked up on a fractional movement of her eyes as she stopped herself from looking meaningfully toward the door and beyond it, to Iseult. Kelly was retrieving her own notes from a side bag, but she was listening. Tash went on: "Right now, we're just checking it out. Nothing reckless. We did a lot of poking around yesterday, and we don't want to draw too much attention. Well, no more than we already have."

"Iseult was covered in more blood than anyone else, and that's with all the medical people working double-time," Nick said. "I think it's safe to say the S. S. *Attention* has sailed."

Tash shook her head. "There were practically gangs of volunteers springing out of the woodwork, including bikers," she said. "We weren't the only ones doing our best to help, covered in blood and tears."

"I almost gave myself away," Kelly said with uncharacteristic timidity.

Nick looked at her with pride but said nothing. He was more than happy to have the whole world see what Kelly was capable of, though he knew better. He didn't think the comic books had it right — he wasn't sold on the idea that people knowing about powers would cause a blood bath. But it only takes one lunatic to abuse a situation.

Kelly was looking at Tash and didn't see his pride. But she felt his gaze on her and was warmed. Tash looked between the two and drew her own conclusions. She let a heartbeat go by before asking, "Were you safe?"

Kelly blinked.

"Were. You. Safe."

"I think so," Kelly said, and regained confidence as she spoke. "I don't think anyone noticed-"

"That's not what I'm asking," Tash cut in.

Kelly and Nick looked at each other.

"You saw what Abby's gift did to that wayhouse," Tash went on. "I'm sure you've caught bits in the last half a year. From me, if not from crossing paths with Victor. Look at the following Gavin had. Remember Quinn. Yes, I want us to stay under the radar for as long as we can, but sooner or later the rest of the world is bound to catch on that there are people who can do...more. So yes, it's important. But don't get yourselves killed to keep secret today what everyone might know tomorrow."

Kelly looked at her nails. She'd done them in sunrise colours, beginning bright at the quick, and looking at those colours helped her cheer up. "This isn't about our identities — not really — is it? I mean, Iseult can knock people out just by touching them. If anyone comes at us, Nick will see them coming..."

"Oh, sweetie," Tash started. "No one can fight the world-"

"Why not?" Nick cut in. "Isn't that what you and Victor have been doing?"

Tash wiped her forehead with one hand and shifted some of her materials with the other. "Are you hungry?"

"I could eat," Nick said without missing a beat, "but don't change the subject."

Kelly giggled and Nick felt it in his toes. Tash watched them and she was reminded of so much study, of textbooks and photographs, of archaeological sites. She couldn't place it, but it was like they were still on the beach, the sand beneath them thrumming with history.

"Oh, but I'm not," she said. "We talk, we have our feelers and our connections. We pick up on the rumbles."

"Is that why you chose this place?" asked Kelly. "Or were you looking for somewhere where we won't make rumbles? Are we hiding or running?"

"I know it's not margaritas and Caribbean blue sea, but I really wanted this to be a get-away."

"I'm sorry," Nick said, as a weariness settled onto his shoulders like wide-awake anaesthesia. "I just…this is a lot."

"The therapy helped," Kelly offered. But they hadn't had a session since they left Georgia.

"Nothing happens here," Tash said.

The couple looked at each other.

Tash continued: "That's why I picked Kodiak. Police and firefighters help get cats out of trees or give a stern talking to kids who leave burning bags on doorsteps. I mean, they have their struggles, but there's no Gavin here."

"You don't think we can handle this," Kelly blurted. It took everything she had not to try to pull the words back into her mouth.

Tash shook her head. "Actually, I'm afraid you can. No one's scared of an empty nest — they're scared of seeing more beaks and claws in the world."

In the room across the hallway, Iseult knelt in the bathtub. The bathroom door was locked. The door to the room was also locked, but that didn't matter so much; Tash and Kelly would have the key. Her tablet was on one of the beds, full of browser tabs about suicide bombers; victims unifying in the face of tragedy; improvised medicine; field dressings and First Aid; medical school. There was one about geocaching, simply because she was curious. More tabs covered subjects like survival skills, exploration, navigation in the wild, and music: Florence and the Machine.

Right now, she was using a ghost knife.

On herself.

From here, she couldn't hear the other three talking. She told them to go to breakfast without her because she needed some time alone. They thought they understood; everyone had needed time alone in the last few months. She called up room service, and Kelly texted her that they were going to the other room to chat. She could join whenever. She ate, she studied, and she cut herself.

When they'd been helping at the hospital, she used her gift to heal. At a touch, she learned things. Things others could miss. Things she shouldn't be able to know.

She recognized blood clots that wouldn't have shown up from tests in time.

She saved the life of someone with recently developed diabetes who hadn't known they had the condition.

In one case, she had to keep finding excuses to stay

in arm's length of someone who was bleeding internally from a ruptured kidney in order to slow and redirect enough of the blood flow to let platelets do their work. She hoped the patient got the surgery they needed the minute the hospital was re-opened because they'd survive if they did.

As she watched the blood well up around the edges of her wounds — always small, always clean — she did her best to bring her power to bear.

It never would work on herself.

She had an elaborate process for hiding the evidence of what she thought of as her experiments. Oddly, it gave her an opportunity to practice her skill with bandaging. Never had blood or bandages shown through her clothes. These operations concluded, she left the bathroom in a state of feeling somewhere between lost and satisfied.

Iseult placed the ghost knife in a leg strap but tucked it away rather than wearing it. She returned to her tablet.

Kelly wondered and worried about Iseult, but everyone had to deal with this in their own way. She wondered and worried if she was like Iseult, and if she was not. "So your network has nothing?" she asked.

She was already close to getting lost in this kind of thinking when Tash answered: "I'm still waiting to hear back from Victor and the others. They have their own matters, and we're not even sure yet what questions to ask. I mean, it looks like an isolated tragedy. If there is such a thing."

"What are you thinking?" Kelly asked Nick.

He was staring in Tash's direction, but Kelly knew he hadn't been seeing what he was looking at. He regarded

Kelly for a moment and drew out his phone.

A minute later, Iseult walked into the room, still holding the phone to her ear. "Reporting to the Bridge, Captain Carry," she said into it even as she stood to attention.

The trio laughed despite themselves.

"Feeling better, I see?" Tash asked.

"Something like that," Iseult said, hanging up her phone and helping herself onto the bed with Kelly. "This one's mine now," she said to Nick with a wink.

"I'm into it," Kelly grinned.

Tash rolled her eyes, but had to stifle a chuckle when she looked at Nick.

He looked between the two, opened his mouth to say something, ran scenarios in his mind, and went crimson.

Kelly opened her own mouth, but Iseult took charge: "So I guess this meeting's now in session. We're a little late if we're actually gonna look into this hospital stuff." She nodded at Nick with such solemnity that all the joking vanished. "But I get you. That was...a lot. For all of us."

Everyone nodded.

Tash said, "We don't have to go any farther. But we should take precautions."

The youths looked at each other, but Tash got the impression that they were consulting themselves.

"Here's the thing," Kelly started, "I don't think what I can do is any different than having a talent for guns, or kung fu, or all that hunter trapping stuff. I have a talent that can hurt people. It's a little unusual, but really, how am I gonna put that on a resume? 'Experience as a human taser. Excels at re-establishing current even when electronics appear to be broken. Proven reliability in making the best caramelized apples ever.'"

"Trained in First Aid and emergency preparation," Iseult added for herself with a grin. "Volunteer experience with an emphasis on weird blood pressure voodoo."

Nick wanted in too. "Could probably see a speeding bullet. More powerful than a microfiche reader. Able to read tall pages in a single…uh…flip?"

Tash shook her head. "I'm kinda surprised you know what a microfiche is."

"That's what you question?" Iseult asked through the tightness of restrained laughter.

"Once I realized what my gift means for reading, I figured I should take a look around. I wanted to see how much I could push that," Nick explained.

Kelly blinked. "Was this before…us?"

Nick shook his head. "When we took turns for therapy in Atlanta over the winter. I usually ducked into the public library down the road. You were helping Tash with stuff when you weren't doing the Freud thing, and I didn't think about mentioning it. No big deal."

An instant passed as this information was digested.

"Is that part of why you needed time?" Tash asked. "To absorb everything that you've seen?"

"Sort of," and he rolled and flipped his hands awkwardly. His mouth moved wordlessly.

"When I first…" Iseult started, wrestling as much with her own story as with making sense of Nick, "…realized… it was with a friend when I was a kid. I knew they had hemophilia before they told me, but I didn't understand why I knew. I started picking up on other things, too."

"But people expected things from you," Kelly said,

remembering her own self-discovery. "You have to be polite, but you don't wanna be prissy. Clean, but not a neat freak. Like this guy," and she poked her toes out at Nick. Her foot couldn't reach him.

He pantomimed tossing long hair over a shoulder, giving a limp and feminine flair to his wrist.

Tash, of all people, stuck out her tongue.

Once the laughter subsided, Tash looked at them all in turn. "I don't think this is about us or the things we do."

"No," Iseult agreed, "but we still need to know."

Tash's expression was quizzical. Nick added, "Nothing happens here, things happen around us all the time, we come here, and a hospital explodes? Doesn't feel like a coincidence."

"Now don't you blame yourselves for a second for this," Tash admonished.

"It's not our fault," Kelly said. "But you gotta admit, something just doesn't ring true here. Even if someone wanted to make a statement blowing up a hospital, why do it in such an out-of-the-way place?"

"What makes you think they're making a statement?"

Kelly played with a strand of her blonde hair, running her hands through it in an oblong line that came away from her forehead. Nick picked at his own hair and looked around the room as though something somewhere would give him direction. Iseult gently traced a finger over one of her bandaged, self-inflicted wounds. Her dressing was flattened with medical tape, so anyone who was watching her would have taken her motions for a scratch or an adjustment of the sleeve at her upper arm.

Nothing to see here.

It was Iseult who broke the silence: "I couldn't get much about the bomber. It was mostly just...fear. We had lots of gear for the pain and the bleeding, but we couldn't treat the fear."

Kelly dropped her hair. "I tried to go everywhere," and she watched Tash now. She couldn't put her finger on why she needed Tash to understand this, didn't know what she was hoping for, but she couldn't stop herself from pushing for some obscure kind of approval. "I helped with the machines a few times, but I'm not a power grid." She didn't even notice that she was sitting straighter, head held high and legs evenly spaced on the bed. When did she put her back to the wall? "I tried giving shocks to everyone who was...who was..."

Iseult held her hand.

Nick opened his mouth, but Tash gave him a quick glance. How'd she even know he would try to speak? He didn't until the words got stuck in his throat. But something about Tash's look told him that he shouldn't try to push those words through.

Iseult had Kelly's attention. She said, "For what it's worth, that's not how it works." Kelly was caught up in the moment and her eyes revealed some confusion. Iseult continued: "A working heartbeat is like playing piano. It's not just hitting notes, it's about timing. That whole thing you see on TV where they get the defibrillator going after the flatline? Yeah, that's like the conductor going nuts with his wand when the orchestra has already left. A shock fixes the timing, but someone's gotta be playing or it's just a conductor in an empty room. No music."

"Do orchestras have pianos?" Nick asked.

Everyone looked at him.

He flushed. "Sorry."

"What else did you do?" Tash prompted Kelly.

To Kelly, Tash had a surreal quality. Here the woman was, occupying the bed closest to the door of the hotel room, ranging from short black hair through a lithe and tall frame to long and immaculate feet. She was surrounded by notes, a tablet, and the atmosphere of a working mother. This despite the fact that she wasn't their biological mother and none of them knew what she did for money. Kelly tightened her grip on Iseult's hand. She'd have to sort out those feelings later.

She took a breath. "Well, you saw some of it," Kelly said. "Running around and such. Talked to people, calmed them down, asked questions. Most of it was side comments and half-answers. Everyone was shook up." She turned her eyes to Nick. "It was hard to look past all the fear, the shock, the just…basic needs of it all. You know?"

"I saw a lot of hands," Nick added, since Kelly seemed to be reaching out for help. "Twitching, searching, just trying to hold on. People were taking things that didn't always make sense, like I could see people had stuffed things into their pants or shirts or pockets or backpacks or whatever."

Kelly said, "What kinda stuff?"

"IV bags," he said right away. Iseult blinked hard. He hesitated before continuing: "Pens, stationary, gloves that were too big for them, clocks — those square alarm ones? — and things like letter openers that could be used as weapons if you had to. Teddy bears. Things that they were holding like weapons but wouldn't be good for it, like paperweights and thermometers and curling irons. And I saw someone with a Medic Alert bracelet who'd stuffed a bunch of candy bars wherever they could fit them." He said this last as though it were one of the weirder options.

"Well, that makes more sense than you think," Iseult said. "If they're having diabetic problems, adding more sugar doesn't do much real harm against hyperglycemia but not having sugar for hypoglycemia could kill them."

Nick was absorptive, though no one believed that it was for medical knowledge. Kelly desperately wanted to shield him from everyone, from the questions, from the burden of having better eyes than all three of them combined. That much, at least, she understood about Tash. It was why Kelly used to do laundry when she'd been with the cult. She was no one's servant, not even Gavin's, even then. But even in world-class hospitals, or when you're part of a group of people with extraordinary abilities, there's laundry. There's a satisfaction in being the caretaker.

Everyone was looking at her.

She swallowed and shook her head as though to clear it. She realized what Nick was really doing; the details he just described were manifest versions of what she'd dealt with that day. "People sometimes asked weird questions, mostly because they didn't know what to do. Some people wanted to help, but others were just helping because doing was better than not doing. A few people had to be stopped because they were going around asking things they had no business asking. It was like everyone was on autopilot. Well, not everyone, but…"

"Even so, I must say I was impressed by the compassion and community I saw," Tash remarked.

Everyone nodded.

"From what I could tell," Kelly said, "most people are guessing as much as anything else. It's one of those things, you know? No one knows what to do, or how to explain it. A lot of them were just asking why, over and over. Some people saw other people who they thought were sketchy, but…"

"They suspected who they wanted to suspect," Iseult added.

"Well, there was some of that," Kelly said, "but most of them suspected what sounded like the same guy."

"Weirdo wearing band shirts who kept coming back and saying weird things and staring at people a little too long?" Nick asked.

"Yeah!" Kelly said.

"I didn't get much on that," Iseult said. "Some people talked about band camp, but I was too busy with… well…"

"I'm proud of all of you," Tash said. They all looked at her. "You see a need and you do what you can to help. Whatever happens, I'm glad you haven't gone cold after everything you've been through. Just the fact that you care is enough."

All the youths shifted uncomfortably.

"You were right and you were wrong earlier," Nick said, looking at Tash. Her jaw straightened in that way people have of waiting for a person to continue. He did: "We don't have to look into this, we don't have to get involved. But we do. Because we need to know. Like Kelly said, it's all just too…off."

"I couldn't piece everything together," Kelly said, "because a lot of it was people talking while their brains tried to catch up. But they were talking about Band Camp as a nickname. It was a person. The weirdo, from what I could make of it."

"I saw a lot of strange glances," Nick added. Kelly looked him in the eyes. He didn't notice the other two in that moment. "Band shirts got extra looks, and they weren't kind looks. People were covering up their band stuff, like baseball caps with band logos. Some of them looked confused, like they didn't know why it was wrong, but they covered them up anyway. It was social pressure," he added, and he finally took in the full view of the room. "They had no direction, a lot of them were under-equipped or whatever, and they followed along with this band symbol stuff because it was better than nothing."

Tash saw it. She saw how Iseult and Kelly grasped what Nick was feeling. She saw how they made the same connections and had the same doubts, but processed them differently. She saw the way he kept glancing at his copy of *Sherlock Holmes* with what she'd thought was disgust, but now realized was envy. Who or what did he really envy? Holmes? Doyle? Or was it something about the story, some metaphor that made sense to a teenager? That spoke to Nick in particular? Maybe she wasn't being fair; his age might not have anything to do with it. She wondered — not for the first time — if she were really teaching children. Was she teaching?

Were they children?

"I'll tell you as much as I remember about every detail I saw," Nick said to the women, though his gaze was directed at Iseult. "But I think you're all relying on me to pull a rabbit out of a hat. I remember the way Jaycee used to talk," he continued, and he could have sworn that Tash had flinched if a person could flinch with their eyes alone. "And it was like that small-town stuff he mentioned once or twice. Like people would be content with a rumour if it answered enough of their questions." He looked at each of the women in turn, but again returned to Iseult. "I looked at the building a lot, too, and the people running around outside of the crowd of the hospital. There were plainclothes authorities securing the perimeter. It was like someone did surgery on the building. It was like the town was cut open and no one knows what the surgeon took yet. There were still exposed wires that could start fires, but that's not the scary part."

Nick buried his face in his hands. "I could give you all the details in the world, and when we can't find an answer, you're going to think I missed something."

CHAPTER 04
KARAMBIT

FinTech Server Farm,

Undisclosed Location in Europe

He was not there right now.

The server farm, effectively one of the international computing hubs that makes the Internet possible, was surrounded by rocks and emptiness for miles in any direction. Waste heat was a giveaway for server farm locations. They were ideally located in cooler areas; it made it easier to prevent the servers from overheating. They were generally kept hush-hush, especially when they were used for financial technology, to reduce the chances of attempted infiltration or destruction.

So the server farm, like Karambit himself, was hiding in plain sight.

"Can't believe you don't just use the bunks here. There's nothing for miles!" said a person who was also working in one of the server rooms. Karambit knew her because it was his business to know everything everywhere he went. He knew that she was transgender, that her name was Perange, the broad strokes of her transition.

He even knew her dead name.

Her favourite book in English class had been *The Stone Angel*, by Margaret Laurence. Perange settled on her new name because it meant "stone angel." Everyone was surprised by her gender identity not because of the identity itself, but because she was so dry in her interests and humour that it seemed too colourful a thing to do. This sentiment, once expressed, led to many arguments. Karambit knew all of this, her education, and even her blood type, allergies, birthplace, and various numbers such as driver's license info.

To Perange, Karambit was so familiar that he was like a brother or childhood friend. It was all too easy to keep that up, with the extent of his knowledge. She was, as such, far too embarrassed to admit that she couldn't remember his name.

He was so familiar, she had no idea they'd never met before today.

"Technically, we're not here right now," Karambit replied. His voice was not monotone, exactly, as he was conveying the tone of a joke. But it was familiar without a root connection in actual memory, and so hard to remember.

She laughed. "Isn't it liberating?" she continued talking while she switched up some wires and used a laptop to coordinate some minor maintenance routines. "It's like being a teenager and trespassing just to hang out."

As they chatted, Karambit was moving up and down multiple aisles of the server towers with his work case, making small adjustments, adding the occasional thumb drive, or removing one or two minor components. His efforts would be noticed if Perange continued her task much longer. "I know!" he said as he rounded a corner, coming out at the opposite end of her aisle. "Every day is an adventure. Say, are you working the jurisdiction provenance subroutine?"

Blinking, Perange looked up. "Why, yes. How'd you know?"

"You're the third one this week," he lied smoothly, and put on a mask of frustration. "That's why I've been doing so much sector defragmentation," and he pointed to the aisles he'd been working.

Perange was deadpan. "At least there's no pressure. We're just computer jockies, but--"

"...but we're the ones holding it all together," he finished with a smile. It was a trained smile, one he'd practiced with the same principles that were used for the plastic surgery performed on his face: defy facial recognition software; evade the frames of reference the brain uses for analysis and memory; let the viewer fill in the gaps so that multiple accounts will conflict. Some part of Perange's instincts, something balancing ice cubes in her brain stem, told her that he was always a little off. It wouldn't be until later that she'd scramble for memories of him before today.

Without missing a beat, Karambit continued: "Never mind how good we are or any of that. We don't make the decisions."

An old sentiment, and not really fitting for a professional environment like this high-tech and low-profile facility, but Perange had had her merits so ignored and unappreciated — even been told to her face that she wasn't who she said she was — that it was hard to resist fall-

ing in with what the man was saying. Karambit's rhythm
was a constant, his motions confident and smooth. She
was already getting out of his way and moving on without questioning that he was taking over her position. "I
should look into that," she said, by way of being useful as
she moved for the door.

"Oh, I've reported it every time. I've scheduled a meeting with the Deputy Director of the Storage & Retrieval
Division." Karambit did not bother looking up from his
work. His statement was precisely the sort of tactics he
liked: both false and true, because he'd never had any
such reports or meetings but had altered the records —
including signed documentation indicating who'd been
the stenographer and the minutes they'd filed — to line
up with his statements. "I'd be grateful, though, if you'd
help smooth over the process."

While he continued working with one hand, he reached
into the work case he'd set down by his leg to produce a
sealed eight-by-eleven document folder. "If the trains are
on time, Herr Erstgradt should be finishing his coffee and
debriefing with the Department of Cryptography when
you get there in about twelve minutes."

"Trains…?" Perange stammered, taking the document
from her "co-worker" in something of a daze. She wasn't
feeling excitement; his familiarity wasn't attraction. She'd
be sure to reflect once she got the chance to decompress.
What in heavens was his name?

"Inside joke," he shrugged. "And I know the stairwell
left of the door will get you there in five, but they're doing repairs because of a coolant leak." He encompassed
the room with a sweep of his free hand before punching

several keys and then adjusting hardware by switching cables and adding a thumb drive while removing another. "These things happen, but there are cables under the Atlantic Ocean just to shave milliseconds off of stock trades. You'd think we could avoid coolant delays."

The time it would take. That must have been what was throwing her off. How silly of her. This must just be an off day. "Getting paid by the hour isn't what it used to be." She felt awkward making the joke, but she'd clambered up a mountain of ambitious years to get to where she was. She wouldn't be left in the dust just making conversation.

Karambit's obligatory laugh loosened her tension and made her feel that she was still a respected part of the team. "That's what I like about you," he said. "You always know what's really going on. Thanks for your help, and I'll be sure to bring some chamomile for our evening break!"

Chamomile was her favourite tea. And some people, including Perange, often met after the evening shift change at the north skywalk. Clearly he was a mainstay. What the devil was his name? "Thanks! You're a doll!" she said as she strode out of the server room. It didn't occur to her to even take a peek at the compromised stairwell, despite her usually curious nature, because she was so swept up in the adventure of the day. "I've never been to see Herr Erstgradt!" she breathed as she went.

Once she arrived at the Office of the Data Security Manager Rafe Erstgradt, she stopped and envisioned herself going directly and at a strong pace. Sure enough, when she checked her watch and reflected on the time she'd taken, she saw that the man had been right: it was about twelve minutes to get there. But she was tall and had a longer stride than he did. Surely he couldn't have reckoned upon that?

"Can I help you?" asked a secretary.

"Hm? Oh!" Perange stepped forward, holding the folder dutifully in front of her with both hands. She stood firm and confident. "I hope I'm not disturbing Mr. Erstgradt, but I was sent with some papers to help along a server editing process from Sector 4-D."

"You just missed him," the secretary replied. "As soon as he was debriefed, he got called on to answer some questions from surveillance. Apparently the coolant leak down the hall ruined a bunch of camera data." Their eyes continued the conversation — surprise, curiosity, and the disdain unique to people who don't have to take responsibility for the problem.

Perange didn't know what to do with herself. She took a deep breath. Emergencies and blips in the radar were so common in data management of this scale that she wasn't alarmed. She just had to make sure that all the financial information they were responsible for got where it needed to be and nowhere else. "Sounds just like my neck of the woods," Perange replied with a courteous smile. "I was under the impression that these documents would keep things going, but if he's gone…"

"Oh, I'm sure he'll be back momentarily," the secretary said with a smile of his own. "Why don't I pass those papers along for you?"

"Much obliged!" she said as she handed them over.

"No trouble at all!" The secretary waved a small hand.

"Have a lovely day!"

"You as well!" Perange replied as she took her leave.

Seven minutes later, as she rounded a corner in the corridor leading back to Sector 4-D, she walked past a man who she dimly recognized. He was familiar the way a bus driver was familiar; she'd have noticed if he were absent but didn't think twice to see him there today. She stopped. "Pardon me," she began. He paused. She asked, "Have you heard of the coolant leak just past the stairwell?"

"If you mean the one near the server room," Karambit replied, "I didn't come by that way. But one of the metadata specialists from Sector 7 was telling me that it was a simple maintenance error. Now I'm afraid I'm in a bit of a rush..."

"Of course," Perange replied. "Take care!"

"You too!" he said over his shoulder.

Perange returned to the server room to find that everything was nominal. Even her laptop, as she picked it up, was just where she'd left it. She had so much to catch up on that she dove immediately back into her work. She never gave another thought to the man who'd been in the room with her.

Later, she met with friends in the north skywalk and one of them had a chamomile ready. It wasn't the same person who'd promised it to her, but she didn't stop to remember that part; a friend had promised chamomile, so nothing was unusual. She was so busy. There was a minor error in the record for the number of thumb drives used in the server room during her time there, when the camera was damaged, but she thought nothing of it and answered her superior's questions easily.

Two maintenance employees received disciplinary write-ups due to the camera and coolant system problems.

It never entered anyone's mind that anyone had seen a man that day they hadn't recognized, who hadn't belonged there, or who had never been there before or after that day.

No one noticed the complete disappearance of all records of financial account activities of any kind relating to shell companies, offshore accounts, affiliates or subsidiaries of Engen. In fact, despite billions of dollars in Engen's European connections spanning many months, there was no indication anywhere in the financial systems of the continent that a company by the name of Engen — or by the searchable names of shells and related organizations — had ever existed.

The name Karambit did not appear in any context.

He did not exist.

Engen did not exist.

The financial technology infrastructure registered another normal day of business.

That was not the end of Karambit's day. Once his work for Engen at that location was concluded, he calmly made his way to the helipad on the roof. Few guards stopped him, except when they were required to check every person's ID. He made himself so familiar to most people in the facility that he was like the wall — always there, so nothing to look at. But whenever ID was required, he stopped to provide it. His identification always worked while in the building, but once he was gone, the name he used would not have been found in the system.

Not that anyone would have thought to look.

The facility's dress code made it all too easy, even with the cameras. With his face surgically altered to not be memorable, even in the cameras he was just another person in the crowd — without even needing a crowd. That he stopped to give ID meant that no one saw anything unusual.

He arrived, as he'd timed it, just as a group of operatives were loading sensitive data storage equipment onto a helicopter. They finished and he got in the vehicle with them, sitting for all the world like an authority figure. Everyone recognized him the way they recognized power: I've seen this before and must tread carefully.

No one made conversation.

They saw to their respective responsibilities, and Karambit to his own. The flight was uneventful. It landed six hours later, well into the evening, in the United Kingdom. From there, Karambit joined the train of operatives at first. But the dispersion of such material is a complicated affair, and he was soon walking alone. He procured a heavily encrypted $40,000 portable computer using clearance that didn't exist. Each operative thought Karambit had gone with someone else, and no one thought any more of the matter. The attendant who gave him the computer didn't even look up; everything was par for the course for the kind of executive he was claiming to be.

Karambit never crossed the street in fifteen steps if it could be done in fourteen. He kept his trail clear. He was always mindful of cameras, such as those in the tech building he just left, but he preferred playing to their expectations over hiding from them. People stood out when they tried to hide.

He walked into a hotel, carrying the computer in what was designed to appear as a normal briefcase. It was much heavier than that, but Karambit was athletically muscled and so heavily trained and coordinated that he moved as naturally as though the briefcase had simple paper and folders in it. Every person in the hotel, no matter how many times they'd seen him before, either passed him by as a stranger or exchanged introductions for one of countless first times.

He checked in and was provided with a piece of confidential mail that had been sent to one Kyle Andross of room 67.

"Have a lovely evening, Mr. Andross," said the night auditor.

"Thank you, and the same to you," Karambit replied in a Welsh accent.

"Kyle" went to room 67 and locked the door behind him. He removed from the briefcase the sophisticated computer and from the package an external boot drive which he proceeded to attach to the computer. He used the boot drive both to partition the laptop's hard drive and to use powerful stowaway software for connecting him directly to a highly encrypted black market satellite system.

As part of this setup, Karambit included a microchip he'd obtained from the server farm that allowed him to fake a continental proxy such that anyone trying to trace his signal would conclude that his was a dummy connection to the impenetrable financial data framework.

In short, his signal looked like a private message in one of trillions of daily financial transactions.

Throughout this operation, which he conducted like a ritual, he was reciting in his head. The Knives of Engen followed a set of guidelines called Apothegms, which ran over and over in his mind like a mantra. Each one he repeated four times before moving on to the next, and he started over after completing all four Apothegms.

Perfection is Engen is perfection.

For the rest of the evening, the Knife improved upon various skills such as his Spanish language fluency and the most up-to-date information and strategies for national and international law, especially pertaining to food trade and distribution; franchise and multinational business development; the terms of NAFTA; and various logistical policies and procedures. He used tools ranging from elite tech to simple RSS feeds to accumulate these resources and sharpen his knowledge and skill in their use.

He also checked in on a unique self-erasing digital signal. In the unlikely event that anyone else were ever to detect it, they'd have thought it gibberish. A deletion cycle, most likely, as part of the infrastructure's upkeep protocols. He knew what to look for: a series of points that could be converted to a simple RTF file to create ASCII art. Should anyone find it, they'd see images of knives and just think someone was playing a joke. He saw a ghost knife, a switchblade, and a cyclone blade. He added his own: a karambit.

Status optimal.

In the morning, food service arrived as he'd previously arranged: plain and well-balanced food with water and black coffee, left on a service table outside of the room. There was no knock, but he did not require one, and did not wish to be disturbed or to get the attention of other hotel tenants. Once he was certain the hall was empty, he retrieved his meal and only after locking the door behind him did he produce the computer equipment again; it was not the sort of material to leave about for easy viewing.

He followed breakfast with more ritualistic behaviour, repeating the Apothegms and performing Qi Gong exercises. Included with this was an array of body weight exercises so that, after the ninety minutes required, he was both fully prepared for the day and well-honed from a reasonable workout. An additional hour cleaned and maintained his tools, which ran the gamut from common to illegal.

Engen is white space. Form the picture but leave no trace.

His reflections upon this one centered around his exploits in the server farm the day before, where his own presence and all the financial activities of the organization he represented were deleted. He'd reroute shell companies with other shell companies and re-launder and double over all the re-labelling and deletion until it got to the point that there was no longer any hint that anything had been altered. The only times Engen was known were when it wanted to be, and it was not known the next moment.

This morning, he concentrated his electronic espionage upon international waters and many of the nations that dealt in oil exchange through supertankers. He tracked myriad trades and the nationalities and companies involved, and used his influence to provide two ships in particular with multiple avenues of re-labelling or disappearing.

Part of these investigations and arrangements was a brief mention of restricted waters between north-western Canada, the United States of America, and Kamchatka. The Americans had issued a Red Alert in Alaska because of a hospital explosion. He hadn't expected such an extreme result from Engen's power suppression project. Fortunately, he didn't have to worry too much about covering the organization's trail. Americans and their terrorism. They made this so easy.

Still: he tripled the surveillance resources there and arranged for agents to stake out the area. Obtaining the remains of a suicide bomber would be too risky, but some genetic samples could find their way to Engen's databanks without too much trouble. Karambit sent his orders to connections in the medical and mortician circles of Kodiak.

Engen is the end. Be the beginning.

Karambit had had lunch at the hotel's restaurant, making a show of chatting with a few people who thought he was a friend and getting in some time with a newspaper and discussions with the locals. One never knew what there was to be found at the ground level.

He spent the afternoon as a satellite network stowaway. Coordination was done through temporary, re-routed, encrypted messaging. Ongoing investigations and back-up initiatives between Knives — even Knives from different Sections — was done through this and other systems. Because of some blips in his network in eastern Europe, he investigated the name of Sebastian LeGaea, but found nothing.

Once again, Sebastian had eluded Karambit's world-class webs and networks. Karambit had to acknowledge that he was impressed.

Using one of hundreds of online aliases, the Knife set about re-directing online fora, comment threads, social media shares and hashtags, and e-mail communications in order to call attention to various conspiracy theorists, journalists, watchdogs, and the like. Some of them were talking about food distribution in the United States in ways that were inconvenient for Karambit's employers.

One strategy was to get them in touch with tabloids and similar media. It didn't matter if they were turned away; often just having it known — again, through well-placed comments and shares — that an activist had been contacted by a tabloid was enough to damage their credibility.

Some he silenced with other means: website sabotage, creating correlations with known terrorist cells, falsifying data so that the very watchdogs reporting on industries such as ____ were now buried. No industry had been influenced by any shadow organization; these were just poorly-thought-out hacker attacks. In some cases, Karambit actually worked to improve the credibility of crackpots and conspiracy nuts, just to make the waters murkier.

He also used manifold dummy accounts and online-arranged hard cash meetings to hire contract killers.

Engen's agents, representatives, or pawns were coincidentally the ones readily available to occupy the vacated positions of influential people who had retired with varying degrees of free will.

Engen is the helix. Build it and climb it.

Room service brought "Kyle Andross" his supper. He made previous arrangements for tipping. They were more than happy to accommodate his busy schedule. Guests holing up like this for days at a time were a common occurrence for a big-city hotel, so he was left to his devices.

Door 67 ate and returned to his work. He was in the process of electronically inviting himself to a clandestine train ride in two days that would include the most prominent geneticists of more than a dozen countries. It had been arranged to look like a tourist attraction that ran for a month in each season, so to see one day entirely booked was not unusual.

Some would have seen a day spent with such productive computer-generated influence as a tour de force in hacking, but to Karambit this was like the paperwork of a police officer: necessary, enormous, and undesirable. He much preferred being on the field, such as his work at the off-the-grid server farm. He was looking forward to that train ride. Still, he'd erased billions in Europe-centered Engen finances and covered their tracks in a dozen countries just by using an on-loan laptop from a nearby tech conglomerate. He only stooped to using the hotel's Wi-Fi when he wanted his activities to be picked up by investigators who would draw conclusions.

He'd of course be long gone by then.

The Knife's evening had two people on the agenda. In the morning, he'd return the computer to the company with no trace of his activity. Records would eventually show that the laptop with the serial number he was using had not been removed from the building during those days. An unlikely loose end, since he wouldn't have gotten it out of their secure framework if they could notice a problem, but he left nothing to chance.

First up: Jacinta. He'd been the Knife to discover her in Portugal years ago. Shame about the disappearance of her husband and son; they'd have been useful. He'd already done some work to her benefit the day before, when he was protecting the *Huginn* and the *Muninn* from attention or interception by most other ocean-going vessels. Unless matters had changed, he expected her to still be operating out of the *Huginn*. Most likely playing the lead surgeon both in and out of the O.R. if he understood her at all.

Understanding people was part of his business.

For the last five years, Karambit had had to dedicate frequent attention to Jacinta. Someone was looking for her. It started with Circe, an organization that shares his specialization: not existing. Even with his considerable skill, gifts, training, and resources, Karambit had failed to dig up their reason for pursuing Jacinta. She'd gone off the radar more than a decade before that; why were they looking now? Or had they been looking for so long that they'd finally caught the scent?

That seemed more likely to the Knife.

He'd faked her death quite well; how had they learned? Though he'd thrown their search enough that they didn't appear to have learned that Jacinta was a part of the ocean Section, they did enough damage to him — his information networks, his data, his body, and his connections — that Karambit had had to lie low for a year. He recovered his missions for Engen easily enough, but the search for Jacinta was an ongoing problem. If she weren't such a success, he'd simply have removed her from the Ships, since one person was not worth risking the whole operation.

Her husband disappeared from Shane Industries not long after Karambit extracted Jacinta well over a decade ago. Karambit's investigations found the false story that the husband had been killed by criminals and that lye was used in the disposal of the body. He'd also found that the death records showed subtle signs of tampering. He suspected the husband was still alive but had found no leads since. Until the efforts to find Jacinta, this was treated like playing a jigsaw puzzle after work: merely a curiosity.

Their son had vanished entirely. Obviously, there had been at least one name change. Was he the one searching for Jacinta? It seemed the obvious place to start. Though digging them up was proving just as trying as keeping Jacinta buried. Karambit rubbed his face and tapped his chair in frustration. Governments, businesses, nations, and networks were where he was comfortable. These little one-person rat races were beneath his role yet thwarted him at every turn.

He had field agents at his disposal, of course. There was only so much a laptop in a hotel room could accomplish, no matter the programs, skill, or hardware. His best networks were with his core efforts in Europe, but that only gave him a place to start. It was another of the benefits of joining the geneticists on the train: they were headed for Portugal, which was where Jacinta's story started.

Strangely, his agents, contractors, assassins, and other subordinates ran into endless amounts of trouble whenever they pursued Jacinta's family. He launched attacks and counter-attacks against Circe, of course, because it kept them on their toes. But they were not, as far as he could tell, the only player involved. Once again, his efforts to find the husband were thwarted.

One of the agents found something before being sniped, but only part of that agent's message got through: foster. And something about a drug lord. Foster wasn't enough by itself. Was it a name? Karambit checked in with other tendrils he'd put out. Some had been arrested, and thus used cyanide tablets. One was committed to Black Springs. He'd have to look into that. Several others were killed in firefights or tried and failed to turn coat.

Traitors never lasted long when a Knife of Engen was involved. On the rare occasion that it happened, they often died within minutes of the crime. Most never even learned that they'd been discovered.

Karambit opened a three-minute line directly to the *Huginn*.

A Vietnamese face stared with some surprise at their own surveillance equipment. "I-I'm honoured..." the woman started. She didn't recognize him, but that was how she knew.

"I chose you because you are the Overseer of the Excommunication Division. How is it that you are surprised to see me this way?"

Was this a test? She was humbled and awed, but also shocked; the Knives were talked about on the Ships the way that elfs or spirits were talked about on land. They were powerful, even magical, and could be the groundwork for whole cultures. But they were myths. Metaphors. Surely they weren't...

"Well? You have two minutes twenty-three seconds remaining."

"Yes, sir. Sorry, sir. It's just — I thought you were a myth." She flushed, though even thinking about it later, she would not have been able to say if she were proud, embarrassed, somewhere in between, or both.

"As it should be."

"Not everyone will believe-" she started.

"To the point, Quynh," he said sharply.

Quynh was accustomed to being the almost lordly, consummate professional. She strove to recover that identity, even as she floundered in a sparkling heartbeat. "This is quite outside my experience, sir," she started. It was a testament to his power that even though he was taking the risk of exposure or compromise by contacting her through satellite link and they were under pressure to conclude their business quickly, she felt utterly constrained by his patient silence. "I was concerned with operations, not…"

"You thought us invincible," Karambit said.

Swallowing hard, she nodded with shame.

"Take heart," he said. "I have monitored your intelligence work, and it is remembered. Now, we must be brief: I seek confirmation about the surgeon Jacinta."

Quynh was shocked. "I wouldn't dare question…" she began.

"…but you wonder why I didn't contact the Overseer of the Surgery Division," he finished.

She once again nodded in helpless silence.

"I have my reasons," he said. "You are forgiven for questioning a Knife, but you will be removed from the operation if you do not prove more perceptive in the future. Remember the Apothegms."

"But I am not-" Quynh started.

"All of Engen lives by the Apothegms," he corrected her. "The Knives merely treat it as the code, rather than merely implied by our culture of supremacy. Now: confirm."

"She is still a part of the operation, and — now that I think about it — she embodies the Apothegms well," the Overseer answered, recovering still more. "Her loyalty and accomplishment are without peer or question."

"The chances that she has been tracked, contacted, or compromised?"

"Less than zero," Quynh answered firmly.

"How so?" Karambit was legitimately surprised by the idea of negative certainty.

"Only you or another Knife could contradict my words," she replied. This carried many implications. Karambit was pleased.

"Thank you," he said. To be personally thanked by one of the Knives! He knew she'd be riding that high for a month at the least. "After this conversation, you will find instructions in a file I've attached to your device. Make no hard copies of it. It will delete itself in twenty minutes. I expect you to have those instructions memorized. Use them for a one-time means of contacting me should a Knife need information you possess — especially concerning Jacinta. Mention this conversation to no one. The consequences for wasting my time shall be severe."

"Yes, sir. Thank you, sir."

"Engen is the end," he said.

The connection had terminated before she got the words "Be the beginning" out of her mouth.

Karambit sat back and pulled at an ear as he thought. He would make more in-person investigations concerning the husband and child.

The second person he was investigating — since he thought of the previous efforts as only really amounting to Jacinta — was in the United States. Normally he'd have left such a person to the Knives in the USA, but this person was a special case. A hacker, and so very much of a spirit with Karambit himself.

It was now well into Spring. It had been December when Karambit learned about a place in the American State of New Mexico called Towerton. The situation was so bizarre that no one would touch it, even when a State of Emergency had been declared.

It was…complicated. Most of the matter — inexplicable, widespread agoraphobia; riots and deaths; a lopsided economy; and hundreds of reports of missing persons — was of little interest. Towerton was a crossroads community, amounting to little more than a glorified gas stop and camping resupply centre. Much of their appeal was in mechanical work like replacements and repairs.

It was the drones that had caught Karambit's attention.

They came from a competition between a larger drone company — which has been putting significant amounts of money and effort into distancing itself from the incident — and a small, independent start-up. The start-up used some surprisingly clever tactics and tools to keep its leadership under the radar and utterly vanish after the incident. Karambit had tracked the owner down to an online persona called Incendio. But the drone business and all Incendio activity ceased when the problems of the town became public.

Information was fragmented because the whole town had a kind of mass hysteria, but that was part of the appeal. Karambit was seeing all the signs of a person with a gift, a power of some kind. Building the Helix, as the

Apothegm went, was all about recruiting talent. The Knife found enough evidence to suggest that "Incendio" had had help, but that was not surprising. Field agents turned up some intriguing details, but nothing on Incendio or the helpers. Multiple stories in the community and from neighbouring centres like highway patrols and convenience stores came up with conflicting details but one common thread: someone escaped in the tumult. Different parties in different directions.

Ghost and Switch, two Knives working Stateside, were too occupied to pursue the matter but helped him narrow down some details. Incendio had clearly changed their name and switched up some of their software and hardware to mask their transitions to new locations. If not for the other two Knives, even Karambit might have gotten lost. But they found a pattern in hacker activities moving northwest in the USA.

To State authorities and some federal organizations, these activities appeared to be separated by too many weeks and borders to be the same person. Since it didn't look like terrorism, they had a low priority on the government front. But the combined efforts of three Knives of Engen, through infiltration and extraction, were enough to piece together Incendio's rough direction.

The trail ended in Idaho. But then, it was a tenuous connection. Like a constellation, just drawing lines between unrelated stars. It took a patient, tireless eye to watch enough to make the connections without being shown.

Karambit was just that. He hid in unusual places, moved in curves, and could stay sharp for a long time.

CHAPTER 05
HOW FULL THE NEST

After New Mexico

December?

He was already losing track of the days.

"Do you know how expensive my hardware was?" Thatcher asked. He was in his mid-twenties, Hispanic, overweight, and well-groomed. He opened the glove compartment as he spoke and found, among other things, a car knife.

"We both know you don't care that much about money," Soto replied. Though also Hispanic, this man could pass for white if he put in the effort. In fact, he had the skill to pass for many things he was not. He was in his late forties, looked mid-thirties, and maintained a buzz cut. He was easily half a foot taller than Thatcher and carried himself as the rock around which a river flowed.

"I do when I don't have any," the younger man retorted. He turned the tool over and over, glancing occasionally out the window or the windshield. He didn't look at his athletic counterpart. "And I don't have a lot of time for sight-seeing. Where are we, anyway?"

"Colorado. For now." Soto didn't look at his companion but kept his eyes on the road as he spoke. "I've had your businesses investigated. You did well."

Thatcher's widened eyes scanned the older man, then narrowed and returned to the passenger window. He ran his fingers over the different parts of the knife. There was a button for flipping out the blade, a knob for breaking glass, a flashlight function, and even a component for starting fires. "We've been to hotels, camps, shelters. You've even had us sleeping in the car. For how many days now? And why? I can't rest like this!"

"Don't you want to know how I tracked down your work? You tried pretty hard to cover your trail, and you were clever for someone untrained."

"No," he said. He looked at his hands and fought his best not to admit to himself that in fact he'd love to know. He absently flicked out the knife, reset the blade, and repeated this sequence. "You're like the Santa Claus, except you have to explain why you thought of that present and all the things you did to get it."

Soto pursed his lips but couldn't deny a certain amount of truth in that. He cast a quick glance at his passenger and tried to mask it as checking the traffic on the other man's side. "What do you mean, 'the' Santa Claus? If you're trying to play yourself off as a foreigner, you're preaching to an Atheist."

Thatcher allowed some silence to thicken the distance between them before he decided what to say and what to keep to himself. "…it's a good habit."

"Your mother wouldn't-"

"Don't." Thatcher's tone was sulphurous.

…

They drove in silence.

After Colorado

Winter. Definitely winter.

Thatcher was in the bathroom with the door open, fastidiously grooming his curly black hair and black goatee. His nails — both hands and feet — had had his meticulous attention as well. He liked to shower in the mornings and then run through these ablutions because they made him feel human. Sometimes it felt like his hanging belly conflicted with that. He ran through his situation in his head for the millionth time, indexing his hopes and problems.

Soto entered the room carrying hefty paper bags that smelled wonderful.

Thatcher emerged from the bathroom with criticisms on his lips but mispronounced them. Instead of the intended questions about lying low, his words came out as, "Is that Thai?"

Winter layers shed and stowed, Soto was already busy arranging the meal on Thatcher's bed. He took his to his own bed and sat with his back against the board. "I haven't forgotten, you know," was all he said as he dug in.

Thatcher's helping was Joke, a common breakfast food in Thailand and his favourite way of starting the day. He processed Soto's words as he ate, sitting cross-legged on the centre of the bed, and offered a *"gracias"* halfway through his meal. He honestly couldn't remember a time when he'd had Thai around Soto.

"De nada," Soto said once they were finished. He con-

tinued in Spanish: "It would be better if we spoke in our home tongue, don't you think?"

"All I remember is growing up in the States," Thatcher responded in English.

Soto frowned. "You could meet me halfway once in a while, you know. I know you're not used to-"

"I'm not trying to be that stand-off-ish," the younger man interrupted. He said that last in an odd lilt; like many bilinguals, his tongue chose strange places to get tangled. While he usually avoided these verbal brambles, he chose that one to emphasize how differently he spoke. "I don't remember Portugal or Spain, and they put me with the Mexican kids. Sometimes I think America expects entire languages to have skin colours."

"Their system saved you, you know."

Thatcher looked the older man square in the eyes. "Geronimo Gualtier?"

"Don't be cute," Soto admonished. "And no, I won't be using that one anymore. You should know, 'Incendio.' What kind of name is Fire, anyway?"

Thatcher got a perverse enjoyment out of this exchange. It reminded him of "flame wars" — arguments on the Internet that got out of hand. He resisted the temptation for vitriol all the same. "So," he said after assessing this unusual man with the skill to look normal, "Was it you I was dodging so much? Kudos for tracking me to New Mexico. Did you have help?"

"You have no idea," Soto replied. "But no, I found you through your drone product supply chain. My fieldwork was part of how we were able to track down your online history after the fact. You did well," he said with pride.

Thatcher was pleased by the praise and resented that pleasure. But he set that aside, as he had other things on his mind. "All right, then, who was it?"

"When we noticed we weren't the only ones looking for you, we put in a fair amount of effort to throw them off your trail."

Setting the empty bowl of Joke aside, Thatcher stretched out on the bed and cupped his hands behind his head so he could stare at the ceiling while they spoke. "How kind of you," he remarked.

"You know I want what's best for you," Soto started.

"Don't give m-"

"Yes, I damn well will!" the older man declared. It wasn't a shout, but it was the deep-chested raw energy of a muscular man who had no time for disagreement. "You have no idea what I sacrificed for you, how hard it's been to protect you!"

"I've taken care of myself, thank you very much. And I didn't see all that much protection while I was in foster care, now, did I?" This was more than antagonism; it was intended to sting.

The fire and lightning of wrath is what he expected. This wasn't their first exchange on the subject. But Soto's answer was cold: "The foster care *was* your protection."

After Wyoming

"What are we looking for?" Thatcher asked. He was wearing an aviator hat, a second-hand parka, the heaviest boots he'd ever seen in his life, and two pairs of gloves: one on the inside that was more like hand socks than proper gloves, and invincible sealskin mittens. An unused camera dangled like an amulet from a lanyard around his neck.

In theory, they were part of a tourist group. There were eight or nine people, including themselves but not the guide. In practice, the cluster was made up of several cliques of various sizes and connections. Thatcher and Soto simply appeared to be a pair. Thatcher had insisted that they tell the story that they were business partners when they signed up for the SNOW (Shuttle Network of Whitefish) bus. This was his first attempt at conversation since.

Soto was silent as each of the cliques (including him and Thatcher) were dispensed hot chocolate and spread out. A group unrelated to the tour were congregating around one of the artfully maintained trees in this section. Strands of worked boughs stretched above the street like living tinsel. Vehicles were interspersed along the immaculate winter wonder road, most likely belonging to the employees, skiers, and hikers of the resort. Most of the others from the tour group were stretching their legs, taking pictures, telling stories, and exploring various nooks and niches. Even when Thatcher regarded him expectantly, he didn't at first meet the gaze. Finally, just when the younger man was accepting that there would be no response, the older replied: "I've never bugged or tagged you, you know."

"Didn't say you did," Thatcher responded. He took the cover off the lens and started taking pictures with no thought to where he was actually pointing the device. Inwardly, he wondered if he could trust that statement, but he wanted to believe it. It would be a relief to be sure he was more than cattle. "But what-"

"No one's gonna believe your little display, you know," Soto cut in.

"Huh?"

"You just took a picture of the open sky."

Blinking, Thatcher stopped to look back at his previous shots. Sure enough, there was a corner from the heights of one of the nearby resort buildings on the lower right corner of the image, and nothing but sky for the rest. "They don't know what I'm getting at," he said lamely. He barely took in the breathtaking scenery: snowy mountains; tufts of alpine greens; resort buildings with the cozy cabin aesthetic; ice sculptures; red and green craftworks like paper bells on the bough-lines. Several patches of real estate were left clear on the hill they occupied so that tourists could indulge in the hibernal spectacle. The pair alternated between hot chocolate and lukewarm words.

"You must be much more comfortable in front of a computer, eh, *Grumete*?"

"Never call me that again."

"Sure thing, Grumete."

Thatcher stopped, let the camera dangle, and turned to foist his most powerful glare upon the older man. "I'll find a name for you if you keep that up," he said.

"I have many names. One from you would be a pleasure," Soto replied with a smirk.

"You still haven't told me why we're here," Thatcher pointed out.

"Surely you're not conceding defeat that easily?"

"What makes you think you won anything? It's not like we're doing anything in straight lines here, anyway."

"We've been going more or less north. That's a straight line," Soto said.

"Running off to Canada, are we? I think not." Thatcher quipped. "Is this about my drones?"

"I get the feeling," mused Soto aloud, "that you're grasping at straws because you want straight answers."

"Who doesn't?" Thatcher retorted. The older man gave him a sideways half-nod in acknowledgment of his point. He went on: "I can't get anything set up this way, you know."

"Meredith Heaney survived, by the way," Soto said.

Before the younger man could say anything, the group were called back to the SNOW bus. It looked like a blue moving van with two sets of modular treads. Thatcher was just about to get back into the conversation when a beefy White man — the sort who clearly skipped Leg Day many times and thought protein was the only important nutrient — stepped into their view. "I think maybe you gringotts should stay here," he said with a smirk.

Soto and Thatcher looked at each other in surprise, though each had a very different reason. Thatcher was afraid; he didn't even do much fighting in video games. Soto, by contrast, could see not less than seven ways to render the troublemaker helpless. He stood ready and wore an expression like that of a childcare worker dealing with a delinquent.

"You watch too many movies," Thatcher said. Soto gave him a glance and the walking protein powder commercial frowned in confusion. "Gringott's is a Harry Potter thing. You mean '*gringo*,'" he elaborated with an accented flourish, "which sort of means White person." Part of him was expecting a beating, and part of him wondered if the bench-presser knew his mockery for what it was.

"You wish you were White," the brute replied.

The tour guide cleared his throat and made some distinct sounds with his gun to indicate that there was one. It was holstered. For now. "Way I see it, it's high time we all got back on yonder bus," the guide drawled.

Thatcher sighed with relief once the big man turned around and headed off with a cluster of men trying to look tough. Patches worked into their hats and coats, aggressive and predatory posturing, leers at female attendees, face and tattoos — all manner of hints and symbols that Thatcher felt little inclination to explore. While the groups united on the bus to begin the next leg of their tour, Soto muttered, "Was that necessary?"

The younger man shrugged. "Who's Meredith Heaney?"

Soto blinked. "Drone company?"

"Oh. Right. Wasn't she with the other two?"

"Didn't you keep tabs at all? I know you've stolen glimpses by grabbing people's smartphones when they weren't looking," Soto continued.

"Those were smaller questions. Like figuring out where we were at the time."

"I've had to leave you alone long enough a couple of times now. You must have gone to coffee shops or libraries or those computer brothels."

Thatcher actually laughed, but he also made the barely conscious decision to switch to Spanish. He doubted anyone on the snow coach could speak it, but they weren't likely to be overheard anyway; the coach was old, reliable, and loud. Everyone else was talking, too. He was conflicted about speaking Spanish to this man in particular, and didn't know Portuguese. It came down to heritage and identity. But then, he also had a British name. What had his mother been thinking?

These emotions flashed through too fast to have words attached in his head. They were more like the rumbling of the coach. While the vehicle's activity naturally generated all that rumbling, the rumbling itself wasn't important for moving the vehicle and it wasn't there to be examined. It was simply a part of the process.

All Soto saw of this was a distasteful curl in Thatcher's lips as the younger man spoke: "Do you mean gamer cafés? Computers aren't prostitutes, old man."

Soto smiled for a little too long and said nothing.

"...what?"

"Is that what you call me in your head?"

"Not what I meant."

"Why are we still talking about this?" Soto had to express some disappointment. He liked the Spanish more than the English, but still: "We're missing out on the scenery."

"You realize there's not a lot I can do with those public computers, right?"

"I think you can do plenty with them," Soto corrected. He still had that irksome smile, like he'd gained something or had a burden cut away. Thatcher couldn't make sense of it but didn't puzzle it out.

Instead: "I'm sure you're having me watched somehow. While I'm using them, anyway."

"Don't be paranoid," Soto said. "It's rude. Besides, I'm

watching over you. It's not the same."

"Sure thing, Big Brother. Now: what aren't you telling me?"

"Do you want to walk the rest of the way?"

Thatcher stared. "It's a two hour ride back to civilization!"

"That's the kind of walk we'd need. I'm not holding back by choice, you know."

After Montana

January?

The hardest part of espionage, as far as Soto was concerned, was looking common. This meant no obvious signs of authority, no unusual tools unless they could be easily explained as something else, and having his face openly exposed. As he walked the gangway of the hotel, he knew the location of every camera in a sphere of at least thirty feet. He had a rough idea of their field of view and resolution. He knew the locations and ranges of the nearest four cell phone and radio towers and wi-fi networks. He knew this information the way that someone entering a mall for the first time in an unfamiliar city will pick up on the signs, both literal and metaphorical, of what's available and where to get it.

He wore light blue jeans and an untucked dress shirt under his winter coat. Winter boots in the hiking style. It was hard to tell if the Americans would bat an eye at this or not; they had strange ideas here. He opened the hotel door and spoke even as he was closing it: "I've been called in on a mission." The statement was punctuated with the click of the doorknob. Still without looking behind him, he checked the window and door for slivers of light: opportunities for forcing them, or viewing himself or Thatcher. "We've lost contact with agents in Ghana. How do you feel about a field tr-" he turned about to take in the room properly.

The beds were made. By itself, this was not unusual; Thatcher liked to be clean and organized.

The remote was under the corner of the TV, next to the power button. The dresser was closed and clear of stray socks, wrappers, or other detritus. No one had changed the garbage basket. Used towels and cloths were placed next to it for replacement. Thatcher hadn't had any bags or other gear, so he was picking up things on and for the run — such as disposable grooming supplies. All the hotel items formed a scene, but no play.

Soto had only ducked out for twenty minutes. He'd stepped out like this in various places during their travels. They didn't always use hotels. But this time, he knew something was different. He couldn't find the details to support it, but the change cut off his words.

Thatcher often left the bathroom door closed. Even when he lived alone. In fact, he always left every door closed until he needed to be in another room. So it wasn't unusual that the door to the bathroom — the only door in the hotel room other than the one opening onto the gangway — was closed.

He opened the bathroom door and found the emptiness he expected. After years of searching, he'd finally found Thatcher. It went against all protocol to take the man with him for any mission, or even to be in his presence for any extended period of time. Clandestine operations rarely worked well with company.

Soto cursed with nothing short of fluorescence in Portuguese.

Thatcher was gone.

After Idaho

January.

It took all of Oregon before Thatcher was sure that he was alone.

At some point along the way, he'd overheard a radio conversation about the New Year. He hadn't caught any of the specifics, however, so they could have been talking about yesterday or next week or even a month ago. He'd been dreaming about a city covered in swarms of flies the size of drones.

He had to be fast and clever. Someone with Soto's skills and resources wouldn't be easy to lose. It would have to be more than a foot race. Which was good — Thatcher had to count himself as extra baggage because of his weight. Or so he thought to himself. Fortunately, there was a lot of growth of Latino peoples in the region. He didn't know if that included Hispanics or not. The western States could be different about their words. Nevertheless, both were lumped together as often as not, and even their experience of being welcomed was prone to variation.

He found himself in an abandoned bus.

At first, he was scared. But he looked around at his homeless fellows: most just wanted a night's sleep; no one carried weapons as far as he could tell; there was muttering; most were either of African descent or shared his ethnicity; and someone on the roof of the bus was ranting. He wasn't going to get an opportunity to clean his clothes without stains or memories. Surprisingly, he was one of the few without a cell phone.

He sat up helplessly. Hands on knees, he looked out windows or roamed his gaze over the other occupants. One of them, an elderly Latina, sidled over and spoke her mother tongue: "Let me show you how to get set up." Her accent was Puerto Rican, though Thatcher couldn't have named it. He'd heard it once or twice before, and she sometimes dropped in English words like mismatched socks on the bedroom floor, but he could understand her. She curled her hand toward herself a few times, and Thatcher realized she was coaxing him out.

Once he was out of the way, she stowed her cell phone and slowly went about the process of detaching the back of the seat so that it could be placed atop the bottom cushion. She explained each step as she went. Then she pointed out one of the seats behind the pair, where a man with big feet was sleeping in a fashion similar to what she'd just set up. "See how he's bent? You'll need to limber up in the morning, but it'll do."

"*Muchas gracias,*" Thatcher said. Then: "I wish I could give back somehow; you've all been kind. Even the weirdo on the roof."

The lady chuckled. "We gotta look out for each other."

The next morning, Thatcher awoke to find that a woman with a burn scar on the left side of her face was standing over him and assessing him. "AH!" he declared bravely, then nearly fell into the floor space between seats.

She giggled and walked away.

Shaken, Thatcher sat up. Daylight and semi-clean windows filled up most of the space for him. It was surreal. Something about the abandoned bus in early morning light was haunting in a way he didn't have words for. Most of the heat came from himself, blankets, and the combined body heat trapped in the vehicle. Doors and windows were kept closed in the winter, he'd been told. The smell was less unpleasant than he'd have expected; it was a sweatier, more metallic take on pleather. It was warm enough to sleep, but getting up in the morning came with a chill. Felt in the bones, that chill was as much about vulnerability and pasted-together domesticity as it was about the winter or any amount of clothing.

It reminded him of growing up as a ward of the state. Short stays in foster homes, being juggled by residential treatment centres and group homes. In the system, he was labelled a problem child. He always thought it was because of his race, that they were mislabelling him intentionally. Disruptions happened around him — to him, as often as not — but they'd hear none of that.

His hands rubbed along his pants and shirt. There was nowhere to wash them and no soap, anyway. Nothing to be done with his hair. He was glad there were no mirrors. He expected an echo, but when someone near the front spoke, there was none. He didn't tune in enough to hear what anyone was saying. Most of them were muttering to themselves.

There were blankets, but they stayed in the bus. Those were the rules.

After a deep sigh, he managed to get his bulk under him and get out of his seat.

A small cluster of people in a mishmash of clothing stood near the front of the bus. Between them was an oil drum that would house a fire at night. During the day, it was just sort of a place to stand. Thatcher slowly turned a full circle. Some of the homeless were wandering away in each direction, though they rarely collected much past the occasional duo or trio. In fact, as he watched, even those slowly separated or dispersed.

He'd be leaving shortly, but what was the rush? He would be no less visible moving than he would be staying with a group like this. That frightened him, but there was a thrill and a kind of ego boost as well. When you're at the bottom, it's not all that different from flying high. Don't look up.

"Why do you only get together at night?" he asked in English as he approached the oil drum.

Two of them looked up at him while another three did not. One of those three was fiddling with something small and black. One of the two who looked said, "Who wants to know?"

Suspicion? Now? After being in a bus for the night? "Uh...just me?" Unconsciously, his hands tugged down on his shirt to make sure his belly wasn't exposed.

"You a cop?" asked one of the three. She didn't look up.

"Are you serious?" Thatcher asked, looking meaningfully upon his woeful condition.

"You aren't homeless like we are. You're new to this."

"Yes. I'm running. Am I the first?"

"To be running?" asked the man who was struggling. Bald, Black, and very tall. "No," he went on. "You're no first. Wouldn't be no first cop, neither."

Flustered, Thatcher did his best not to look how he felt. He focused on his shoulders and tried to keep them high and broad. He almost tip-toed. One of the five in front of him snickered. "I can help with your phone," he offered.

Several glances shot up at that. He heard a few people approach from behind and to his sides. Before him, they said, "Really?"

After twenty minutes, those who he could help without tools had working and optimized phones. In return, they explained that too many homeless people in daylight made "cacklers" edgy. *What's a cackler?* They also gave him a run-down of nearby locations for food and other help, and rough maps drawn in the slushy dirt to give him a sense of where to go next. They couldn't offer much for getting access to computers, except for social supports to help find jobs. There weren't a lot of those for people who couldn't manage a certain level of hygiene.

Well, he was definitely off the radar.

As he travelled through Oregon, he had had a lot of time to think. He was somewhere between running and hiding, yes, but there was something else to this. In New Mexico, he'd seen things that should not have been. Talents. *Regalos.* Though not convinced, he was starting to wonder. He'd been in Towerton for something like three or four months. Then things became…a problem.

Now that he thought about it, most of the fosters, groups, and other homes were the same. Never more than four months before he had to uproot. He'd talked to other

kids from time to time. Assessments. Temporary wards.
Most lived that feeling of being juggled or boxed up for
inventory, so he chalked up his experience to the same.

One of his early foster parents showed him the magic
of computers.

Now he was hitch-hiking on the side of a highway
in Oregon. At least, he thought he was still in Oregon.
A mountain foamed out of the earth to his right. It was
stupendous and repulsive at once, like the shoulders of
a crowded club where he was not welcome. He was desperate for a computer. Growing up, they kept the chaos
away. He could go to the public library and play on the
computers. Or the devices of foster parents. Even schools,
sometimes. Computers didn't have emotional whims.
They had their quirks, yes, but they never tossed you to
the curb. And somewhere, if you looked hard enough and
learned how to see, you'd find their problems and there
would be a sense to them.

There was no sense in people.

Soup kitchens and homeless shelters blurred the days
together. Sometimes the shelters would provide (more or
less) new clothing. Not always a perfect fit, but they were
on budget. He helped where he could because for reasons
he couldn't quite explain, he detested a free meal. Maybe
that was what had led him to a business degree.

There weren't many opportunities to flee back into
those computer sanctuaries. Once or twice, when he got
more presentable clothes and the shelters actually had
something that passed for soap, he managed to clean up
enough that he could go to gaming cafes or public libraries. Those days were glistening islands with pristine caves

to keep out the rain.

He also had run-ins with underbellies and criminal groups. They looked at a vulnerable Hispanic man, someone grim and alone, and saw an easy opportunity for a drug mule or even low-rate bodyguard. He actually laughed at that one. In all his life, the only things he'd ever beaten were buffets.

Still, he took some of the jobs.

It was like cleaning vomit out of a rental car and hoping the owners wouldn't notice that anything had been amiss. He hated resorting to such primitive crime, no matter how "victimless." Once, he actually got his hands on a poncho and a sombrero. He wasn't Mexican, but a depressing number wouldn't know the difference. If he was going to fall into stereotypes — after so many years of seeing himself as an upstanding American — he might as well do it in style. Not everything he trafficked was drugs. Sometimes he bussed around parcels full of Don't Ask.

They tried to keep track of him.

But if he was able to slip the net of a professional spy like Soto, then getting out of some of these criminal "networks" was a joke. He did it enough to get a day's pay and he was gone, covered in some social fluid that reeked of prejudice and false hope. Sometimes he fell in with Hispanic groups of various types. One was a traveling group of masked performers.

Thatcher couldn't sing or play any instruments, but he did the stuff behind the scenes and loved them for the opportunity. When he fell in with a group he was proud of, like this one, he introduced himself as Braulio. When he was with the criminals and other such enterprises, he gave them made-up names. Like Gringott, at one point.

"I don't think you're from around here, are you, Braulio?" asked the man in the fox mask.

Thatcher shook his head. He didn't trust himself to speak. He was helping them put away their elaborate makeshift stage, and currently had his hands full of rope.

"You ask him yet?" called out a woman in a bear mask.

Some of the audience, made up of Black, white, and Hispanic people, had dispersed. But there were enough strangers milling about that the performers hadn't yet taken off their masks.

Thatcher put two and two together even as the fox answered that he had not asked. "I can't come with you," he said with a heavy heart. It was tempting.

"Why not?" asked the fox. "Surely you find no fault with our cooking?"

Thatcher chuckled. A younger member of their troupe stepped into their conversation wearing a stylized owl mask. "I'm proud of my cooking!" he declared. "Papa, can we stay another day and stage a cooking contest?"

Thatcher opened his mouth to speak, but a fourth member, this one wearing the mask of a beaded lizard, cut him off: "That was one time, Alvaro!"

"But it was SO GREAT!" Alvaro replied as he started to take off his owl mask.

The one in the bear mask stopped him. "Not yet," she said.

"You're careful about your faces, but not your names?" Thatcher asked. He sporadically shot glances around himself, looking for signs of being watched. There were stragglers — mostly white people — doing just that.

"Names can be changed, Braulio," answered the fox mask.

Fair enough.

Just then, a deep-voiced woman spoke from behind Thatcher's shoulder. "If y'all lookin' foa new playa, I'd like a step or two down dat route," she said.

Thatcher whirled around. "I know you! The gamer cafe a few days ago!"

Delighted, the newcomer gave him a hug. "Dis one done fixed all the computas! H'was a mahvel!"

Thatcher jerked a thumb. "Elodia here used to be in a travelling circus."

"Sounds like you're a long way from home yourself," the fox remarked to her.

"'Tween roofs," Elodia smiled. To Thatcher she said, "I thought odd you up an' went wit da wind. Ain't it summin' we meetin' a-ghen?"

"Even in the wild," said the mask of the beaded lizard, "there are connections that can stand long distances. It would be a shame to see you gone," this to Thatcher.

"I...don't know how to explain it. It would be wonderful," he started, and gestured inarticulately at the others in the conversation. "But now I'm holding you up," and he started trying to distract himself by sorting out the rope some more.

Elodia laid a gentle hand on his, pressing it down so he couldn't continue. She held up her phone and wiggled it meaningfully.

"I...don't..." Thatcher felt himself flush.

"You don't have a phone!?" Alvaro was shocked. He

adjusted his owl mask, then ran off to one of the chests the troupe was about to load into their van.

The bear and the fox looked at each other. "Seems fitting," fox said. The bear could only nod.

As the boy returned with a lime green cell phone, Thatcher experienced a kind of electricity inside him. Lime was one of his favourite flavours, and he loved the green by association. But then he realized what was happening. "Oh, but I couldn't-"

"We lost someone on the road," said the beaded lizard mask. "He got between some police shooting at some coloured folks who happened to be in the...well, it was wrong, no matter time or place."

"We know how it feels," said the fox. "Needing the road."

"But I don't—" Thatcher started.

"You're not the first we've met like this," cut in the bear mask. "It's been beautiful working with you for the last couple of days. We're not newborns, we know you got a destination haunting you."

"Dun' hauntin's come from past?" asked Elodia.

"Sure do," said Alvaro. "But sometimes needing to get somewhere can weigh you down like that."

Thatcher looked at the boy in a new light. "You've seen some things. All of you have."

"Hard not to," answered the bear mask. "Times as they are."

"We've kept all the stuff for the mask of the Bonefish," said the beaded lizard, "but we don't need his phone. We'll keep in touch with you, help you keep it set up."

Thatcher's lip shook. "This is a lot, just for a couple of days..."

"It doesn't take much," Alvaro said. "Sometimes you just know."

"Best be gettin' my numba," Elodia said with a grin.

"I…" Thatcher looked at the phone, then each of the people around him in turn. "I'm grateful."

"Good," said the bear mask. "Now, we don't doubt you'll be heading your own way when we hit the road again. But you don't have to reinvent the wheel every time you need a ride."

Thatcher frowned at that.

"What we mean is," fox explained, "don't start over thinking you've lost all your work. Sometimes you've gotta cut away a lot of wood to make a mask, and sometimes you gotta start that mask over. But all that cutting taught you how to make your new mask better, even if this one didn't work."

Thatcher looked at the phone in his hands for a long moment and swallowed. "I'm…more of a tech guy than… uh…"

"Yeah," the bear mask said, "we heard Elodia here. I don't know much about these cafes she's describing, but it sounds like you play a different kind of music than we do, if you know what I mean."

Thatcher smiled. "I like that."

"Y'know," Elodia started, "I friends in Seattle." With her accent, it almost rhymed with "beetle." Sometimes Thatcher struggled with accents he hadn't heard much, but this one he could piece out fairly well if he had the chance to give his full attention. He followed her as she continued: "Some actin' scene dere, I'll give numbas later. An' dey computas…!"

Now armed with a direction, Thatcher suddenly felt

his spirits rising. "When I'm set up," he said, speaking to the troupe, "call me. Anything you need that can be done with a computer."

"I think perhaps your mask wears you," the beaded lizard remarked. "You're more than that one thing."

"We only really need to grow our name," added the fox. "And she's right: you have a gift for feeling out other people."

This sent a chill through Thatcher for a moment, but Elodia cut in then for a conversation with the troupe about where she'd fit in for their immediate future. No one noticed that he was nonplussed. He ran a hand through his hair, fairly clean but un-styled. What they were talking about fell more under hacking than Internet navigation or software manipulation. He missed his work with business and business with work. But he couldn't go back to those drones. If nothing else, Soto would be keeping tabs on those circles.

He had his skills with digital technology from passion and sheer time investment. But he felt awkward in human society and at a disadvantage when navigating emotion. How was it, then, that people told him about a gift for emotion? What did that mean? He didn't feel he understood the feelings of others, and certainly couldn't influence them. He thought back to his time with Soto, and before Soto had found him, and could find no answers. Always he looked for a base of operations.

Never could he manage more than four months.

But Seattle was as good as anything. And what he had now looked like friendship. It looked like something more than just passing on the road. And surely the odd phone call wouldn't hurt?

CHAPTER 06
BLADE PROTECTORS

Seattle, Washington

1 March

Thatcher sat at the small table that passed for a desk. It was squeezed between the real wall of the building and the partition of a cubicle. It had a computer, a stool without back support, and a wireless Bluetooth headset that required the computer when he'd started a month ago. He'd since replaced that headset with a proper wireless phone setup. He was a "go-fer," as the desk jockeys called it: an entry-level employee who would go for whatever a more established employee or group needed.

He'd put on brown slacks and an untucked off-blue dress shirt. As the resident Mr. Fix-It, his ruffled presentation was expected: no one at the company generally noticed the guy with a headset crouched in the corner reprogramming the fickle printer or helping an older employee navigate the e-mail system while talking through tech support on his phone.

There was a knock behind him. "This is the SS Stewart, requesting permission to dock!"

Thatcher shook his head as he turned. The other man had about ten years on Thatcher and wore suspenders and thick-rimmed glasses with a taped bridge. "You could just say 'hi' like everyone else," Thatcher chided.

"Pretty sure most people just tell you what they need," Stewart pointed out with a cheer that didn't match the statement.

Thatcher shrugged. He had to admit, the man had a point. "What can I do for you?"

"Ah, c'mon, Braulio," Stewart said with mock offense. "You really saved my keister with that virus, and I'm the one who pushed to get you this...uh...I mean, it's not an office, exactly. Well, sorry about that, but you had to just walk the halls before, and..."

Thatcher laughed as Stewart stumbled over himself. "I really am thankful to have this," he said. He wasn't joking; in the last few months he'd dealt with Towerton, Soto, soup kitchens, and sleeping in buses — all while phone-hopping between the troupe, Elodia, and her friends in acting circles. Next to that, a regular paycheck and a place to sit while he worked at a tech firm were practically magical.

Stewart rubbed his hands contentedly. "See? We're buddies now!" Thatcher was warming to the having-friends idea, but he didn't know yet how he felt about this poindexter from Accounting. Stewart pressed on: "Just thought I'd say Happy First Month!"

"*Gracias*," Thatcher said. One of his hands was gliding over the computer keys as he was gearing up for the day's responsibilities. Then: "Any luck with the dating scene since?"

Stewart had gone a little too far down the online dating rabbit hole on a work computer. Thatcher had handled the consequences with discretion, but the accountant was left a little embarrassed. Although Thatcher hadn't done anything quite like that himself, he knew embarrassment well enough. So he chatted with Stewart at the other man's workstation from time to time, and made an effort not to be mean. He didn't know if he wanted a work friend, but he definitely didn't want a work enemy.

In response to the Hispanic's question, the painfully white employee scratched the back of his neck and looked around awkwardly. "A few false starts, but nothing. I know most people don't find my job exciting, but I love playing with numbers and keeping everything running, you know?"

They'd had all this out before, so Thatcher had no interest in talking about it yet again. Apparently his continued half-attentions toward the computer and asking small-talk questions wasn't getting the message across. "Yeah, I hear you. Has anyone been tracking Jake? He wasn't at his office when I came in, and you know he makes me nervous."

"He's already a conspiracy nut. If he finds out we're all keeping an eye on him, he'll be vindicated forever." Stewart sighed. He wasn't aware that he was a social benchmark at Spindle — if you couldn't get along with Stewart, the problem wasn't him. Everyone else knew, though. "We think he has a frenemy in Bevis."

"I don't know which is worse," Thatcher chuckled, "the fact that someone actually called their child Bevis, or the fact that we can use words like 'frenemy' at work and no one bats an eye."

Stewart laughed, a quick and high-pitched sound. "Steel said that, too! I was talking with her, Aim, and the Patriot earlier. One of those 'liaising' meetings. Anyway, we're all on board for keeping an eye on Jake. And we were thinking we should get you into a work thing."

Thatcher leaned back and let his suspicion show.

"Now, now," Stewart said with hands raised. "I-"

"We should get you a cake," Mashaka interrupted. She leaned over the wall of Thatcher's half-cubicle so that he was looking up at her. She was so lanky she made this look easy, and her folded arms on top of the partition were incongruously graceful for what she was doing. "A whole month!"

Thatcher visibly beamed with Mashaka's appearance, but his lips flattened: "Should I be worried that making it a month is a big deal?"

"Well," Stewart fumbled, "it's just that-"

"Ain't no white dudes — even starting out — who get this cheese grater to work in," Mashaka said bluntly, making a sweeping gesture with one hand. "But you knew that, eh, Brau?"

Thatcher nodded once. "How's my favourite trouble-maker?" he asked to change the subject.

Mashaka made as to be offended. "Now, good sir…"

"Y-you have lovely hair today," Stewart said. He was fidgeting with a pen. He didn't have a pocket protector, despite the stereotype, but Thatcher thought he wanted Mashaka's approval. Thatcher made a mental note to ask about that later.

"Thank you," she said after a moment's pause. "I think

I fixed it pretty good. I was going for a Beyoncé vibe, but that obviously didn't work."

"I didn't peg you for the Beyoncé type," Thatcher remarked.

Mashaka shrugged. "I don't know about type, but if I like a look, why not?"

Thatcher conceded the point with a sideways shift of the head and a bumping up of the lower lip. "What's next fo-" he started.

"Three's a crowd," said a voice like parchment from behind him. Thatcher now had a real wall on his right; a self-conscious Stewart on his left; Mashaka above the partition in front of him, wriggling her fingers in greeting behind Thatcher as she checked her phone; and behind him…

"Liam," Stewart greeted. "Thanks for helping me with the D&D database."

"Jolly good!" the other man replied. It wasn't clear if this meant a Good morning, a You're welcome, or both. Liam was a metadata specialist. A white man in his fifties, he was most likely the shortest employee at Spindle but wore his height with dignity. He also wore a tweed jacket with patched elbows and a button of the Vietnam flag, visible on his shirt under the jacket. He was bald on top, with wild hair ringing it like a divided snowstorm, and had piercing blue eyes.

His Vietnamese heritage came out in his cheeks and jawline, but otherwise it was his Irish descent that showed. He wore the frames for glasses, but a sharp observer would notice they didn't have lenses. He wore them this way because he didn't need glasses but he liked the look, and this compromise amused him. He was holding a paper tray of coffee cups.

"Welcome to my one-month *fiesta*," Thatcher smirked at the older man. "*¿Que pasa?*"

Liam actually blinked. "You're coming along! You weren't talking much at first. Delightful! At any rate, we have a new user testing meeting this afternoon. I thought I'd stop by, since I forgot my morning coffee after cleaning up after the cat. Hairballs! Where did evolution get that one?"

"I think you forgot the question, Doc Brown," Mashaka said with a wink.

Liam frowned. He'd have connected the reference if he thought about it, but Thatcher nodded to Stewart and said, "I know you aren't a coffee fan. Thanks for the little celebration. Does accounting need any help today?"

"E-mails are under control, and you're a miracle-worker for setting up the Leone Link. Cute name, by the way. What's it mean?"

Thatcher was horrified. "You don't know Sergio L-"

"Is that a triple-double for me?" Mashaka cut in. This gave her a coffee and Stewart a welcome out.

"Black for Mr. García," Liam smiled at Thatcher.

"Ten thousand thanks," Thatcher replied. "But what's this about user testing? There's nothing in software development for this month."

"Your simplified 'Leone Link' e-mail stunt got people talking," Liam answered with an air of sympathy. "Three division managers will be there, along with me and Marketing."

None of them spoke enough Spanish to know what

Thatcher said to that, but they all had their guesses. "On that note," Mashaka said, "I'm gone to break some lines. Break a leg!" And she left to do her own programming.

Not long after that, the day itself seemed to wake up, and everyone went about their business. Even the white noise made Thatcher acutely aware of the fact that most of the people working at the company were white. There's something about white noise in a place where you don't feel at home. But he didn't dwell on that. Once lunch hour arrived, he tossed out his empty coffee cup on the way to getting his meal from the fridge. He microwaved it, then took his warmed meal downstairs to the hallways leading to employee parking. There was an alcove he liked. No one came around this way during break hours.

He was on the phone, speaking Spanish with most of the troupe he'd met in Oregon. He used to feel that having been exposed to Spanish in the foster care system allowed the institution to pigeonhole him, especially because they kept calling him Mexican, but now it gave him connections beyond simple ideas of skin colour. "I have to say," he remarked to Fox, "this is a breath of fresh air."

"That White, huh?"

Thatcher had to laugh. "I didn't even mention anything about the place yet!"

"We're a traveling Hispanic troupe in the USA, Braulio," Fox replied. Thatcher felt a swift sting of guilt for keeping up the lie of his identity, even with this group of new friends, but his time with Soto had him wondering who else might have tracked him. Fox, unaware of this, continued without missing a beat: "We know what a fish out of water sounds like!"

"Thanks," Thatcher said. He hadn't missed the undertones. "How's Alvaro?"

"Feeling much better," the other man answered. "I'd put him on the line, but he's mending one of the displays with Elodia. He's bouncing back much better than the rest of us after…the passing."

"I've never met the man in the bonefish mask," Thatcher replied, "but I think of him every time I use this phone. I wish I could do more to honour his memory."

"It's enough that you carry it on," Fox said.

There was a moment of silence.

"The others say hi, of course," Fox said. Thatcher thought he caught an emotional shift. A sober note, maybe, or moving out of a grim mood. He didn't have time to unravel that. "Have Elodia's friends helped much?"

"Oh, greatly," Thatcher answered enthusiastically. "Some of it was their own stuff. I couch surfed with them for a little bit. But they also got me some contacts for papers and such. I had to get to a computer a couple of times to fill in the cracks, though."

"You must be all set, then!"

"You know it. And if you ever need help," Thatcher said, phrasing himself carefully, "I can get you just about anything now. New names if you need them."

"We're proud of our names, and our masks," Fox said. But his tone was kind.

"I know. It'll take more than a month for me to forget…a lot of things," Thatcher said.

"Have you found what you're looking for?" Fox asked.

"I'm still getting settled in," Thatcher said. "And I

know this probably sounds weird, but I'm beginning to think that it can take a while just to figure out that you're looking for something at all. Does that make sense?"

"More than you know," Fox answered. Then there was a slip of his lips as he cracked out a smile like a sunrise and said, "If you had a mask, what animal would you represent?"

"I-" he stopped. He'd thought that the animal represented the person, like how white people thought of spirit animals. Maybe he should look up animal symbols or something.

"Lio?" asked Fox. Then: "Perhaps the lion?"

"Never been a lion person," Thatcher replied. "They take everything and then just sit around being king."

Fox laughed. "Lions can surprise you, though."

"Anything can surprise you," Thatcher said, and he thought that he might want to remember that notion. Then he pressed on: "My favourite animal is the civet," he said. "Is that how it works?"

"Favourites? Sometimes. You've gotta be careful about favourites," Fox said. His Spanish was different from Thatcher's. Thatcher couldn't put a finger on it, but something had him feeling that it wouldn't be appropriate to ask where they were from. He suspected that they had connections to Mexico at the least. Fox added, "When you like something — a creature, a symbol, a quote — you need to wonder if you're identifying with it because of how you see yourself or what you want your future self to look like. What is a civet?"

Thatcher was surprised at first, but then, no one could know every animal. He found out about them when he was researching colognes as a teen and learned that civets used to be the source for a lot of scented products, especially perfumes. "Let's see…" Thatcher filled his mouth while Fox had a half-heard conversation in English with Elodia about their use of puppets. Thatcher continued as though there hadn't been an interruption: "They're related to cats, weasels, and ferrets. Picture big ferrets that listen to heavy metal."

Fox got a hefty laugh out of that.

Thatcher took the opportunity to finish his meal, the corners of his lips so high that he had to be careful not to spill through his smile, while he waited for the other man to level off. He was still chewing as Fox audibly wiped away his humour. Then the trouper said, "I think that is a good way to describe you, my friend. But you should think on it. The mask is an important commitment."

"But you know I don't…I mean, I can't join you…" Thatcher wistfully pointed out as he collected his detritus and set himself in a mindset to work.

"That's not my point," and Thatcher could picture Fox's wave of dismissal. "If we didn't have any of our stuff — even our masks — we'd still be the troupe. We'd get new stuff, or find a different way, but we'd still be us. That's not what the mask is for."

"Thank you," Thatcher said as he was walking back to the stairs. As often as he could, he took them instead of the elevator. Baby steps. "This isn't my usual lunch talk."

"They say a good fox is clever," the other man said. "Let us know if you meet anyone looking for a troupe. The bigger we get, the bigger we'll be!"

"Will do. Take care!"

"And you," answered the Fox.

That conversation stayed with 'Braulio' for the rest of

his day. Especially for the meeting about his little e-mail interface trickery. He didn't consider it all that interesting or intelligent. He'd done more by pranking fans of prominent figures he didn't like.

He wasn't Mexican, but the people making speeches about Mexican immigrants and refugees were the same people who had him looking over his shoulder when walking home at night. And those people went after Mexicans for the same reasons they went after him. So he'd create a porn download loop in their wi-fi network if it wasn't properly secured. Or he'd reroute online complaint forms for sensitive topics so that messages from disappointed customers or people with anonymous medical questions would flood the inboxes of racist senators.

At least, he used to.

Nowadays he had to be careful about his hacking. He did it through computers he could get his hands on, without people peering over his shoulder or the possibility of being tracked. He only used public library computers as a last resort, because he couldn't come back there afterward. When he did use them, he was fixing things for himself to smooth over his life in a new identity. If he didn't want to be tracked, having a pay cheque connected to the SSN of his real name was a poor strategy.

As he walked home, he passed a moving van. It was a street two or three blocks away from his workplace. He made himself not stare. He didn't look long enough to see anything that was in the windows. He wouldn't have been able to describe the faces of the moving workers; they were overalls carrying items covered in cardboard or plastic. He saw and heard the flashes and slashes of retractable work knives getting through ropes, plastic straps, or stubborn covers.

Forty minutes got him to the front of the apartment building where he lived. He never wore anything with a hood — even when it rained — if he was coming to or from work. Streetlights and transparency guided him and kept the accusations away. He dressed reasonably for work, if on the shabby side, because being too clean and professional had people assuming he was part of white collar crime or a drug lord. Too shabby, and he was small-time crime. He got used to minimalist travel, no bookbags or other large containers. A tasteful briefcase had to cover his needs.

A lock on a glass door stood guard for the first entrance to his building.

Instead of producing keys, he simply walked through the broken space where glass used to be and passed the number pad for calling tenants for entry. He used his keys on the second door, set into a stone wall, and entered the first floor. As he stepped — neither too quick nor too slow — into the stairwell to the side, he looked up. Knees and feet played with his pain like a tennis game, but they weren't as vigorous as they'd been in Oregon. He could move comfortably, and he'd sleep tonight. He was getting used to the activity.

The stairwell always reminded him of the corrugated shipping containers used by intercontinental transport ships. He'd heard that refugees could sometimes refurbish those containers into something passing for a home. If they were stacked up and connected with stairs, they'd feel like this part of the building. Dust motes weakly protested his passing. Since the elevators were out of order most of the time anyway, he was getting used to stairs.

Now he was on the fourth floor. A hallway stretched out to his left like another container, surprisingly unmarked. Not new, yet it featured no graffiti or noticeable damages. It lacked signage or windows, all the lights were properly covered and lit. All the doors had their numbers. Except for an emergency fire alarm and extinguisher, it was a plain yellow stretch of access to living spaces.

Thatcher didn't even know what his neighbours looked like, though he knew the other rooms were occupied.

Room 432 opened for his key. That number stuck out to him. Descending order. He dismissed the thought and set his work materials aside. His apartment was divided into places with or without boxes, with a space against the wall hosting a tower of collapsed cardboard. He hadn't had much more than the shirt on his back when he first arrived, but these boxes were part of the life he was building.

He'd gone to thrift shops, yard sales, and events for donations to the poor. He'd gone to immigrant support groups, despite his upbringing in the United States. As a minority who couldn't use his real name or sleep with a roof over his head, he was an immigrant in the eyes of the system.

He had a chair, a table for food and boxes, a bed without a frame. It had scrupulously clean and neatly made bedding with a pair of cheap pillows. A corner was dedicated to his house cleaning gear, used daily. The beginnings of a custom computer build were still in boxes, and the empty case sat waiting for innards. He walked past all of this. Next to the kitchen was a collection of hard copy books for self-help and cooking. Basic, healthy eating. No fads.

Next to them was a calendar.

Past the bed was a second-hand armoire he'd acquired to serve as a closet. In it hung two nice shirts, two belts, two nice pairs of pants, and — piled on the bottom — his casual/ non-work attire. One of the belts was the one he'd just put there: his work belt. The other was the one he'd been wearing when he was larger. It didn't have holes for a small enough length, now that he'd lost a few inches of waistline.

He removed the old belt from the closet and wrapped it around himself so that the buckle was just under his belly button. Once he'd brought its full length around, he lined up the tongue with the buckle. Using an Exacto-knife he kept nearby, he cut a mark in the tongue. It was part of a long series of marks that, if the belt were straightened, would look a lot like the wall record a child makes of their height over time.

Thatcher sat.

On one side of him was a satellite radio, which he'd turned on to a Spanish-speaking news station. That radio was one of his first acquisitions. He knew the computer would be expensive and need waiting time for payment and shipping of parts. He thought about getting into video games like some console amateur, but he belonged to the growing Internet mock-religion that hailed the PC "master race." He needed something electronic to keep him going in the meantime.

He sat on his bed with his back against the wall and listened to the radio while he perused a cookbook. Progress had been slow, and he usually just resorted to microwave dinners in which he tried to find something with a vegetable and kept his calories down. But he forced himself, at least three times a week, to make a simple meal with real food. If he had to get new (to him) kitchen paraphernalia, then so be it. Aside from rent, this and the computer were where his money went.

He did not buy what he could trade for, and fixing computer problems counted as barter material. Knowledge was a currency for him, in a sense. Phones were computers. Music was computerized in so many ways, from DJs to iPods. So he'd program, edit, reformat, access, conceal, or clean hard drives or systems and take payment in parts, kitchenware, a table, a nice set of clothes, forged documents.

He was also determined to get his weight down. Sometimes it plateaued, sometimes the line was farther from the head of the metaphorical snake. That part didn't always make sense: he was staying active and keeping his calories down. He might have had one cola. How did his weight increase between measurements? Everything else was so thin. Budget, apartment furnishings, purpose.

It wasn't fair.

He looked down at what he wore. Hygiene he had in spades, but he could never dress well, and not for long. It was difficult to find something comfortable. He gave an outfit back to a thrift shop as often as not if he lost too much weight for comfort. There wasn't much sense in buying more than two at a time. So far, he didn't think anyone at work noticed; they didn't say anything. He was playing the ruffled tech guy.

A radio news broadcast summarized the world. Some technical difficulty kept an oil supertanker on the coast of Africa for a lot longer than scheduled. There was no spill, but reporters weren't allowed close. There was some stuff about tabloids and conspiracy theories, and he took that time to get a shower and cook. If the best they could manage was some disgraced watchdog talking about money channels disappearing, he could afford to miss some details. Thatcher had his business background, and he knew embezzlement was real, but intercontinental corporate dealings left too many memories and footprints to vanish so fast that trillions of dollars over decades didn't even leave the name of a business behind. No cover-up was *that* good.

Loco.

As Thatcher pulled himself out of bed the following morning, he set about his wake-up routine of basic calisthenics before breaking his fast. After some dusting, meal prep, and other chores that went quickly in his tiny living space, he set out for work.

"We will be shelving most of the non-necessary projects currently in play," said the CEO. A sweaty Thatcher was still marvelling that the CEO himself was here to unveil the company's change in direction. He was sitting on a folding chair in one of the meeting rooms. The conference rooms and even cafeteria had been annexed for the CEO's speech because everyone in the building was expected to be a part of this announcement at once. Video feeds had been set up, and the areas without TVs simply had conference calling set on their phones. Thatcher had spent the morning running this way and that to help with the slap-dash last-minute technical aspects of the arrangement, which was why he was dishevelled.

"There will be press releases and further announcements in the coming weeks," the CEO continued, "but don't let PR distract you. This promises to be the single biggest contract for a company of our size in the industry. I shouldn't have to tell you that discretion is paramount. We will be handling the system cleaning and computer security for Surimp, seafood division of the transport conglomerate Hydropolis Industries. Surimp accounts for more than 70% of the west coast's seafood intake, export, and processing!"

He paused. Thatcher looked around the cramped meeting room, wondering if there should be applause. Without a TV, all this room got was the voice of a man who rarely had direct interaction with the daily operations of anything or anyone in this building. Many were standing, as there hadn't been design — much less time — for bringing every single employee to bear on a company-wide announcement. He was only sitting because Ciel insisted, in light of his fatigue. There was one landline phone, a large oblong table, eight rolling office chairs, six folding chairs, and a line of people leaning against three walls. The air was stale, and the heat was the grey-white of too many people and a cubicle work culture.

The CEO lectured for a while about the importance of not posting about their work on social media. "Is this guy for real?" Ciel said to Thatcher out of the side of her mouth. She was a website designer from the same division as him. She was three inches shorter than he and leaning on the wall to his right with her arms folded. She wore slacks and a wrinkled button-up with the sleeves folded to the elbow, collar loose and a button undone. Along with hazel eyes, she and Thatcher even shared a degree of fashion. Any further resemblance ended with how she spoke, however: "We've even got custodians and cafeteria staff in on this speech. Hasn't he heard of gossip?"

Stewart, standing on the other side of the room, looked painfully awkward. His arms were at his sides and his posture was almost straight. His black hair, normally a Caesar cut to help with his invisibility in an office setting, had a few spikes from how often his hands had wiped at sweat. A pocket protector nestled a pen in his shirt. He was watching more of Ciel than Thatcher, and the resident Mr. Fix-It was having some trouble reading the poindexter's expression. When he spoke, his mousiness had a twang that came from the meeting room walls and an effort to be heard in a crowd without being too loud. "Isn't the phone set for conversation?"

"They're all muted," Thatcher answered, and even he could pick up on the relief that flooded the room. Suddenly there was such a chorus of people sounds that the words of the CEO were lost to him. Everything from sighs to shifting chairs. Thatcher kept his business face on, but had to wonder — what kind of *bobos* was he working with?

Ciel was the only one who showed no response.

Once the announcement concluded, everyone was afforded a break before they'd have to dive into the new operation in force. They flooded out of the rooms and many made a beeline for the doors and the promised land of the smoke break. Ciel and Stewart stayed with Thatcher, and the three were joined by Jake as they walked the corridors of the building looking for windows they could open. The first three corridors were fairly blocked by people looking for fresh faces and air, so the four of them continued until they'd passed the employee workout room and found themselves at the other corner of the building.

As they walked, Jake assaulted their ears with his notions. He was White, bony, gaunt, and taller than all but Stewart — if only by an inch. He looked shorter than he was because he stooped and hunched all the time, as though someone had dropped an ice cube down the back of his shirt and it got caught in a time loop. He had salt and pepper hair and, though his eyes were blue, they were more oily than watery and almost looked grey. "I was just stumbling through a ream of stuff — a ream! — in the blogosphere," he started.

"Scram," Ciel replied with her usual diplomacy.

"There's a trail of bodies running through Atlanta," he ignored her, "that connects to a bunch of cult stuff from late last year. They say even the dead were up in arms, so they had to cover up a bunch of stuff that went down in this big ugly house full of teenagers."

Jake's voice had a high-pitched, wheezy quality, as though his body was being piloted by a rat that didn't have enough space in the cockpit. "I don't suppose they were Mexican mafia?" Ciel quipped.

"Don't be silly," Jake said. "Mafia are Italian. Besides, Mexico here knows more about that than I do."

Thatcher sighed but couldn't be bothered to respond.

"He's not M-" Stewart started, but Thatcher gave him a long-suffering look and shook his head as Jake, unperturbed, continued:

"See, we get this CEO in here telling us there's a huge computer attack…"

"A virus, or possibly a backdoor security breach. There aren't really compu-" Thatcher started.

"…we've gotta clean. Make sure all their data is 'safe' and be sure to 'serve and protect' and all of that. It's like the Atlanta thing." Jake's intonations rose and fell in strange ways, and his emphasis often seemed to have a very special significance known only to him.

"You know you can't talk like this outside the building, right?" Stewart reminded him.

Jake seemed to be looking right through Thatcher and didn't pay much mind to Stewart. Ciel ground her teeth, Thatcher seemed to take it in stride, and Stewart was so continuously upset or uncomfortable that it was hard to tell if this conversation made him more anxious than usual. "Figures they'd want us quiet," Jake said. "Don't you think all this is a little much, with all the other suppressions? Shane Enterprises, those disappeared oil supertankers, Port Haven Institute? Even today there was a fishing boat just van-"

"You should consider..." Ciel started, and pointed to the gym as they passed it. Jake looked at it and shrugged, curling his lip in contempt. "It would be good for you, maybe work off some-"

"I don't need a hamster wheel," he said. "I wanna know why they think they can fix such a problem with a bit of computer scrubbing."

"You'd be surprised what some good computer time can do to fix things," Thatcher said.

As if the other man hadn't spoken, Jake went on: "We're one of the biggest IT and cybersecurity firms in the western US of A. Why are we dropping everything for grunt work? And you want me to believe they've just got some random attack that might influence financial data and employee confidentiality? And why only Hydropolis Industries? You can bet I won't be having shrimp any time soon!"

CHAPTER 07
BLIND TRUST

Kodiak, Alaska

Nick ordered the shrimp.

They were getting comfortable at a table for four at a restaurant-and-bar near Chenega Bay, a short drive from the hospital. Iseult pulled in her chair on the non-Nick side of Kelly, who came in hard and excited with the tray of drinks she'd taken from the server on her way back from the washroom. As she slipped into the group, Kelly brushed her leg against Iseult's. Kelly wore ripped denim, black leggings showing through because she wanted a bit more warmth. Static sparked where their legs met and Kelly glanced at her, but said nothing. Nick and Tash couldn't see it under the table.

"It's on special," Nick said, "and I like trying something a little local and far from home."

Tash seemed oddly flattered. Though taller than the others, it wasn't the lanky woman's height that set her apart. She had a stage presence, a confidence when in charge. She said, "Can't argue with that. I'm interested in seeing what they do with their salads here." She seemed to glow a bit more than usual, and Iseult wondered if it was the casual mention of home, the implication that they now had one with Tash.

Kelly handed out their sodas and iced tea, keeping her leg slightly in contact with Iseult. Iseult, already feeling out of her depth, was self-conscious. "Thanks," Iseult said as she got her Sprite. "Speaking of," she said to the other two, "We're a long way from Atlanta. Didn't think I'd miss it after…"

Kelly squeezed her hand, and Iseult wasn't sure if it was acknowledgement of the thanks or her reference to October. "I miss it, too. Even with the therapy. So much for vacation, huh?"

"Oh, it'll be a vacation, all right," Tash asserted. She was next to Iseult, the tallest next to the shortest. "You're all gonna relax!" Her chin was tilted up so that she looked at them with a slight angle and a downward, commanding cast.

"It was like a free preview of working as a doctor," Iseult said, hoping for a laugh. Nick and Tash smiled weakly.

There was an awkward moment of silence. Iseult crossed her feet, toes inward, and bumped Kelly's foot when she did it. "That's the spirit," Tash remarked. "Let's try to keep this in a positive light. But no work talk at dinner."

"Can I mention the elephant in the room?" Nick asked.

"We'll poach it otherwise," Iseult warned, managing the nerve to look Tash in the eye. Everyone did chuckle at that.

"All right," Tash said, holding Iseult's gaze warmly until the young woman looked away. "I'll bite: what's the elephant?"

"You took us on a vacation to get us away from where... all that happened," Nick said. "Even with a bit of therapy, we can't..." he moved his hands about.

Now Kelly was squeezing Nick's hand. The pair had a bond, something valence and electric, that Iseult didn't know if she wanted or envied. Maybe it was in between, like a reminder of a hope gone thin from hunger. More than the background humdrum of voices and shuffles, it was the utensils clinking here and there that stuck out to the young woman. Even her brown hair was between Kelly's blonde and Nick's black, and no one at this table had utensils. Maybe she was just...on edge.

It wasn't obvious if Kelly was correcting Nick, Tash, or both. "We can't get back down to earth just by coming down from the second floor of that place, no matter what we say about Quinn," she said. Iseult hadn't seen what happened with Quinn, hadn't been there for that. If she had, could she have stemmed enough of the bloodloss? Kelly went on: "It's like we need to breathe again, but fresh air isn't enough, you know?"

Their food arrived.

Nick was wearing his steely blue contacts, and he was watching Tash during this exchange. "Thank you," he said. The timing was wrong for it to be about the food. Tash, her plate untouched just yet, looked at him in surprise. He rarely felt conscious of being the only male in their group, but he was now. "I can see your pores opening. This talk about what we're carrying, it weighs on you.

I'm just...I'm grateful."

"We all are," Kelly said.

Iseult looked at Tash and nodded vigorously, blushed and looked down, and began poking at her fries. She liked to get at the small bits first, before tackling the centrepiece like a burger. Or, well, bigger problems.

Tash, despite everything, beamed. "I love you," she said to all of them.

Nick's reply was to begin attacking his shrimp platter. Kelly had one of those moments — Tash and Iseult could see it — of falling in love with him all over again. She put her hand on his thigh, high enough that he looked at her. He was still chewing. She was watching his eyes until Iseult nudged her. "Um," Iseult said, "you might wanna watch his hair."

Static had started lifting it.

Mortified, Kelly pulled away. "I'm sorry!" She said, "I didn't mean…"

Tash had an elbow on the table, her face in one hand, watching this unfold with the rhythmic shake of suppressed laughter. Nick himself was unphased. Iseult looked at Kelly's untouched stew and watched Tash return to the salad before slowly nibbling her way through more fries. She started low, her voice muted by her self-consciousness. "Does anybody…"

Tash, who hadn't heard Iseult, decided to try a different tack. "Have you all given any thought to your ambitions? Education? I haven't forgotten, you know."

"Do we have to go to Victor when the law says we're adults?" Kelly asked. "Could we, like, become teachers or something and stay with you?"

"You can't play my heartstrings that easily, young lady," Tash said, pointing a finger at those electric blue eyes and trying to be menacing. "And you don't have to stay in this life. Iseult's been keeping up with distance studies. At this rate, she'll have her GED before she's seventeen."

Tash was turning the attention to Iseult, whose head was mostly down. Iseult felt uncomfortable looking at anyone else in the bar, a discomfort that transcended her usual shyness. "Uh, guys, I-..."

Nick had looked all around him as though he couldn't believe what he was hearing and didn't realize Iseult was trying to speak. "Really? What, we need to think about scholarships on top of everything else?"

Kelly, shocked by his bluster, put her hand on the back of his neck in an attempt to be supportive. He got a particularly sharp jolt of static electricity and turned to her. His expression juggled wounded pride, a lost look, annoyance, and outrage.

A server walked by the table, passing closest to Iseult, who shuddered hard and looked swiftly at him. He proceeded to the next table, a boisterous crowd in jerseys and flannel, and set down the heaping plates of nachos he'd been carrying.

Tash was focused on Nick. "That was uncalled-for, young man."

"I'm sorry!" Kelly said. "I didn't mean-"

"Do you really want schooling all that much?" Nick was absorbed in Kelly. She was all he saw. He stopped short of voicing his disappointment, but she knew him better than to need his words for that.

"I didn't mean to spark," she said, clasping her hands in her lap.

Tash, who'd been watching the two, was struggling to make sense of the exchange until then. "I don't think this is really about-" she started.

Iseult slammed her glass on the table hard enough that the Sprite bounced up in a liquid cloud. Most of it made the way back to the glass, while the rest splattered over her hand. She blushed as everyone looked at her, but sat upright and looked each of them — including Tash — hard in the eye before she spoke. "Kelly," she started, "does your...talent include sensing? Do you feel anything off in the room? Don't look!" She said that last in a harsh whisper, to everyone at the table.

Kelly and Nick looked at each other in befuddlement while Tash stole various surreptitious glances. The young woman could be mistaken for meek, but she took command when she was ready. If only Tash could reach her like she could the others...

"Not really?" Kelly answered. "I mean, I can't tune into a TV or phone just because they're electrical, if that's what you mean."

"That's one of the things I mean," Iseult clarified, "but I'm talking anything at all. Nervous systems? Magnetic fields? Something more metaphorical, like emotional static or social currents or something?"

"Now that you mention it," Tash said, "there are a few people here who seem touchy, nervous, or agitated. The server, for one, and there's a woman — don't look, like Izzy said — over in the corner who keeps staring at lights. I thought she was just spacy when we came in, but..."

"Yeah, she's one of them," Iseult said. When she was called Izzy, she shuffled in her seat with the warmth of someone unused to compliments.

Nick, preoccupied with glancing around to see if he could pick up anything, was a little slower to pick up on that phrasing. Kelly's attention was internal, trying to find some kind of electrical sensing, but Nick grabbed her hand and moved it to her plate while he absently munched on more shrimp. Tash was ahead of him, continuing to eat so as not to draw attention to their table.

It was Tash who asked, "One of what?"

"I was too caught up in the...um, everything, at the hospital to say anything," Iseult started. "Some of the people here have a…" her hands, resting on the table on either side of her plate, wriggled their fingers inarticulately before she took a big bite of burger. She had to chew for a while because there was so much of it, but she tasted nothing as she alternated between staring into space, glancing at the other customers, and watching her table-mates.

Kelly shovelled some stew into her discomfort. Her attention was now on Tash, across the table from her, as she hoped for some guidance. Nick was clearly feeling the strain since October, and Kelly had inwardly been wondering about the future for a while. Somehow she doubted they'd be throwing on some spandex to become a superhero squad, so what was she — what were any of them — to do once their unusual upbringing came to an end?

Tash chewed on thoughts and leaves, her fingers steepled in front of her, and led the group in waiting for Iseult to speak. Kelly recognized the tactic for what it was. Iseult was about to speak when a server stopped by their table.

"How are we liking our meal tonight?" she asked. She wore understated lipstick and a poofy hairstyle straight out of an 80's movie, but was otherwise just as much in uniform as the others. She seemed for all the world to be honestly interested in their well-being. Iseult quickly shoved three more fries into her mouth, staring at the edge of the table and nodding vigorously.

"It's lovely, thank you," Kelly said. Nick and Tash had their mouths full and simply held up a thumb. "Could my man here have a beer?"

Nick sputtered.

The server looked at Tash with a raised brow. Tash, just swallowing, said to Kelly: "Adorable." To the server she said, "We'd appreciate a top-up of my iced tea and this one's Sprite. It looks like the others are good to go, but if you have a coal for a Christmas stocking…" and she tilted her head in Kelly's direction.

The server's laugh was the only giveaway that she was putting on a performance, but she did well and went off to see to their requests. Nick and Kelly squeezed each other's knees and watched Iseult. Tash, after giving the couple a well-meaning mom-squint, turned her attention on the talented but reclusive youth as well. "She's not icky," Iseult remarked.

Everyone blinked. Iseult didn't generally use childish words like "icky."

Iseult looked at Tash. "Did your contacts mention anything about this place?"

"Do you mean the town, the hospital, or this restaurant?" Tash asked. When Iseult shrugged, Tash chewed her own lip for a second before saying, "They've been looking into things, but more for our safety than anything else. And we can talk about the police situation when we get home. Nothing here, though." She drew a circle in the air with her fork.

With those words barely out of her mouth, Tash cringed as a rowdy group of people on one end shouted and whooped, one of them slapping the rump of a passing server. Closer to the group's table, the party with the nacho platters got into an energetic argument, full of burns and laughs, about sports. Football, as far as Iseult could make out.

Kelly leaned her head over to snug into Nick's shoulder, but this was an excuse to bump her leg into Iseult's again. There was no spark this time, which took some conscious effort, but she could feel it: an inconspicuous bump that spanned a short length. Iseult was not so oblivious as to think this move an accident. Her eyes widened slightly when she looked at Kelly, who pretended not to notice. Nick was watching the kitchen and serving area through a rectangle cut in the wall, as though he thought the suspicion should be directed there. It didn't stop him from his shrimp, though.

Tash watched Iseult darting her eyes about, tracking the servers and the woman eating fish & chips in the corner. The one who kept staring off at the lights. She also studied two or three other people, and Tash picked up on the fact that everyone who caught Iseult's eye had passed by the younger woman at some point. "So, what's on your mind?"

Iseult subtly shook her head, more with her eyes than the actual neck movement. "Good thing we got in our beach visit when we did," she said. "It was nice to see and play with the locals."

"Yeah," Nick said. "Do we wanna try fishing next? See if I've got the eye for it?" He grinned.

Kelly seemed a little confused, but Tash played along: "I was hoping to get in a museum visit tomorrow. They have a display about all the boats and ships in local history going on right now."

Kelly caught on when the server reached over her to provide the freshly filled glasses and take away the empties. Once the server was gone…

"I can't make out why yet," Iseult said, leaning forward, "but some people, when they get close enough that I can pick up on their blood flow, feel all wrong to me."

Nick made a show of a long, slow stretch so that he could get a good look at about 270 degrees of the room. He did two sidelong adjustments to play off looking over each shoulder to fill in the rest of the space. Kelly slowed her eating; she was almost empty and didn't want someone coming by to take away her bowl just yet. Tash began playing with her phone, but it wasn't clear if she was pretending or actually getting caught up on some details.

"Wrong how?" she asked.

"I can't put my finger on it," Iseult said. "I know how that sounds."

"We trust you," Kelly said.

"Yeah," Nick chimed in. "I can see a lot, but I've never picked up on someone having a stroke or heart attack before they even knew something was up."

"I'm proud of you," Tash said. "Go on."

At moments like this, Iseult felt like she had black-and-white lungs. The white one swelled with love, company, belonging, feeling appreciated. But the black shrank, spewing doubts. Did she really have a place with them? Maybe they were just being nice. Civil, empty. Like the server. Obligatory. She shuddered and realized everyone thought it was about the "ickiness."

"Sorry," she said to Nick, who looked confused. "You know when you get those guys who are handsome but not too handsome, real polite and charming, but the other girls give you the nod that he's up to no good?"

The other women nodded.

Nick looked at each of them, stopping at Iseult with his mouth just a little too open.

"Oh, honey," Kelly said. She kissed his cheek. He swallowed. Sometimes Kelly had a way of letting him know where the walls were. He couldn't see them, didn't understand, but he had faith in her, and let it lie.

Nick opened his mouth to ask if it was just the guys right now, and realized it was the wrong question. He closed his mouth and looked helplessly at Tash.

"Do you think it's about their intentions?" Tash probed Iseult.

"Well, no, but, I…" Iseult floundered. She held her glass with two hands but didn't take it off the table.

Nick leaned one arm on the table so that his opposite shoulder angled away, giving him a look of confidence in the vein of a sitting swagger. "All right. We're with you. I know you've stayed out of the 'field work,' so to speak, but we'll have you when you're ready."

"He's right," Tash said. "And no pressure. Do you think we're in danger?"

"I can't tell," Iseult said. She'd finished her burger, and popped one of the remaining fries in her mouth while she processed her thoughts. "Maybe they're in danger, though they're healthy as far as I can tell. One of them has a mild heart murmur, the woman by the door with the fish has some circulation trouble in her feet. Nothing major."

"Well, I haven't picked up on anything beyond the usual foibles of people," Tash said. In another context, that remark might have been dismissive. But these three knew about her training and experience. Iseult remembered Tash's anger while Chad was helping with an Internet search about a cult, but that was both late last year and a lifetime ago. "Nick?" Tash added.

"Same," he said. He looked at Iseult. "The ones you mentioned have a lot of the signs of tension and worry, more than what you guys can see. Micromuscles lining or bunching tightly, pores opening, pupils widening to take in more so they can see danger."

Kelly raised her brows. "Just seeing them doesn't mean you know why they're there. Like the pupil thing. Have you been reading up on this stuff?"

Nick simply nodded and continued speaking. Kelly kissed him on the cheek, which he allowed but didn't stop for. "Some people here show the signs of physical jobs. Slight changes in range of motion, or pain mild enough they don't notice it but it shows in their micro-expressions. Bad posture, bad joints, I think one of them is missing a toe."

Tash put her phone away and the youths collected themselves as a server approached. "Would you folks like anything else today?"

There was a round of "No, thanks;" they tidied up, Tash handled the bill, and they made their exit. Iseult was hugging herself and kept her head down as they walked.

Tash draped a comforting arm over her shoulder. "We believe you, and don't worry. We'll get to the bottom of this."

Iseult wanted to tell Tash about the warmth and the gratitude, but she only managed a weak smile.

As they got in the car, Kelly stopped Nick so she could get in on their side. "You've got shotgun this time," she said, and drew a line down his back with her fingertips. He shrugged, brushed her hair with the back of his hand, and obliged.

It was an old, brown Camry Tash had rented for the trip. She didn't have the same hang-up Victor did. "I haven't let the subject drop, you know," she started with the car. There was a pregnant pause. "We know Iseult's going to be some kind of doctor. Speaking of," she said to the rearview mirror, "What kind? Surgeon?"

Kelly, in the back with Iseult, glanced significantly at the thigh with the knife strapped in under the pants. Iseult had arranged herself so that the knife didn't show, opting for an outfit with cargo pants and a vest under her jacket so that she'd look a little more like some of the locals. Still, it was only possible because the weapon — or was it meant as a tool? — was small and slender. Kelly wasn't an expert, but she knew the difference between a strapped-on hunting knife and a blade that was designed to be hidden. She spoke to cover her obvious curiosity. "Even after the hospital?"

"Especially after the hospital," Iseult said, and she

was almost a new person now. Being in an enclosed space with people she trusted, she seemed more in command and self-assured. "I'll bet my gift, or talent, or whatever will be helpful, but I want to be real and help no matter what's up. You know, with knowledge and skill and not just something I can't show anyone."

"Can we just call them powers?" Nick asked.

Iseult shook her head. "I don't feel powerful. And remember Abby? That's powerful, but I don't like calling that a power."

"That's fair," Tash remarked as she hit the highway. An occasional car passed them because, though still going highway speed, she was only just. "What about hematology?"

"Too obvious," Iseult said. "And I'm sure they'd test each other's blood for fun. Med students get zany because of all the pressure."

Kelly, threading the boundary between passing into Iseult's trust and getting a hold on her inner motives, played it safe. "You could learn about your gift that way," she reasoned, "but I suppose nothing happens in a vacuum, huh?"

"Nope," Iseult replied. "And I like the idea of the research side of it, but I'm not sure it's for me. Even just doing the first aid stuff, and helping with the blood flow of some of the...victims..."

"It's what you want," Nick said. It wasn't really a question.

"What about you?" Iseult asked Kelly. The blonde's heart beat a little harder at that. Was this a sign of comfort in her? "Any big dreams?"

"Y'know," Kelly thought aloud, "I've been playing with that idea lately. After Atlanta, and my dad, and realizing that not everyone is a human Tesla coil, I'm just not really sure what's in store for me."

"I think it's pretty obvious that we're not on this earth to become accountants or have 1.5 children and a white picket fence," Nick said. "And don't get me wrong, we're really thankful, Tash. Really. But it's kinda hard to do the therapy stuff when…"

"It's hard for everyone who needs it, though," Tash pointed out. "That's the idea."

"But when we have supe-...special abilities and I don't want a day job because it's my destiny to make the world a better place? Talk about Black Springs…" But Nick was fidgeting.

"You're bad at this kind of bluster, sweetheart," Kelly said as she rubbed his shoulders from the back seat.

"I'm raising you to be well-rounded adults," Tash said to Nick, "not training you to be soldiers."

Iseult shivered. Kelly glanced at her out of concern. Tash took them off the highway and towards their hotel. Nick huffed. "I'm sorry. It's just...a lot."

"I know," Tash said, "and I do want to try therapy again once we get sorted out. But you're right: it's hard to dig into everything when we can't actually talk about a big chunk of your lives without spilling the beans about pow-...gifts."

Iseult reached forward and across to grab Nick's arm. He knew the difference between her touch and Kelly's. "What's up?"

Iseult sat back and looked at Kelly with dread.

Kelly's mind raced. He'd seemed irritable, hadn't dealt well with the talk about their futures. They were all a little off after their struggles in the last few years, but the others in the restaurant also seemed uncomfortable. The ones who gave Iseult the crawlies. Stifling her fears, she reached between Nick's seat and the door so that she was teasing her nails over his arm. "How you feelin', babe?"

He turned his head so that he could look at her over the shoulder, which pressed him awkwardly between the headrest and the side of the car. "I'm good, sweetheart. It's all been kind of a lot, and that whole hospital thing was unsettling. How you holding up?"

Kelly and Iseult glanced at each other. Tash chimed in: "We're here! Let's have a proper once-over once we get into our rooms. Maybe throw on a movie or something."

"Yeah…" Iseult said. "Maybe it's just nerves."

On their way through the building, they made some attempts at small talk that fell flat. Iseult was okay with talking when it was natural but didn't care much for forcing it. Tash opened the door she shared with Nick, and the other ladies piled in behind her. Kelly stopped once they were through and watched Nick with alarm.

He was bracing his weight against the doorway, a hand on each side, and his face was a rictus of fear. His eyes were wide, the steel blue contacts jutting this way and that in line with his attempted sight. They were searching for nothing.

Iseult turned, close enough to Kelly that she could feel the other woman's heart leap to the throat. Tash, sensing tension, marched back into line of sight from the other end of the room. "What are you doing?"

"I…my eyes," Nick started. "I…I can't see!"

CHAPTER 08
RANDOM PIECES OF BROKEN THINGS

Kodiak, Alaska

Iseult was holding her hands on either side of Nick's head. Her legs were draped over the side of the bed, as though riding side saddle, and Kelly was pacing at the foot of the bed. Tash was using what few tools she had available to examine Nick.

He was trembling and sweating.

"Tell me everything you can about how you're feeling," Tash said.

Iseult's eyes were closed. Her mouth trembled a little every now and again, and she had goosebumps. But she'd been there for a solid fifteen minutes, with no sign of changing.

"Nick?" Kelly asked. She stopped and looked at him, laid out on the bed. She took his shoes off because no one had thought of that.

His voice was dry and the wrong kind of steady. "I'm... scared." His posture was straight, feet shoulder width apart, his head and upper chest elevated with pillows.

"Just breathe," Tash said, and set aside her flashlight.

They'd removed the contacts he used in public, revealing sclera and nothing else. There were no pupils or iris to respond to the light in a way she could check. There weren't even any visible blood vessels. So she changed tactics. "Focus on my voice." She got up, motioned Kelly to his side, and handed his lover a hotel towel.

Wordlessly, Kelly began patting down the worst of his fear moisture. She made some calming susurrations, but other than that, she just stroked his face and hair and patted him down. When she squeezed his hand, he clasped and didn't let go. It hurt a little, but she let him cling. It was all she could give him.

"In through the nose," Tash instructed. "Out through the mouth. In six, hold two, out four."

"My lungs aren't the problem!" he objected tremulously.

"In. Deep breath. Slow count to six." Tash was so firm it was almost cold.

While Tash coached Nick on relaxation techniques, and Kelly did what she could to be supportive, Iseult was giving her all to feel his blood flow. She was trying not to alter anything; she witnessed the whole circulation of his brain. Followed the flow through the skull-shaped network of muscle and skin, dwelled in the sinus cavity, and even kept her focus on the vessels' interaction with cerebrospinal fluid at the base of the skull.

Most of her time and attention was spent at the occipital lobe — the big span of brain at the back of the head responsible for vision — as well as his retinal nerves and the eyes. His visual cortex took some getting used to, because he wasn't built for vision the way normal people were.

She opened her eyes. "Nicholas," she said. No one in their group called him that. She sounded for all the world like a medical authority. A surgeon, maybe, or the well-versed bedside manner of a nurse. "I'm gonna get real close to you for a while, and then I'm gonna put my hands over a few places. I'll go step by step, but I need you to work with me on this, okay?"

"You were doing that at my temples forever! What did you find!?" None of them had ever seen him so utterly afraid.

"I'll tell you everything once I'm done," she said, and her tone left no room for argument. "Now, some of this is gonna feel a little weird…"

It went on for a while, with awkward comments and moments of panicked resistance from Nick. Kelly had to give him a one-finger shock at one point to get him to snap to it and let them examine him. Tash kept pulling his attention back to progressive muscle relaxation, breathing techniques, and concentration tricks to help him keep his cool, with mixed results.

She tried another tactic: "Let's have a little low-pressure talk game, since we're so attentive to each other right now."

Nick's face quivered in a few places, but his breathing was level and his hands were still. Kelly and Iseult looked at each other, glanced at Nick, and focused on Tash. "I'm thinking hobbies. Not the usual ones we already talk about. I'll start," Tash said. She folded her hands on her lap and stared at nothing for a moment. "I started taking an interest in anthropology and archaeology in high school. I was always sort of into gardening, but it kind of changed flavours as I got older. What started me down the road to my university days was awe. I wanted to collect moments of awe, if that makes any sense. I was really into statues, monoliths, monuments, and that sort of thing when I was in my undergrad."

Nick's facial tremors subsided as he focused on her words. Kelly smiled a little smile, and Iseult's toes and attention turned inward in a bashful way. Like she'd walked in on someone in the middle of changing. Nick said, "Why awe?"

It was Tash's turn for a bashful smile. She was never vulnerable with them. Not like this. Even Nick, who couldn't see it, felt a change in the room. Tash did her best to answer: "Some of it is a little much to get into right now, but there was something about it. I tried poetry events, open mic and what-not. Spent months going to synagogues, churches, and temples; checking out prayer books and spiritual websites and on and on. There was just...something to it. Before we got all industrial about it, it was like people saw magic in the world and packed it into every stone or plank of wood they worked on."

Tash waited to see what they would do with that. Nick and Iseult closed their eyes. She was still examining him, but her breathing became more rhythmic. He'd already started relaxing because of Tash's distraction, but Iseult's comfort — if that's what it was — came from somewhere else. "I used to collect keys," the medical talent said as she worked.

Tash raised her brows. Nick and Kelly both had a melting of the cheeks, a kind of candlelight through body language. Iseult continued: "I had a framed cork board in my room. I even had the old scan cards mo-...my parents had…" her voice became meeker as she went, and she hitched on that point.

Nick grabbed one of her hands and squeezed it. Tash resisted the urge to gather up the shy young woman and coax out her confidence. Kelly said, "We'd love to hear more. Take your time."

Iseult blushed. "I didn't like lame holders like thumb-tacks. They had to be ball-tipped push pins, like you see for maps? I had a system: I only got the push pins with the balls that looked like birthstones. So each one was the month of the year when I found the new key. So many afternoons disappeared in craft shops with…" She swallowed and sighed through her nose. No one said anything. "My favourites were what I called inn keys. They were the long wrought-iron ones that you see in movies. For treasure chests and old-timey inns."

And her body language returned to work mode. The change was subtle; mostly angles and a practical pose. The way she shifted her ponytail to hang on the opposite side of her neck from Nick.

Tash was eager to hear from Kelly, who was the newest to join their group. Even with Nick, who she'd latched onto pretty quickly, Kelly mostly kept to the surface of things for a long time. She took Nick's hand and kissed it.

"My turn, then," Nick said. Tash adjusted her sitting position on the small table to stop herself from throwing up her hands. One of Nick's feet started tapping, though there was no floor under it to actually rap off of. "I'm... uh...kinda still looking, if you know what I mean. I played a bunch of sports a few years ago. Lots of basketball. I liked a good game of pool."

"I remember," Tash said. Kelly took her hand as she stroked Kelly's hair. Iseult blinked at the pool remark.

"When I was a kid, I kinda thought I had to be a manly man. Not really sure where I got the idea. I started hanging out at garages and talking to mechanics, trying to be a car guy. Tried getting into weightlifting for a while, but I didn't like workouts that weren't also, you know, actual activities."

"Functional fitness, you mean?" Tash said.

"Is that, like, a special type?" Kelly asked.

Nick shrugged. "Yeah, I guess. That's where workouts are all things that actually bring your muscles and nerves together for real activities. Like running and climbing to train for sports. Anyway, all that manly man stuff was why I learned how to barbecue and tie a bunch of different knots for dress ties. What about you, babe?"

Kelly shivered. Iseult cast her a glance and then focused on Nick. Tash perked up, but no one noticed. "I... well, I mean, you already know I'm into fashion."

"That was hard to miss," Tash confirmed. Iseult ducked her head.

"I've concentrated on the everyday stuff," she started. "You know: laundry, reading up on what kind of stuff to have in the medicine cabinet," Iseult nodded at that. Kelly wondered if the other young woman even knew she'd done so. Kelly went on: "Some house cleaning and repair stuff. How to shop — and not just for fun," she said with a twist of her lips. Nick closed his mouth meaningfully.

"You guys know how I've been spending my time

since I joi...since we…"

"We're happy to have you," Tash said in a tone of serenity Kelly didn't think she could feel even if she worked at it.

"I was into found art for a few months," Kelly said.

"What, like you just went looking? With a metal detector on the beach?" Nick asked.

Iseult giggled, opened her mouth, but produced only silence.

Kelly frowned for a moment, then her face lit up. "Oh! No, no — you find stuff like sticks, bones, animal eggs, random pieces of broken things, glass, nice rocks. Then you put them together. To make art."

Nick absorbed this without comment.

"I always thought found art was cool," Iseult said. Her eyes avoided Kelly, but her voice leaned towards the other youth.

"Why did you stop?" Tash said.

Kelly dropped to a whisper. "The other kids made fun of me when they found out. I just couldn't anymore. I used to be so embarrassed."

"Maybe we could go hiking or spelunking sometime, make found art together," Tash offered.

No one said anything.

Tash watched each of the youths in turn. She sometimes squeezed Kelly's shoulder, or stroked a length of her hair. Kelly hesitated a moment longer, then nodded. If Tash hadn't been watching her, she'd have missed it. Nick stared at nothing. Tash wasn't sure what to make of him. He was still a wire drawn taut, but there was less panic. Iseult was Iseult; hiding behind her actions and trying to keep her actions quiet. But the room had changed. The paint was a warmer yellow.

As all that had gone on, Iseult had been tracking the muscle movements around Nick's orbital cavity. She tested facial reflexes, and sequentially put her hands on places that helped her track blood flow to important areas: kidneys, liver, spleen, major glands and lymph vessels.

Eventually, she sat back and took a breath. Kelly and Tash stopped their ministrations, and everyone sat close. Nick swallowed and made a visible effort to pull himself together.

"That...discomfort I've been feeling? The one I sensed from some of the others? It's in your whole vision system."

Nick focused on not crying.

"What does that mean?" Kelly asked.

"Eyes, optic nerve, brain. Everything connected to actually seeing. Not the muscles, though. At least, not much. But there's no extra activity from any of your cleaning systems," Iseult said. Her brow was furrowed, and she sometimes poked at her nails — which were poorly kept but clean — or fiddled with her hair. Most of the time she kept that pulled back, because a ponytail was easy. Her tone was far away since she was puzzling the situation together even as she spoke.

"Kidneys, liver, lymph...?" Tash prodded.

Iseult nodded. "All of it. All of the immune responses you can get by tracking blood vessel, pressure, and flow behaviours. Even the brain activity is normal. It's like..."

"Say it," Nick said. Kelly felt a surge of hope; his fight was returning. "If I'm gonna fight this, I need to know what I'm up against."

Iseult braced herself. "It's like your body thinks there's nothing wrong. All systems go."

"If I get us on the next flight out," Tash mused, "I could use the equipment I have at the farm. There's a lot more we could learn."

"Why not another hospital here in Alaska?" Kelly asked. "There must be one a highway drive away somewhere."

"No," Nick said.

Iseult got up and walked to the dresser across from the foot of the bed. She leaned there and watched him. His hands were folded on his stomach and his feet were shoulder-width apart, his legs straight. He looked for all the world like a casual teenager lying on his back and staring at the ceiling.

Except for his eyes.

Kelly slid up to the head of the bed, tucked her legs under her as she lay on her side, and stroked his hair. Tash sat on a folding chair, composed but troubled. Everyone waited.

"I know we've got a great little home base in Georgia," Nick said, "but we came here to get away from what happened in Atlanta. And we're not always gonna be able to just run home and play safe. Izzy, you said you felt a weirdness, right?"

The other women looked at her. She leaned on the dresser and hugged herself. "It's not in the rest of us, if that's where you're going."

"And no hospitals," Nick said. Kelly opened her mouth. Nick shook his head in her direction. "They'll have to look at all the parts involved in vision. They'll instantly see that I'm wearing contacts and ask me to remove them so they can look at stuff like pupils."

"He's right," Iseult said. "Looking at pupil and iris response is right after checking for discoloration, like a black eye or jaundice."

"They'll have a pile of questions long before they get to the nerves and brain," Tash said. "But Victor's more worried about keeping p-...gifts under wraps than I am."

"I don't want to be a lab rat," Nick said.

Kelly was trying so hard not to wring her hands or fidget with her hair or show other obvious signs of stress that her whole body was stiff. Tash got up and walked around the bed as Iseult said, "You still have rights. They can't just pull you out of a hospital for human experimentation. This isn't a comic book movie."

"You don't know that," Nick said.

Tash, though slender and elegant, was too tall to gather Kelly up in her arms with Nick also on the bed. So she moved the lamp and radio off the end table between the twin-sized beds and sat on that, leaning over so she could soothe Kelly by stroking the younger woman's hair and caressing her shoulders and back.

Nick continued: "We don't know how people will act. They coul-"

"Exactly," Iseult said. "You never know how people will react. What they could take from you, what they'd allow to die. And it's not like there'll be a new bomber at every hospital."

"Whose side are you on here?" Nick asked.

Kelly, despite her anxiety, put her hand on his bicep

and gripped firmly. "That wasn't fair."

He took a shaky breath. "I'm sorry, Izzy."

"Don't worry about it," she said. She didn't realize Tash was watching her, because her attention was wholly on Nick as she strove to puzzle out what to do. Tash felt a lopsided swell of pride and worry for this young woman, so professional and possessed of faith in everything except herself. Iseult elaborated: "You're scared, and that's fair. But we'll get through this. We shouldn't take a hospital off the table, no matter what they might think when they realize you're different. Patient confidentiality counts for something."

"But they wouldn't be my doctor," Nick said.

"What do you mean?" Kelly asked.

"The privilege of medical information isn't just about your own doctor," Tash pointed out. Kelly added some quick nods, small enough that only Nick noticed them.

"Are you guys filling the air to calm me or yourselves?"

"Both," the women all said together.

Everyone shared a brief, tense laugh.

"I think you're right about going back to Georgia," Iseult said. "What if this is temporary?"

Tash looked between the bed and the dresser. "What if it's permanent? We can't risk speculating when there's so much at stake."

"Whatever this is, it's probably not happening everywhere. We'll have to ask more questions about that." No one was quite sure who Kelly was talking to. "We'd be safer in Georgia, if we can be safe anywhere." Tash flinched. Iseult pretended not to notice. Kelly was focused on Nick.

"But we'd be leaving behind whoever is struggling here. How far is this going?" With that, she turned her eyes on Iseult.

"I didn't notice anyone in the hotel who felt icky," Iseult started. "Or do you mean since we got to Alaska?"

"Everywhere," Kelly answered.

"Ever," Nick chimed in.

She wracked her brain. "Just the restaurant, that I can think of," Iseult said. "No! That's a lie. I felt it a couple of times while we were...while the hospital was..." Solemn nods spread throughout the room. "But there was kind of a lot going on, so...yeah. And I have to be close to people to pick up on stuff like this. All the ones I told you about were either people who walked by me or people we passed while we were coming in."

"None of them were blind," Nick pointed out.

"No," Iseult whispered as her attention blurred inward, to memories of their meal. "But all of them seemed uncomfortable or something. Nervous, maybe angry in that weird way people get when they're threatened. Lots of glances, like they were searching or jumping at shadows. The server guy looked real tense, and I thought he was obsessively checking his hands. Maybe I'm reading into it. I mean, you gotta look at the stuff in your hands when you're working that kind of job."

"The woman you pointed out in the corner," Tash said. "I just took her for another one of those people you see in public places. They're everywhere. The ones who mutter to themselves at gas stations, whether they had a car there or not. That guy at the mall. Even when I've gone to digs and other expeditions, I've had fellow anthropologists who were like her."

"Exactly," Iseult said. "That's why I'm having so much trouble."

"Can't put your finger on it," Kelly said.

Iseult nodded, looked at Nick, and realized her mistake. "Yeah," she said.

Nick took a long, shuddering breath. He covered his face with his hands.

"There's only so long I'll wait," Tash said. Iseult stood upright. Kelly lay down and curled into Nick, and it wasn't clear who was giving or receiving support between them. Tash returned the lamp and radio to the end table and sat on the other bed, hands on its edge, facing them. "I can't pull the equipment for a whole lab out of a hat. I can only call in or ask for so many favours. We'll have to go to someone at some point."

"What about Victor and his troopers?" Kelly asked. "Maybe we could bring them in, catch a lucky break?"

"Chad and Abby have been having a little trouble lately," Tash replied. "They followed up on Towerton, which has so totally cleaned up that everyone has a different story about what happened. Some people are saying that the whole drone thing was an art project, and they tried to claim it was Banksy's hometown. It's so covered up in tabloid nonsense that Abby's uncomfortably remembering P-H-I. You know about Jaycee. And Victor's so skull-deep in whatever's on his mind that he's in his sandstorm phase."

"I don't remember much about Victor," Iseult said. "Only really saw him a couple of times, and briefly. He looked at me funny. What's his sandstorm phase?"

"Yeah, he looks at a lot of people funny," Nick said. His tone was desperately casual. "He's pretty insightful, likes to study them, I think."

"It's when he gets so focused that the whole world could be in a sandstorm and he's still in his little cave, studying the paintings on the walls," Tash replied.

"Kinda feels like what we're doing," Kelly said.

"That's not fair," Nick said. He actually grinned, though only with half his mouth.

"I'll be asking around a bunch tomorrow," Tash said. "We'll work out a schedule of bringing Nick between rooms."

"Why?" Iseult asked.

"Room service and cleaning," Tash said.

"Yeah, the vacuuming is good for the eyes," Kelly said with characteristic sarcasm.

"That's the only freebie you're getting," Tash warned.

Iseult swallowed audibly.

"I'm gonna go crazy if I have to just lie here," Nick remarked.

"We'll figure something out," Tash said. "We've got more leads than you think."

Nick frowned his doubts but said nothing. Kelly curled into him tighter. Iseult took to the folding chair beside the bed. "We'll be going to bed soon," Tash said as the younger woman sat. "It's getting late, and we all need our rest."

"I don't think I can sleep like this," Nick said.

"No, but we all need our rest," Tash said again. "I believe in you all, you know."

Each of the youths reacted with alternating stiffness and slouching, as if they were equal parts flattered, offended, and lost. They all wanted to speak, but no one wanted to say anything.

CHAPTER 09
SIKLOON

Lake Volta, The Republic of Ghana

He sat in a shabby boat. It was practically a shanty that didn't sink.

A child entered. She spoke Akan, his mother tongue. "They're ready for you, Mr. Sikloon, sir."

"Excellent," he replied in that language. It had a long and complicated history, with an influence reaching as far as Jamaica, and shared a heritage with the stories of the spider trickster Anansi. His clothing had spent munitions cartridges worked into it so that he looked like a heavily armed warlord. It doubled as cheap, flexible, and surprisingly effective armour. "Have you been assigned?"

"Yes. I'm to carry your name." This was a coded phrase in Sikloon's human trafficking and slave operations. It meant that she worked on cyclone knives. His name meant "cyclone" in Afrikaans. Unsolicited, she continued: "My name is-"

"-irrelevant," he said.

She bowed to the floor of the boat in apology.

He watched her there. Even on sound earth, such a

posture wouldn't be comfortable for long. He waited. She began to tremble but did not dare move. She wore a simple cotton dress of mostly red, yellow, and purple. Despite her dark brown skin, her hands looked almost chalky from many hours of hard, calloused work. She was not so malnourished as to be deformed by it, but like most of his work force, she was smaller than her age because she'd been so long underfed.

"Stand," he said.

Flooded with gratitude, she rushed to her feet. Only to stumble and nearly fall. She got up slower this time once the faintness had passed. "Sorry, sorry, sorry," she said, looking down. "They taught me. But I'm…"

"It is an honour to speak with me directly," he said. This was not a question or command, but the closest he came to kindness. He understood why she was so out of sorts. "You've had a moment for that, which is fair. Now, I expect a full report when I arrive."

"You will have it."

"A woman for my entertainment."

"You will have her."

"A meeting with my people."

"You will have them."

"The head of the spy."

"You have it already, and you will see it."

"Good," he said. Sikloon smiled, but there was more tooth than muscle in it. "You may go."

She bowed again and left. Sikloon bore no insignia that connected with Engen. Nor did the girl, the boat he rode, or anyone in his operation. Any money that found itself in his hands, or the hands of his work force, turned into vapour.

His slaves were the white space. They formed a picture, crossing from as far as Egypt and running in lines through to Nigeria, Ghana, and the Congo. Here on Lake Volta, there was a forest under the surface. The whole area had been flooded for the dam, and fish were plentiful from the white and black rivers. Fishing nets still got caught in trees under the water's surface. And there was no trace that he was a Knife of Engen.

Many workers were part of the show when his vessel reached the shore. It was tied onto a stump that had been left on the bank intentionally. Not only did the roots help hold the earth together, but it served as an anchor, a seat, and even a reference point. Most of the fishers were either on the water or operating out of several supply points elsewhere around the lake. Some people were working on boat engines; some were making repairs to wooden or metal planking; others were working on setups like winches, wagons, barrels, and surveys; and a few performed maintenance related to the hydroelectric dam.

People involved in ownership, significant money handling, and other forms of business rarely came this far into the front lines. Other than a scattered overseer, then, there were few white people. Most outsiders who looked upon all the people around the lake would have concluded that there were two types: Brown and Black. Sikloon was not so ignorant and knew the variety and diversity well. Religions, languages, cultures, countries.

The Knife was barely a half-dozen steps away from the boat before a Muslim woman sidled up to him. She was wearing a hijab. They looked ahead and not at each other as they spoke:

"It is the end, and from there, the beginning," she began. This was the third Apothegm among the Knives, but she used it only as a code.

"What have you got for me?" he asked. His footsteps were commands. Whether they were slaves or not, everyone obeyed.

"The loss in product has been staunched."

"Good. I expect I'll have confirmation of the leak." He looked out over the lake as he listened to her. The sun cut through the blue and glistened off the water; he couldn't see the trees beneath.

"That is where you go next." She handed him a file folder. Sikloon saw how anyone in eyeshot decidedly noticed no such exchange. They hauled fish or worked on one project or another. Nothing to see here. The woman continued: "Albinos have been rare even for their nature. The last one we've found was from Egypt. He is in transit."

Albinos were their term for people with powers, prodigal skills, and other stand-out features or abilities. Since actual, pale-skinned albinos had a history of murder and persecution, it worked well for plausible deniability. Sikloon took this all in even as he watched the overseers, slaves, and workers going about their day. He was looking for slackers, spies, assassins, exceptional workers, and opportunities.

"Excellent," he said. It was the closest he came to Thank you. This covered the first three Apothegms, though he'd want to put more time and effort into their various kinds of scouting. "But the whales will still be hungry." If the

Ships, *Muninn* and *Huginn*, came up, they were named as the whales.

"We will feed them well. The Knives will be kept sharp," she said. Her path parted from his without any obvious signs of order or departure.

Sikloon soon found himself in an industrial tent. Similar to field hospitals or military command tents, these were thrown up from time to time to offer a place for everything from gutting fish to hosting meetings between traders, slavers, and various leaders. As he entered, a man approached with a briefcase handcuffed to his wrist. A special flap had been set up beside the entryway. Sikloon stepped in first. The man then stepped in, curtly opened the case so that only Sikloon could see it, then closed and locked it before leaving the tent and from there, the country.

Sikloon was not one for taking chances.

In the case was the indented foam padding one might expect for carrying vials, tubes, or weapons. There was a karambit, an extended switchblade, a high-end ghost knife, and a cyclone knife. Sikloon was pleased that all four of the Knives were in operation and uncompromised.

The cyclone knife that was his symbol was an unusual weapon in that its edges were not intended for cutting. It had three of them, winding up from the handle to the tip. Along each edge stretched two angled sides of the blade, perforated at regular intervals with holes that connected through the core to the bottom of the hollow handle. The handle was capped.

Sikloon proceeded from the flap-covered enclosure to a small table on which was situated a TV and some equipment for transmission. Nothing was recorded. He opened the folder provided to him as his subordinates set up the apparatus and a news broadcast came on. The broadcast was in Arabic, but Sikloon wasn't listening to the reporter.

On the screen was a man, tied to a chair, with a cyclone knife driven into his side. Even if he'd been found alive, his chances for survival would have been slim: three entwined, curved edges formed a wound that was difficult to close. The holes in the blade channelled the blood from the body, through the knife, and out of the uncapped handle like a spigot draining sap from a tree. In the folder was the file of the dead person, including a photo, and an explanation of how it had been rigged to look like an assassination between rival crime lords.

There was nothing to show that the victim had been a spy who'd infiltrated Sikloon's network. Even as the Knife of Engen set fire to the file he was holding, a subordinate stepped forward with a metal can in which to place it. "Who was he working for?" Sikloon asked.

"He held out for longer than most," one of them answered. "There is some honour in that." Sikloon nodded acknowledgement but allowed the other man to finish. "We're of course looking into it. All we've found so far is the mythological reference. We're not sure if it's an individual or a group."

"His last word was 'Circe.'"

CHAPTER 10
KNIFE DEFENCE

Seattle, Washington

1 April

Thatcher closed his apartment door behind him. He filled a glass with water and sat at his computer desk. On his left side, in a seemingly random portion of the bachelor space, was a small, third- or fourth-hand armoire for his clothes. Just beyond it lay his bed — or rather, a mattress and box spring. Assorted items littered the wall leading past the counter into a tiny kitchen.

The chair for his computer desk, and the desk itself, were each more expensive than almost everything else in the apartment. He found it easier to move the bed when he needed some room for calisthenics and a frame was just more expensive, anyway. The chair and desk were large, ergonomically designed, and high quality because that was where he spent the lion's share of his time.

He sat next to his computer and pulled up the self-help book *Overcoming Agoraphobia*. He'd gotten it new, two or three days after moving in, and it was ratty from re-reads. It took him a while to get some of the habits and strategies down, but he'd learned from his time in New Mexico. It wasn't exactly getting easier. At least, not in a way he could feel. But he was getting better at it. It was one thing to be walking a highway or sleeping on a bus full of fellow homeless people when you were fleeing something or someone. It was quite another to be walking the streets of a city, one large and mostly unfamiliar to him. To go to work. Every day.

He sat next to his computer, reading from a book worn to threaded edges and cracked soft covers, drinking water. He'd taken it a bit easier today. His finances had been pretty thoroughly planned. He'd enjoyed being an entrepreneur, had been proud of his drone business, and missed it. His business degree from MIT had literally gone up in smoke. But he'd chosen to leave it there. He'd cut out Soto and planned to keep it that way. And he was trying to cut down on his waistline.

Thatcher sat next to his computer, representing his skills and life blood. He had to be vigilant to keep himself from falling back into old habits, though he sometimes struggled to work out which of those habits had been harmful. A second glass of water helped get the reading down. The exercises from the book created healthier thinking and provided strategies for getting through the day.

The next day, he went to work.

The inside door had an employee card reader, as there was no reason for the general public to enter. Posters — not just sheets of loose-leaf taped to the glass of the foyer, but actual laminated meant-to-be-there-long-term posters — indicated that job search efforts should be made over the phone or online, with e-mail, website, and phone number info provided. None of this was particularly remarkable.

Nor was it remarkable that Thatcher stopped before rounding the corner to the security gate. This gate was largely ceremonial, as fraud was unlikely and the public should not have access, but here it was. Thatcher had stopped to take an extra breath, tidy up his hair, adjust his shirt, and have his ID card readily available. He squared his shoulders and proceeded.

"Hi, Eryx," he started casually.

Most people called the outgoing security officer Eric because it was easier. But Thatcher took pride in making a point to get it right. Eryx had shoulders "for days," as some of Thatcher's online friends would have said. The man was the human version of the jaws of life, average height, and in his late twenties. His chin was Roman and soft, his cheeks hard, his nose and forehead prominent. Green eyes and short, curly, black hair topped him off.

"Hey," came the reply. The tone was quick and sounded off. Eryx usually called Thatcher Leo, the Spanish Lion, or Mr. Roar. Thatcher stopped, his expression flattened, and he faced the Greek head-on. Eryx's explanation was already under way: "You can't take your lunch in that parking hall anymore."

What? "Why?" Thatcher asked. He kicked himself; he didn't want it to seem like it was all that important.

"New policies coming in. I've been at more meetings and signed more forms in the last week than all of last year." Then Thatcher registered that, behind the holed glass of the security post, Eryx's workspace had a dishevelled array of post-its, official notices, papers, a full waste basket, scattered pens, an empty mug of coffee, empty go-cups of coffee, and a computer with its monitor on maximum extension. It was angled so that passers-by couldn't see the screen. The Greek rested his elbow on the sill of the windowed door and leaned closer to the glass in a conspiratorial manner. Thatcher stepped close for the lowered voice: "And you never heard this from me, but a pile of zeroes fell out of a Panama account and into ours. I wasn't supposed to hear that, so I didn't."

"Hear what?" Thatcher said with his best grin.

The other man had a weak smile under eyes glimmering with paperwork and thinned-out caffeine. Thatcher wondered if he'd been awkward or if the jaws of life really had been overworked. He waited a moment longer, trying to feel out the situation, but Eryx seemed just as uncomfortable as Thatcher felt himself. Both men were projecting a stoicism neither felt, so they each nodded and continued about their business.

Once he had navigated the halls and elevator to get to the break room for his area, Thatcher came upon Ciel and Liam as they were rounding a corner. The metadata specialist stood a half a foot shorter than the website developer, but was never one to be troubled by his height. Liam's shoulders were stiff and just a little too high, however; it was like he was frozen in a mobile state of huff. By contrast, Ciel had darting eyes and rubbed her hands together continuously. Her smile was half-cocked, like a movie character who'd just picked up a shotgun, and her hair was now platinum blonde with highlights of blue, red, pink, and purple.

"Don't know what you're so worried about," Liam was saying to her in his fatherly way. "You said she kissed you at the end of the date. I've heard half a dozen people in the break room guess your age and…"

"Hi, Braulio!" Ciel said. Liam regarded Thatcher without blinking and made no comment on the interruption. "Don't mind this fuddy-duddy," she said with more levity than she felt. She'd jerked her thumb at her colleague. "Jake gave him a case of Trojan War over his racist nonsense."

Thatcher looked between them helplessly, unable to put his finger on the fact that something seemed amiss. All of Spindle's employees were becoming increasingly stressed because, he assumed, of the roll-over for the contract with Surimp. "Not gonna lie," he said, "I usually find that mildew like him doesn't change on its own. But I want to try with him. I've got a hunch that he'll do some good if he can stop watching truthers on YouTube."

Liam adjusted his glasses, which didn't reflect the lights of the hallway because they had no lenses. "Mildew?" His tension and frustration seemed to be disarmed.

"You know," Thatcher said, "white muck."

Ciel grinned. "That's racist."

"He racisted first," Thatcher said in his most childish tone. Though Liam in particular never really shared that kind of humour, the three of them had a moment of awkward half-positive friend energy. There was a flood of relief: Thatcher wasn't the only one struggling to keep on a face.

"I wish you the best of luck with…uh…cleaning the mildew," Liam said. "And, for what it's worth, congrats on your second month here. Sorry that it won't be getting any easier."

Thatcher's forehead tightened. "Thanks, I'm doing what I can. But what do you mean?"

"We've gotta get going," Ciel said. "Just came out of a huge debrief about both Spindle's website and a bunch of the front-end presentation for Surimp."

Liam fingered the Vietnam flag pin on his tweed jacket. "Now, now, I told you already — this isn't a war." He locked eyes with his Hispanic friend. "All the preliminaries are out of the way. You were on a list of all the people who got shuffled around or promoted. They're even cutting through paperwork. I've never seen the bureaucrats so nervous."

"You should have seen Aim at the printer!" Ciel chuckled. "He almost transformed from a grey blob to a real, live human!"

Thatcher took a deep breath. "All right. Thanks for the heads up!"

"Don't hesitate to reach out for help," Liam said. He'd always had a certain professorial vibe, and he had a reputation for being great to have in a storm.

Ciel hugged Thatcher and the pair continued to their next task. Thatcher swelled inside, though it would be a while before he'd identify that feeling. He couldn't remember the last time he'd been given a casual hug. He glanced over his shoulder. The pair had a lighter step, more relaxed body language, and he heard Liam's throaty laugh as they took another turn.

Thatcher began looking and watching more attentively, even checking to see if some of the wall decor had changed. It had: framed as though they were proper pictures, there were inspirational statements and reminders of ethos and ethics. Was this a contract or a takeover? He barely got out of the lunch room after putting his meal in the fridge before Stewart swept him up into a brisk power-walk.

"This whole situation's got everyone on edge, huh?" Thatcher asked as they went.

"Yep," Stewart said, fidgeting with his pocket protector. Thatcher glanced at him and realized that the bulge wouldn't have been a pen even if it were long enough to reach the top of the accountant's shirt pocket. "We'll need Steel for this meeting."

"Y'know," Thatcher remarked as they passed a long stretch of cubicles, "I've been here two months and you haven't actually told me what's up with that." A chorus of office supplies — phones, papers, printers, carts and wheeled desks, garbage bins, filing cabinets, and so on — played in the background. There was next to no talking.

"Up with what?" Stewart asked. "The contract's still got some ink drying. This is gonna be a long haul."

"I meant your…" the Hispanic tapped his chest where a shirt pocket would be. As usual, his own button-up didn't have a pocket in the chest area. One button was undone, the shirt was untucked, and his whole outfit looked more crumpled than wrinkled. Like he'd jumped into the dryer with his clothes.

The incredibly white man replied, "Oh. Lavender perfume. My aunt wore something like it on a cruise when I was a kid. Helps my nerves."

Thatcher couldn't remember ever smelling lavender anything from Stewart. Or had he thought one of the women nearby was wearing it? The workplace was scent-free, but…

They had to make three cramped turns. The cubicle they were looking for was tucked within the masses and too far inside to directly connect to any of the main walkways. It was like a secret speakeasy in a back alley. When the pair reached the opening to the cubicle, they saw a name plate reading "Steel." A one-word name, like Beyoncé or Madonna. On the cubicle panels were pictures featuring a man with a receding line of chaotic green hair. He was dressed in a bizarre black-and-white-striped suit. Some of the images included a younger woman, whose features were dark, sane, and pretty. What looked like cartoony versions of both characters were also among the images, and there were figures and bobbleheads of the male — known as Beetlejuice — positioned on the computer or around Steel's desk.

She pushed her chair back and turned to face them. She was probably slightly older than Stewart — who was in his mid-thirties. When standing, she reached just over six feet. Her build was muscular, and she'd told Thatcher recently that she weighed about 170lbs. Platinum blonde hair framed an angular face with grey eyes. "Braulio," she said with a hint of a German accent. "Didn't I see you yesterday?"

"You see me every day," Thatcher replied without a proper smile. He put his hands in his pockets, though, and the slight change from his normally stiff posture practically changed the very light in the wide, cubicle-stifled room.

Stewart stood straight and leaned a little more towards the computer specialist, as though his spine were saying "I'm with him." His hand went to the pocket of his shirt, stayed a fraction of a second too long, then scratched as though it realized too late that it had to explain its presence.

Steel, herself a computer networking technician, leaned her elbows on the arms of her chair so that her hands dangled over her lap. She had to be careful moving her chair because the space — small though it was already — had a collection of modems, ethernet cables, and dongles arranged in what Stewart hoped was a system secret to her. Otherwise, it was chaos. She wasn't bright and smiley, she was not quite cold, and she was entirely professional. Like a set of high-end kitchen knives. Including a cleaver. "New pants," she said to Thatcher.

Stewart looked down at his friend and realized it was true. "Yeah, Braulio, good job on your weight loss stuff," he said to the floor.

Thatcher resisted looking, but his eyes shifted in Stewart's direction. Steel pretended not to notice. Stewart was mousier than usual, and while Steel could be...commanding, she seemed ready to flex at any challenger right now. Took a lot to put her on edge. "Do you know what this meeting's about?" he asked to take the edge off.

"Not yet. But I've been talking about some of the tweaks and strategies you've been putting together in the last couple of days. Diagnostics, that little twist you did with the software mirror. They say you've been making a name for yourself and getting along well for a guy who likes his privacy." She hadn't stood yet. Her phone showed an update from a stylized heart-in-flames symbol Thatcher recognized as a dating app. He pretended not to notice, and she turned her phone over without taking her eyes off the men before her.

Thatcher shuffled, uncomfortable with compliments,

and turned halfway out of the cubicle.

"Yes," she said, standing like a crane and stepping through the space vacated by Stewart. "Let's head over."

Stewart kept to the wall opposite her, putting Thatcher in the middle. He didn't generally mind, but it meant he was the one who ducked behind or moved ahead of one of them to allow passers-by as they made their way to the elevator.

As they waited for their floor, Stewart broke the silence but not the awkwardness: "You know Steel's real name is Betelgeuse?"

Thatcher blinked. "Beetlejuice?" He looked up at her in surprise.

While her lips stayed even, there was a lift of her eyes and brows. It was partly amusement, and partly something he didn't know how to name. Affection? "It's true," she said. Then: "After the colour."

"Wow," was all the response Thatcher could offer.

"Is that why you like the character?" Stewart asked.

She shook her head. "That's asking a lot."

"Where does Steel come from?" Thatcher asked as the door opened.

Mashaka was standing at the water cooler across the hall from the elevator. Betelgeuse said, "When I started working out and rock-climbing, some scumbag at the gym started up this joke that I was a steal. Something about being hot and pumping iron. It was one of those chimpanzee dominance things."

Stewart, brows furrowed, opened his mouth. Thatcher knew the posture of objection and spoke first to stop Stewart from stepping on a metaphorical mine. "It was one of those taking-it-back things, then?"

Steel seemed impressed. "Something like that. Where does Braulio come from?"

They were getting closer to Mashaka, who was leaning away from the white man talking to her. The man didn't have a water cup. "Seattle," she said to the man with a tone Thatcher couldn't place.

Not many asked him much about himself, other than Ciel and Mashaka. And the troupe, of course. A brief warmth tingled through him, and Mashaka and Stewart both seemed to relax. "It's Spanish," he said. "It means 'Shining.' It's also a…" he made a rapid swiping gesture toward himself, as if he could waft in the word he was looking for.

"No, where you really from?" the man asked. Thatcher cringed on Mashaka's behalf as the group stopped to absorb her. He'd had this conversation. That was what distracted him from the word he was looking for: digestif.

"You got me," she said. "I'm from Madagascar."

"It's a drink you have after meals," Stewart said in an effort to be helpful.

Mashaka and the man looked at him in confusion.

"Our colleague was just on her way to a meeting," Steel said, nodding toward Mashaka as she spoke to the blundering white man who wasn't Stewart. "I'm afraid you'll have to-"

"That's okay," he said, "I can walk you there."

"We're right h-" Steel said with a dangerous frown.

Thatcher simply continued with the right turn that would lead to their meeting room. Stewart, nonplussed, looked back and forth between the rest of them and dithered for a moment before following his Hispanic friend.

"I'll have a postcard sent to your cubicle," Mashaka

said to him as she turned to join Steel.

"Okay," he said. Smug was the only word for him at that moment. "I'm at-"

"We'll find you, no trouble," Steel said. "You're a stand-out guy."

He walked away thinking he'd done well. Mashaka, halfway up the hall, looked over her shoulder before elbowing Steel and making a half-laugh that came more from the shoulders than the lungs. "Damn, girl!"

Steel's only response was to match step with Mashaka. While Mashaka was slightly taller than the men, Steel was taller again. Enough of that height was leg that falling in line with anyone's walk was practically a political move for her.

Thatcher waited a moment, as much for Stewart's benefit as the women's, so that everyone was more or less in line again. "Well, good luck in there," Stewart said.

Mashaka smiled. "Don't look so disappointed, Braulio. I got you. Stew's got his own team stuff goin' on. Finance must be swimming in caviar!"

Stewart shuffled his feet nervously. "They tried to give Freedom a dressing-down over some of the public image stuff. It was spending, which wasn't really her thing."

Thatcher was taken aback. "Is there a person named Freedom here?"

"Most everyone calls her the Patriot," Mashaka said.

"For some reason," Steel commented, "having a name like Freedom makes people uncomfortable. She has red hair, she might be the only person here even whiter than I am, and blue eyes. Red, white, and blue."

Thatcher actually chuckled at her description, more out of surprise than real humour.

Stewart managed to detach himself from the group and they opened the door to the meeting room. Thatcher realized he hadn't asked about Stewart's general discomfiture with Mashaka just as the door was closing. Already seated were Bevis, Jake, and three others.

Jake sat at the head of the table and began as soon as everyone was seated. "Thank you for coming, everyone. As you all know, our recent contract is unprecedented, and we're here as part of a series of team divisions. This is about focus. I'll be the lead for this team, and my name is Jake." He then set about introducing everyone in the team, referring to a sheet to describe the people he clearly didn't know. Thatcher already forgot the names of the three new team members.

It was only now that Thatcher realized that he had no idea what the conspiracy nut actually did with the company. Everyone just knew Jake as the resident quack. The man was hunched on his chair like a hyena overlooking a meal he didn't trust. And hyenas will eat anything. Slightly sweaty, with blue eyes so oily they looked grey, the only part of him that spoke of real professionalism was the thoroughly ironed button-up shirt with suspenders and a black-and-white tie that matched his salt-and-pepper hair.

"...and now we have Braulio," Jake said. He'd been left for last. "I'll get into our objectives shortly, and I was hoping not to have a Mexican as part of such a-"

"I'm American," Thatcher pointed out. Again.

"...sensitive information security operation," the other man finished as if not interrupted. The Hispanic's outrage was like the high noon sun on black metal. Though there was somewhat less intensity from the three newcomers, everyone at the table glared this heat at Jake.

Lifting and tensing his shoulders, Jake shot peeks at each of them in turn, and gradually lifted his folder full of papers as though erecting a wall. Thatcher made a mental note to chat with HR, but all he said was: "What will I be doing, then?"

He'd intended it as a rhetorical jibe, expecting Jake to explain himself or remember what Thatcher did for a living. His surprise was complete when the team lead responded, "Cybersecurity Specialist. You've been promoted and it had to be delivered as a footnote in this meeting because of everything being in a rush. And to fast-track Gary Azure's replacement."

Steel and Mashaka applauded. Bevis made a shocked remark that was lost in the clapping, but the tone of his voice matched his scowl. Hubbub bubbled from the others. Thatcher was flattered, mildly offended by the sheer wonder everyone was expressing, bewildered, and uncomfortable. How had he gotten on such a radar? The limelight made him self-conscious, the attention made him vulnerable. Some part of him registered that the others began to squirm or shift in their seats, fidgeting with hands and papers and phones, and he took this to mean that he'd taken too long to respond.

"Um...wow. I...uh...thank you, I'm honoured. It's... that's..." he frowned and sat up. "What do you mean, replacement?"

Jake did a poor job of hiding a grin. "Your position is subject to review, of course. We're plugging a hole for now. Mr. Azure hasn't been answering any of his contact info. His daughter reported him missing a couple of days ago. Don't worry; I'm sure we'll find a suitable candidate soon."

"Jake...!" Steel said in consternation.

He raised his eyebrows. Bevis folded his arms and leaned his chair back on its rear legs, one of his feet anchoring him from the cross-braces under the table. Mashaka leaned forward, left palm flat on the table and right forearm placed like a crossbar in front of her. Thatcher was reminded of passionate pundits or gangsters with commands to bestow.

She said: "You get away with a lot of stuff when it's you and one person in the break room, when you're in the halls and no one's looking, when you're manspreading with your ridiculous corkboard. But you'll keep a civil tongue, y-" Steel put a hand on her shoulder.

Thatcher had a flood of gratitude for her pride and supportive outrage. But he'd only ever seen her talk to authority like that — or anyone at work, for that matter — when she'd had a rug pulled out from under her. Full of a mixture of concern and relief, he related to her and set about lining himself up with the table and the meeting. It was time to stabilize the boat. There was general agreement.

"Right..." Jake said, with the tone of a child soured by the fact that no one wanted to play his game. "Sorry. It's... this is a lot."

Bevis collected himself as well. "I 'spect y'all wanna get on with this. I'm not any happier than you are." Bevis was now slightly more rotund than Thatcher, a fact in which the new cybersecurity specialist took grim satisfaction. With blue eyes, blond hair, a collection of gun magazines, and a computer hardware specialization, the man was a cross between military-grade impact plastic and a fourteen-year-old obsessed with "yo' mama" jokes.

Steel glared at Bevis in disgust, but slowly fixed herself into a cold and stiff posture with her hands placed on either side of her collection of papers and notes, her thumbs at the top of the hand. "I'm sure there will be suitable condolences arranged concerning Mr. Azure."

Jake nodded a few times, his eyes on his own sheaf of papers. "Yes, yes. Now: I have a few other housekeeping points, and then we can get into why we're all in the same room." He shot a barbed look at Thatcher, who kept his attention on Mashaka and Steel and pretended he'd seen nothing.

"It goes without saying," Jake began, "that discretion is paramount. There's no guarantee that the seafood supply chain is really compromised. You all know that computer infiltrations can happen for all kinds of mischief, and we're working closely with the FDA on this."

"Not us pacifically, I reckon," Bevis put in. No one corrected his pronunciation.

"No, there's another team for that," Jake confirmed. "And if the public found out…"

"What's your take on a possible leak to the public, Braulio?" Mashaka asked.

Again with the spotlight. Several throats cleared. Thatcher felt like he was sitting on a bucket of worms and had to keep that secret from everyone. He adjusted his shirt collar, and registered that he was the only man present not wearing a tie. "I don't think that's the plan of whoever did it," he answered.

"We haven't started the real investigation yet!" Jake ejected. His glare was mistrusting and contemptuous. "How would you know?"

"If you're taking out someone's computer security," Thatcher replied with as much calm as he could muster, "you're either hoping to be invisible or making a statement. If they were going for stealth, they might already have whatever they wanted. Obviously, no one's caught them, so my guess is invisibility was their goal. If they were making a statement, it would be obvious — sending a letter to some editor, a random note, declarations over radio or TV or the Internet."

"Unless the message wasn't meant for the public. Maybe it was obvious for a private interest," Steel put in.

Thatcher shrugged. "Yeah, that could work."

"Anything else we should know before we dive in, boss?" Bevis asked.

"Yeah," Jake said, shooting a look at Thatcher. He shuffled and glanced at a few sheets, scratched off or checked a few things, then went on: "Everything we're doing will be remote. They've given us the required access. Spindle is sending a team to the warehouses and plants, where most of our hardware specialists will be. We're keeping you," he nodded at Bevis, "so that we have a kind of eye-in-the-sky who might recognize evidence of hardware tampering that teams like Cybersecurity might miss." Thatcher, Steel, and Mashaka clenched fists or teeth. The three strangers offered less intense responses, like soft sighs and eye rolls when Jake wasn't looking at them.

As Thatcher opened his mouth, Jake pressed on: "I'm sure we'll be wanting piles of input from Braulio once we get underway. And for those of you who are wondering, the hardware team won't be announcing themselves as part of a system-wide prelim from Spindle. They'll be representing responsibly. Routine maintenance or something. They're not even allowed to show the company logo. I know; I thought that was strange too."

"All of this sounds like a massive PR risk for Spindle," Steel pointed out. "Why would the Board of Directors allow such a sweeping deal? This isn't business as usual."

"You're darn tootin'," Bevis said. Thatcher wondered if he was playing up the redneck thing, or if this was actually the kind of person Bevis was. Maybe both, somehow?

Jake actually smiled. Was that genuine approval of Steel? "Money answers reams and reams of the questions we could all come up with. I'm doing some digging on my own time, to be honest, but that's not really what we're here for. You're right, though — nothing usual about this business."

Before he got into what their team would be doing for this investigation in great detail, Jake outlined various PSAs and other memoranda that were obviously parcelled out to each of the team leads. The usual branding and mission statement reminders, non-disclosure agreements, and notes about mental health topped the list. He even got into recent news stories, including: citizens throughout the western seaboard reporting bursts of strange behaviour; odd incidents involving animals, lights, and unnatural events; rising crime levels; a trend reporting school shootings as "unique"; seemingly good news about the burgeoning fintech industry that had experts asking about the potential risks of computer security; even evidence that there were anomalies and disappearances within the seafood companies, subsidiaries, and surrounding workforces.

"That's a big part of why they hired us," Jake explained.

"That evidence was planted. They suspect a frame job, or some kind of planned public outcry. They'll have more updates for us on that in the coming weeks."

Thatcher had to wonder how much of this stuff was inserted by Jake himself, and had no mention in the paperwork or team lead meetings Jake had received or attended. He also noticed that, in the last week or so, other people working at Spindle had started showing signs of strain. They were often wan, pale, and taut. Some were obsessive, others lethargic. But everyone seemed more concerned with body image. More people were talking about diet, exercise, and the like — and he'd been doing that stuff for a while now. He was making progress, but still.

Except for Bevis, who had actually gained weight, most people were losing it. Some were also showing the early warning signs of, well, losing it. For the rest of the meeting, Thatcher found himself wishing he had a notebook. He didn't usually need something like that. He felt a little naked without his headset. His unexpected promotion was like having his moorings cut.

Part of him wanted to run and hide, and he had to remind himself to take things in stride. He realized his attention had drifted during the meeting. There were questions, debates, and conflicts of personality. By the time he got home, he wanted to defragment himself the way he would a computer.

He secured a glass of water with freshly squeezed lime, which was helping him with the weight loss and his nostalgia for lime soda. Once planted on the chair at his computer desk, he set to work.

By now, he'd abandoned his search for Chad and

Abby. He just didn't have enough info. For all he knew, they were using assumed names. In fact, his habit of checking up on Towerton — the incident, and what was happening there now — was fading away entirely. Soto clung to the back of his mind with the same temptation as drunk-dialling an ex: an unwise part of him very much wanted to know. But the very act of looking was risky. He might be counter-traced. And then there were the emotional risks.

A pop-up he'd programmed reminded him to practice mindfulness. He grabbed his nearest hard copy book about agoraphobia and held it, without reading, as a kind of talisman as he spent the allotted ten minutes on himself. He couldn't afford to fall back into his old mental space. Maybe he'd take a late-night walk later. Ten minutes. Fresh air. Fight the temptation to get comfortable. He had to carve carefully around the edges of comfort. You could drown in your comfort zone.

He'd hoped to use the intranet, hardware, and infrastructure of Spindle to piggyback his hacking activities and Dark Web usage. Now, though, it looked like their internal security was ramping up just as much as their investigation into the mainframes used by Hydropolis Industries. Even with a robust VPN and other privacy and security measures, he didn't like trying anything heavy with his own hardware on his own network. That felt to him like stealing something on a train, taking a seat in the same train, and holding the stolen item on his lap for the whole ride.

Thatcher rubbed his face, scrabbled his hair with his fingers, drummed them on the desk, took a sip of the lime water, tapped his feet a bunch, and checked his belly.

He stopped.

Jumping from his chair, he grabbed the belt he used as a reference and measured his waistline. He thoroughly examined the fit of his clothes, and realized he'd have to pick up new outfits again; his weight loss was going well. But that wasn't what got his attention. He turned the radio to his preferred Spanish-language news station and returned to his desk.

He took advantage of his bilingualism to maintain connections and observations in online communities in both English and Spanish. Though the latter was his mother tongue, he had to work to stay connected to it, as he didn't have a local Hispanic group to welcome him. Or rather, he hadn't made a great effort to reach out. Baby steps. In any case, he focused his online exploration on local trends in behaviour, consumption, mental health, and businesses related to health that ranged from gyms and nutrition supplements to those seen-on-TV weight loss strategies and classes.

In the background, he had bots clambering over the Web in service to his search for information on strange occurrences. Jake had been helpful in this, as the conspiracy theorist's rants were basically name-dropping exercises that gave Thatcher a place to start. Every once in a while, he'd get a notification connecting him to a website, article, tabloid, police report, or other piece of information accessible through the Deep and Dark Webs and well-placed hacks.

Most of these blips were nonsense, hoaxes, or so tangential and incomplete that he couldn't do anything with it. "Blur spotted in field." Okay. Do these people realize how little that is to go on for cryptids like Bigfoot? Some of them seemed real — as far as he could make it — but not really useful to him. Some little place in Maine called Coral Beach. Apparently Jake was on to something with Port Haven Institute. Stoneville was so classified he'd have to risk detection to get through those defences. He made a note to try it at some point in the future.

"What am I doing?" he muttered aloud.

The radio reported various Seattle goings-on that he didn't much care for. As far as he could tell, they weren't picking up on the stuff he'd seen at work. But why was he looking for the strange incidents? Surely Soto had been yanking his tail about him having some kind of power. Hacking was power enough for him, thank you very much. None of this loosey-goosey feelings stuff. Here he was, however; looking for signs that special abilities existed.

He finally started picking up on messages, data, and other signs from medical watchdogs, blogs, restricted professional communities, and the like. So far it looked like only people with their fingers on the pulse had anything to say. But it was happening: Seattle, especially the business district bordering the Denny Triangle, was showing a spike in problems related to body image. Gym memberships; dietary aids and programs; weight loss supplement sales; demand for dietitians, personal trainers, counselors, and mental health experts. Oddly, violence against transgender people was rising, and tensions were increasing in and around LGBT groups. Thatcher didn't know what to make of that.

Then flags started popping up in his system before it automatically shut down as part of his defence protocol.

Someone was trying to track him!

CHAPTER 11
HAND-WRITTEN

Kodiak, Alaska

They weren't really tracking the days now. Fear became furtive and timeless as they watched the news, visited police and private investigators, talked to journalists and spy contacts, and alternated their hotel rooms. They brought Nick back and forth so that each of the two rooms could be cleaned by the staff without calling any attention to the fact that Nick himself was not out and about. His eyes had given out... three days ago?

Maybe four?

Iseult was in the washroom of what used to be the room she shared with Nick. Though that had stopped mattering; Tash was letting Nick sleep however he wanted and spent a night with him herself to keep tabs on him and talk him through it. She did maintain two people per room, though. She didn't want any of the hotel's representatives to get curious or push for more enforcement about who had what room.

Most of the conclusions — even from what could be garnered about his private and online life — showed that the Providence Bomber had been "disturbed." Iseult turned this over in her head as she finished patching up the wound she'd cut in her own leg. Even when wearing shorts, the cuts were easier to hide on the legs than on the arms. She rinsed and dried the ghost knife she'd used for the purpose and secured that in the sheath strapped to her other leg. Once she got another private moment, she'd want to oil and whet the blade — as much for the Zen of the exercise as for maintenance.

Once her ministrations were complete, she headed to the room proper and arranged some of the groceries Kelly had brought in the day before. Tash had been against it, aiming to fly low, but they'd had fun — and Iseult argued that they were supposed to be on vacation. They had to look like they were loosening up. Living a little. People had stopped going to the bar or public areas for news specials about the explosion. Things were far from normal; this was a small town. A single stabbing could stay in the local news for a week. But they could pretend that normal had returned.

And so she did. She pretended a butterknife all over the bread, with mayo and pepper she shook onto it. Three meats adorned her normality: sliced turkey, shredded turkey, and some of those microwaveable room-temperature slices of bacon. Lettuce. Cheese. Cans of pop were plentiful in the other room. She took a grocery bag full of what basics she might want from this room — a change of underwear, her e-reader, toothbrush, and the like — in case the cleaning crew took longer than she'd like. They had to make it look like they were just absent for a while; if their suitcases and discarded clothes also shifted all to one room at a time, it would be a little much.

Upon slipping the closed and wrapped ingredients into the bar-fridge, she tucked the butterknife under her thumb and splayed her fingers under the plate with the sandwich. Supply bag in hand, she shouldered across the hall to the other room. As soon as she entered and kicked the door closed behind her, she swung the bag into a bedside toss and squared up to present the sandwich to Nick. The butterknife was now in her free hand.

Nick heard the sliding of the knife, blinked, and squinted in Iseult's direction. "I'm not hungry."

"Bullshit," she declared. "You only forced down what Kelly gave-"

"Look, I appreciate it. I do. I haven't forgotten how you held down the fort while we all…"

"That's not what this is." She set the plate on his lap. He tried to move it and she promptly put it back on his lap.

He aimed his face in roughly her direction. "What is 'this,' then?" He braced the plate in his lap. A slight shift in one hand tilted it a little, and he heard the butterknife slide.

She sat on the other twin bed. Her leg stung a little, even though most of the cut wasn't directly touching the surface or bearing any wait. Tension was strain enough. Her plaid shirt was unbuttoned, and the sleeves rolled to the elbow. "Not many people have Mom's Tash powers. Or Tash's Mom powers?"

Nick's hands fluttered about the plate and the sandwich. Iseult's joke fell flat. "To be fair, not many people have what she has. It's not just the smarts, the fist-fighting, or all the hard work and loyalty. I mean, those help. I'm glad she's there for Kelly. And even for me. But I don't know about calling her Mom, not yet."

She let sit the fact that he'd already used the "M" word in her hearing. "I'm sure you can cut off your own crusts, or slice it up, or whatever," Iseult said.

"Why do I get the feeling you're wearing flannel right now?" He actually managed a little smile and took a bite of the sandwich.

Iseult let out a hard reverse sniff, as much laughter as he'd get for that. "I kind of thought they'd be back by now."

"Kelly said she was itching to go to a mall. I tried to warn her about small towns." Nick was taking smaller bites than usual. It made talking easier.

"I think she knows. I don't think they're really shopping," Iseult said. Her shoulders were hunched as she sat with her hands on the edge of the bed, fingers sliding over it like a waterfall. The T-shirt between the plaid buttons held the image of a bear in the style of some new artist. She probably got it at a flea market, but couldn't much recall. "I can take that for you, you know."

He'd been wrestling with taking and returning the sandwich to the plate. Nick's hands were like cat whiskers, splayed out and always going first. Always looking for where the walls were. He sat, lay down, slouched, brought up his knees, turned and twisted over the covers. The sandwich had been as much about getting him to sit still as about nourishment. He handed the butter knife over to her. "Thanks," he said. He wasn't talking about the knife, or the food. "You know... when we first met," he started, moving to brace his back against the headboard, "I thought you were her daughter. Like, flesh and blood. Maybe with Victor."

Iseult moved back a little on her bed, her hand dangled over one knee of her cargo pants. Her feet were bare. She loved hotel carpet on bare feet. Hand and butterknife played out a continuous dance as she chatted: "That wouldn't be the worst thing. Victor feels more like an uncle, though. I can picture him arguing about politics over Thanksgiving dinner."

Nick did chuckle at that one. Which confused her, as she hadn't meant it to be funny. Over chews he said, "Well, you feel like her daughter. I mean, you're a good fit. We make a bit of a family, don't we?"

Where's this coming from? "I guess?" She stopped moving the knife. She'd wiped it before bringing it out, so there wasn't much grease or anything, but she held it by the blade without realizing that she might have gotten her hand messy. She didn't want to say how much that would mean to her, the family thing. "Have you had any new symptoms? Any changes?"

"Oh, no. You're not changing the subject that easily," he said. "Where did you come from?"

"My family's from France, at least they were. Been in New Hampshire since my gran's day," she said. "Or do you mean why did I join our little troupe?"

He hesitated and took a bigger bite. Iseult had nowhere to be. The room was no different than any of the others: stock framed pictures, a desk with a TV, obligatory overpriced bar fridge, and the beds. Nick said, "Well, yeah. I guess. It's just...you're always in the background. Doctor, not cop, I know. But still. You don't seem as messed up as the rest of us, like me and Kelly."

He thinks I'm *the healthy one? Adjusted?* She watched her toes as she spoke, wriggling them or waggling them around. "My...uh...the people who raised me were doctors. Probably worked during sleep through muscle memory. Could've been on the cover of Ostentatious Homes Monthly, and my brother was like them. All money and grades and dinner jackets. Dressing the part. It's like, have you tried acting the whole?"

Nick had never heard her talk this way before. He placed the empty plate on the end table and sat with his own legs dangling over his bed. "You're sure not the rich type."

"I wouldn't be, no matter how much money I had. It's just not me," she answered. "Anyway, I had a friend. And not like that — actually a friend." Nick opened his mouth but thought better of whatever he was going to say. He closed it and nodded, and she went on: "Charlotte. She had hemophilia."

"Did she tell you that?" he asked. Iseult didn't miss the undercurrent of connected questions.

"Yeah, but I already knew. It was because of her that I realized that I was...that I had…"

They shared a silent moment. Even if they had the words, they wouldn't have bothered using them.

When the air between them changed, Iseult finished her story: "Charlotte was LGBT. I'm not doing details right now." Nick shrugged. What could he say? She twisted the butterknife as though wringing a towel. "My family wasn't into that. Or my survivalism stuff. They thought I was being a petty tomboy. They worried Charlotte would 'rub off' on me." Again, he opened and closed his mouth. "There was a school field trip. My parents were chaperones for our group. She got hurt and they...they dragged their feet."

Nick didn't need to see in order to stare.

Iseult shifted uncomfortably on the edge of her bed, wrestling with what to say. Talking about such ghosts, such transformations of pain, could make them real. Real in a way she couldn't swear she was ready for. She was reminded of ripping-the-band-aid medicine, walking rope bridges, dealing with sickness in the woods. Some things you just can't be ready for. "You know it wasn't your fault, right?"

At first, she thought those words were hers. She'd grappled the idea often enough. But she blinked and looked at her friend.

Nick had that echoing silence she could never find a word for. Micro muscle tension, maybe, or just some emotional energy. It was the silence of someone who'd just spoken.

She clasped her hands in her lap. "Yes," she said. "I know. But what makes you so sure?"

This took him aback. He was prepared for the victim-blaming, the self-doubt. Kelly had shown him more than a little of that. After her father and his bottles of fermented abuse. After Gavin, who led an exodus of angels. A religion without spirit. Nick never could get a handle on the difference between Iseult's shyness and her quiet, fierce, unpredictable confidence. He sat back. Though not a giant, he was tall enough that his feet touched the floor while his knees wrapped over the edge of the bed. His weight was seated on his palms, his fingers pointing to the wall behind him. Except for underwear, he hadn't been bothered to change his clothes in two and half days. Shorts and a tank top. He'd have fit right in with a basketball court.

"Hard to say," he said. And he meant it; she always kind of fit in, but also was kind of background. Not a wallflower. She was the person at house parties who sat on the couch, was a part of the conversation, wouldn't have been turned away, but just kind of...didn't stand out. "You wouldn't belong with us if it were?"

"No, I don't think that's it," she said. Nick didn't even realize he sat a smidge straighter with her response.

He rubbed his eyes. The blur had changed from completely black to a murky, meaningless brown. He wasn't less blind than before. Or was he? He didn't feel right about changing the topic with that. "We've had times when we've all sat around reading. Kelly was the antsy one. But you? You managed to keep your eyes on the page every time, and even managed to get the ants out of her pants. That's just...you."

She was flattered, but vaguely suspicious. Of herself? She pressed her hand against the ghost knife strapped to her leg. "Yeah, it is pretty nice what we've got, huh?"

"You know Kelly worries that you never come to the movies with us?"

She raised a brow, though she knew he couldn't see her. "Is it really Kelly you mean?"

"Oh, yeah. I think Tash gets you. Not that we don't..." Nick wondered how much he should backpedal here.

Iseult chuckled, and she meant it. She tossed the butterknife flipped into the air, then caught it in her other hand. She gathered herself into a cross-legged position and played with the knife as though it were a see-saw, her hands on either end. "Did Tash tell you two how we met?"

"Nope," he said, openly relieved that his foot was only partially in his mouth.

"I disowned my family after Charlotte," she said. Nick visibly shuddered, and she chose not to see that. "Mom — Tash I mean, the important mom — straight up walked in on me helping a bunch of homeless folks. They had swelling, cuts, scrapes, all sorts of blood flow issues. You know adrenaline can cluster with long-term anxiety? People who are all wrecked, they sparkle to me. It's not ugly until you think about what it means. Like a stain on the sidewalk, you know?"

That was so out of his experience that Nick had no idea how to begin with it. "Uh, yeah. Hard stuff."

"Real hard," Iseult confirmed. "Tash had been on the phone, something about high-stakes poker. She saw what I was doing, stepped into a sub shop on the corner, and came back with a big platter. Sandwiches," she added with a grin. Nick didn't move from his seat, but he was conscious of the empty plate he'd set down. "She got me talking, and here we are."

Nick digested all this. "How did we get here in the conversation?" he said with an inhaled laugh. "Why haven't you talked about this stuff before?"

Before she could respond, Kelly and Tash swept into the room.

"I found nail polish!" Kelly declared triumphantly.

She was wearing a taupe, one-shouldered bodycon dress. She took off her camel coloured sandals as she sorted her bags. Iseult's grip shifted to the handle of the knife. Everyone looked at Kelly. "We're all gonna celebrate Nick's recovery by doing our nails," she pressed.

"Well…" he started.

"I brought you an audiobook," Tash said, shooting Kelly a look that was all wide eyes and narrow mouth. Iseult knew that look well. The audiobook was a collection of the works of S. E. Hinton.

Kelly huffed, but she kept up an unflappable air. "It's good to have some ideas about what to do with your inevitable victory, you know. You're not gonna sit around pokin' at your pooter," she said with a grin she didn't quite feel. It was a habit from Georgia; pronouncing "computer" as "pooter" tickled her.

Tash sat beside Nick's bed. He was still on the edge facing Iseult, though, so this put Tash behind him and on the other side. With her elegant and sylvan form, her place between the bed and the wall changed the energy of the whole room. "I trust there haven't been any changes?"

Nick gripped the edges of the bed on either side of him and stayed where he was, feet on the floor and shoulders hunched. His face was down. "Instead of all black, it's all brown," he said.

Iseult's face turned sharply. "Why didn't y-"

"See?" Kelly said. "We got this. Also, I got us party snacks, Jenga, and some bandanas we can use as blindfolds."

"Blind Jenga?" Tash said in disbelief.

Nick's lips were so tightly squeezed together it was

like his mouth had become a surgical scar. Iseult knew that feeling. Whenever she took the knife to herself, she felt that way: the combination of numbness, helplessness, indignation at life, and being shrunken large. It was like turning into a baby the size of a room. "It looks like Tash has some more stuff she wants to run through," Iseult started, thinking quickly. She gathered the plate and knife as she spoke. "I've got some ideas I'd like to research about the...browning...and we should probably get everything a bit sorted," she said, looking at Kelly. "Let's hop over to the other room."

Kelly, unaccustomed to Iseult taking charge, tensed her grip on the bags she'd brought with her. Doing her best to stay untouchable, she shrugged. "Sure," she said, and marched over to Nick. He sat up, his left hand lifting in her direction but setting down again immediately. Her hands full, she kissed his forehead.

He reached up and guided her to his lips. His eyes were closed. "I won't be long," he said, shifting his way back to leaning against the headboard. He turned his face to Tash. "Some vacation, huh?"

Tash's lip trembled once as the two young women sorted what would go and what would stay, then moved to the room across the hall. As they left, the last thing they heard from her was: "My connections will need time to get us set up with tech, so finding a more populated..."

The women closed both doors.

"So," Kelly began, "I've been worrying about that knife you're carrying."

Iseult stopped and frowned at her friend. She spoke as she set the bag on the bed and the plate with the butterknife on the TV stand. "Hi, Kelly. Glad you're feeling better after your trip with Mom." She removed the band from her hair so that it tumbled behind her shoulders. She tousled it with both hands and listened to Kelly.

"Ha, sorry. That's fair. Hellooo!" Kelly had set down the bag she'd been carrying and produced a high-energy hand wave. "And sarcasm's *my* thing."

"Yeah, well, you made it look like fun, so I thought I'd give it a-" Iseult retorted until Kelly wrapped her up in a sudden hug. Her forearms, exposed because her sleeves were rolled to the elbow, were held aloft behind Kelly's back. Iseult looked around the room as though it would explain something to her, then slowly embraced her friend.

"We're kind of like sisters, you know," Kelly said.

Iseult had a brief wave of guilt. Too quick for her to describe, it went unnoticed, but it came from some obscure feeling that she didn't deserve this. She wanted it but had to play fair for it. Earn it somehow. She suddenly clung to her new sister. Hard, and for a little too long. "That Providence Bomber," she said as she held on. "It's like he stabbed the town and we're the ones who should be sewing it up. People don't know about powers. He must've had them, y'know, from the talk…"

Kelly stayed in the embrace. She couldn't have said what had possessed her to do it, but she was glad she had. Iseult didn't smell like hotel, fresh laundry, or rigorous cleaning — despite her high standard of hygiene and care for Nick. The young woman smelled like a working person. Metal, a hint of sweat, fabric that has wrestled with underbrush. Kelly pondered that as she said, "I know,

I know. But any scumbag can walk into a hospital or a school with a bomb or a gun. We can't be that kind of crusade."

"Are we some kind of crusade?" Slowly, Iseult released the hug.

Kelly, tempted to renew it, gradually let go of the embrace as well. "I guess? I don't think too much about putting a name on what we're doing." She climbed onto the bed, ignoring the bag for now. "Are you gonna tell me about the knife?"

Iseult took the folding chair and sat backwards on it, a bare foot and a leg of cargo pants on each side as she rested her arms on top of the chair. Slipping her hand into her pants, there was a click as she undid the clasp, and she produced her ghost knife. "It's for survival stuff," she said. She turned it so she could hold it by the blade, leaned forward with arm outstretched, and gently tossed it so it made the extra foot to Kelly's bed. The other woman half-sat so she could lean down and pluck it up by the skeletonized handle. Iseult continued: "Super light, compact, meant for living in the woods and week-long hikes and that sort of thing. What did you think I had, a switchblade?"

"The only people I ever heard of who carried around a knife in their pants stole cars for a living. You're not that. So I didn't know what to think."

Iseult folded her lips and nodded. It was a bobblehead style of nod: a casual but complete acknowledgment. "Well, here's how I see it: ghost knives are tools. They're useful. Switchblades have moving parts, so they can fail and need more attention for maintenance. But you only have them for stabbing people. They don't brace the blade well for anything you'd do on the go, like first aid or cutting moving boxes or trekking in the woods. It's like having your hands super-glued into fists."

Kelly turned the knife around in a bunch of directions and angles while she considered Iseult's words. She tested the blade and the edge, weighted it. She didn't actually know much about knives, so all she really learned was that it was sharp. "How long have you had it?"

"I ordered it to arrive here for a day after we would. Kinda thought there would be more room for a hike in the woods or something," Iseult said. "I didn't think it would bother anybody."

Kelly pursed her lips and played with the knife some more, as if weighing its meaning or brandishing trust. A spark flashed and Iseult caught a whiff of ozone. "Ah!" Kelly said, and she quickly put the knife back at the foot of the bed for her friend/sister to retrieve. "Sorry."

Iseult took the knife and handled it more deftly than the other young woman. Her left hip leaned more into the chair so that she could slip it back into its sheath on her right leg. "No worries," she said. "Still having some trouble, huh?" She wiggled her fingers as she asked.

Kelly looked at each hand, played her fingers over each other, and readjusted her whole body with minor lifts, bends, and twists. "I'm trying. I managed at the hospital. With the machine?"

Iseult tilted her head back and forth as she thought about that. "We should get you a defibrillator sometime."

"A what?"

Iseult pantomimed rubbing the paddles together, lifted her fists up and apart, and said, "Clear!"

"Oh!" Kelly laughed. "Yeah, that would be fun."

"We could start calling you the Queen of Hearts," Iseult grinned.

"Check mate!" Kelly said. "Wait, wrong game."

Iseult got a good long laugh out of that.

Kelly hugged herself and watched her friend. The other woman had terrible nails; Iseult clipped them with a pair of scissors. Not even any particular pair, but whichever she had to hand when she decided her nails were too long. But Kelly fuzzed up inside to see genuine glee in her often-distant friend. Iseult was still smiling — more on one side of the mouth than the other — and it didn't so much reach the cheeks as skip to the forehead. Iseult's emotions came from the full face, almost fey. "Once all this settles down," Kelly said, "We should go on an epic camping trip."

Iseult's face opened. She sat up a little straighter, and inwardly put a clamp on feeling too excited. "I...yeah. That would be nice."

For the rest of the day, the four of them switched about. They gathered as all four, various trios or pair-ups. They did some reading, Nick listening to the Hinton readings with earbuds. Tash insisted that the reading be recreational, for relaxation. "No research," she'd said as she wagged a finger at Iseult.

It was worth a try. None of them could focus. It felt like quarantine, but there was nothing contagious — as far as they knew, anyway. Nick was working hard on the therapy techniques he'd been given in Georgia. Radical acceptance. Relaxation. Don't try to fight what you can't change.

Their anxiety tossed words and body language all over the room.

They slept.

The next day, Kelly and Nick were in the room the two women had shared for their conversation about camping and the knife. They'd asked Iseult to give them some privacy. She didn't ask for details. Iseult's feet were folded over each other on the bed Nick had been using when he ate the sandwich she made. She had her eReader, with a book about eyes and eye-related genetics, lying on her left side. On her right was Tash's laptop, which the mom had left to assist Iseult's research. On her lap was a notepad and pen. Thinking things through, looking for answers, making connections.

She got a text.

Tash:

In the car. How are the kids?

Neither of them used the barbaric abbreviations of textspeak unless they had to, so they mostly wrote in full sentences to each other for texts.

Iseult:

Not dead. Playing Jenga.

Tash:

Come out to the car. Let them rest, goodness knows they need it.

Iseult didn't reply to that one. She closed the laptop and put her research materials away before leaving the hotel room. As she got into the car, she had to move a carpenter's knife — price tag still attached — from the seat. Tash was staring ahead, drumming her fingers on the wheel.

"Did you even know it was me?" Iseult asked.

"Oh, yes."

"You didn't look up!"

Tash closed her eyes tight for a few moments, then opened them as she turned to the young woman. Iseult was holding up the knife with a look of concern, and just now realizing how Kelly must have seen things. Tash felt a little foolish then. "Sorry," she said. "I guess we all need a break. I had to buy that so that the people at the store wouldn't think it was weird that I was wandering around and playing with this."

She held up a short-range walkie-talkie.

Iseult put the knife in the glove compartment. "Yes, because randomly buying a knife that looks like a straight razor on steroids will surely allay their suspicions."

Tash gave that one a brief laugh, then shook her head and scrunched her fingertips along the roots of her hair. She got the car in motion and continued talking: "I was making contact with someone in my network."

"Weren't you *texting* your spy friends a few days ago? Why go all covert now?" Iseult watched the road. She couldn't help but look at the small, distant hospital. Tiny moving shapes represented the repair crews at work.

"The problem is bigger than we thought," Tash said.

"Like, how big?" Iseult asked.

"Five states so far."

As they went into town, Iseult snuck glances at Tash and asked questions, both about the woman herself and about what she'd learned. Tash was long, elegant, and a shaper of things. So far, all the evidence in Tash's networks suggested that only people with special abilities were affected. She parked the vehicle in the lot of a shopping centre.

"Not that I don't love your company," Iseult eventually said to her hands, voice low, "but why are we-"

"Excuse me?" Tash asked an approaching pedestrian. They weren't far from the restaurant quarter of the town. Iseult doubted that was accidental.

He was a portly man of colour, wearing a cardigan and a beret. "Hm?" he said.

"Do you happen to know about any sports happening in town this time of year? My daughter here needs to flex her muscles."

Iseult tried to run with it. "I...um, like rock climbing," she said. "But with everything..." she waved her hand in the direction of Providence Hospital. She also stepped to within arm's length of the man in order to talk comfortably. He didn't seem to mind.

"Afraid I can't much help you ladies there," he said. "Been here most of my life, but the closest thing I know about sports is bird-watching. Heh heh!" He patted his belly with both hands. "Now, if you've got a mind for a spectacled eider, I've had quite a find of one!"

The women looked at each other. "I'll think about that," Iseult said. "Thanks, though."

"No harm, no harm!" he said, lifting his arm as he continued in a farewell wave.

"Lovely fellow," Tash remarked. She was looking down the road, in the direction of the restaurant where Nick had had his fateful shrimp.

"He didn't have the icky," Iseult said. She felt childish

and uncomfortable calling it that, but couldn't come up with a more accurate name.

"Hm," Tash said, and continued walking.

They chatted, between themselves and with random people, for another hour.

"Is this the plan?" Iseult asked. "There's been one, uh, icky, since that cluster of joggers went by. With the ones in the restaurant, and I think a couple at the hospital, I wasn't expecting to encounter so many who might have... gifts."

"Yeah," Tash mused, turning to regard the young woman contemplatively. It wasn't clear if she was answering the question or acknowledging the remark. "It's hard to know what to think. I know I'm being a little dodgy, and I really am sorry about that. I've never heard of power suppression before."

Iseult's face slackened as she looked her adoptive mother more directly in the eye. "You've been doing this how long?"

"Long enough."

They resumed walking. After some trepidation, they ate. Other than to avoid shrimp, they weren't sure what to do. They needed food, after all, and their best guess was seafood. But how far did that extend? Did it include products that used seafood? Nick had been asking about possibilities, and they did what they could with that. But they had had to turn his attention elsewhere and accept that there wasn't enough info. For example, anchovies could be found in many sauces because grounding them into it was a cheap way to salt foods like pizza. Cross contamination was a thing.

They chose a vegetarian eatery.

Once they were on their way again, Iseult asked her new mother: "Why is Nick dressed like he's ready for a basketball game?" The young woman glanced away. It pinged Tash in the heart to see the girl still shy with her, of all people.

"Tell me first about the restaurant."

Iseult shook her head and wrung her hands, staring at her feet. "I have to get too close. Do any of these people even know they're affected?"

Tash nodded. "Many are adults before realizing they have any kind of…" she looked around to make sure no one was in earshot. "…talent. Even then, some have their doubts. I'm sure plenty go their whole lives not even knowing."

Iseult frowned. "How?"

Tash shrugged. "Imagine that you can breathe underwater, but you've lived in a desert all your life. If you don't have a swimming pool or live near a reservoir, how would you know?"

"Is that a thing?"

"Breathing underwater? I've never seen it, but that's not a no," Tash said. "Just an example. And he used to play as a kid, before I found him. I think it comforts him somehow."

It took Iseult a flash to realize that Tash was talking about Nick. She began pulling her hair down over one shoulder, smoothing and collecting it so she could tie it in a ponytail. "Five states, huh?"

"Yeah, but we're only talking about one case in most of them. Hard to know if it's more widespread or not, because these were just the cases where people did something extreme. Even then, most didn't blow anything up. We're talking about spectacularly quitting their jobs, intense and incoherent public rants, big and strange posts of text or video on the Internet." Tash checked her phone and stopped.

"What is it?"

"Watch my back," she said, and put her phone in her small purse before producing a burner phone from a pocket inside the light jacket she was wearing. Iseult, in an old hoodie and jeans, had left her knife in her suitcase. It would be too hard to hide in this outfit.

The young woman moved to a bench and sat, casually looking about and making sure no one would get in hearing range of Tash. Iseult was at a bus stop while Tash had found a little space between some trees. Iseult's own phone buzzed. She ignored it and waved off the bus. This went on long enough that Iseult was getting uncomfortable. She'd had to talk her way out of encounters with passersby several times. Finally, Tash began walking away from the trees. Iseult left the bench and made her way over, wondering where the woman was going until Tash turned at a public garbage bin and Iseult heard a thump.

"Come with me," Tash said.

They continued into a neighbourhood, away from the direction of the car. Iseult waited for Tash to speak, looking about this way and that and not even taking her attention away long enough to check her phone. It buzzed again.

"I'm sure you know who that was," Tash said. Iseult

nodded; Simon was their go-to. But they never talked about what they learned in the same place where they learned it. They also didn't make their way back and forth any more traceable than they had to. Tash went on: "Jury's still out on whether this is an issue for just people with abilities, or if people without them are still affected somehow. And you couldn't tell much from our forays, could you?"

"To pick out if someone has powers? No," Iseult admitted. "And who knows how many other reactions could be happening? Some of these people could be getting the icky because they have an unrelated allergy or something. I've never felt this stuff before now, but that might be because there's a rare allergy that's more common in this town for some reason. We need a lot more info."

"Right. We don't even know what counts. Does pickling foods matter? Is sushi okay?" Tash wondered aloud. "Anyway, we've at least got some leads. There's a whole bunch of tracking, odd online behaviour, exotic computer crime, and cover-ups happening in Seattle."

"That's kinda far away. Is it that much of a seafood place?" Iseult asked with some surprise. They went up a small hill and took a left into what looked like an average small-town neighbourhood. But it put them back on direction for getting to the car.

"Not really?" Tash hesitated. "Yes, it's a port city. Lots of seafood goes through there. But it's more about the information and business stuff. The networks for foods in the entire western seaboard must be going through there. Or at least, they're one of the big players. That's where Simon got those clues, in any case."

"Anything about cures or remedies? Is it permanent?"

Iseult asked. She rubbed her hands together nervously.

"They haven't tracked down any surviving cases yet, and the smokescreens are going up immediately. Tabloids, evidence showing mental instability. You know how shootings always turn the conversation away from gun control? That sort of thing." Tash had to keep slowing her roll. Iseult was an energetic, sporty person. As long as she wasn't in the limelight, she walked quickly — even when going from the couch to the fridge. But Tash had over a foot of height on her, all leg, and she was powered by worry for Nick and the weight of the world.

"I miss Quinn," Iseult said suddenly.

Tash stopped. They'd all talked about Quinn, of course. Early in the therapy, after what happened in Atlanta. But Tash hadn't really appreciated that, as the unofficial nest-keeper, Iseult was the one who stayed at home and did what she could to help and support their most troubled youths. Iseult was in the background. She stayed out of their adventures most of the time. So she was the one connecting with everyone at home base.

She was the one who made the beds, and sometimes they stayed empty.

"Nick won't be like Quinn," Tash said.

"You can't promise that."

"I won't allow it." They stood on the sidewalk. A group of people on fat bikes rode by, unnoticed. The women held each other's gazes.

It was Tash who started the hug.

When they separated, they collected themselves. Caught their breaths, adjusted their clothes. Neither noticed that they'd responded to the same emotions in a surprisingly similar way. The difference would come later, when Iseult wrote on herself. But for now...

"The other incidents, tarred and unreliable as they are, all have notes like the Providence Bomber," Tash said as they resumed walking. "Saying stuff that makes sense to us if we plug in an unusual ability, but sounds like lunacy to most people. If it shut down Nick's visual power, then it makes sense that he can't see. It's just how he's built, after all."

Iseult, who'd worked with Tash at the farm in Georgia, had gone over the medical testing and equipment for examining the others. Quinn, Nick, Kelly, herself. She only had records for Hunter, which Tash showed her to help improve her experience and solidify Iseult's role. As such, she knew these matters well.

Tash continued: "My contacts, especially Simon, have tracked down some strange computer infiltrations around Seattle. There's a new and unusual business arrangement there between a seafood company called Surimp and a security firm called Spindle. Eating disorders and exercise mania have started creeping up in the area, and seafood for a lot of the western intake has been concentrated there for some reason. More than average. They've started to track someone who was trying to hack from his own home. They don't usually do that."

"Desperation?" Iseult suggested.

"Maybe. He certainly can't be the cause of the whole thing. Who contaminates the food system to target powered people — if that's even what's happening — by hacking from his bedroom? He's probably not the major player. But he's a lead."

Iseult nodded several times, slowly, as she digested this. "What's his name?"

"Braulio García. Simon says the guy's identity is fake, but it's clean. Well done. Holds up enough for employment, taxes, credit. But he doesn't have the in-person stuff. The little things the spies can dig out. We have García's apartment, his mailing address, and some of his work info. He's apparently a loner, very careful, but not...social. Whatever he's got going on, it's tied up with Spindle's flurry of sketchy activities. Siaz's team can't get close. Someone else is in play. We should be able to get to his apartment and investigate the city without much trouble because we're an unknown. For now." Tash looked over her shoulder.

"What else?" Iseult asked.

Tash's gaze darted to Iseult, but she didn't object. She'd had to wait for the youth to catch up yet again. Taking a breath and forcing herself to appear calm and collected, Tash answered: "His network intercepted some suspicious movements and communications heading for Kodiak. Something about tracking down volunteers and contact-tracing. It isn't safe for us here, especially if they catch wind of-"

Iseult checked her phone now that they were in sight of their car. "Holy crap!"

Tash looked at the younger woman.

"Kelly's been trying to get a hold of us. Nick can see!"

CHAPTER 12
THE TWINS

After January

The *Huginn*

It didn't look like a seafaring vessel from the inside. Staff could go topside to experience air, sea, and sky, and maintain a semblance of sanity. Belowdecks, though, it was a state-of-the-art facility. Here, the pair were walking a corridor. The floor was blue tile, and the walls and ceilings were variations on white paint, grey walls, transparent glass, and stainless steel.

"No, but then, I wouldn't expect it so soon," she was saying. Her name was Dr. Jacinta Serrano. Her accent was slightly British, but she came from old Spanish lines. She walked and spoke as a person with knowledge, comfortable with her power. "The Section has integrated our operations with the extraction industry quite smoothly. The altered specimens have been introduced already. I look forward to your positive report, *navaja de muelle*," she added as they rounded the corner.

Aside from HVAC systems and massive vault doors, the breaks in the corridor came in hall intersections, stairwells, elevators, and the observations and experiments behind the panes that looked like glass. Dr. Serrano cast clinical glances at the latter as she went, occasionally making notes on her clipboard. Sometimes threats, weeping, cries for help, and other sounds came from her research materials. Her flats clicked on the blue tile. Like most of the people working in the facility but not handling materials, she was wearing a white lab coat and professional attire.

"Just Switch, if you would," said the other woman. She was of Chinese descent, wearing a boat cloak over a tactical wetsuit. They got into an elevator as staff dressed in scrubs left it. "I trust the Section Head has briefed you on the activities of the other Knives?"

"The last I heard, Sikloon's supply chain is running smoothly. Karambit's managed the finances, legalities, and the like. Well, beyond the usual Section responsibilities." Dr. Serrano kept her eyes on the doors. This was simply how she went about her day: she had many projects, operatives, goals, and ideas — and little time for mere human dalliance. "Is there anything else I should know?"

"Not yet," Switch responded. Unlike the other woman, she was restless; she examined the surgeon from head to toe. She studied the entirety of the elevator, noting things others would be unlikely to see. For example, areas to unlatch or dismantle for escape, or means to compromise the electrical system. There wasn't much to find. Unlike an average city-constructed building, everything in the laboratory had to have robust design and construction for biohazard containment, ease of cleaning, and meeting specific needs. Switch continued: "My sister and I will ensure that only the information we desire will rise to the surface."

"Engen is the white space," said the surgeon.

"Engen is the end," Switch replied.

Idaho

Engen is the helix, she thought to herself.

She had reached a hotel that had been visited by two Hispanic men around the cusp of the year. They'd used assumed names, because they were apparently not stupid, and she had little to go on. As soon as she'd closed the door behind her, she began her investigation. This woman, the Knife named Ghost, looked identical to Switch. Sikloon had reached out to them because of spy infiltration in his Engen-related operations in Ghana and Nigeria. Engen's mid-tier and expert agents had failed to dig up an explanation for how and by whom their network had been penetrated.

Karambit's tracing efforts had garnered several leads, one of whom was contacted at this hotel.

Ghost had taken on the mission of tying loose ends and, simultaneously, tracking down recruitment opportunities. The fact that she was here at all was because of a hunch of Karambit's. There was only supposed to be one person, and the presence of another could have meant several things: she had the wrong guy, he kept a decoy on hand, he was socializing, or the spy could have been part of a network.

She needed more information.

As soon as she shut the door of her hotel room behind her, she produced a cigarette, removed the lid of the disposable coffee cup she'd brought with her, and set the cigarette on top of the lid. She performed this manoeuvre with the swift flow of constant familiarity. The cigarette stood, unattended, and burned. Ghost put down the parcel that had been timed to arrive shortly after she had, as well as a tote bag.

She began her process with a sweep of every nook, cranny, and fixture. There was no evidence of bugs or cameras. A UVLED blacklight, about the size of two stacked C batteries, revealed only the usual carnal histories and poor habits. She slipped a notebook out of her tote bag, opened it, and compiled a complicated series of software applications. They set out to connect with and scan every vulnerable connection in its boosted radius. It did the same with the protected ones, after penetrating them and removing most traces of its presence. Anyone who looked would have concluded that some amateur was trying to gain remote access. Meanwhile, she removed one bottle of rum from the minifridge, dumped its contents in the bathroom sink, and tossed it into the trash.

Naturally, the computer found little that Karambit's impressive digital tools could not. It was always worth a look. Ghost stepped over to the coffee lid just as the embers were reaching the butt. It was laid flat and moved to the rim as the second cigarette was placed and lit. In the parcel was a perfect replica outfit of the hotel's housekeeping staff, from the shoes to the nametag and a wig. The nametag corresponded to a whole file of a fictitious new hire with her modified photo, all of which would disappear in twenty minutes so cleanly that anyone who asked about her afterward would have been left questioning their own imagination.

She only made a few quick adjustments — mostly with the eyes and brows — which, along with her outfit, were coordinated to make her complexion seem paler than it had been in her previous attire. She stood straighter, put on a bubbly personality, and went through the front reception area and behind the desk just as the previous attendant had left. The shift change had put a new employee on his first independent night watch. She swept in and out so confidently that it never occurred to him to question her, and even showed him some of the ropes while she moved to "double-check" the records.

She was back in the room just as the second cigarette seared its last wisp of smoke.

Upon igniting the third cigarette, she placed a call with Karambit using a $20,000 satellite phone she carried in her tote bag. They compared notes, including local conversations and camera records, as well as her appearance an hour ago as an officer of the Idaho State Police. They arrived at a conclusion: their target had left in a private jet which had been found at a crash site on the east coast with no bodies to be found.

Without loss of life, both Knives knew that their target was alive and had changed transports. They suspected that the agent they were tracking was headed for Sikloon and the human trafficking operation. Karambit said he'd handle it from here. Meanwhile, there was a cybersecurity expert in Seattle sniffing around a little too much. Also, the person their target was with had split off and gone to ground. The third cigarette seared out.

During the fourth cigarette, Ghost set about cleaning contact points so there wouldn't be fingerprints or hairs that could identify her. Not that she was in any database, but there were networks out there with unusual resources. Part of this step was the removal of chips and remotely trackable components in the satellite phone and notebook. These she crushed with a small hammer she kept among her effects. She swept the bits of them in with the ashes of four cigarettes and an empty coffee cup, collected herself, and left the building through the back for all the world like an employee who'd finished her shift.

In the waiting car, not new but new to her, was a replacement set of the chips she'd disposed of. Clothing, gear, and makeup sat in a package on the back seat. She drove for fifteen minutes to find a dark corner, changed, and turned herself into a grease-streaked mechanic, and proceeded on the highway.

After February
West Coast, USA
Switch loosely tied the bodies with rope, fishing line, netting, or whatever else came to hand in each case. Most of them hadn't known she was even aboard, much less behind them, and some had been chatting without knowing that their mates lay dead nearby. She was in her tactical wetsuit and required very few tools as most of what she needed was already available on the fishing vessel. Some of her agents were removing the labels, numbers, postings, and other records indicating the identity of the ship; it had no name now.

As she went about her business, she used the same military-grade double-action OTF switchblade on the ropes and lines as she had to eliminate the captain and crew. She only used the deathstrike locations that avoided possible blade-to-bone contact. The bodies were only loosely tied; they wouldn't stay strapped to the interior for long, but it would be enough of a delay that anyone who discovered them would have little evidence to go on.

Switch emerged on deck as her team were finishing with the erasure of the boat's identity. She retrieved her boat cloak from Nuri, a Black woman wearing a waterproof field poncho over heavy rain gear. While the pair got into a shuttle to return to the *Rain Shadow*, Switch's agents operated tugboats pulling a barely submerged shipping container. It was surprising how many of these lurked just beneath the ocean's surface, and how often colliding with one could doom a ship.

Nuri's accent was rich and complex. She spoke an English that was deepened by her Afro-Puerto-Rican roots and trickled and danced with the influence of her Spanish mother tongue. "This is to be my ship?"

"Yes and no," Switch answered as they boarded. "In three hours and fifteen minutes, you will arrive in Hawaii. You will corroborate the story we've built here as the only survivor of an unfortunate accident. Your accommodations as a crew member of the *Rain Shadow* will follow shortly afterward."

"So I am unofficial." It was not a question.

"Our communications will change, and my agent will provide you with the necessaries," Switch replied. They sat in the mess room and lowered their hoods. "I will leave your name to your preference."

Nuri nodded her assent. "I shall be average to the point of invisibility."

Switch's answer was a brief silence. She wasn't merely accustomed to command: the world around her laboured in her service and hoped for the reward of not being re-buked. "Keep us informed of any more misguided moral-ity. They're paid too handsomely to question which parts of the sea produce their food."

"I shall also have an eye out for...other talents," Nuri said carefully.

The women studied each other. "Perfection is..." Switch said.

"...Engen is perfection," Nuri finished.

"You will retrieve your instructions at the bridge," Switch said.

Nuri considered her dismissal praise and accepted it wordlessly.

Switch pressed a finger against the state-of-the-art ear-piece she wore. "The bodies and the ship have lost their names."

Ghost replied that the MIA notifications and comms scrubbing were already underway. Then she informed her sister that they'd have to "make arrangements" for someone, or possibly several someones, who were snoop-ing around the computer networks in Seattle.

Switch eyed the windows and doors of the mess room. "Are these all Intranets? Is there Internet access to these trails?"

Ghost's answer was complicated. Multiple false iden-tities had been created, and she was sure most of those were unrelated petty crimes. Many she'd already traced to larger financial crimes, which were still petty to her. There were sloppy attempts at accessing the deep web and the usual conspiracy nuts and other whack jobs. Still others were far slyer.

"If we arrive together…" Switch suggested.

But her sister was vehemently opposed to that idea. She missed her and they worked well together, but they kept their distance because of their…unusual gift. Instead, Ghost suggested that Switch head to Seattle. She'd be keeping hands-on tabs on the operation anyway, and who better to snip some loose ends? Meanwhile, Ghost was accessing her contacts.

"I miss you too. And if you're not careful, you'll lose your touch," Switch teased. "Besides, all this computer stuff is Karambit's bag. No, I don't care much for Genblade, but I have to admit that I envy his insouciance. I'll oversee the operation, then. Any luck with the New Mexico thing?"

None. Ghost was impressed; there weren't many who slipped by the Knives. She suspected Circe involvement.

"Figures. Well, I'm still on counter-espionage. Sikloon's sent his message, but he's not confident it's been received. Will follow up."

Atlanta, Georgia

"I saw them, Mom," Iseult said. She was sitting on a swinging bench behind The Farm, which had been Tash's refuge for years. It was less a true farm than classical architecture of colonial persuasion, a lovely three-storey building that might have been a plantation in the midst of land spacious enough to be farm-like. Iseult, wearing a light jacket and snow pants, was hugging a body pillow. "I saw them get up. I didn't go in. Didn't even know why I went there. I couldn't help. I just…"

"Oh, darling…" Tash said. She'd set down three cups of fragrant tea. She hadn't really brought them for anyone to drink; they created a soothing atmosphere. It wasn't her way, but a trauma-informed response wouldn't be usual. She'd worn a dress — also not her usual thing — in an effort to look matronly. It meant wearing a heavy coat over it all, though, so that her skirts lingered with the wind like a whispering gravity.

Nick was pacing and fidgeting. He'd been working out with a reflex ball earlier. His speed had been awe-inspiring, but his face was like his mind — peeled back, raw, and stiff with a coldness like dark water. He kept glancing at Kelly, torn between wanting to impress her and wanting to run. Not just with his feet, but his whole being. Run the way the landscape blurs if you're driving too fast and only seeing it peripherally.

Kelly was stillness. She stood on the ground, on the opposite side of the steps where Nick was pacing, with Iseult on the other side of the railing lining the rear patio. Her name was Ms. Saunders, her name was Kelly. Her name was not Princess. Her arms were at her sides. "Tash…" she said, stuck between wanting to call her mom and fearing that the label was accurate. "I'm sorry, I…"

"No more of that, now," Tash said as gently as powdered sugar. She stepped to the other side of the top of the steps, so that the four of them now formed roughly the points of a square. She kept eye contact with Iseult as she spoke to Kelly. "I won't hear any of you blaming yourselves."

"But I-" Kelly started.

"You're a survivor," Tash said. "You have every right to pain, fear, shock. But not blame. Not guilt. Never that. No matter how many times you twitch it out, like a reflex, I'll stop you there. It's not your fault."

Iseult barely swung her seat. It was like she conveyed a tremor to the furniture. "It's been months," she said, resting her chin on the pillow. Her feet were flat on the seat of the swing. "All that therapy, and we can't even talk about it!"

"I know it's hard, and I wish you didn't have that burden…" Tash said.

"We do," Nick said, without stopping in his pacing. His hands and feet echoed and prickled with fatigue and tension. "We do have it, and how do we even start? 'Excuse me, I saw the dead walk and a shed with green light and…and…' I…" He swallowed hard.

"I've made some calls," Tash said slowly. None of them registered that she'd taken on the same cadence as soothing down something feral. "All I need is your go-ahead, and I can set us up for a trip. The other side of the country. Get away from it all, fresh air, clear your heads."

Nick stopped.

Kelly and Iseult looked up, then at each other. Iseult's eyes turned back to the floor of the patio. Kelly watched Nick, who was looking at Tash. Kelly wanted him to look at her, then, and didn't know why.

"If this is the world, how can we just go to another

place? The world is everywhere," he said. But his tone was hollow.

"We're never going to be a white picket fence," Iseult said. She kept staring at the floor. "We can't just get mall jobs and plan the prom and look forward to two-point-five children. There's no normal for us."

"You're all so much more wonderful than normal, but you can have all the normal things the world can give you," Tash said, keeping her tears in check. Equal parts determination to help these young souls and cold fury for the cultist responsible. "I'll give you all beige clothes if I have to!"

Normally, Iseult at least would have given that one a giggle, but the joke stayed in the air like a poorly timed fart. It was Kelly, with a voice like ozone and electric blue eyes, who surprised Tash with her sudden surge of resilience. "Where did you have in mind?"

"My contacts have confirmed that it's pretty isolated, beautiful, and as uneventful as a wheat field," Tash said. "A small town over a big land, called Kodiak…"

After March

Seattle, Washington

It had only been a few days since Thatcher got his promotion, but they'd cost him. He was sitting in the break room, feeling miserable. He could only call his friends from the troupe when he was at home now, as he didn't feel comfortable doing so with an audience. He spent more time at work and less anywhere else. He'd forgotten his belt this morning as he'd rushed into a cab to make it to work on time, so he felt vulnerable. He went around with his hands in his pockets to try to hide the fact that he had to hold up his pants.

His own exercise and food regimens were going well, and he was at 230lbs; the lowest in his adult life. News specials covered the health craze in a significant portion of Seattle, centered around the Denny Triangle and spanning much of Belltown and Downtown. Gyms were pushing capacity; bicycle sales were through the roof; joggers were creating pedestrian traffic problems; restaurants were seeing lower turnouts; dietitians were being called in; diet crazes like no-sugar, no-fat, and intermittent fasting were hitting grocery stores, magazines, newsstands.

News pundits were calling it Seattle Feeds, a play on the phrase "Seattle freeze," which referred to how distant but polite Seattleites tended to be. Looking into this development was why Thatcher had been late to work.

He wasn't permitted to eat alone. No one was. Security checks happened at entrances, exits, the breakroom, gatherings and meetings, and even washroom doors.

Corporate policies for privacy and data control were getting out of hand. It seemed every passing day, the confidentiality issues got more paranoid. As they escalated, so did his suspicion that there was something more going on. It felt like his paranoia was spreading, too.

But that was preposterous.

Thatcher rested his elbows on the table, setting aside his finished salad of spinach and avocado topped with Google results. Rubbing his face, he tried not to think so much about the illegal data mining software he'd developed. That was incredibly risky, and he was acutely aware of how his ethnicity might weigh him down in court. This software, bundled in the thumb drives he'd smuggled into the building, gave him untraceable access to records decrypted and analysed for evidence of viral activity and other tampering.

He sat back, sighed, and took his eyes off his side of the table to discover he was not alone.

"Braulio," Stewart said by way of greeting.

Thatcher resisted a grimace, to see his friend in such disrepair. Stewart appeared so pale that the contrast with his black hair and even his dark brown slacks made him seem gaunt. There were no bags under his brown eyes — he was sleeping, at least — but the micro muscles of his face outlined a topography of tension, mistrust, and undirected need. He kept smoothing out his clothes and adjusting his position in his chair. It was like solitary confinement was following the man around.

"How goes the war?" Thatcher asked, as much to restart Stewart's whimsical and inflated phrasing as to make conversation.

"I'm not even following the contract anymore," Stewart said. He looked at his shoes and fidgeted with his belt. "The money is enough. No idea what I'm gonna do tax season. They've got an army of financial officers, payroll managers, fiscal engineers, and consultants swarming all our cash divisions. They've been helping a lot, and they're super nice, but…"

Thatcher nodded. "Any word from Liam?"

Stewart looked around the room, not really watching anybody, and stared at the counter space with its coffee-maker and two sinks. "You talk to him more than I do, don't you?"

He had to acknowledge that with a shrug. "He's far away now, if you know what I mean. He works on Vietnamese language apps on his breaks, and only drops in to do his tasks and moves on. I can't really corner people," the Hispanic added helplessly, "so it was hard to get through to him. Steel says he's been avoiding her, only calls her Betelgeuse now, and has started wearing…" here Thatcher struggled for words. He held up his index and thumb with a large space between them. "The shoes. For being taller?"

"Platforms," Stewart said. "Yeah. And now that you mention her, Steel's been hitting the gym and stuffing herself with protein. It's been getting results, but…"

Thatcher traced the muscle groups around his eyes with his fingertips. Liam taught him that; it was great for stress and prevented headaches. "Nobody expected this contract to be so hard," he said.

But what he was really thinking was that he was approaching three months of being in Seattle. He was remembering New Mexico, around the time he'd spent three months there. And he was thinking about Soto, a car ride to nowhere, a conversation about a past he didn't believe in.

He wanted to cut all of that out, like so much excess weight, and he could see a frightening amount of precisely the same pressure sliding along the social crevices like water beading in through failing seals. Bevis, in the opposite corner of the breakroom, threw on the TV. That was unlike him; he was usually the one playing sports programs on his phone without the courtesy of using headphones.

But the news cut to an Alaskan reporter and got everyone's attention.

"Early reports suggest that the death toll is ballooning. The work of what they're calling the Providence Bomber has done far more damage with its aftermath as the hospital's power systems and life supports failed, and people already vulnerable have been experiencing…"

Woodinville,

Outskirts of the Seattle Metropolitan Area

"…heart attacks, strokes, and post-op complications. The community response…"

Switch turned off the small TV screen in the car. This was Seattle's wine territory. The cybersecurity specialist, Greg Azure, died here the week before. There was no sign of powered people, suppressed or otherwise; no odd happenings, people making bizarre claims, or demands or outbursts like what had happened in Kodiak. "Woodinville is clear," she said in Cantonese through her earpiece.

Ghost acknowledged and said that she was in northern Oregon. The specialist's investigations into the seafood industry networks had been suppressed, as had his blog. His e-mail had been scrubbed, and to all appearances, he'd taken a plane to Greece and disappeared after arriving there.

"As expected," Switch said. Ghost thanked her for the praise. Then Switch said, "I am en route to the East Side, and I will systematically rule out the boroughs. If you're this close, do you expect to need to meet up?"

Ghost answered that she did, but they would have to be careful. With so few kilometres between them, their gift of transferring energies between each other would work too quickly for one to warn the other. The eastern seaboard appeared to be secure, though they rarely used it because they wanted to put the continent between their work in Seattle and Sikloon's operation. There was no evidence of intrusion, and setbacks were mostly logistical. There were rises in racial tensions which her network had traced to people acting out. Desperation in the face of power suppression was suspected. But the west…

"We should at least be able to coordinate which neighbourhoods we investigate. If we're caref-"

Sadly, her sister would not be able to avoid the city, and Switch's presence would also be required. It was becoming increasingly obvious that Circe was sniffing around, though it was hard to say if they knew anything. Ghost couldn't track down the activity or even net any names, but the specialist was not the only one attempting intrusion.

"There will be risks. Though I cannot deny that I would enjoy a reunion."

That much was agreed. Ghost's initiative to use Spindle as a shell for expunging suspicious data was going well, but there were loose ends and potential breaches. There was at least one internal intrusion. Even with their expertise, they might have overlooked it, but they'd been keeping an eye on the replacement cybersecurity specialist – one Braulio García – as a precaution.

"Gutsy. I'm almost impressed."

So far as her sister could gather, several access points

within the organization had been used for decentralized investigations using software Ghost had never heard of before. As a Knife specializing in infiltration, that was rare enough that she could say with confidence that it had been custom-made. A hacker, likely working alone. Or as the only hacker on the team. It left nothing she could pinpoint, and not even enough evidence through absence to send along to Karambit. They must have been using hardlines and ports belonging to other users to mask their trail.

"I stand corrected; I am impressed. Do you recommend sticking entirely with Seattle? That's a little much for two Knives, isn't it?"

California was secured. Engen's influences in tech hubs and seafood centres were personally overseen by Ghost, and she'd been in talks with her informants and contacts in Colorado, Virginia, Florida, Louisiana, Hawaii, Wisconsin, Michigan, Massachusetts, and the Carolinas. But most of those were testing grounds and control groups; the largest focus of the first wave of their years-long project took place in Seattle. For reasons Ghost could not yet determine, someone had caught on to the fact that something was amiss.

Whoever that someone was, they either hadn't uncovered Engen specifically, had stopped at a lower level of the shadow organisation's activities, or simply wanted more hard evidence. Regardless, they weren't going public. Yet.

CHAPTER 13
"DEAR DIARY..."

Kodiak Airport, Alaska

Tash

She had to get them out of here. The Providence Bomber was, as far as they could tell, an isolated incident. Internet videos he'd posted showed him talking to his pet lizard and getting remarkable responses, but most people took that as more evidence that someone should have seen his attack coming. Never themselves, of course. But someone.

She didn't want to abandon his case or give up on the vacation, and the kids weren't ready to go home. Tash wanted them to have some happy memories, some forgetfulness, and some rest before they returned to therapy and life in Georgia.

"Shouldn't we be doing something?" Nick asked. They were all sitting in the waiting area after going through security. He'd noticed Kelly pat her hip and look at Iseult with a raised brow but didn't get what that was about and didn't have the attention to spare. "Aren't we supposed to be strapping on our boots and getting magic swords from a woman in a lake?"

"I'm raising you to be family and find your way in the world, sweetie, not training you to be Green Berets," Tash said. She sat with a jacket folded over her arm and a small, tasteful purse at her side. Iseult was sitting across a line of seats with her head in Kelly's lap. Her expression as Tash responded was inscrutable, and Tash saw that Nick was looking intently at Iseult. Were the young woman's emotions that complicated, or had his eyes not returned to form yet?

Tash elaborated: "This isn't our fight. I brought you out here to-"

"Run?" Kelly suggested. "Hide? Protect Willy Wonka? I'm glad we're going to a real city. We could use a mall. And other humans. No offense."

"They have rock-climbing businesses and stuff, too," Iseult put in, obviously trying to take some of the bite out of Kelly's sarcasm. "And I'm sure they have basketball courts and bookstores." She glanced at Nick with that. "But what about you, Mom?"

It occurred to Tash that Iseult might be using the word to distance herself from her past mother, rather than tighten a connection with her new mother. She shook and played it off as adjusting her seating. Guilt sat on her shoulder and whispered about Nick going blind on her watch. She rallied herself. "Never been," she began her lie, "and I hear it's got some great sightseeing. Plus, the museums and archives have got to have some interesting stuff, and I was thinking we could check out the Rep."

"What's their medical research like?" Nick asked the floor. "I mean, I guess there's nothing I can do for that anyway. 'Hi, I have a super-power and that's totally a thing. Can you give me a sci-fi voodoo scan, please?'" When Tash had told them all that her contacts suspected there would be more high-risk P-O-I's and warned her to skip town, Nick had been the most accepting of that advice.

Kelly watched him with torn eyes. He was in a solitary seat, not far from everyone else but not close enough for a reaching hand. She heard his belly growling last night. And the day before.

"I've been making some calls," Tash said. They all gave her wry expressions; she'd been stepping away for calls as often as not since Nick's vision returned. "We'll have more advanced equipment and some discrete specialists once we get back to the Farm. I know it's not enough, but…"

"Is it so bad if people know?" Nick asked. "I mean, there could be advances. People might benefit from me."

"And from me," Kelly said, "but I don't want to be a science-y pincushion for the rest of my life. And people benefitted from me at Gavin's. It's not all it's cracked up to be."

"Kelly!" Tash admonished with undisguised shock.

The blonde lifted her chin defiantly. Iseult grabbed her arm and she looked down at her sister-friend. Nick crumpled like paper at the mention of Gavin.

Iseult said, "My whole family — from my past life — were medical professionals. Top in their class, top in their field. Our house had four people and seven bathrooms. I've seen what their conversations looked like for medical research. The meetings, parties, fundraisers, applications. They took me with them for symposia, conferences, conventions." She rolled her hand with this as though they would tumble on and on. "People talk, in person and online. Academia can be like Gossip Corner with an overpriced sweater and a logo. Rumours alone would eat us alive, never mind media and the people playing games under the table. Why do you think I like survivalism so much?" Everyone was watching her. Even Tash was caught off-guard. It was a raw day for everyone, it seemed. "Rocks don't have agendas. Forests don't have invisible strings."

While they all expressed their feelings, often striking out verbally or seeming to rebel, there was a tacit practice of order among the three youths. Forced into adulthood early, they were navigating conflict with efficiency so powerful it was sad. Tash ran a hand through her pixie cut, sitting tall and elegant. "I'm proud of all of you," she said. And smiled at their looks of surprise.

Sky, Pacific Ocean
Nick

The aisle of the plane separated Nick and Kelly on one side from Tash and Iseult on the other. While the other two women were resting, Kelly was doing her best to get through to Nick and he knew it. He was reading an on-board newspaper with shaking hands. He was so pale, with so much tension suffusing his body, that his eyes appeared rimmed with blue beneath the surface of the skin. Blinking constantly, he'd get three or four pages in and have to restart because he hadn't absorbed a word.

"Honey…" Kelly said gently, rubbing the back of his neck with one hand, "Come back to me."

"I'm right here," he whispered. He didn't mean to whisper, but his mouth was dry and his heart was worn. "I need something with Google. Or a library. Maybe if we just pick up some more stuff on eyes, on food stuff..."

Kelly kissed his temple and traced his forearm with the tips of her nails. Normally, this would send shivers through him — even without her electric gift — but it was like tapping the armour of someone mid-battle: it wouldn't have gotten through even if he'd thought to feel for the touch. "I don't think a textbook on genetics will help us, Nick."

He blinked and looked her in the eye. Maybe using his name got through? "Do you think it's genetic?" he asked, and her hopes were dashed.

"Even Tash didn't know what to do," Kelly reminded him. She turned to face him directly and tried to pry the newspaper from his hands as she spoke. "I think she's right: we couldn't stay there. At best, it would happen again, or affect someone else. And for what? This is bigger than we are."

"I don't care how big I am," he said. He wouldn't let go of the newspaper, but he also didn't take his eyes from hers. Though her hair was blonde and her eyes blue, her pale was very different from his pale. She was like seeing a cloudless blue sky behind a sunflower. He was the white of a dental office: sanitized and infused with fear. "I don't care how much reach we have as a team. Cats can't take a mouse's eyes away. Not even elephants or whales can do that."

"You're not a mouse, dude," she said.

That actually stopped him; she'd never called him

"dude" before. It was like she was talking to some jerk at the movies.

She went on: "I know you're scared, but don't give them more than what they already took. They knocked you down, but you got back up, and you found your way back to seeing without anyone's help."

He clasped her hand. The tightness was intense, but no longer powered by adrenaline and muscle. This was a grip from the bones, from kisses stolen in the patches of dark between streetlights. "I had help."

A current, quick as forgetting, made his hand jolt. "Sorry," she said, and started to pull away.

He held.

His contacts, steel blue again, looked at her, at the women across the aisle, at the passing stewardess. He shook his head, but Kelly got them two juices and some crackers. When they were alone again, Nick was forced to drop his newspaper to accommodate Kelly's placement of their goods on the backs of the seats in front of them. "You're going to eat and you're going to drink and I'm not taking my eyes off you until it's done."

"How can you guys keep trusting what you eat after...?"

"Look," Kelly said, "maybe our suspicions are right — maybe Iseult had the right idea — and you got it from the shrimp. Maybe it's not from food. But we can't just sit around being scared. You went after me, didn't you?" Meaning what happened in Atlanta.

"Maybe it's just me…" he said.

"Do you believe that?" Kelly kissed his hand as he ate a cracker. He was so slow that Kelly requested a water in addition to their juices and thanked the flight attendant for her assistance. The woman offered Nick a sympathetic smile and said that their company hadn't had a plane crash in its history and went on her way.

Nick shook his head when she was gone. "If it was me, why now? I mean, sure, people start feeling sick out of nowhere because of something that had been brewing. Happens all the time. But I just don't think so. I believe Izzy's got more going for her than just a medical talent and the willingness to keep house while we're out. Her blood flow thing is cool, but I think her real gift is knowing the pulse of things a bit more...uh…"

"Spiritually? Metaphorically?"

"Something like that."

"I'm with you," Kelly said, "and in more ways than one. Now, I need you to stop looking at your eyes in reflections and doing those tests you do."

He sat up a little straighter. "I don't know what you me-"

"You can't lie to me, buster. Like that one where you make a triangle with your hands? You know that doesn't work for you, anyway."

"I don't think I have a dominant eye…"

"That's not the point and you know it."

His colour was starting to return. He didn't realize yet that she was making him feel better. "I can't keep dragging you all d-"

She'd grabbed his face with both of her hands. She was kissing him. He was the eye of her storm, and utterly lost in the meshing of their lips and the way her breath caressed him with each transition. But while she started it, he soon lost track of where one ended and the other be-gan. All time was sliced away with the strands of her hair and the undercurrent of their muted voices.

Ballard, Seattle, Washington

Iseult

Tash's resources never ceased to amaze the young woman. Though Iseult had spent her early years enjoying the wealth of a family in medicine, she was used to things coming from conventional places. Tash, by contrast, ac-complished a great deal through...other means. She ap-peared to operate in an economy of favours, with coinage like timing and influence. She extolled the law often, but also pointed out that their whole need for secrecy about the abilities that brought them together came from an un-just system built upon a foundation of prejudice and per-secution.

Which justified introducing a degree of flexibility in their interpretation of the law.

That, more than anything, was what had brought Iseult into Tash's fold: trust in the woman's integrity. It was the spirit of the law, not the letter of it, that made the difference.

Iseult was standing around the corner of the wall di-viding the apartment's living room and tiny hallway lead-ing to the front door. Tash had snagged the apartment on the phone before they got on the plane, and they were set up with keys a little over an hour after leaving the airport in Seattle. Apparently, the apartment had been vacated last-minute by the recent widow of a fisherman. Couldn't take the memories.

Iseult understood.

And Nick's distress in the Kodiak hotel had resonated with her. There was so much love and support in their family. It had only been six months since they'd even met Kelly. But when he was vulnerable and the chips were down, here they all were.

Perhaps it was time.

So she stood by the divider, wearing shorts — and feeling intensely out of place in them. She hadn't worn shorts since she was a girl. She listened:

"Nothing like what you've got going, babe," Nick said to Kelly. Her nails were coloured like candy corn.

"No, something simpler, I'm thinking. Black is a little too punk or emo," she replied in a musing tone.

"Maybe he has some goth in him," Tash suggested, and Iseult could almost hear the lanky woman's dimples lean into a smile.

"I was more of a billiards guy, actually," Nick said. Iseult resisted a giggle; she knew that baritone tweak he put in his voice — just a hint of depth — when he was trying to be bigger and beefier than he was.

So Tash's response surprised her: "That's true. Bit of a shark, actually," and she chuckled. He must have made a face.

"You never told me you could play!" Kelly slapped his upper arm.

"What can I say? I'm a man of mystery," Nick replied.

There came the tell-tale *mlah* sound of Kelly sticking out her tongue as Tash said, "You're about as mysterious as toast."

"I am cosmopolitan toast!" Nick retorted, and they all laughed.

Iseult took the opportunity to sweep into the room, standing behind the high-backed chair in which Tash sat. Nick was on a pair of milk crates, and Kelly was sitting on an end table they'd found left behind in the master bedroom. Most of the apartment had been empty, but the widow had cleared out so fast that there were still assorted oddments kicking around: a whiteboard; all the big items like fridge, stove, and washing machine; a broken barbecue; a storage room packed with the random things they didn't have the time to toss.

Iseult had been in another room for the last few hours, connected to the Internet they'd started arranging before they even left the airport. They had wi-fi before they had keys. Tash went on at some length, stressing to them the importance of not committing to a place and setting it up without previous inspection and in such a timeline as they'd been doing. Everything was hectic and awkward, but they had to set up quickly — which was why Iseult was hitting up Kijiji and the like for furniture and other items.

"How are we doing, dear?" Tash asked Iseult over her shoulder.

"Well, there's the bed we already have in the guest room, and I've managed to get a fold-out couch and a futon. It's not great, b-..."

"I mean, how do you feel? It must be a bit of a whirlwind," Tash said. She'd turned back so that she wasn't straining her neck. Iseult didn't need to see her adoptive mother's face to know that she was taking in the other two with her eyes.

Nick grimaced and looked at his hands. Kelly beamed and held her hand up, back-facing, and wiggled her fingers. "We're all getting our nails done!"

Iseult managed a giggle. "Even Nick?" She doubted that was why he was looking at his hands, but maybe he needed to pretend?

"I'm thinking the same shade as Ash's shotgun from Army of Darkness," Nick said with his best casual voice. "This is my boomstick!"

"Cobalt blue?" Iseult asked. She hadn't seen the Evil Dead movies.

"Gunmetal grey?" Tash suggested. She'd seen them, but out of order, and hadn't cared enough about the gun to study it. She'd been intrigued by all the background activity, the settings and unnamed characters. Anthropology was more a lifestyle to her than a career.

"Both!" Kelly and Iseult said together.

It was Nick who laughed the most at that. "All right," he said, "I'm in. What about you, Mom?"

There was a flash of interest from Kelly as he spoke, as though she were wondering what was behind his words. They seemed simple enough.

"I'm a purple gal today, I think," Tash said with a dignified air.

Iseult fluttered inside with love and insecurity. She took a breath as Nick said, "What about you, Izzy?"

For a fraction of a second, she froze. But she was committed at this point. They'd see if she walked away wearing shorts, anyway. Now or never. "Actually, I…"

The air in the room changed instantly.

Even though she was taking control, and this was a moment for her, Iseult was at a loss for words. She'd played the conversation out in her head ever since she'd helped Tash with the incidentals following Quinn's...end. Months of shower sessions evaporated in the limelight. So she merely stepped around Tash's chair to take a place where all three of them could see her.

She turned her right foot outward, levering the leg a bit so that they could see the marks. "I've..." Iseult swallowed, stood straight so that her feet now pointed at the three most important people in her life, and said: "...they're self-inflicted."

Self-consciousness and the distress of a shattered family had a way of slowing time. In the flutter of a butterfly wing, the whites of Kelly's eyes became a highland sky: far-reaching, looming, quiet with thunderous surprise. Nick's bottle of nail polish hit the floor. Each of his lips quivered independently as he walked a tightrope over a chasm of loving rage and shamed grief.

Tash leaned over the arm of her chair, even as Nick's bottle was rolling, and placed her own nail polish on the floor with the emulsified articulation of ink in the ocean. She sat as on a throne, her fingers flowing over the armrests like tributaries. Cold and untouchable, her pulse was regal. A queen's tears streamed freely and shivered with the earthquake of heartbreak beneath the skin. They'd seen her mourn, but none of the three youths had ever seen her so devastated.

Who knew bedrock could slither away?

Ballard

Kelly

She actually giggled.

They were sweaty, breathing heavily, and had just re-dressed in the dark amid heavy shushing of each other and the gentle rocking of the tugboat they'd stealthily boarded on the Ballard Locks. It had been exciting to colour so firmly outside the lines, but neither of them felt brave enough to test their luck with a languid departure.

They walked hand-in-hand, boldly traversing circles of light. Kelly's ankles and hips bobbed in unison to an undulation no one else could have seen. Nick's grin belonged on an idiot. Since it was after dark, most people avoided them and they avoided in return.

At one point, they crossed paths with a middle-aged man. He wore a shirt with one too many buttons down, his hair coiffed into a promontory above his forehead, and he had a gait with a distinctly heightened anchorage. They stopped because he stopped, and he gave them the head-to-toe. His eyes met Kelly's. "Nice," he said, and gave Nick a lingering look as he continued about his night.

Kelly blushed so hard her hair began to lift and frizzle. "That's handy," Nick remarked as they started up again.

"Hm?" she bubbled helplessly.

"You get to make that static outside of you. You don't have to describe what it feels like. But I feel it, too," Nick said.

She didn't just look at him, she *existed* in his direction. She stepped into him as she walked, their hands forming the point of a "V" as it closed at their shoulders. "We're gonna be late for curfew," she said. And then felt foolish; would he — could he — not know that she was starlight stretched over the street right now?

"We need to make Izzy feel how we just felt," Nick mused aloud.

Kelly giggled. "I mean, I love her too, but I'm not looking to spice things up that much just yet."

When Nick blushed, it was less colour than surface tension. It was facial expressions all over for him. Kelly stopped him long enough to kiss him fiercely on the lips. After a trio of footsteps in willowy directions, Nick managed to collect himself. "Isn't she ace?" he asked.

"I think so. Your shirt's inside-out." She thought her tongue would turn to Flubber any second.

"What are we gonna do?"

"Can't we hold onto the magic a bit longer?" she asked wistfully. She knew he was right, but there was a reason they felt such a powerful urge to get out of the house. And not just that urge.

"Pretty sure the magic will be holding onto me for a long time," Nick said. "But I can't help...I dunno...looking around. At the world, or life, or my life, or something," he added.

Kelly soared inside, but there was a blocky weight about that emotional flight. It was the combination of looking at the land far below the airplane with awe and – paradoxically – being cramped in a pressurized metal tube. "I don't like leaving Kodiak just because it was too dangerous," she said. Would he think she wasn't trying to be understanding? Should she console him, or...?

"Can we not think about that right now? I know I look

like I'm scared about the food, but being stuck in that hotel room was like being handcuffed with darkness. I just...I can't. Not yet."

She popped a kiss onto his cheek. She wanted to look over her shoulder. They could've gotten in trouble with the boat. But she also didn't want to be that young blonde woman out after dark, looking over her shoulder every two steps like some helpless movie damsel. Was it Nick who rescued her in Atlanta? Did she rescue herself, and he had good timing?

"I used to do the laundry. Back then, I mean..." she said.

Nick furrowed his brows.

"I'm just, what I'm trying to say..." Kelly huffed with brisk frustration. "Izzy holds the fort and all, and that's lovely. Tash is our fearless leader. But I kinda get both of them, even with just a few months. Doing the laundry, it gave me something I could give for the others. Or do for them. It was a community thing. Wasn't that what was under your skin about getting degrees and doing day jobs?"

"I...sort of," Nick answered. "If you've only got one mechanic, and he put in all that time and money for learning all that stuff, why is he inside doing the laundry? Shouldn't he be fixing the car?"

Resentment flashed through Kelly and left ozone. But she swallowed it for now. "I wanna track down this Braulio guy."

Nick's face flattened and widened. "Really? Doesn't he remind y-"

"It's one thing to have a screw loose and bomb a hospital while you're wearing the bomb. Maybe he had a personal beef, or something super unfair was happening. I don't see how hurting innocent people helps with that, but still. Maybe there's something to that. But Braulio? That's planning. Calculated. Long-term. If he's part of whatever happened…"

"Well, if it's that big, why don't we leave it for the CIA or FBI or UN or some other bunch of alphabet…soup…heroes?" Nick said. He ran his thumb along her hand while he held it. His tone was coaxing.

Kelly wanted to call him childish. *He wants to dodge everyday responsibilities like jobs, taxes, and education – but have some…what? Vainglorious soldier romance of fighting vague big-bad-wolf conspiracies and chasing down powered folk who don't agree with us? But was she any different?* She took in a deep breath, hugged his arm as she let it out slowly through her nose, and tried something else. "I'm not sure either. About Braulio, about any of it. If there's such a deep corruption or whatever you wanna call it in the food industry, we can't just call the cops or the FDA. They'd be the first problem the conspiracy would have to fix. So Braulio's kinda obviously the bad guy, and we sorta have to chase him. No one else will. And I'm not a hundred percent on Tash, either. Is she taking us out of fires or jumping between frying pans? You've seen how she talks; you've heard some of her conversations with Victor that end up getting just out of our range."

"I just…" Nick said. But it wasn't his words that really hit home for her so much as the look on his face, the pace of his feet and his breath. He wasn't just hearing her. He was listening. Willing to be wrong. "…I'd like to keep my eyes on the same puzzle until I've worked it out. We keep jumping around. Even when we were staying at the farm, there was…" he flapped a hand about, at a loss for words.

"I know," Kelly said. "Hectic, but nowhere, too."

"Yeah!"

"And then there's Iseult."

"I don't know who I'm worried about more."

"My fighter," she said. "I don't think this is that clear-cut. Maybe leaving them alone together helped?"

"Maybe they just need time," Nick conceded. "At least, y'know, for each other. But by themselves? Tash is…and Izzy can't…"

Kelly squeezed his hands a little tighter. "At least we got some of that furniture in earlier."

"About that…"

"Yeah, maybe she means to give us a lot more time here. Like, we can't just keep jumping and running. Sooner or later we need to lick our wounds and sit down and stuff," Kelly affirmed.

"I don't think she really left the Providence Bomber behind…" Nick said to the night's sky.

Kelly didn't have an answer for that. Her skin still hummed, but the bounce had faded from her step.

When they got to the apartment, they stopped at the door and — by unspoken agreement — listened. It was so quiet in the hallway that they could hear someone a few doors down cussing out their cat over the cheers and commentary of a football game. Still, nothing came from the apartment. Kelly took a deep breath, as if screwing herself up for action, and nodded toward the door.

He frowned. "Don't you have the key?"

It was the first time he'd seen her straight-up facepalm. As Nick shuffled self-consciously, Kelly texted Iseult, who showed up at the door so quickly that Nick started. Her eyes had the gelatinous squalor of crushed hope. Kelly thought her heart would break with the sight, but she couldn't make a step before Nick had wrapped his friend in his arms. They were blocking the door now, with Kelly awkwardly out in the hall.

Iseult's shudder came from expended sobs and pent-up disappointment. "I'm sorry, I—"

"Don't be," Nick said.

Iseult spoke quietly. "You shouldn't..."

Nick released her and moved forward into the apartment. Kelly slipped in and closed the door behind her. They prevented Iseult from turning to the narrow hall to the storage room, or into the partial wall making an angled fold over the kitchen. When she tried to duck to her room, Kelly slung her arm around Iseult's waist and they performed a three-legged, stubborn, wordless wobble into the mostly empty living room.

Sleeves. That's what had stood out to Kelly. Iseult was wearing track pants and a thin, long-sleeved shirt. With a thumb and middle finger, Nick reached for his own eyes, plucked the contacts, and tossed them aside.

Kelly, meanwhile, kept Iseult from fleeing the room. The back of her mind squirmed with the realization that her hair was a mess, Nick's shirt was on backwards, and hers was on inside out. Tash took up the rest of her mind.

A nurturing leader and natural mother, Tash was the genetics of their experience. She was how they knew that there were others like them, and not just because of unusual abilities. Every lost, damaged youth is its own species in an ecosystem of coping mechanisms.

Kelly wasn't sure Tash was coping.

Without the romance of a throne, Tash merely sat in the armchair, facing an unadorned wall of egg-yolk yellow. Maybe she hadn't moved since Iseult's confession (revelation?) a few hours before. Though there was an emptied wine glass (when did Tash get wine?) on the divider between the room and the kitchen.

Kelly squeezed Nick's hand and Iseult's shoulder. Then she stood before Tash, arms folded. Tash's eyes flickered unwilling acknowledgement of presence but sought no connection.

Everyone was startled when Kelly plopped herself on Tash's lap!

"I want a horsey, and a Sephora gift basket, and a nice scarf to go with a cute beret. Oo! And some new magazines," she said as she draped her arms over Tash's shoulders.

"Stop that," Tash said haphazardly. Her eyes slowly closed as her head drooped, and she ineffectually flapped her hand at her adoptive daughter.

Kelly poked her newfound mother in the nose with the tip of her finger and didn't intend to create a current. But Tash's eyes widened and she sneezed, shaking her head vigorously. Her hair became mildly frizzled. Short, dark, and sleek, her hair resisted static poofing more than Kelly's.

This got some more life back into Tash, who made a more insistent full body shoving resistance against Kelly.

"Not sorry," Kelly said.

She heard Iseult try to sneak off behind her, and Nick's calm but firm denial of that plan. One dimple tweaked as she was just a little proud and oh so full of love.

"Izzy," Kelly began. She stood and kept her eyes on Tash as she spoke. A shift and something like a gasp acknowledged the fact that she was using Nick's nickname. "I want to be there the next time you cut."

That got Tash's attention.

"Now hold on a s-" their mother began.

"It's a little more complicated than that," Iseult murmured. Nick lifted her chin with the knuckle of his index finger.

"We've been through enough that we can stand proud, no matter how messed up we are," Nick said.

"Actually, it's real simple," Kelly said. Between her Texas upbringing and her time in the state of Georgia, her drawl crept in from the back of the throat instead of the jaw. Nick stood up a little straighter, and Iseult tried to steal a glance at Tash. Kelly was the atmosphere of the whole room, but not because of any electrical gift. This was raw humanity. "I don't care if we're on a plane, or I'm in a restaurant bathroom with the shits, or we're stopping some lunatic from going after a hospital. You only bust out that ghost knife of yours when I'm here."

Tash stood then. Kelly stood her ground, woefully unequipped though she was for Tash's fierce will. It was like she moved from her spine rather than her arms or legs. Her knuckles were white on empty hands. "You knew?"

"Only about the knife," Iseult said sheepishly. Her voice was a bent but vibrant blade of grass. "She bumped me by accident in the restaurant."

"Which restaurant?" Tash demanded.

Iseult clasped her hands together, stood straighter, took a quick breath through her nose, and cast a meaningful glance at Nick.

"...oh." Tash concluded. The white went away, but her hands stayed clenched.

"I'm surprised that we're all so surprised," Kelly said. "I know it's a hard conversation, and no one wants that right now, but even my safe place is the Farm by Atlanta. Twenty minutes' drive to that house, if the traffic's good. That house, where we almost went all *Lord of the Flies*."

"I should have kept us up on the therapy..." Tash admonished herself.

"It doesn't work like that, either," Iseult said. Her tone had changed. She spoke with a nurse's command of the room. "I'm not your fault, Mom."

Tash's lip quivered as though she'd been struck a blow. She was speechless, and Kelly guessed it was the guilt of having overlooked something important.

"None of us are okay," Kelly said, "and that's just what's up. We can't whittle the rot away and then just keep shaping the wood. It's not the same wood now."

"You're not rotten. You got hurt," Tash said. This was the woman who'd pulled the chambers of Kelly's heart back together. Maybe better than Nick had. Kelly wanted to do the same for her.

"We should get some sleep," Nick pointed out. No one moved to check the time, but they were all exhausted. Things had gotten dark before the sun went down.

"Look," Kelly said, "we're not going to heal on our own. And it's not something like a cut where the skin comes back together and you move on with your life. We're all gonna be different as this goes on, and it's not gonna finish like a degree or something. It's practically a lifestyle."

"I won't be a victim," Nick said. "I didn't come this far just to spend all my days hugging a pillow that says, 'Poor me' on it."

Iseult put her hand on his shoulder.

"Then we'll all work on that healing here. We've got this," Tash said, spreading her arms to encompass the apartment, "and we've got each other."

"We're helping you, too," Kelly said. "This is a forward base to you. You're not here for sightseeing; you wanna do more about Providence."

"I'm the adult here," Tash said, "and I'll take care of that sort of thing. Besides, Victor's team should really be doing more on that."

"Pretty sure he's got his hands full with Theo right now," Nick quipped. "Besides, we're already here, and all we need to do is scout and stuff. Nothing too intense."

Tash opened her mouth but Iseult, meek yet firm, said to the floor: "Not even therapy can help us with the fact that we can do things normal people can't. We can't even bring it up!" Suddenly she looked at Tash, who wasn't meeting her eyes, and she reached into her jogging pants to produce the ghost knife she'd had strapped there.

Tash's eyes flashed. Nick gaped at her. Kelly didn't even turn.

Iseult declared, "Whatever's going on, we'll have a say in it."

Kelly backed her: "We'll choose where we make our cuts in life."

CHAPTER 14
HUNTING KNIVES

Onyx site, Leuk, Switzerland

What happened?

Karambit slipped out of one of the janitor's facilities on the site. He was dressed like a custodian, his previous clothing included beneath the refuse in the rolling bin he was pushing. He knew an alarm had been tripped because he had a special dongle attached to the last computer he'd been infiltrating. It sent a signal to a key fob he had in his pocket that caused the light to blink. He'd arranged his belt and the many-pocketed overalls to include his indispensable tools and weapons. The rest he'd disposed of.

"You!" someone called behind him in German.

Looking for all the world like a calm and casual custodian, Karambit turned. "Yes?" he responded in German. His accent was clearly standard, rather than Swiss German — but that wasn't unusual enough to be noteworthy.

"What's your name and employee number? Have you seen anyone here in the last five minutes?" The speaker, whose accent was Swiss, was accompanied by an armed security detail.

"I never caught much," Karambit answered as he presented a fabricated identity card. That was when he noticed that one of the guards in the detail wore a distinct pin the others did not. He knew it as the logo of Circe, a spy organization. But why were they wearing it openly? He continued speaking and made no outward sign that he'd noticed anything. "I was in the supply room." He pointed to the door down the hall, with a translucent pane. "Someone ran by. I thought I caught the bounce of a ponytail, but it could have been a cord or strap. It was quick."

The guard — if that's what she was — with the logo spoke: "I can take this one, sir, if you'd like to keep looking." Her German accent had Dutch influence.

"Rejoin us at Muster Station C," the leader responded and kept the group moving. Karambit knew what that meant: the entire complex was in lockdown. There would be no way to enter or leave without passing through security checkpoints. He was trapped.

"Can I...?" Karambit asked, indicating the waste bin.

Her response was curt. "No. Return with me to your supply room. I will examine your effects and get your full statement. Then you will proceed to the next security checkpoint."

Wordlessly, he obliged her, and turned the waste bin around. Once they were in the room, she had him remove each item in turn so that she might inspect it before he placed it aside. He knew where the items were that he'd used before, though. As he handed her a bundle of clothes, he positioned his hands so that he was holding a removable hand grip for climbing. Her surprise was complete when he threw it in her face by whipping his hand in a rolling arc above the bundle. The clothes immediately followed. He was out the door before she finished the fraction of a second of getting the clothes out of her injured face.

She gave hard pursuit. "It's him," she said into a radio. "The intruder is dressed as a janitor." She rounded the corner in the hallway, following the sounds of a man crying out, to find a janitor she didn't recognize picking himself up from the floor. About twelve feet ahead were two doors, one swinging and the other closed.

"Report to the nearest muster station," she told him when she gave him a good look and didn't recognize him. Then she was off. As soon as she was out of sight, he collected himself, returned to the supply room to tidy it and remove any signs of disturbance, and proceeded to take a left where the right would have led to the hall with the opened door.

Right on schedule, three explosions went off in different sections of wall around the compound. The plan had been for all of them to serve as diversions. At least, that was Plan A. Now that the Circe operative was aware of his rough location, they'd converge on that section — where one of the explosions had made a hole to the outside.

The halls were markedly empty because everyone was either at a muster station, out of the compound, or looking for intruders. As usual, he'd carefully studied the plans of the facility before engaging in his mission, so he made his way to the emergency fire suppression equipment. Normally, this was locked down in a breach, but its locks were released with the bombings as a failsafe. He'd just donned fire safety gear when two others joined him, and he helped them into their outfits.

"Hey!" one of them said in German. "Sorry, I know I should know your name…"

"Gustave," Karambit improvised. "And don't worry about it; I get it all the time."

Because he'd caused them to see him as familiar, he spent several hours with them as they cleared out any fires and secured the area against any potential follow-up attacks. He was soon out of the compound, planted Engen agents helping play out a scene of him joining his office friends now that he was wearing business casual clothes he'd hidden in a men's room as a Plan E back-up.

His extraction only left him with minimal relief; how had Circe known this facility would be of interest? How had they intercepted him? Were they working with the FIS — the Swiss Federal Intelligence Service?

Naturally, they would find nothing to compromise Engen. But he would have to lay low for now; he couldn't be the eye in the sky for the other Knives if someone was watching through him.

∞

Congo Basin, Republic of the Congo

Sikloon was murderous and showing it.

"Why are there so many delays!?" he demanded in Afrikaans.

He was deep in a section of rainforest, personally overseeing his transport operation. Apparently the example he'd made in Ghana hadn't sent a loud enough message; someone was interfering. Sikloon was on a one-man motorboat, moving himself between each of the vessels. The person at the head of the large riverboat he'd just connected with had yet to respond to him. Sikloon's mind was a cutting board, subjected to all manner of dicing and the slams of jagged edges: logistics; anticipating the enemy; news and weather patterns; cultures and how to play them off of each other; money; warfare and tactics.

He'd had all of the assets that were smuggled into the country's train operations withdrawn, which had eaten profits and thrown some of his power structure into disarray. His pet dictators and cronies liked to be the biggest fish in their little ponds. His moves were starting to remind them of where they were in the food pyramid. It made them antsy and the wrong kind of courageous. Now he had a massive land-bound line of people on foot, motorcycles, bicycles, sleds, quads, jeeps, and whatever mounted animals he could get his money on.

Boats paralleled this line, and the pair of lines traversed the Congo River. Zaire, as he liked to remember it; that was what they'd called it when Sikloon was a boy. The boats went from mere canoes and rowboats right up to the biggest supply ships the river could sustain. Only the open ocean could keep bigger vessels afloat. Materials and quality varied just as much: wood, fibreglass, metal, and even clunkers made of a mix of animal bones and hides. It was a wonder some of them floated at all.

Sometimes his people failed to answer straight away because they were terrified of him. Maybe there was a language barrier, though he'd given specific orders that only speakers of his native tongue should be used as forward guards for his line of ships. Now that he was nearing the stern of the larger riverboat with the speechless guard, he called on one of the crew to help fasten his boat alongside so that he could board.

Movement from the shore caught his eye.

He didn't have to watch his hands as he assisted the others in getting his boat attached to the side of the larger vessel, so he had no trouble spotting the newcomer: a gorilla.

He was up in no time. "Where's the gem?" he asked as soon as feet hit deck. It was code; they called slaves with powers 'gems.'

"In a cell we built under the trapdoor by the netted boxes," the crewman answered. "You'll find her just past the rations."

"Go to the guard at the starboard bow," Sikloon instructed. "I want to know why he didn't answer me instantly. Come to me sooner than you can with the answer."

The man went as fast as he could safely run on the deck.

Sikloon tied off the rope that held up the trapdoor and descended. As he came upon the boxes of rations, loaded into crates and accessible in a way similar to the strong-boxes at banks, he withdrew one and accounted for it in the tracking sheet on the nearby wall. He opened it without looking, stepping with the confidence of command until he reached the cell he expected.

Within was a woman of mixed descent — in itself a brand of shame in many of the racially-contested countries of the region. Her hair was long and scraggly, and her manner was wild and snuffling. Not surprising; time in a mostly lightless cage made people hard and glassy in eye and mind. Her clothes were an odd mishmash of leathers, hides, and western casual. Sikloon spotted an Adidas logo. "I see they've shown you courtesy," he remarked.

She perched in the middle of her cage when he spoke. The position was awkward. It wasn't like any kind of animal Sikloon had ever seen, but there was something in her expression — in her eyes — that reminded him of beasts he'd encountered in Ghana. It was less comfort than resignation; she'd gone somewhere beyond fear. The Knife cursed inwardly; it would be harder to bring her power to bear — and to tame her — now that she'd gone beyond humanity and animality, into raw survival.

Her lips moved. Like a wind that had been squeezed into the space of a whip, they snapped at the silence and clawed at the empty air. He'd heard the Sango language before, but it had been one of many languages spoken by overseers. Or slaves? Townsfolk in his travels? There were so many tribes, so many people just struggling to get through the day. He did not know. But she obviously wasn't speaking Afrikaans.

"Work for me," Sikloon said in Akan.

Wariness.

"What is your name?" he tried in accented English.

She began walking, or maybe it was prowling, around the perimeter of her cell. She rambled in Sango. At least, it sounded like rambling to the Knife. He noticed that her fingers twitched expectantly. He noticed that she kept glancing at the wall.

Was it a particular section? A bar of her cell, a panel

of the hull?

Sikloon tilted his head, listening for activity beyond the square of sky in the ceiling. No one was approaching the trapdoor. No one was talking. Distant crying, some of what was likely begging. Instructions. Cursing in at least a dozen languages. Typical for a human trafficking lineup. But nothing from the deck. He didn't like it.

"The gorilla on the bank," he said in his mother tongue. He imitated the sounds and motions of an ape and pointed with emphasis in the general direction he meant. He was grateful none of his troops were here to see this; it was beneath him. But he couldn't call for a translator, since he was fairly certain the person he sent running was dead.

She watched him with her head tilted and moved forward, emulating the gorilla-style movements.

"Yes! Yes, that," he said. Then he pointed at her. "You?"

She watched him.

He pointed more at her, and in the direction. He even did the chest-thump. Then he pointed at her again, and did his best to look inquisitive.

She hopped with more positive energy than he expected, pointing to herself and in the direction of the gorilla. Then she said something in Sango.

"I don't know what you're saying," he replied in Afrikaans.

She made a sharp remark — some tones can do wonders for bridging cultures — and marched to the door. She yanked at it with both hands, faced the trapdoor even though it was out of her view, and pantomimed climbing a ladder. She pointed again in the direction of the gorilla.

What does she take me for? "Tell the gor-" he started, and there was a silenced gunshot.

Most wouldn't have heard such a shot. Even without subsonic rounds, it would have easily been drowned out by the sounds of so many boats on the water, so many people, and so many animals in the distance. But Sikloon was running a human trafficking operation, on an international scale, as a Knife of Engen. He could overhear someone dreaming of a pin dropping if it might affect his work for Engen.

He'd expected the peon to report by now.

The woman in the cage had gone rigid. Did she know about guns? She was an adult, and it was a big world even for isolated communities. So maybe. Perhaps she had a primal gift for picking up on danger. It didn't matter. He looked at her, pulled the cyclone knife from its holster at his side, and ran its three spiralling edges over the back of his other arm. He had to draw out a long line to span each edge, and did his best to keep the penetration shallow.

She didn't step back. She was watching the trapdoor. How did she know he wasn't planning to stab her? Most were disturbed that he'd put an edge against his own flesh, but she barely acknowledged what he was doing. He'd want to probe this one some more.

He inwardly shrugged as he worked. As soon as he finished with his knife, he set it against the keyhole. All three spiralling edges converged at the tip, which was a struggle for him to sharpen, but he'd managed. It was metal tip against metal keyhole, and he let the edge do the work. He had to pull the knife out partway through the process to refine the edges again. He chose to pull up a leg of his pants for the flesh he'd need, then resumed when he was satisfied with the keenness. The metal of the cell's lock splashed away from the edge like squashed cake. There were shouts from the deck as he worked. One voice he knew was one of his troops, but there were at least two others.

And they spoke Spanish.

If they'd been from Equatorial Guinea, there might have been cause to wonder. But their accents were European. The only ally Sikloon had who might have been in Spain was Karambit, and this was clearly not his work. Too sloppy. "We're leaving," he said to the woman in Afrikaans as he swung the door open. Panic sounded from his product line with wild abandon; slave and minion alike were being dispersed or confused somehow.

As soon as he started moving, she made for the trapdoor, but he grabbed her arm to stop her. Their eyes met and he gave her a curt shake of his head as he immediately headed deeper into the boat. She made no acknowledgement he could detect, but went along with him.

There was a preamble. He knew this war song well. It was tinkling and bumping, followed by the light dying as the trapdoor shut and the few electrical lights belowdecks went out. He knew the war song would have a loud, flashy finish — and didn't intend to stay here to hear it. The woman hissed as darkness filled the hull. Though they weren't touching, she always managed to stay close. Could she see? He didn't need to; he knew his fleet well. Even in the dark, he found his way to the cargo door and heaved it open.

They jumped into the river just as the grenade exploded.

Soto saw it and wasted no time. "*¡Misión fallida!*" he shouted into his radio before leaping into the water himself. His teammate on the riverboat had been killed, and he was going to have to trust in the infiltrators from here. His job had been to distract Sikloon and the Knife's troops; make them think the primary agents were foreigners, to throw off the scent.

It was chaos.

Freed slaves ran every which way, overseers and troops sometimes fighting them and sometimes joining them. Soto had had to jump from the next vessel in the line. Emerging at the riverbank and turning, he saw their best sniper — a Latina stationed in the trees across the way — being torn from her perch by gorillas. There were the tell-tale, oblong flashes of throwing knives in multiple directions.

Pitchforks, lit torches, gunshots, grenades, tossed bodies, fistfights.

Smoke.

The line of boats and vessels was beginning to recover a semblance of order even as Soto leapt into an off-road SUV alongside another agent. One of the refurbished military buses in the entourage also disengaged, heading off in a separate direction. Their rendezvous point was several hours away, of course, so they had to split off now to thwart too much pursuit.

Sikloon stood over the body of the sniper and saw only the tools and evidence to be harvested. "Train her in," he said as he jutted a thumb at the woman who spoke both Sango and, apparently, Gorilla. One of the peons led her away. "Fetch me my case," he said to another, meaning the one with the encrypted satellite phone.

He had a slate to wipe clean.

Seattle, Washington

"Switch," she said in Cantonese to a sophisticated satellite phone. She'd wired the phone into a TV studio's broadcast equipment to boost the signal, but the real power would come from global satellite networks — not the phone itself. She was in one of the studio's maintenance rooms, dressed like a nondescript operator/maintainer.

"Shaving the whetstone," she said, this time in English.

It was a code, meaningless by itself, that attempted to establish connection with the other Knives.

Instead of a standby signal, response, or busy code, she got what she'd feared: a mishmash of numbers in mixed languages. Gibberish to anyone else, the Knives had established this as a simple message. The words for zero in Afrikaans and Filipino meant that Sikloon and Karambit had gone to ground.

Switch let out one profane word. To an outside observer, it might have seemed casual. Even monotone. But it expressed an intense rancour, with a tone tinged by something like admiration. A single Knife was unaccustomed even to delays. But two of them? And gone into hiding?

Shane couldn't have done this. Was it a Knife from another of Engen's independent Sections? They were known to compete. Yet theirs was a unique operation; four Knives for a single Engen project was unprecedented. Who of the other Sections even knew about the *Huginn* and the *Muninn*?

No matter.

Her work here was done. She'd visited Surimp to investigate the weak link in their chain personally. Spindle was next. Her sister's line connected.

A line was most secure when it was never used. Expensive equipment and razor-sharp encryption helped. Mixing up languages, frequencies, users, and voice filtration added layers of protection. But safe communication was like the value of a new car: pristine until it's in action. Then depreciation hits.

Ghost answered that there was a free agent in the mix. The Twins were in the same city now. She was getting into a falsified mail truck. Ghost had taken possession of all the necessaries: a false identity, the vehicle itself, its plates and other documentation, passable fake mail, and an outfit.

"Aren't all of Circe free agents in some way?" her twin replied in their mother tongue.

Of course, being expendable and being independent were not the same. Furthermore, Ghost wanted to focus on the spy's network once the Twins finished tidying the mess.

"What do we know about this agent?" Switch asked. They'd agreed the night before that they'd wait until Karambit and Sikloon reached out to them; it wouldn't do to inadvertently tip off their enemies by digging up their allies.

Ghost had gotten hints of intrusive activity as she'd

finished with the Azure business.

"Is this really worth the risk of us being so close to each other?" Switch asked. If one of them encountered so much as a shock from carpet static, the other would produce it instead. It would happen too fast to send warning, and if the one receiving the static charge was working on computer hardware...

Ghost was on edge. She was en route to the replacement specialist's apartment.

"Why?"

Spindle's system logins stopped making sense when he was promoted. All the records showed that he was Braulio García, but Ghost and her agents tracked him to nowhere. He used a VPN and other countermeasures, so they couldn't get much about his activities from home, but he'd used his workplace access to search out unconventional interests. Odd happenings, tabloid stuff. Foolish from an outside perspective, this was a red flag to the Knives. And his home system shut down when the free agent she'd been tracking tried to contact this Braulio person. He might never have been noticed without a Knife on his trail.

"I assume I'm to look for him when I get to the primary target," Switch remarked.

Ghost confirmed that and said that she planned to contact Switch again once she'd checked Braulio's apartment. She parked the mail truck across the street from the apartment building.

She left it locked and crossed the street. If anyone had cared to look, they'd have seen a mail worker a little later in the morning than usual. But that would only have authorities barking up the wrong tree. Heads would roll, but that wasn't her concern.

She'd have preferred an operational elevator. Ghost had two more floors of stairs to ascend when a group entered the stairwell from the ground floor. She had the tools for getting by the locking system unremarked, so they were probably residents.

"But, like, what does Siaz think we'll actually get from that Braulio guy?" came a female voice.

That got Ghost's attention. She slowed but continued up the stairs, careful to keep as quiet as possible and snug to the wall.

A man said, "Tell me we've got more than 'spy links hacker interactions to IP?'"

Another female voice, this one meeker: "I've been tracking the developments online, and I did some triangulating. Around this building, or at least the neighbourhood, is the centre of all those eating disorders and exercise crazes that have been getting out of hand. And something about a big contract in the fishery?"

"There were cover-ups," said another woman. This one sounded more mature. She had a nurturing, measured cadence in her speech. "Tabloids have been exploding for the last few weeks. Shady disappearances, weird happenings, impossible tales."

"Why didn't we talk about this in the car?" came the sulky, male voice.

"You were the one who didn't want to talk," and Ghost was surprised by that response. It came from the cottony voice. She could picture a teenaged girl muttering at her shoes.

"That's rich. Been cutting at anything else we should know about?"

"NICOLAS CARRY!"

This was Ghost's opportunity. While this apparent family got into raised voices just one flight below her, she dashed up and slipped through the door as quickly and quietly as her elite training allowed. As she reached an apartment door, advanced tactical infiltration tools slid between fingers, muscle memory, a lock, and a deadbolt.

She was in so smoothly that she'd barely lost stride and slid the locks back into place as she heard the slamming of the stairwell door in the hall. She wasn't listening to the voices — something about medical school — because she was on a mission.

Thatcher's minimalist and tidy lifestyle meant that she'd covered the drawers and cupboards, as well as most of the boxes, by the time the group had sorted themselves out and knocked on the door. The mother called out, "Braulio? If you're there, please answer. We don't want any trouble."

There was additional muttering, but Ghost was concentrating on what to look for. Mr. García, it seemed, was trying to lose some weight. There were self-help books as well. The only thing the Knife could find that might be of value was the CPU tower. She wasted no time disconnecting it and lamented that there wasn't time to remove the hard drive. Then she carried it to the wall behind the door just as someone on the other end was finishing with the locks.

They'd been using far more primitive tools, though she knew from the sounds that there was skill behind them.

Who were these people?

"There's a heartbeat in here somewhere," the shy one said as the group hustled in. "You're all too close for me to te-"

It was the one called Nicolas who looked back first, despite the fact that he had to adjust for the blonde who was holding his hand. Ghost had managed to step around the door but stay behind the group, and was just about out before he cried out, "Hey! Stop!"

The tall woman with the pixie haircut surprised Ghost; few could react so quickly and skilfully in her experience. "Who are you!?" Pixie demanded as she caught the door before it could shut, pushed it back while still on the move, and snagged Ghost's sleeve.

"The beginning," the Knife answered in Cantonese as she kicked Pixie in the gut and made for the stairs.

"Mom!" someone called out. They were crowded with the other two youths in the small and awkward space of the doorway.

Though the Knife had made good time down the stairs, even with the computer tower in her arms, the tall woman with the pixie cut actually hopped over the rails at the turn of a landing. Ghost had to toss the tower down the stairs to defend herself from a kick, and then the two were fighting all the way down the flight. The taller woman produced a collapsible baton — was this the free agent? — and fought with impressive vigour. But her skill was odd; Pixie's hands seemed to do the thinking for her. It's not that she fought foolishly, but the Knife was a cut above.

She could tell when someone fought without the

trained mind of a warrior. She'd seen many powered people in her day and knew the limits of superhuman reflexes or unnatural muscle memory. Ghost disarmed the other woman with a swipe running the base of the hand just as they reached the next landing, where the computer lay. All she needed was the hard drive, and she cursed these interlopers for their timing. As soon as the baton left the tall woman's hand she came in with an elbow, but Ghost produced a taser.

The mother drove her knee into Ghost's forearm, and the taser went flying high — to be caught by the blonde.

In her bare hand.

The Knife was so astounded by the young woman's lack of response to the charge that she looked directly at the blonde for a fraction of a second. Which was all Pixie's fist needed. Even as her face snapped away, Ghost noticed the young man managing many little manoeuvres. He caught the meek one from two separate trips, shifted the blonde so she didn't collide with Pixie, kicked away broken pieces of CPU casing three times, and managed to keep his footing. All while calling out, "Don't let her reach her legs! She has hidden weapons!"

How? Was he clairvoyant?

Ghost kicked the CPU tower down another flight and used foot-trapping techniques to throw the taller woman off-balance even as she landed subtle strikes. When Pixie collapsed on the steps and Ghost leapt for the next landing, sparks and arcing electricity went flying all around her. She cursed in Cantonese and recovered with a breakfall technique. Wedged awkwardly between her body and the wall was the CPU tower.

Pixie and the shy one were piled on the floor, and the young man rushed to help the women.

The blonde's left hand still sparked.

Accepting that she could not pacify all four of these people and keep the tower, Ghost grabbed it while she got her feet under herself and heaved it at the blonde.

...who cried out when she caught it because her electricity sparked — a defensive reflex? — and the computer case let out a high-pitch wine. There was smoke, the smell of ozone and molten plastic, and lots of crackling. She instantly dropped it, both hands going up with fingers half-curled and palms skyward.

As soon as Ghost passed the front entrance to the building, she threw off her hat and jacket and ran around the corner instead of crossing the street. She heard the other four in hot pursuit and headed toward a fuel truck that was parked nearby.

"Your knife!" the blonde said.

"What will you...?" the shy one responded as she awkwardly continued in a loping run so that she could produce a glinting edge from her pants.

"Trying something!" said the blonde.

Ghost glanced over her shoulder and couldn't believe her eyes. A ghost knife was making its way through the air, tied to the blonde with a line of electrical energy! Though the buzzing light did nothing for the knife's flight, it gained focus; the electricity would go where the knife landed. Thinking fast, she looked around, found a beer bottle on the sidewalk, and shattered it batting away the flying lightning knife.

Into the fuel truck.

"NO!" the blonde shouted, but lightning was not a rope that could be pulled back. The knife itself did nothing significant, but the current it transferred flew over the surface of the truck. Was it damaged? Had someone been careless in closing off all the valves?

Ghost's gift protected her, sending the truck's explosion to her twin sister instead. Tash and her wards only saw or heard suddenness. For all they knew, she was gone. But Ghost was in the same city as Switch, and even in the same district. That was close enough to transfer the energy too fast for Ghost to even warn Switch.

Who, at this moment, was just walking up along the side of the Spindle building. She could do nothing, and hadn't been prepared for this possibility. Who gets caught in an explosion when they're breaking into an apartment to steal a hard drive?

Only after the explosion had rocked the side of the Spindle building did the screams even begin to register to her.

CHAPTER 15
CUT TO THE QUICK

Spindle Building, Seattle, Washington

Ground Level

Switch stood on the sidewalk, waiting for everything to clear. Some of the heat, dust, ashes, and grit remained. Smoke seemed farther away than it was but filled her nostrils just the same. Her senses swirled: car alarms, horns, screeches, and screams. Lights were everywhere, lambent from the building beside her as it melted, crumbled, splintered, and burned. Headlights, streetlights, office lights, and the surreal glare of the sun. Traffic was congested, backed up, uncoordinated, and confused; some people were getting out of their vehicles to help, investigate, duck into a nearby store, or harass other drivers.

Pain.

Her nerves were red, her skin shocked with bits of concrete and glass. The sidewalk and some of the asphalt were impacted, cracked, and scarred. She could taste the flat, cold panic of citizens dumbfounded. This was the sort of thing that happened at night, Somewhere Else. The world was so fast it seemed slow. Rushing like incisions of glass were voices in mostly English, with some Spanish and peppering of other tongues, punctuating the slithering glitter of disruption.

Part of Switch wondered if this was how anglophone tourists felt in downtown Hong Kong.

All of this registered in the span of her turning her head, patting herself down, and touching her earpiece. In Cantonese: "Ghost! What happened? Where are you!?"

Her sister reported that she was safe, but trouble was on the way. Ghost began outlining a plan for them even as the background came alive with the crunching flutter of a run and the slips, bumps, and bonks of going through a door and readying a vehicle.

"I'll have to be quick," Switch added as she made her way through Spindle's own doors. "We have dangerous opportunities."

Iseult and the others were rushing into those opportune dangers. She was driving the rental Tash had acquired for them and focusing on the radio, tuned to the spot news about separate and simultaneous explosions of a fuel truck and the Spindle building. Her jaw was tight as she strove to hear it over the din of the others.

"If you're careful," the announcer was saying, "you can go around at the Ren and slip behind the building. Obviously, authorities are asking that you give it a wide…"

Kelly was gripping Nick's hand to keep from floating away. She was staring out the rear passenger side window, but seeing nothing. "Yes, officer, a postal van. I know, I thought so too. Across from some run-down apartments. There's a blown-up gas truck around the…"

Tash was riding shotgun. Iseult had hoped for a co-pilot. As the radio was updating her on traffic problems, she did her best to remember the street maps she'd studied whenever she'd gotten the opportunity. "I don't belong here," she murmured. She hadn't even known she'd said it, she was so absorbed in getting them around blockades and through intersections before traffic could lock down.

Tash swelled with pride in the children, a feeling so powerful it was operating in her spine and not taking up the limited real estate of her mind as she juggled plans, news, and details. "Thanks, Siaz," she said. "How long since they went dark?" Only bits and pieces got through to Iseult between the sharp turns, the radio, her memory of the map, and Nick and Kelly behind her.

"...Braulio, too. That's where...really? How did y-nevermind....but if both explo-" The car screeched around a turn. Police lights sparkled up. Traffic started jamming around a crash just ahead, so Iseult cut through some green space and flew crossways through an intersection. Tash glanced at her in terror and astonishment, but she was watching enough to know it was the only way they'd have gotten through the next two blocks. She gave Iseult a congratulatory pat on the shoulder.

"Really!?" Nick demanded. "If I tried that..."

"Could we be dealing with an infinite?" Tash asked her phone. Iseult didn't need any special abilities to know Nick was stewing behind her, but he didn't miss a beat of his own. He rattled off the licence plate of the stolen or false postal van for Kelly.

"We urge citizens not to try any gutsy driving moves. Just let the authorities get the situation under control; a little patience can..." the radio host went on.

Nick tapped Iseult's left shoulder, over the seat separating them, and said into her right ear: "We're gonna close in on a gap under the burger sign. Brake for the biker, but don't stop. I'll say when."

"'Kay," Iseult said.

"All right," Tash said as she put away her phone. "Siaz has access to a news helicopter. Don't ask. It looks like that truck blew up the same time the Spindle building took fire out of nowhere. There were witnesses at the fuel truck, but all the stories are conflicting. We're in the clear, but there's no news about the woman at the apartment, either. Kelly, any luck on the van?"

"They said they're looking into it," Kelly answered. She had her hand on the back of Tash's seat. "And I'm texting Victor at the number you gave me. Nothing from Abby, but she says they're doing what they can between stops."

"Stops for what?" Iseult said over her shoulder.

"BIKER!" Nick called.

Iseult hit the brakes, watched a motorcycle blur through the opening she'd created in traffic, and instantly got back up to speed to swing into the space that had opened. The truck behind her blared its horn, but could do nothing.

No one wasted a breath.

"I've been trying to get a hold of Chad and even Theo," Nick said. "Are you sure you gave us the right numbers?"

"Hard to say," Tash said. "They were right at the time, but they might have had to change the numbers or the phones. Victor messaged me this morning; looks like they're too tied up for a visit to the Space Needle."

At the front of the building, the traffic had been forced to one side as emergency vehicles made their way through. Fire trucks and ambulances made up most of the response. Some police dotted an arc in front of Spindle, but people were less accommodating to the officers as they were to the actual emergency responders. Some people had started looting, attacking cars in the traffic jam, and attacking the police.

There was so much chaos surrounding the entire incident that Ghost had had little difficulty inserting herself and her agents in the ambulance fleet, using some of her Engen resources. She leapt out of her vehicle and led efforts to designate an area for triage. Two fire trucks, in coordination with emergency medical personnel, were lined up side-on to the building as they fought the blaze. A third blocked off most of the street on one side, and their firefighters were helping the paramedics with the triage. Another space was being cleared for gargantuan yellow inflatable objects which, so far, were formless.

As she went, Ghost was maintaining communication with Switch whenever she could.

Behind the building, authorities were having a harder time locking things down. More of the police had gotten to the scene, but they were unprepared for what awaited them. They thought they'd be receiving people who welcomed them, relieved to be safe from some bomber, shooter, or other terrorist.

They were utterly overwhelmed as well over eighty people, mostly dressed as custodians or office workers, stampeded them. Many just wanted to get past and keep running. Some tackled, bit, or threw officers. Some even wrestled away guns.

It went downhill from there.

Tash parked the car at an empty café across the street and turned to the teens. "You're all staying here." She raised a hand for silence as all three protested. "Going to an apartment for a suspect is one thing. Marching you all in that is something else," she added as she tilted her head in Spindle's direction. "I think you all know a riot like this doesn't just happen. The best way to get to the bottom of this is to go into the belly of the whale, if you know what I mean."

"Going alone is suicide!" Nick said. Kelly nodded with this.

Iseult stared at her hands on the steering wheel.

"One person might manage, but we'd never be able to stay together as a group. Now, no argument. You're all staying here. Look after each other, try to keep up on everything that's happening. Call or text if there's anything I should know. I'm only looking for info, so I'll be as safe as possible. I won't leave any of you alone." She placed a warm hand over one of Iseult's, pressing it tight to the steering wheel, as she said that.

Then she was running.

The three looked amongst each other in the car as the door slammed to.

Tash slunk along the side of the next building and witnessed as the situation become an atrocity, but did her best not to get too many details. Thankfully, such buildings rarely had children around. She stepped over a rail and lowered herself down the concrete wall beneath it, letting go so that she landed on more concrete. She was at a rear corner of the Spindle offices.

Losing no time, she grabbed a fire exit door as more mob spilled out. None of them looked, turned, or stopped to find out how the door was staying open. Many were weeping or crying. Some, incredibly, were laughing. They scattered as the first gunshot rang out.

Tash heard begging, screaming, angry shouting, and a megaphone that got cut off mid-sentence. Once she was inside, she only heard the odd metallic pop from outside. Now: to find Braulio and whoever else was behind this.

Not even Simon Siaz had been able to dig up any intel on these spies or operatives or whatever they were. Terrorists? Had they engineered this tragedy?

Tash would have answers. It couldn't be coincidence that Siaz's network had also traced suspicious activity in Hydropolis Industries to this building. Or that his agents have been turning up dead or going to ground in the last few days.

What she hadn't considered was her own network.

"But Tash said…" Iseult began, leaping out of the car to chase the couple.

"Those were gunshots!" Nick said, as though that explained everything.

"We can't stop a mob fighting cops…" Kelly thought aloud. "…but we might use the distraction."

"We could be a liability!" Iseult objected.

They hadn't followed Tash's path; the police were locking down the road in that direction. There was already smoke rising from what looked like some kind of tunnel on the other end of the building from them. Multiple vehicles, out on the road ahead of the carnage, were struggling in multiple directions. Police, rioters, reporters, and other people too hectic to identify were all clustered in patches.

"It's underground parking!" Nick said, pointing at the tower of smoke.

Iseult dearly missed her knife. Metallic flashes sparked and flared all over. Some were cameras or glints of sunlight. Some were gunshots. She even saw a swinging aluminum baseball bat.

I'm a doctor, not a cop.

"I'm not leaving Tash alone in that!" Nick barrelled forward.

"Izzy?" Kelly asked, struggling to hold Nick back and help Iseult keep up. "Do you feel that...uh...ickiness?"

She blinked. It hadn't occurred to her to look. Er, feel? As she jogged in their direction, she allowed herself enough distraction. "...yes! That cop we ran by, on the ground!"

"...guys?"

Her feet decelerated one pounding step at a time as she threw her gaze around. "Nick? Kelly?"

A terrified swarm came for her and she leaped over the trunk of a car just as they thundered by, more police cruisers spreading in to meet them. Out of the corner of her eye, Iseult spotted a S.W.A.T. vans.

She got turned about several more times and looked up as a high window splashed open, an office worker performing a concrete dive. A voice forced her to realign her sight:

"You there! Freeze!"

She ran into a pair of large, muscular cops. With no time to think, she put her hands on the bare skin of an arm of each of them as they were grabbing her.

"On your kn-" one started.

"Stay ca-" the other began.

Their eyes widened and rolled backward as they slumped to the ground.

"Please…" was all she could manage to ask of them as she pushed on. Hopefully, she'd only knocked them out. It was like a sleeper hold, but done with the blood flow alone.

Iseult ducked under a concrete wall, waist-high, that ran down into the ramp to the underground parking. Someone on the grass ahead was shouting, and she was scared.

"Freedom! That's enough!"

"Dammit, Jake, let go! HEY! OFFICER!"

Crap.

"OVER HERE!"

She climbed over one of the vehicles blocking the access ramp. There weren't many people here now, though she didn't dare think about what might happen if more people decided to flee from the building this way.

"The cops are in on it! Don't you see?"

"Shut UP, Jake!" Iseult couldn't tell if it was the man or the woman who was more hysterical.

"FREEZE!"

"RUN!"

"WAIT!"

Iseult had been continuing farther into the parking area and had a terrible feeling about that conversation.

Which was confirmed with a pistol burst.

She dashed into the most obscure section of the basement parking garage that she could see.

"Did you see where Izzy went!?" Kelly demanded as they neared a section of the building. Vehicle traffic had made the trek to the main exit door harrowing. Human traffic, billowing out of the door like smoke, was worse still: rioters, innocent bystanders who'd been outside beforehand, and cops with batons. The smaller fire exit at the opposite corner, which Tash had used, might as well have been on the moon from here. People were peppered among the grass and concrete where she was, and she tried not to see them as she collected a maintenance ladder left beneath a broken second-floor window.

Nick was fighting off the few remaining people who were nearby. Whereas Tash fought with muscle memory, his efforts were almost entirely reflex. He glanced over at the first opportunity. "What!? When did we get separated!?"

She started hefting up the ladder. "How could you not notice?"

"C'mon! No one can see *everything*!"

"HEY! You there!"

They both glanced over in time to see that some of the mob in their area had been contained, and one of the police had noticed them.

They rushed up the ladder.

"STOP! FREEZE!"

They were inside.

Inside the Spindle Building

Switch marched up to the security gate. While the foyer was in disarray after the blast, Spindle's personnel were collecting themselves and setting things to order. Several employees were in tears, gibbering at their phones. Switch was largely ignored until she reached a burly young man with olive skin and short, curly black hair. His name tag read Eryx. Though average in height, this only accentuated his weight. She guessed it at around 175lbs, definitely no more than 185, and he was musclebound.

He was also pale, trembling, and practically pupating in a cocoon of sweat.

"You will see me inside," she said without hesitation.

Eryx's lips quaked between terror and humour. "I... excuse...sorry?"

"I am CFO Husan-Tainai," she explained with measured patience. While it was natural for people to be unsettled, shocked, or even horrified by a sudden explosion, what she saw in the staff here was something else.

While Eryx stared at her, temporarily vapid, she put a hand to her ear and said something in Cantonese. Then she snapped at him, "I will proceed through the stairs. Escorted. Where's the manager on duty?"

Stammering and hammering the keyboard, Eryx struggled to hold himself together. "Apologies, ma'am, we're having communication problems. I didn't see a name like yours in today's briefings or lists. I think this was planned."

Switch frowned. It certainly was not. But she could make use of that assumption.

"Eric!" one of the other staff called out. Switch, ever the stiff-spined professional, turned to glare at the other man. But she said nothing. "Liam's on the seventh floor! He's managing to pull some people together, but it looks like a riot!"

A riot? In an office building?

Switch swept forward, glanced at Eryx, and tilted her head at the door he'd have to buzz her through. He buzzed, and as she opened it, she said: "Everyone out. This is over all your heads. The authorities are here." She looked at the Greek and softened her tone. "Look for a paramedic who looks just like me," she began once everyone else was out of earshot. "We're sisters. Don't ask. Tell her I sent you, and that you're influenced."

"In...influenced?"

"Just go. She'll help you."

And he went. What else could he do? He'd been bored but anxious, and couldn't place his anxiety, until suddenly everything was brimstone and screams. Nothing made sense. He had to hide, but couldn't sit still. The paramedic.

Eryx was the final staff to step outside of the building, and his last vestige of self-control crashed into the roof of a car off to his left. He wet himself, lost track of whatever his mouth was doing, and soon found himself clambering along the side of an ambulance, muttering, "I can't believe it! I can't...this isn't..."

"You!"

It was the CFO, except dressed as a paramedic.

"It was Aim!" he babbled. "Payroll! Out the window, landed on a car! Why isn't there more fire?"

Ghost was about to have him carried off when he said, "I'm influenced!"

"What's that?" she said.

"Your sister...I'm...oh, gods…"

She waved over a police officer. He had a full head of thick, light brown hair and golden earrings. The unusual look didn't register. In his head, he was fixated on the payroll officer. Aim was bland, hard to know, a little boring. But to see him crash into the roof of a car like that? "Influenced…" he muttered as the cop guided him into the squad car and closed the door. He blinked. "Wait! Sister. Liam?"

He wasn't sure if his words were trying to make sense of his brain or if it was the other way around. Then there was a distinct metallic point in his side. "You're not…" he whispered to the growing dark.

As Switch was first encountering Eryx, Tash was bursting out of a stairwell. She didn't know if the elevators worked and dared not try them. Already a thick sheen of sweat unfurled over her; she had nothing to go on but a floor-by-floor. And there were many floors. "What have we got?" she said into her phone as she sped down a hallway, opening a door and glancing around before moving on to the next.

"They're setting up inflatable escape slides by breaking through the windows of the second floor. More people are getting out, but most are frenzied or panicked. Emergency services can't secure the perimeter, so we've got people from the surrounding buildings and neighbourhoods trying to help or take advantage of the situation. Military is on the way and treating this as a terrorist attack. Still no word from my contacts inside. My team assumes they've been eliminated," Siaz answered. "And we've just started picking up on multiple intrusions in the computer systems, at least the ones we can access remotely. I've never seen anything like it."

"Nothing on the woman at Braulio's apartment?" Tash said as she opened an office and found two adults. They were...enjoying each other. On the desk. She quietly closed the door behind her as she turned away. A riot in an office building wasn't her idea of romance, but to each their own.

"The postal service verified that it was a false vehicle. Whoever's behind it has impressive resources. Nothing on your P-O-I. Is that...?" Siaz marvelled at what he was hearing. And seeing. And learning. This whole situation showed both incredible precision and professionalism as well as a bizarre absence of intention. What was going on?

"Yeah, nothing makes sense here," Tash said as she went on her way. She knocked out someone who was trying to start a fire using supplies ripped from a maintenance closet. "I think it's all fear, but it's like everyone's taking that fear differently. I've studied mob behaviours and histories of social collapse, and I've never seen this before."

"Shit," Siaz said suddenly. "Reconnect later," and the line went dead.

Tash had enough time to blink and put her phone away before she began inching her way around a corner to a massive length of cubicles lined on one end with windows. There'd been all manner of noise the whole time, but she tuned it out as best she could; the building's acoustics made it hard to make sense of volume and direction anyway.

But this…

At least four different windows were taking beatings from separate people who were trying everything: fists, feet, chairs, sliding desks or tables, throwing printers, smashing a person's face on the glass. A fire extinguisher went flying. One person succeeded in breaking a hole through the glass and immediately ripped at the freed pane, tearing themselves to shreds, before making enough space to get through.

It was much too high for hope of survival.

People were beating up cubicles, trying to get into the panels of the ceiling, fighting each other, screaming, shouting, tearing clothes off themselves or each other, laughing, weeping, struggling to hide, and running all over the place. Tash could go back or head for the sign of another stairwell on the other side of the wraparound wall.

She did her best to go unseen, dodging garbage pails and navigating misshapen cubicles as well as furniture in every kind of disarray. She rounded a barrier and encountered a scene:

Splayed on the floor was a tall, remarkably well-built woman — a wrestler, maybe? — with distinctly platinum blonde hair. It was messed up, but not as much as some of the men and women groaning or unconscious nearby. She had a black eye, blood dribbling down her chin, and the wreckage of clothing that comes from hand-to-hand in office attire. Looming over her was a white man, just out of middle age, wielding a broken length of pipe.

He raged something incoherent about "rights" as he set himself to jam it into the woman.

From the side, around another barrier, a smaller woman emerged. Her hair was a panoply of colours and she sported numerous rug burns and a nasty red-purple splotch on her cheek. "Steel!" she shouted as she pounced the man, armed with — was it?

Yes: a letter opener.

Tash had some footwork to her name, but she couldn't get to the pair before the smaller woman...finished.

"Ciel," the tall blonde croaked. "It's...well, it's not okay. But I'll manage. We need to…"

"Ciel," Tash repeated. That got the woman's attention; she'd been knelt over her handiwork. Weeping. "Take your friend. Go down the hall," Tash turned to point behind her, "I just came from there. It's safe enough. There are escape slides below."

Ciel spent the way to the slide in a daze. "I had to…" she kept muttering.

"I know, sweetie, I know, it's okay, you did good," and it got to a point that Betelgeuse — known in the office as Steel — was no longer paying attention to her mouth. Was she trying to comfort herself?

When the pair reached the ground outside, all they saw was pandemonium. It wasn't much of an improvement from what was transpiring inside. Someone got pushed into a police car. Didn't police have to keep their hair shorter than that? And who wears earrings like that?

Lights everywhere. People in uniforms, professional attire, armour.

Military armour.

Iseult was alone, armoured by an enclosed metal space, listening to the alternation of havoc and silence as she ascended to the top floor. In the back of her mind, the mundane ding! gave her a modicum of comfort. It was short-lived. As she stepped into another cubicle space, floor-to-ceiling windows lining the other side of the area, she noticed a military helicopter with a spotlight just as it was ending its trek at one end of the windows and rounding the building.

Silence.

The building was tall enough that little of the pandemonium below reached her. There was some flashing of emergency lights that had made its way to the ceiling where it joined the windows. She tried her phone as she explored the area. Tash got her a busy signal. There were spilled coffee cups, dropped briefcases, splotches of blood, overturned chairs, scattered papers, and endless disarray.

There was nothing discrete in the silence. Even when she found a server room near the end of her tour of the floor, they had laptops, exposed cables, and various bits of inserted hardware like thumb drives and even what looked like external hard drives attached with cables. Unless they were caught by the frenzy in the middle of maintenance, she suspected tampering. But she didn't have the time to discern anything for certain, even if she'd had the know-how.

A group bustled out of another elevator just as she was nearing the stairwell at the end of her exploration. She slipped in and tried to catch sight of them through the narrow window in the stairwell door. All she could make out were suits and muffled voices. Definitely not Tash, Kelly, or Nick. She wasn't interested in accosting that Braulio guy. Not by herself.

Her hands fluttered over her as she descended to the penultimate floor. A casual observer might have thought she was adjusting her clothes, but she was touching different places where she'd cut herself. Taking a dark comfort in that, she slowly inched her way through the door as she watched for unwelcome company.

"AH!" she cried out when a gunshot took the quiet.

"GO BACK WHERE Y'ALL CAME FROM!"

More shots. There was also cracking, shattering, pinging, and splintering — depending upon where the missed shots landed.

Other sounds told her some of the shots hit the mark.

"...the hell, Bevis!?"

"Run for it!"

"Are you okay!?"

"That bastard...!"

"Mashaka! NO!"

Iseult ducked into an empty office with an open door. Footfalls, weeping, shouts, thuds, and bangs resounded.

Hands shaking, she checked her phone. Missed calls from Nick and Kelly. From a few minutes ago. Must have needed a second to get to her because of the elevator. She texted:

Shooter Floor 49. ppl gone to roof, idk why. You find mom?

Send.

Another shot, and then a special kind of silence. It shattered the noise like a fault line in a glacier, and it had the distinct tang of distress. There was a series of metallic bumping thumps, muted by impact with carpet. She guessed it was a tossed gun, probably empty.

She peeked out of one side of the door, ducked back in, slipped to the other side of the opening, and peeked out again. The only sign of people was a brown foot on the floor, partially dislodged from a high heel shoe. The leg led out of view, and didn't move. Ever so carefully, Iseult made her crouching way to that wall. She put her back to it and sat, struggling to keep her breath quiet. She was close enough to sense the other woman's heartbeat.

There was none.

Fear leaked from her eyes, but she kept her lungs and throat under control.

"Go on! GIT! Yer white, yer not the problem!"

Three terrified pairs of feet scrambled through the door, now down a hallway from her, that led to the stairwell she'd left behind. Closing her eyes, she crawled past the turnoff. She didn't want to look at the person sprawled on the floor. Didn't need the end of that story. Spanning her hands on the floor, she stayed on her knees. Only one set of footfalls now. At least, that she could feel. Heavy breathing, but she couldn't be sure where it was coming from. It sounded far away, but how many walls would it take to muffle it like that?

She made her way to the next turn.

"Bastard," came a voice.

The hallway had an intersection not far ahead and a counter to Iseult's left. She made her way to it and heard a man's voice — the shooter's voice — from the other end of the counter after the turn.

"Proud of yerself now, 'shaka? Shouldn't've sided with that Mexican."

"Braulio's American, douchebag."

He actually laughed.

He laughed!

Iseult, too shocked to make sense of all this but too afraid to do nothing, used the cover of his laughter to push through the swinging half-door of the counter and cross diagonally. The other half-door was already wide. A line of blood led from it to a door three feet ahead of it, to Iseult's left.

She didn't want to know.

She peered from the edge of the counter. Ahead was a small sitting area worked into the hallway. Lying with her back to the wall and a blood-smeared hand over her abdomen was a lanky woman with rich brown skin. One leg was bent and the other straight. This was what Iseult could make out between the legs of a blond white man.

He was standing over who Iseult thought might be the Mashaka someone called out to earlier. Neither of them had noticed Iseult yet. The man was rotund, and even from here she could tell that the dark woman was taller than him. He was holding a pistol and had magazines tucked into his pants, over the rump. He was wearing a red baseball cap.

"Any last words?" he drawled.

Iseult dashed at him.

He only had the time to look at her and open his mouth, his gun hand mid-swing, before she planted her hand on his neck.

Mashaka watched in growing disbelief as a short,

white, teenaged girl ran out from behind the counter. The young woman's pale blue eyes were focused upon Mashaka as her hand landed on Bevis' neck and the big man slumped to the floor.

Time slivered long enough for the two to take stock of each other, then snicked back into place as Iseult rushed to Mashaka's side. "Damn, girl," the lanky one said. "You got some hocus in your pocus!"

"You're...uh...probably just delirious. From the bullet," Iseult said as she examined Mashaka.

"Us ladies gotta stick together," Mashaka replied. "Don't gaslight me."

Iseult, taken aback, focused on the wound. "Move your hands," she said. As the lanky woman obliged, the young woman pressed both hands on the injury and leaned hard. It was less about her pressure, though, than making it look normal while she controlled several clusters of blood vessels.

Iseult adjusted herself a few times, wiping blood off on her clothes. This was like the hospital in Alaska all over again, but worse: at least the people escaping the hospital hadn't mobbed the ones trying to help them outside. Iseult gave the rest of Mashaka's body a cursory examination, but as far as she could feel, there was only one bullet wound. No broken bones, bruises, etc. She kept looking about and furrowing her brow.

"Even if I knew where the nearest First Aid room is," Mashaka remarked, "I don't think they keep forceps in there." She blinked. "That...feels better. Cold, but better."

Iseult's mind raced. "I can't get the bullet out. And even if I could..."

"Look, I really appreciate it. I'm grateful. But you gotta go." Mashaka punctuated her words with a downward shift of the chin.

"I can't just…"

"I wanna fight everything right now," Mashaka said. "The walls. The patriarchy. Bevis. Kim in HR. Weight gain."

Iseult looked the slender woman up and down.

Mashaka laughed, coughed, winced. "Get me to the elevator and stop tryin' to be White Jesus."

That was complicated. "Um, I'm not a guy…" But she did her best to help.

"You're not from around here…" Mashaka remarked. She didn't really know how to take this one. Who shows up at an office building during a riot? Was she here already?

"Yeah, there's a whole lot more going on…" Iseult wondered where to start. And where to stop. "There's military now. When did you start feeling the fight response?" *And why are you so lucid right now? Is it the wound?*

Mashaka blinked as Iseult leaned her against the counter and went back, examining Bevis and making an odd expression when she pressed two fingers on his neck. She collected his gun and carried it the way a princess might carry a bucket of slop. Mashaka tried not to think about the bullet, or the fact that more warmth flooded her hands the farther Iseult got from her. It came nearly to a stop when Iseult returned to her.

It was like her own brain and body were in a political debate with her. Maybe it was the blood loss, but Mashaka was struggling to keep her thoughts together. "I'm even fighting myself right now," she started. "Hard to…" she took a few breaths. As they turned to the stretch of hallway leading to the elevator, she saw a wall-mounted clock. Her brain slogged through mental bog water as she pieced a timeline together.

"Can you ball-park it?" Iseult grunted under the effort of helping the taller woman. How long had they been stumbling along?

"Last I can remember the time was hours ago," Mashaka said. "But was that when it started, or am I losing time?"

They were in the elevator. Did she black out?

"You're okay, I got you." Iseult was putting confidence out there as best she could, but it was like using a fire alarm as a light source: too much tension, too much noise, too much context.

Ding!

"I'm a programmer," Mashaka said as they made their careful way out of the elevator. It wasn't quite level with the floor they were on. "All systems were Go until I felt a rumble downstairs. It was small, but only because it was far away, you know? Why was the elevator messed up?"

"Don't know," Iseult answered. She noticed that, at the other end of the hall, some kind of surveillance room had its door swung wide. So many screens… "Was it like the flip of a light switch? When you all went…er, had…I mean…"

Mashaka stopped. Neither of them were really registering all of the thuds, tearing sounds, tumbling, snarling, and so on. What stopped her was her answer: "No. It's been…a month? Anxiety. Weird obsessions. Stress. It was like...emotional termites. This..." she rolled a hand and waved it at her surroundings. "...like the wood collapsing."

Mashaka set herself down without consulting Iseult. That forced the young woman to take stock. It was a mob. No obvious flight of stairs to get them out. No. Wait.

The mob was attacking an Asian woman! Her long, black, silken hair was in a ponytail, obviously thrown together after her previous style was dishevelled. She wore a grey dress suit, now ruined by her combat. But it wasn't Kung Fu or something. This was different. Tactical? Iseult only knew a bit about fighting, because of the injuries it caused.

"HEY!" she cried out as she marched forward. What was she doing?

The Asian glanced over, but no one else noticed.

Iseult pulled out the pistol she'd taken from Bevis and looked at it. She made sure the safety was on. She'd never fired a gun before, but she'd looked up how to remove magazines and turn off full-auto and stuff like that. In her other hand, she had her phone. Her mind raced for who to call. 911? "LEAVE HER ALONE!"

The woman in the grey dress suit was handling herself quite well, but there were so many...

Iseult aimed the gun at the floor, not far from the crowd, and pulled the trigger. With the safety on, it should cli-

BANG!

One of the mob fell in the direction of a leg that had suddenly splotched red. Iseult dropped her phone. Mashaka called out, but it was unintelligible. A flurry of silky black hair and grey fabric caused three people to pile over the person who'd fallen from the gunshot.

Someone dove at Iseult from behind a nearby desk. Her attention was on the gun. She shrieked — at least, remembering it a second later, she thought she'd shrieked — and a heartbeat flashed in her mind's eye as she put one hand on the side of the head of the person reaching for her.

It was a white man, frail. But not as old as he should have been to be so frail. He'd been bleeding, she sensed, so she'd just pushed things more in that direction and turned his head with her hand as he was lunging.

Switch watched in astonishment as a teenaged girl caused a meek man to suddenly and uncontrollably gush blood from his nose. She'd been planning to leave the girl and the brown woman, but this was too good an opportunity. As the Knife dove over the gap she'd created in the crowd, she saw the glint of a phone on the floor, but by now it was too far away. She didn't have the time.

A shame, really.

Switch disarmed the girl so smoothly that Iseult didn't even appear to notice that her hands were empty. She was flimsy and gelatinous with shock. The Knife collected Mashaka as she went and threw the taller woman over her shoulder. "If you can help her, do so," Switch said to Iseult as they artlessly barrelled through the halls to another elevator.

Iseult was so at a loss that she obeyed. What else could she do?

As they stepped onto the second floor, Switch spoke into her earpiece. Japanese? Iseult knew there was a difference, obviously, but didn't know Asian languages.

Iseult was on the slide, with Mashaka falling into unconsciousness, before she realized that she didn't have her phone. When she landed, she was dumbfounded to see the same woman from the building! But this one was in a paramedic's outfit. What was happening?

"She's been sh-" Iseult started, but the woman rushed her to a nearby ambulance as its doors swung open. Her side made a metallic eek that she recognized as a needle prick just as it registered that the ambulance had more straps and fewer medical supplies than it should.

"Wait. What...ish...heah…" She tried to reach out to their heartbeats, but got swallowed as the world became a soft, colourless, timeless gel.

CHAPTER 16
DANGEROUS OPPORTUNITIES

Inside the Spindle Building

Also without a sense of time, Thatcher had come out of a full-on panic attack to find himself in the staff kitchen. He was drenched, hopefully only in sweat or tears. He looked up at the face of a white man slowly coming into focus.

"Braulio! Thank Avandra, I thought we weren't gonna make it!"

He blinked many times. "Avandra...?"

"C'mon, get up, we're still pretty deep in the dungeon." With that, the scrawny accountant struggled to pull Thatcher to his feet.

Despite having made so much progress with his weight loss, however, he was still over 200lbs and dazed. He didn't get up until he'd managed it under his own power. "What happened?"

"There was an explosion. We're still at work. Everyone started talking, then there was stuff on the screens and intercoms, and then there was just...a building scream. I heard it. Coming up from lower floors like, I don't know, an Aboleth or something. I'm just talking D&D because I don't know where to start," Stewart finished babbling. As if that were the hard part here.

Thatcher's insides roiled with caustic despair and a fear that shimmered like desert light. His teeth jittered. "I can't do this."

"Yeah you can. I'm gonna need fresh undies after this, but right now we need to not have more of a meltdown."

"You're hurt!" Thatcher registered as he stood and collected himself. He'd been under a table next to an industrial stove.

Stewart waved it off. "Cuts, scrapes, some pretty serious rug burn. Had a bleeding nose for a while. I think I ran willy-nilly in blind panic, but I don't know why. That screaming, it was the rioting, like everyone in all the offices and halls just started losing it..." The accountant shuddered. "Some people are more organized than others, but everybody's super messed up. I saw Liam while I was looking for you. He looked like he was doing some good leading for a bit. A bunch of people were throwing up. It's like everyone was a different kind of crazy, but all the crazy was moving in the same direction. I saw your used lunch containers all cluttered in front of an elevator door, once I could think straight." He pointed behind him, and Thatcher knew he meant the elevator in the corridor not far from this area. "When I found you, not long before you came to, you were mumbling. Something about Humdroid and a bus trail?"

Thatcher ran through diagnostics, physical and emotional, as he tried to make some sense out of what the world had become. He felt a pang of guilt that Stewart would have been so troubled on his account.

"I'm sorry I couldn't do more," Stewart said, in an echo of the guilt. "But it was all I could do to not run around screaming."

"We need to figure out what's going on," Thatcher said. "And don't worry about it." Then he felt guilty about treating Stewart's rambling as an afterthought.

In the back of his mind, he was recalling some long drives with Soto. Some of their conversations. Talk about "gifts." Soto's crazy theories about Thatcher's part in what happened in Towerton. The moving around he did for most of his youth, almost always in three months. Sometimes pushing four. This health craze that had sprung up just as he was really taking his weight more seriously. Suspicion was a spider walking his spine on pinprick feet.

They made their way through the breakroom, which was a maelstrom. A flat screen TV, tilted on a damaged wall, played emergency broadcasts about the Spindle building. Cracks slipped the length of the screen and there was some scratchiness and snowy portions, but he made out the outside of the building as armoured personnel carriers arrived. There was a messy blockade, thick with ambulances and surprisingly few police.

Scrawling the bottom was a newsfeed about a crippled law enforcement response. The words TERRORIST ATTACK? splashed the headline section.

Thatcher took a deep breath and, with Herculean effort, locked his emotions in a mental cubicle. "We have to get to the security stations and server rooms. As many of them as we can."

Stewart was stupefied. "...why? Can't we figure out

what happened from outside, after everything's settled?"

Thatcher was already on the move, however, so the accountant had to keep up. Because Thatcher had been working tech support and then cybersecurity — along with sneaking in a few things he really shouldn't have been doing — he had a robust head map for the major data access points in the building. Stewart, as the company's unofficial social barometer, knew the flow of people. Where they'd be, where they'd run or hide, the worst and best places to aim for or avoid.

Thatcher knew nothing of the Knives of Engen and had no idea one of them was scouring the building for him. Ignorance was not safety, however; they heard acts of violence, snuck past mobs, avoided areas where they heard voices and saw arcs of lightning. They could have sworn they'd heard someone call out, "Babe! You all right?" right before a flash, a waft of ozone, and a blackout in their section of the building.

Some of the security terminals they found had been infected, shut down, or otherwise compromised. Stewart stood watch while Thatcher repaired or salvaged what he could. They did the same at server rooms and other data access points.

"Are...are you duelling a hacker?" Stewart asked at one point.

Thatcher actually stopped, stared into the middle distance in a flash of realization, and looked at his friend with a flat expression of wonder. "I..."

He didn't have the time to explain that most hacking took long periods of development. Data exchanges representing thousands of hours of reading could flash by in a microsecond; you couldn't manipulate such sophisticated systems at typing speed.

"...yes. Yes, that's exactly what I'm doing." He marvelled at the computer in front of him, took the thumb drive from it, popped in a disc which he refused to explain to Stewart, and they moved on.

Tash was growing frantic for explanations. She didn't know if she was catching whatever was powering the riot — could it be caught? — or if it was traditional terror. "What do you mean, you can't connect with them?"

"The kids have been sending out occasional messages, but there are big gaps. Their phones were reaching out for you or each other a couple of times — both texts and calls — but with everything that's going on..."

Tash's imagination was racing. "If their phones are on, can't you still pinpoint them?"

"To a floor? Maybe, if I'd been prepared for that. There are things you have to set up. The military is trying to create a lockdown where the police couldn't. Lots of questions about la-"

"I don't care about any of that right now, friend." Tash uttered acidly. "Find. My. Children."

"I'm sorry, but they've called off the news chopper. I have a contact in one of the military choppers, but that's not helping for anything inside. None of my people from inside are available. Your best bet is to go for the two hackers and-"

Gunshots. A man whose accent was mostly clear and standard English spoke with noticeable twangs of Texan vowels: "We wouldn't be in this mess if it weren't for you...imm'grants!"

Tash ran for an elevator and pressed rapidly for a few floors down.

"Are you INSANE!?"

"Bevis! This isn't-"

"Shut UP!"

Bang!

The doors slid shut.

She lost her connection with Siaz. Waiting as the numbers blipped downward, typing texts and trying calls, was maddening. As soon as she stepped out of the elevator, she heard the doors partly close and stop. Turning, her phone to her ear again, she saw that the elevator had been shut down. Patches of some of the cubicle sections also went dark. Various lights and the elevator blinked and shuddered.

"Tash?" Simon said as soon as she got a connection.

"What's this about hackers?"

"As far as we can make out, there's two of 'em. On different floors. One is trying to restart or protect the system, while the other is shutting stuff down. Elevators, cameras. Both sides are doing something with data, but it's hard t-...crap." Siaz huffed and slowly exhaled. Tash could picture him sitting back, wherever he was.

"What? What's wrong?"

"One of them locked out remote access. Pretty sure they only blocked out Internet connectivity, and the Intranet is still up. But they could've shut it all down, isolated it all to individual computers. There's not much more we can tell you. They must be using a bunch of hardware they can connect with the computers, servers, and terminals. Thumb drives with a trojan horse program, that sort of thing. You can't attack a system or have a keyboard war with someone else the way they show it in the movies. These two are using pre-built software, as well as leveraging or re-tooling whatever they have access to. They're quite resourceful. One of them is faster than the other and appears to know exactly what they're looking for. The other knows most, if not all, of the access areas in the building. But…"

"…but they're defending? They can only be so many places at once?"

"Not necessarily," Siaz's tone was contemplative. "For all we know, they're competing for exploitation of Spindle. Or they're on the same team but trying to prove who's best."

"A pissing contest? NOW?" Tash had seen some characters in her day, but this?

"Absolutely. Never underestimate the nerds, Tash." She could hear the smirk.

"Anything else?" she asked, grinding her teeth against his humour.

"The thorough one is on Floor 17. Speedy Gonzales was last on Floor 26. I'll call you if I find anything on the kids. Good luck."

He hung up.

Kelly checked her phone. Missed calls from an unknown number. No answers from Iseult. Missed call from Tash. When had that happened? She knelt near Nick, each at a different desk. They heard megaphones, helicopters, sirens, the jeers and cries of a mob, the hollow whumps of control. They crawled together and got to a corner so that they could peek through a window. They looked at each other in alarm. It was a madhouse down there! But more than that…

"That's Izzy!" Nick said. They were on the fifth floor, so it took some awkward angling to get a good look at the second-floor escape slides.

"Where?" Kelly demanded.

"She just got pushed into an ambulance by a paramedic," he said.

Kelly sat with her back to the wall, the windows on her right and Nick in front of her. She hugged her knees. "What were we thinking?"

"Knowing Iseult, she's probably saved some lives already," Nick quipped. "Besides: were we supposed to just sit in the car?"

"YES!"

"I mean," and he kissed her hand in mock high dignity, "that we can't leave Tash in this."

Her top lip was more folded than her bottom one. "I couldn't even handle Gavin…"

He hauled her to her feet and dipped a kiss. "There might not be a Gavin here. Just a really tall shed with a lot more lights."

Kelly slid her hand over his face. "You've always been our fighter."

He took her hand and led her through the maze of cubicles. "Once you get past the fact that you're gonna get punched in the face, you learn how your fists work."

Her foot bumped a discarded fire extinguisher as they went, and it sparked away. "AH!" Nick half-shouted, half-squeaked.

Kelly grinned weakly and resisted the urge to make

fun of him. "Sorry," she said. She really hadn't meant to shock it.

"Don't b-"

"What is it?"

"Look! It started at two!"

The floor indicator for the elevator was rapidly climbing the numerals. Between 37 and 38, the lights stopped glowing. They looked at each other. "I knew we shouldn't trust the elevators," Kelly remarked.

"We'll never get up that many stairs, though..." Nick mused.

"There was another one at the other end of this level," Kelly said, taking the lead and pulling him along. "We'll have to try our luck."

It took four tries. Every time they found an elevator, something went wrong. It wasn't working to begin with; it moved a few floors and stuttered upward until they managed to get out; it ran out of floors on its side and they had to find another one; three or four people had ordered the elevator, were beating on the doors, and Nick had to fight through them.

After that one, the pair pushed forward but had caused enough of a ruckus that more people came as though summoned. They ran, throwing chairs and the like behind them, and found themselves in a pincer attack from two groups of the rioters. Kelly ran to a wall with an exposed power box that still sparked.

"Someone sabotaged...!"

"What are you doing!?" Nick demanded. He was a clever and quick fighter because his eyes and visual cortex took in superhuman amounts of information. With the benefit of adrenaline, he was weaving in and out of the crowd and managing to use their own bodies or surrounding furniture to great advantage.

But they were cornered.

"Just...a little...more...!" Nick heard from behind him. He turned in time to see that Kelly had hauled a power cable, already dislodged by the saboteur, partly out of the wall. She gripped it by the exposed wire and let its power lance out from her other hand.

Nick hit the ground, hands behind his head, and surrendered to hope.

Kelly strove to control the electricity. It was like driving a car with magnetic wheels in a metal hallway. Sometimes she could feel what would happen next, like inertia or some other shift. But all she could accomplish was to briefly withhold the force of lightning and let it loose somewhere else.

Small fires kicked up from stretches of carpet or the fabric used in the cubicle dividers. Several rioters were launched backward, and Kelly hoped against hope that they'd gotten more bark than bite from it. A whole cubicle panel went flying into part of the crowd. A desk somersaulted sidelong when an arc of her electricity landed at its side.

"Babe! You all right!?" Nick called out as a reek of ozone arose. Lights vanished faster than any end a knife could bring.

Before the crowd could recover, Kelly helped him up and they bolted for a stairwell nearby. "You'll have to do all the phoning now," she said as they went. He looked at her and opened his mouth, but she cut him off: "I zapped mine." It registered that she was bedraggled.

They were through the door as Nick tried again for the hospital, Iseult, and Tash — in that order. Kelly kept her eyes on the…

…stairs were all Thatcher could see. All of his thoughts and feelings were geared toward survival. Must survive. Stewart, next to him, was also ascending. What he was thinking was anyone's guess. The man was such a straight-shooter, and Thatcher had just shown him a plethora of computer felonies.

"Braulio! Down!" Stewart gasped just as Thatcher registered that they weren't alone in the stairwell. A flood of humanity was pouring down upon them.

They whirled about and made it back to the next landing down. Thatcher had been so headlong that he slammed into the wall across from the stairs. He was rattled, but mostly unhurt. Before he knew what was happening, Stewart pushed him through the door out of the stairwell and then pulled it shut. Thatcher heard keys he just now realized had been bouncing at Stewart's hip the whole time. Then he heard a subtle, quiet, horrifying click. "BRAULIO! R-" were the accountant's last words.

Bodies piled onto Stewart. Most of the sounds were muted by the door and the sheer press of people. Through a fraction of the narrow window in the door, Thatcher could see that people were pushing by the pile of humanity and continuing down the stairwell. Eventually the pile thinned and continued down the stairs. None of them seemed curious about the door.

Stewart had gone silent long before the deluge of hands, feet, and panic came to an end.

Thatcher tried to open it, but the door was locked. He stood there, staring at the door's narrow window.

It all came together then.

Not just the loss of his friend. He'd seen every idea of home die in front of his eyes, time and again, since he'd been put into foster care when he was six. He remembered the stampedes at playgrounds. Neighbourhoods whipped into a fervour over things newspapers couldn't understand. Protests, demonstrations, bullying, impromptu games that didn't feel right. Soto's talk about people with special talents. Towerton. The last thing he'd been feeling just now was a desperate need that he should stay alive.

And Stewart acted on that emotion.

But if he was putting his feelings out there, if this whole disaster was because he'd put his anxiety, his agoraphobia, his panic onto everyone else…

…why hadn't Stewart been obsessed with saving himself? Why were so many of these rioters angry, or laughing, or running off to be weird in a corner? He'd seen some of them, just off in a corner…

"He called you Braulio."

Thatcher nearly wet himself. "*¿Pero qué demonios?*"

He turned to find himself faced with a tall, slender woman with a heart-shaped face and a pixie-style haircut. She was sweaty, with frazzled clothes and an elegant but practical air. "Let's get away from the stairwell," she said. She didn't touch him, but she didn't have to; Thatcher was vaguely afraid of her.

He closed the door behind him without even really seeing the room they'd entered. He locked it, for what that was worth, but this was a reception area. The door had a large, transparent glass pane occupying most of its top half. Thatcher sat flush to the wall beside the entrance, hoping that he wouldn't be visible at this angle. Tash stood with her back to the next wall, arms folded, looking down at him. This sort of looming, however, he was used to; it was her bearing that silenced him.

"You don't seem terribly self-possessed," she remarked. Her tone was honestly contemplative, but he took offense anyway.

"Something blew up, and then everyone went *loco*," he replied. "What do you want from me? Some Green Beret Jiu-Jitsu?"

"Who are you working for?" she asked. "And don't say Spindle. I don't have time for pedantics."

He stared at her. "Who else would I be working for?"

"We've come a long way to track you down, and you're our best lead. I'm not going to kill you, but I don't think I can simply release you to…"

"Kill me!? I'm not even sure I'll make it out of here! Is that why you're not as crazy as everyone else?"

"You mean to say that I'm not crazy," Tash said grimly. "We don't know yet how far the food contamination has spread, and Alaska might have been isolated, but…"

Thatcher blinked and his face slackened. Then he slowly started laughing. He got to a point of tears and struggling for breath before he could hear a cluster of people laughing hysterically somewhere far — but not far enough — away. "*¡La hostia!* You're serious!"

Tash looked through the entry window despite herself, though there was nothing she could have seen of the mobs from where she was. She shuddered. "I want information, Braulio."

"Me, too," he said earnestly. "Like: who are you with? You're obviously not Spindle, or Secret Service, or anything legit."

She narrowed her eyes. Her phone buzzed, but she couldn't indulge in such a distraction. Not now. "I don't buy it. My contacts have tracked you down through your infiltrations in the building and some Deep Web activity."

He wanted to vomit. He wanted to jump out of a window, no matter how high up they were. In fact, the higher, the better. "I just lost a friend. I can't even check to see if he's still with us because of a *puta puerta*. And then there's you." He strove not to weep in front of her. He'd have some dignity in the end, he hoped. "Why were you spying on me?"

"You're not making any sense," Tash said. "But neither of us can stay here long. We're going to get to the bottom of how they're suppressing powers with seafood and you're going to help."

He jumped to his feet. "So it's true, then."

Tash pumped herself off the wall and into a loose fighting stance. "What?"

"*Superpoderes*." Thin, glistening cracks of despair flowed from Thatcher's eyes. "Maybe I really did this..." and the way that he faced different directions, the way he looked around: he was encompassing the building with his comment.

"You want me to believe that you tripped and accidentally started a riot?"

"Look, *Ciguapa*, I've been struggling for a while to

make sense of what Spindle's tied up in. I just wanted a job with computers because I'm good with them. It's not my fault their big seafood deal went sideways." She opened her mouth and he held up his hand. "Can we just get out of here first? I've got a bunch of disks and thumb drives," and with that he rustled a fanny pack he was wearing under his gut. His clothes were ruffled, and he had some scrapes and bruises, but he largely looked like a fairly clean office worker. Or he would have been, were it not for…

She regarded him with mistrust but pushed a sigh out of her nose. "You're in my custody, and don't forget it. Help me find some teenagers I'm responsible for, and it'll play well for you."

It wasn't playing well for Nick and Kelly. "Do you know Siaz's number?" Nick asked.

"No," she said. "But did you notice? All the mobs are heading downstairs."

Nick frowned. "We don't know that all of them are."

"Yeah we do," Kelly said. Her determination surprised him. "They usually avoid the elevators, and every time I've been able to map out a floor, it's the stairs they're heading for. Every time we've been around the stairs when there was a stampede…"

"…they were going down," Nick finished.

They were sitting in a soundproofed conference room. They'd wound up on the 43rd floor because of their efforts to escape the rioters. They'd also seen elevator activity showing that someone was going more up than down and found several areas with compromised computers and camera systems as they'd wandered the building.

The room in which they were hiding had a transparent pane lining most of one side, so they were nestled in the corner where that pane ended and before the next wall began. Huddled together with Nick's phone between them, her arm around his leg and his arm over her shoulders, they tried to plan.

"You notice how some of them seem to have clearer heads?" Kelly asked. Her electric blue eyes sought his and delved when he met her gaze.

He needed that from her, though he couldn't have put that into words. "Yeah, I've been getting in as many looks as I can for their eyes, their faces, how they work together. It's like every person has their own panic, but the mob..."

"There's only one...uh...personality, let's call it." Kelly felt like they'd been here forever. Was this going to end? And... "Why aren't we affected?"

"I'd say we're pretty affected," Nick said, waving his hands in dismay at the walls around them.

Kelly slapped his leg. "Don't be dumb."

Nick sucked in his lips as though tasting something sour. "Now that you mention it, even Izzy said it when she was on the top floor. They were still running, I think, but they were affected. That high up, would they even notice a big blast of fire from out front like that?"

Nick's phone buzzed. His hand lifted it to his unseeing gaze as it buzzed. He was too immersed in trying to make all this fit, and not letting the situation overwhelm him. Kelly snatched it up. "Mom!"

"Oh, thank heavens," Tash breathed. In the background someone muttered, but it didn't sound to Kelly like English. "Are you all right? Why are you answering Nick's phone?"

"Because he's turning to mulch trying to connect the dots. Yeah, we're good. Iseult got put in an ambulance. Are you okay?"

"Alive. Found Braulio. He's not what I expected." She had an exchange with the man. She must have had her hand over the phone. It sounded like bickering. "How did Iseult get to an ambulance? Is she okay?"

"Yeah, yeah," Kelly said, trying to downplay the situation. Nearly killed in an office building riot, No Big Deal. NBD, nbd. "You know there are slides from the second floor? Like for escaping airplanes?"

"So she was in the building with you. Not in the car." Her tone could have un-toasted bread.

"We couldn't leave you in here alone!" Kelly said defensively.

Nick watched Kelly now with an expression that broke her heart. She'd run away from a home with an abusive, alcoholic father. She'd survived a cult. He'd only seen the tail end of things in Atlanta, and he was part of the cavalry who swooped in to save the day. He adjusted his shoelaces, watched the space exposed by the window-wall, checked his pockets. He examined his knuckles and made sure that he had full use of his fingers, as fist-fighting had a way of bungling such things.

"There's gonna be a lot of conversation when we're all out of this," Tash said. "For now, it looks like Siaz is backing off. He's done all he can." She went on to explain as much of the situation as she understood, with intermittent pauses to talk to Braulio, who she indicated was "one of the hackers."

"Who has a computer duel in the middle of a riot?" Nick said. Kelly could hear his fear like the tension of a fiddle string.

"You should know, I think he's a projective impath. I've never encountered one before, though I've read about it," Tash said. "He needs to know you for a few months, or you need to spend time in his network, before his emotions sort of...become your emotions. Or overwrite your mental state. He says he can't turn it off, and claims he's only now realizing he has a gift. But you should be safe for now, at least from joining this circus."

Nick and Kelly looked at each other as they took all of this in.

"I want to know more about what happened with Iseult," Tash said suddenly. "It isn't like her to just go off with an ambulance unless she needs it. She should be waiting for us."

Kelly looked at the phone and her stomach sank. She played over in her head the scene of Iseult's...departure. Maybe if she knew medical policy and procedure, or something about SWAT or military or emergency response or whatever. Nick took the phone. "We've been making calls. Her phone still works — we keep going to voicemail — but she's not answering. None of the hospitals are saying they have her." He gritted his teeth and tightened his grip on the phone.

"There's going to be a debriefing once we're safe," Tash said. "Don't try to go to the roof."

They blinked at each other; that was precisely what they'd meant to do. "Not that we were, but...why not?"

Nick asked.

"These buildings are designed for escape through the ground floor. You can't Bruce Willis your way out from the roof," she said.

Braulio spoke, and this time Nick heard him: "If you *templarios* were looking for me, then the *contrarios* are too. *Vamonos!*"

"We'll have to get out through the front doors," Tash said. "The authorities probably won't recognize that we were the ones trying to get in, and I'll get us sorted if there's trouble. I love you. Now go!"

"Love you," Kelly and Nick said together.

Call end.

They stared at the opposite wall and took a deep breath.

"Sounds like she wants us to give up on the other hacker. Just let them off," Nick said without looking at her.

"Iseult seemed to think that those people running to the roof had some kind of game plan or expected rescue or something," Kelly mused in return.

He gazed into her eyes. "We're pretty close to the roof."

"I think the mob has mostly gone down to the lower levels," Kelly said. She laid her hand on the side of his face. "Imagine a hacker running into me." She grinned.

Nick smiled. "Just a quick look?"

Holding hands, they looked every which way, opened the door, and checked the areas they couldn't see from inside before leaving. They made their way to an elevator.

The numerals were making their way down, then

stopped at the second floor. Nick cursed.

"Tash wouldn't want to risk Braulio turning on her in order to try for the second hacker," Kelly reasoned as she pressed the call button. "My enemy's enemy is not my friend."

"Are we even sure if Spindle's the enemy?" Nick asked. "I mean, it all sounds kinda specific. Just seafood? Affecting just people with powers? And all we're getting is just this one company and some food industry stuff on the west coast? I don't think the people who blinded me are after everyone."

"So, like, Spindle's a meat shield?" Kelly asked. "The messer-uppers are using its innocence?"

"Messer-uppers?" He smirked.

"Bully," she teased as she stuck out her tongue. She pecked him on the cheek.

"Are we really waiting? There's only a few more floors," Nick said.

"I don't know about you, but I don't want to be exhausted when I get to the top," Kelly said. "And it's been a day already!"

They couldn't be sure the one to go to the second floor was actually the hacker. Or that there were really only two hackers. Or that there wouldn't be anyone else on the way. And they had no idea what they'd find at the top. Not really. Maybe the ones who'd gone up found nothing, turned around, and went back.

"I don't like all the things we don't actually know," Nick remarked as they stepped off the elevator.

"Me either," Kelly agreed. "But what can ya do?"

After a little wandering, they found the way to the

roof. They were just in time: three helicopters were positioned separately, and only one of them was over the surface proper. The rest were near the walls. One of them was military. A second military chopper was just rising above another edge as the couple ran to the nearest helicopter, catching the rope ladder as the last of the suits climbed aboard.

Someone leaned over and looked at them in surprise as he'd been about to pull up the ladder. "Who are you!?" he shouted.

Thinking quickly, Kelly called up "Brother and sister! Our dad's in the other one!" She pointed in the direction of the chopper that wasn't marked as military. It was too far to run to, and the ladder had been pulled up.

The man didn't cut or drop the ladder. The helicopter waited until they boarded.

There were two seats remaining: one for the agent or operator who'd let them climb the ladder, and one that must have been extra. Nick pushed her to it and she didn't argue. Kelly took in the scene and the others in the passenger compartment. The operator guy held out a hand. "Sorry, there's a potential information war," he said. "It's policy: I have to take your phones."

Reluctantly, she handed him the one that had ended up in her possession. "This is his," she explained, tilting her head toward her "brother." To his raised brow she added, "It was a little rough in there."

"I have to search you both."

Nick watched him search his "sister" with a wrathful, laser focus that no one missed. He allowed himself to be searched with far less hostility.

"Sorry," the operator said. "I don't make the rules."

One of the suits called toward the front: "Why can't you just radio the other guy? I don't like strangers, surprises, or surprise strangers!"

"I'm with you there," Kelly said with her best charm.

The operator grinned. The others were stony-faced. Nick was gripping the loops for standing passengers while the chopper was in flight. He was watching through the windows now that the door was closed.

But they weren't moving.

The co-pilot called back, "Stay calm, folks. Looks like the military doesn't like two private choppers showing up like this. Not with…everything. We can't contact the other chopper until they stop talking."

Kelly blinked and looked at the businesspeople who'd gotten to the chopper. They were wild-eyed and bleary, like they were coming down from the biggest adrenaline high of their lives. It wasn't suspicion or mistrust; their knuckles were white with their grips, and their faces gaunt.

They were terrified.

The helicopter started off. Nick glanced back and regarded Kelly from the corner of his eye. She met his gaze long enough to agree: something was going wrong.

They lurched a sudden turn. In the distance, the other private chopper cut in front of them and they pursued. Sounds they didn't recognize and didn't like came from the military choppers who closed in behind. Two of the businesspeople started crying. A dark line formed down the pants of a third.

Gravity moved their guts.

Amidst an unintelligible chorus of shouts and cries, the pilot had switched the comms system so everyone could hear.

"...paid for ourselves, we have a right to get free if we can!"

"Final warning to stand down." This voice was crisp, commanding, firm. "We are authorized to open fire."

"Whoa, whoa, whoa, that's — who's your commanding officer?"

"You don't have authority for negotiations, citizen. Land your vessel."

"I'm gonna comply," the pilot announced through the speakers. Nick swung forward so that he could get a good angle from the window.

"Like hell you are," one of the suits argued. Kelly stared at him, appalled.

The other chopper rushed ahead and dove between two buildings.

Kelly had just enough time to recognize that as a mistake when Nick shouted, "INCOMING!"

She never would have thought before that one vehicle could lurch in multiple directions at once. She tunnel-visioned on Nick because she didn't know what else to do. They were spinning. He was being bounced around like a rag doll with its arms tied upward. But his head movements didn't go with the inertia. "Kelly! To me!"

A lifetime of faithlessness, disappointment, and abandonment reached out its tendrils, tying her spine to her seat. But she cut the pages on which that ink was written. As decisive as a survival knife, she forced away her doubts. She made something new of herself in that moment, though she would be a long time seeing it.

Tearing the straps and belt off, she jumped for Nick just as he'd struggled the door open.

He wrapped an arm about her, waited for the longest fraction of a second she'd ever experienced, and leapt. They were one spinning cylinder in that moment. Ammunition built without a weapon in mind. The timing was breathtaking; they'd landed at a good angle and rolled. It was just the right moment in the falling helicopter's trajectory; such a landing should have been harsh enough to break the bones of someone watching it happen.

As it was, they spent a long time lying there together. While nothing was broken, torn, ruptured, or crippled, neither of them would be standing up just yet. Their surprise was complete when they were both dragged by the collars of their shirts to a shelter behind a stairway leading into the building they were on. One of the military choppers swept by shortly afterward, likely in pursuit of the other craft. Nick did some quick reckoning; the whole area was probably locked down for blocks. With the direction they were in, a crashing chopper should only really land in property damage.

He hoped.

Kelly said, "Who are you?"

CHAPTER 17
UNDOCUMENTED

Seattle, Washington

Tash sat heavily. She was in the apartment she'd gotten for herself and the kids. Thatcher — he'd told her his real name — slumped into the bean bag chair. She'd have argued, but what was the point? They'd have to deal with each other. At least for now. Sleep hadn't seen much of her since the events of the day before.

"For what it's worth, I'm sorry. About your kids," Thatcher said.

They'd had a fair amount of time to talk. To her never-ending astonishment, Tash and Thatcher had both simply walked out. The authorities detained them long enough to determine that neither of them was a threat, but they'd have to set up follow-up procedures to get back in touch with everyone. The building had had more than two thousand employees, visitors, and their families — anyone who'd spent significant time in the building in the last three months or so — go berserk at once.

"Thank you," she said to the living room in general. If it were possible to twist and wring a water pipe, the result would have been how she felt.

"I'm...gonna need you to tell me a lot more. About powers. Or gifts. Or whatever you wanna call them," Thatcher said. "I'm having an easier time with the whole conspiracy thing. If that's what it is."

"The seafood stuff? I'm not sure," Tash said. She sounded far away. "If it's someone tampering without the industry's awareness, then we're dealing with someone who has considerable resources. If the industry's in on it, that's not a whole lot better." Siaz had dropped her one last line: he'd have to hold off for a while. His involvement had gotten someone on his tail. He'd contact her again if and when he could.

"I'll need access to some decent equipment," Thatcher said. "I got what I could, but I only set up my program to look for back doors, what errors and anomalies I could think to look for, and track some of the communications. I couldn't get into the money, unfortunately. I'd give a kidney for that info."

"Me, too," Tash said. "I'll make some calls once I can think straight. You've been at this for months, right? Trying to figure out what's so fishy about the whole thing?"

"More like a few weeks," he replied. "I got promoted faster than I expected, so I wasn't super prepared. And I didn't actually know what to look for. I can't put 'something fishy' in the command line."

Tash's lips moved. It was too weak to be a proper grin. They were like the edges of a wound, still looking for where the knife had passed. "I told you about Nick. You really didn't notice anything off about anyone?"

"Not until everyone was off. Because of..." he wrung

his hands and hung his head in guilt.

"If what you say is true," Tash said, "then you're not alone. And it wasn't your fault. Many people with gifts aren't aware of it, or don't know how to control it."

"You're still not sure you believe me?"

"We both lay down to sleep in this apartment last night," she reminded him. "Different rooms, sure — but I think that says something."

"I slept like a rock. Needed it. I don't think you did, though."

"No."

"Do you have one?"

There was a pause. "If you were me, in this situation, and I asked you…"

"I'd probably lie, even if I did."

She nodded.

"I put a virus into the system, too," he said. "It was the first thing I did. To get rid of everything connected to me. I also destroyed a bunch of other data, and compromised or corrupted whole servers, as a decoy. So they wouldn't find a cut-out of my body in the wall and go looking for someone shaped like me. If you know what I mean."

"I do. Even your images on file?" Tash asked. She was looking at Thatcher now.

"*Si.* I don't know how well it would have worked for payroll, though. I set up a logic bomb in case the payroll system tried to connect to anything about me in the mainframe I had access to, but…"

"…anything's possible." Tash rested her chin on her hand. Hearts beat. "You do nothing on any computer you work on without my supervision."

"I expected that."

"I don't think I need to threaten you."

"No," Thatcher started. "You have everything right now. I can't even use any of the money I've been paid since the last time I accessed my bank account. I can't risk them tracking me." He met her gaze. "Food, shelter, even clothes. I'll need your help."

"We'll have to talk about your gift. I can't promise I can help you if what you say is true."

"I can't promise I can find your kids," he said. "Or anything about the seafood stuff. But I'm in this far."

∞

A Sewer Maintenance Room, Seattle, Washington

"I'm sorry," they said. "You're probably scared and confused. But you're also in grave danger."

This was the person who'd pulled Nick and Kelly out of sight on the roof as the helicopters fought. They said to call them "Liz" and that they were non-binary.

Nick shrugged and Kelly said, "Can do."

"You mean the building and the choppers weren't the scary part?" The maintenance room was either abandoned or — well — poorly maintained. Liz pulled some large plastic-canvas-wrapped bundles out of a few nooks and crannies and soon the couple were sitting on some clean cushions with hot-plate-boiled tea. Nick had expected equivocation at his snarky remark.

"No," Liz answered as they made the tea. "But there's only so much I can do without all three of you. How to ask…"

Kelly met Nick's gaze and then regarded Liz again.

The person had short, wavy, steel-grey hair. Astute, green eyes were set in a narrow face that appeared longer than it was, and Kelly could see how that was so: the style of the hair and funnel neck Margate coat, along with their posture, gave them a vibe of lifting to the point of looming. The coat was open, revealing a thin black shirt and grey-green scarf. It was their gloves, however, that really caught Kelly's fashionable eye: they were the most expensive piece Liz owned, custom-made for hands so long the fingers almost needed another joint. Like the rest of the outfit, however, it was intended to be understated. Nick hadn't noticed and thought this was common attire.

Head to toe, they were probably wearing over four grand in quality brand names.

Nick was looking anywhere but at their rescuer — if that's what this person was — because he was looking for weapons, traps, or things with teeth.

Both of the youths were so occupied in all this that they hadn't recognized Liz's remark for what it was and weren't as conscious of the silence as they perhaps should have been. Tapping the teacup with a long finger, Liz pursued their purpose: "I had reason to believe that I was needed where I was. It's...hard to explain. But I was looking for — bear with me — the knife that cuts itself. It was all rather metaphorical. Something about healing and self-destruction."

Nick and Kelly looked at each other. Kelly started. "Um, no offence, but…"

"You don't trust me, you're afraid for your friend, and you're not from around here." Liz appeared for all the world to be as casual about all this as though they were discussing the weather. "Neither of you have your phone — I don't know why — but you don't know what to do with yourselves now."

"I can see more than most people," Nick remarked, "but how…?"

Liz smiled. "There is seeing and there is seeing." They sipped their tea. "Something greater is afoot, though I don't have the details yet. I'm a private investigator."

"Who are you working for on this one?" Kelly asked with a raised brow.

"A fair question," their new ally (or non-enemy?) replied. "No one, yet. It's a bit like being a freelancer; sometimes you have to sniff out and track opportunities and then look for a buyer of the information."

"We could grill you all day about your business and not get any closer to our own," Nick thought aloud. "No offence."

"None taken. But let's not pussyfoot around the fact that I pulled you out of a helicopter chase. I'm not looking for anything from you. At least, not yet. I can tell you, though, that your knife is in the belly of the whale."

"You know you sound like a cloaked weirdo in a smoky tent with a crystal ball and ominous music, right?" Nick asked.

Kelly elbowed him, but Liz only laughed. "Yes, I suppose I do." They set down their empty cup and seemed to be weighing their words. "The knife that cuts itself, according to my source, was surrounded not by the eye of the storm, but the eye and the storm. Or at least, a bolt or a flash." The private investigator met each of their gazes individually and spoke slowly: "Which of you has a gift for electricity?"

They stood with alarm. "We need to get going," Kelly said.

They were closer to the entrance than Liz. Nothing suggested that the well-dressed stranger would — or could — stop them from fleeing. Yet the standing motions of this odd individual were slow, elegant, confident. That, more than anything else, gave them pause. "I'm asking for your attention. You won't gain much running about the city, at any rate. Did you even know what you were in there for? I mean, specifically?"

Both youths shuffled uncomfortably.

"Please," Liz said, and held out an open hand toward the cushions they'd been sitting upon.

Fingers enmeshed, they sat back down.

"Why are you helping us?" Nick asked.

"Let me put you at ease, at least as much as I can," they replied. "My real name is Yeghisabet Thompson. Liz is just easier. You've told me your names already, and if they're false, you need not tell me. You have as much of my trust as you require. I, too, have a gift."

Yeghisabet let that sit for a moment. The couple seemed to digest the statement slowly. Then they went on: "I've told precious few in my life, even when I encountered the rare person who also had a gift. Of the ones I have told, most didn't believe me. I'm sure I don't have to explain to you the risks of getting them to believe me."

Kelly shook her head. Nick had a brooding expression, but his acknowledgment was in the way he held himself. He still wasn't sure if he trusted them, but he'd found no falsehood yet.

"May we ask…?" Kelly said.

"I don't know if there's a proper term for it," Yeghisabet answered, "but I think of myself as an Odditer. I know the odds of things, but I get that knowledge from the stars."

Nick's brow furrowed. "In Seattle?"

Another knowing, gentle smile. The private investigator's mouth had a soft quality, more in how it moved than in its shape, that reminded the youths of a nurse speaking to a crib. "When I need to look, I find a way to get out of town. It's messy, so I only do it for things that really count."

"So by messy, you mean you can't get clean answers — like lottery numbers," Kelly mused.

As Yeghisabet nodded, opening their mouth, Nick cut in: "Why are we in a sewer?"

"I thought that was clear," their new acquaintance answered.

"Is this, like, a safe space for you?" Kelly asked.

A twitch of surprise. "Why, yes," Liz said. "It wasn't just about protecting you, though."

"It was about trust," Nick concluded.

Another nod.

"This must be important. Someone with hideouts like this is probably a private person, and not just for investigation," Kelly thought aloud.

"Exactly," Yeghistabet confirmed. "Now: there is a strong starlight around a raindrop that casts a shadow." They actually had to resist a laugh at the scrunched-up expressions on the couple's faces. "I've done the leg work already. What you're looking for is a fishing vessel…"

A Diner, Seattle

Tash and Thatcher were also feeling adrift, at a loss for information and thrown together as unlikely allies in a world gone mad. Right now they were sitting at a table in a diner during a sunny Seattle afternoon. Tash's coffee was black. Dark roast. Thatcher had ordered one of the coffees in the Mexican style, with cinnamon and sugar incorporated in the brewing process. He was savouring his more than Tash was hers. He ate more when they had breakfast. He wasn't hungrier or thirstier than she. She didn't enjoy her coffee any less than he.

While he was anxious, afraid, and helpless, though, she was utterly heartbroken.

"Authorities remain tight-lipped about the Wishing Well Riot," an anchorwoman was saying. Everyone in the diner was watching the screens that normally streamed local news, weather, or sporting events. Since the incident at the Spindle Building, the whole city was talking. They were clamouring for blame, for explanations.

Tash watched mechanically. If a world-class spy like Siaz couldn't tell her what she wanted to know, she had little hope she'd hear about her kids from a journalist on TV. Thatcher watched her out of the corner of his eye. He didn't know her well enough to read her. Maybe she was always stony-faced in public.

"Even the name is unclear," the reporter continued. "The circumstances are continuously proving to be bizarre. Tabloids are seeing historically high numbers in social media, daily sales, and high-profile interviews.

Answers for what happened are ranging from aliens and the occult to global warming and capitalism. Law enforcement have been restructuring, and we'll follow up on that in our evening broadcast. After this update, we'll replay the interview in which the riot got its name."

"Thank you for giving me a chance," Thatcher said.

"Don't thank me yet. If you had anything to do-"

"You know I did," he interrupted. "The last thing I wanted was what we got. I didn't try it. I'd give anything to undo it. But it was me. People died..."

She narrowed her eyes at him then. But he had her full attention. "Nick and Kelly told me they'd seen Iseult put into an ambulance."

"We've been over this, *cabeza*. I could put something together for getting into medical records or accessing info about the ambulances, but..."

Everyone's guard was up. All essential services, like medical and mail, were on command for maximum vigilance and high alert status, stemming directly from the federal and state governments. Brute-forcing was out. Even phishing would be risky right now.

Tash wasn't sure anymore if what she was doing was arguing. "Even if they didn't have their phones, Nick and Kelly at least should have checked in by now. They'd have found a way."

They were only half-listening to the news while they chatted, as it had gone on to interviewing average citizens, consulting social media, and describing the rumours that were afloat in the city. "Despite the fact that Spindle's last known CFO is reported missing, has not had a replacement, and was an American man, there have been numerous reports of an Asian woman who claimed to be the CFO. These reports say she had visited the building just as the riot was kicking off." Furthermore, none of the medical authorities could corroborate that there had been an Asian woman among the first responders. The "phantom twins" became an Internet meme.

The screen then switched to a bedside interview in a hospital room with a woman of colour who Thatcher recognized as Mashaka. She talked about unconscionable violence and true heroism. He wanted desperately to reach out to her, but when Tash had told him about the encounter at his apartment, he'd gone to some length to burn every trace of his contacts to everyone. Except for the green phone. He kept its power off and its SIM card out, but he kept it all the same. He didn't tell Tash about it, not yet. But he wouldn't reach out to the troupe until he was confident that no one would be sniffing around his trail.

How had they found him? He'd been so careful!

Tash did start paying a little more attention as the coverage shifted to a story about military involvement. Two private helicopters had been shot down on suspicion of terrorist activity after failing to comply with stand-down orders. That wasn't much concern to her — she was confident the kids wouldn't have gone to the roof — but what got her attention was the extent of the military involvement.

Elsewhere, Seattle

Unbeknownst to either side, Nick and Kelly were watching the same broadcast as Tash and Thatcher.

Yeghisabet had brought the couple to another hideout — an apartment they kept under a fake name — in order to at least give the youths access to the media. "Most of the information about the hacker intrusion has been classified," the reporter was saying.

Nick and Kelly were sitting on the edge of a dingy bed without sheets. Sleeping bags were arranged on the floor. "I've had to call in favours with contacts in the coast guard and the fishery, but I've arranged to get you both on that boat. I can't promise that you will get to your friend-"

"Sister," Kelly corrected.

Liz blinked, but accepted the correction.

"If we have to jump into a fake ID and get some priming from these contacts of yours," Nick said, "why can't we call our mom first? There's no telling how long we'll be at sea, or what it'll take to…"

The news reporter, this one a bald Black man, had said something about Iseult, though he'd mispronounced Izzy's name. Which was fair; many people did. Though they'd caught Nick's shift in attention, Yeghisabet did feel the need to give him a fair answer. "That's why," they pointed at the laptop screen the trio were watching.

It was a special bulletin. "…seen here," the anchorwoman was back again. This time a picture of Iseult was prominently displayed. "The authorities have declared that it's highly unlikely this terrorist worked alone, and they are investigating leads into potential associates as we speak…"

Tash, watching this at the diner, went so pale she bordered on green. Thatcher would have put a hand on her shoulder or something, but he wasn't sure what was proper in this instance. He was used to working — and living — alone. "We'll get to the bottom of this," he managed. He wasn't sure if she'd heard.

Kelly covered her mouth with her hands and let out a small cry of shock. Nick stood, paced a little, sat, and repeated the sequence until the private investigator told him to stay still.

"Your mom's phone might be tapped. I will track her down, and you should give me some info to help with that. Most of my go-to people are muzzled by their various commanding officers. Must be pretty high-profile stuff." Though they were doing a better job of hiding it, Liz was distressed as well. If the highest authorities in law enforcement and military couldn't see that she was being framed — or were prohibited from admitting it…

"They're not stupid enough not to know her family…" Tash muttered this through the side of her mouth, her hand on her face so that no one would see her speak. The diner's eyes were on the screen, but you never knew.

"I could whip up some stuff for your digital tracks…" Thatcher offered.

Tash shook her head. "You'll need all the time and resources you can get for your...project...as it is," she said. Meaning, of course, that he was to help track down her kids. "They're our top priority."

Nick wrapped a silently weeping Kelly in his arms as the special bulletin played snatches of video captured from webcams, phones, and security cameras. The anchor explained, while the images were playing, that the attack compromised some of the footage — which was why the authorities didn't know who the "terrorist" had been working with, or what she'd been up to.

"Experts believe she may be a poison specialist," the reporter continued in voiceover. An employee photo of Bevis was displayed. "This Computer Hardware Specialist was found in the building during the investigation sweep. Toxicology results came back negative, but he now has a new heart problem unlike anything his doctor has seen before. High-profile conversations have raised the possibility of new bio-weapons, and national authorities are on high alert, but so far there is no clear confirmation that there's a ceiling to what this young woman can do."

"Aren't there laws about being so sensational?" Thatcher asked quietly. Every now and again he looked around the room. Tash had to remind him to stop; it was suspicious.

"Yes and no," Tash said. "They're only reporting the facts. Their delivery is a little leading, but you have to remember they're in a rush to cover a big story."

"There's no way Izzy would've hurt him more than she had to," Nick said in the dingy, unadorned apartment. "There's more to that."

Kelly was remembering a large house in Atlanta. She was remembering power, and the people who wielded it. The lies they told others, and themselves. Where could you go if the whole world was a cult?

"I'm sorry about your sister," Liz said. "Truly, I am. But you must realize what it means that they haven't named you or your mom." That got her the full attention of the lovers. "You're being baited. They want you to expose yourself, and your connections, by trying to track her down."

"Won't that put you at risk, even rushing us onto that boat tonight?" Nick asked.

News helicopter footage played of Iseult knocking out the two police officers near the basement parking ramp. It was shaky, grainy, not zoomed in enough. There was so much to take in and no time to properly prep or handle the equipment, but that was Iseult, near enough. "The families of the officers are understandably beside themselves," the anchorwoman said. It was still in voiceover, but most viewers were picturing her based on her tone of voice: the polite despair of someone talking about terrible things that were happening to someone else.

"The officers have been indefinitely detained in a military hospital pending testing and examination for the possibility of new toxins," came the explanation.

"We should get to work," Tash said. She called over the server to pay the bill. Thatcher turned to look out the window. Part of him was heartsick for this woman who just wanted her family safe. Part of him was disgusted with the society outside the window, enjoying the nice weather and going about their day. Part of him was terrified that he might disrupt that very peace any moment, by projecting his worries and fears.

Tash, meanwhile, was planning to harness Victor's fervour. Abby wouldn't stand for what was happening to Iseult, and Chad would join her inquisition if she called on him.

Yeghisabet had plans of their own. "Yes, I'm at risk. But I'm always at risk, and even my getaway cars have escape hatches and back-up plans. I don't know yet why the starlight brought me to you, and I have my own debts to pay. Bills, favours." Blood, they thought.

Static rose about Kelly. Nick, holding her hand, used the other. With his middle finger and thumb, he removed his contacts. He turned to regard the private investigator. Nothing but the white of his sclera was visible. On the laptop, the news program continued with footage of Iseult on a webcam, firing a gun off-screen in a dilapidated section of cubicles. There was no audio beyond the newscaster voice over.

"I'll tear her from their clutches. With my bare hands if I have to," Nick said to Liz. "Just point me in the right direction. I'll stare down the abyss if that's what it takes."

EPILOGUE

Aboard the *Muninn*, International Waters

"I am uncomfortable without my scalpel, Pabulum," Jacinta said. It was the custom to refer to the Triumvirs by their titles or areas of responsibility; whatever name they had before the role was irrelevant. "This ship is not equipped for my work. Why am I here?"

"We've heard of your...unique ideas," the Triumvir of Pabulum said in a thick accent. A person unfamiliar with the Komi people would probably hear it as some kind of blend of Russian and Polish. Pronunciation aside, it was not an answer to her question. She hadn't talked openly about her concept of the Diary of Knives, her musings about suffering and sacrifice. Pabulum didn't give her long to wonder: "But we do not understand it. Your staff tell us you simply sound philosophical." The pair were on a gridwork catwalk, centre and above the aquaculture facilities which occupied about two thirds of the vessel.

Jacinta wore beige slacks with a black turtleneck and a white lab coat. Her hands were clasped behind her back. She looked like a professor torn from her study, and every bit as disgruntled as that would suggest. "My subjects are not a people to be led, like your subjects. Mine are pages to be written on or learned fr-...I see."

The Triumvir with her was not so pretentious as to wear a toga or Roman senator's robes. She presented as a deceptively simple, elderly woman of the Komi Republic in Ural, Russia. Her dress and sash were made up of pinks and purples. She wore a pin, the symbol of Veles. Pabulum walked with her hands at her sides, as casually as though they were strolling a riverbank. What had caught Jacinta's attention was an individual performing Harakiri, or something like it.

The women watched without comment as the man knelt in the process of the ritual, a plastic sheet laid out before him for catching his...remains. It was not the true Seppuku performed in Japan's Samurai days. It had, however, taken much inspiration from the practice. Even the knife was the tanto typically used.

Jacinta didn't have to ask: this was Pabulum's predecessor.

She had other concerns, however: "Surely you don't need a surgical researcher for your succession?"

"I seek to connect with tanto holders from both Sections," she said. She meant the ships inside of which they now walked. A person of proven worth, skill, or importance was provided with the means of Harakiri as both a sign of honour for their accomplishments and a warning: do not fail. "The Triumvirate met after the events of…"

"Yes, yes," Jacinta said. Her impatience bordered on heresy. "Heads have rolled. I'm impressed that both Karambit and Sikloon had to go to ground, though. Who is our enemy?"

"The interruptions have not been coordinated by a single entity," Pabulum said.

Jacinta took her eyes off the man just as he was applying the blade to himself. Around him, aside from the required witnesses, everyone was going about their business. Massive vats of genetically altered seafood were being monitored, produced, transported, labelled, and recorded. The wizened eyes of the faithful senior woman gleamed with a blend of the devoted and the ruthless.

Jacinta was unperturbed by the eyes, but the news… "How? Surely Circe must be behind such incredible counter-intelligence."

"An excellent question." Pabulum put her hands on the railing of the catwalk. "The Triumvirate has communicated with the *Huginn*." By this she meant the other repurposed supertanker, the one on which Jacinta worked. "The Twins remain in the USA and will continue to monitor the situation, but they have caught the scent of an independent entity they are working to pursue."

Jacinta absorbed that with a nod. Not surprising; the Knives would want to ensnare Engen's enemies. No need to enact a clean-up protocol just yet. She resented how this had impacted her own control of her situation, but she held her tongue on that. For now. "Am I to be transferred?"

"Heavens, no," Pabulum said with a scoff. "There is someone we wish you to meet. The Twins sent her."

Jacinta narrowed her eyes but said nothing. They continued for forty-five minutes, walking by the aquaculture containers. They were gargantuan cylinders of industrial glass, metal, and plastic. Some had contents moved to other vats, as they were merely feed for the second set of containers. Others were fed exclusively synthetic nutrients or food components; some had a combination of the two. Eventually, the women reached one of endless numbers of turn-offs from the catwalk. What distinguished it was the surrounding architecture; they were leaving the domain of Pabulum and entering Imprimatur's.

"There are faster ways," Jacinta pointed out.

"But you did not mind. We all have much to contemplate," the Triumvir of Pabulum answered.

The surgeon conceded the point silently. She was led to a series of cells. These looked more like storage vaults, with huge, state-of-the-art metal seals and electrical systems. Next to the door was a sliding window, which Pabulum "opened" with a push of a button. Behind a glass wall so thick it skewed the colour of the room beyond was a young woman.

She was somewhat short. With a little more height she might have been rather thin, but her figure was unremarkable as she was. She had pale blue eyes and shorn, light brown hair. Like the others Imprimatur studied, she was wearing a grey-green jumpsuit with plain white slippers. Her room was utilitarian but not undignified, and she sat on a passable wooden chair at a foldable plastic table.

She looked up from the table when the window opened to see two wildly different women watching her. One looked like a scientist or professor and tapped her foot with her hands behind her back. The other looked like everyone's and anyone's grandma.

"This is Dr. Jacinta Serrano," the grandma said. "I

thought you two should meet. Lots of potential." The young woman wondered where that potential was. What did the grandma mean?

"And this, my dear doctor, is Subject 02—5702 Green. She calls herself Iseult."

**Here ends *Diary of Knives*
Book I of the Knives of Engen series.**

Don't miss Book II: *Red Ocean Strategy*!

ENGEN TIMELINE

With over twenty novels spread over three different series by many different authors, the Engen Universe of titles is growing every day and into genres we couldn't have imagined! From the original ten book *Coral Beach Casefiles* thriller series, its crime novel sequel series *Xander Drew*, our flagship adventure title *Infinity*, or single-novels like *Jacobi Street* or *light | dark*, there's something in the Engen Universe for everyone with more books by more authors on the way soon!

...But how do the events relate to one another, chronologically? While some astute readers have guessed at the potential timeline (some accurately, some not), we're going to finally set the question of the Engen Timeline to rest.

Turn the page for an up-to-date guide of the ever-widening world of Engen, featuring the works of Ali House, Ellen Curtis, Andrea Hackett, Sarah Thompson, Jay Paulin, Matthew Daniels, and Matthew LeDrew!

In the 10 Years Prior Black September

"Reptilia" by Matthew LeDrew
published in *light | dark*.
Danger descends on a small secluded town in the form of a deadly virus with fantastic and terrible side-effects. Can a small group of doctors escape alive?

Compendium by Ellen Curtis
Three short stories forming the basis for the Engen Universe's ties to suspense, genetic engeneering, and the supernatural. Features the stories "The Tourniquet Revival," "Falling into Fire" and "At Midnight, the Dawn."

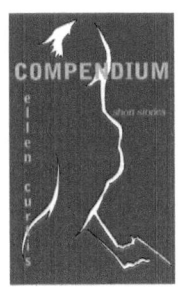

"The Theogony" by Matthew LeDrew
published in *light | dark*.
A tale of young Theo Flaherty of the *Infinity* series and his time admitted against his will to the Black Springs hospital, where he learns to paint, and seeks out his father.

Black September

"Revving Engen" by Matthew LeDrew
published in *light | dark*.
A direct lead-in to both *Infinity* and *Black Womb*, Tasha travels to Coral Beach, Maine on a hot tip about a recently discovered young man with incredible abilities.

Infinity by Ellen Curtis & Matthew LeDrew
Faced with a destiny he's uncertain of, the enigmatic Victor must bring together four unique people with very special abilities… or face the tasks ahead alone. Guaranteed to excite!

Black Womb by Matthew LeDrew
Fifteen years ago, something happened in Coral Beach, Maine that resulted in the present death of a seventeen-year-old boy. Now four high-school students must try to solve the mystery… before the killer picks them off.

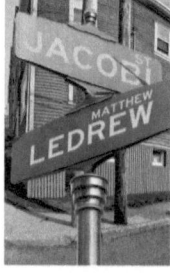

Jacobi Street by Matthew LeDrew
When a mysterious painting shows up at an art gallery he works at, Bob must work with Eddie and Sloan to track down its sinister origins and convince the people living on Jacobi Street of them, before its too late!

Transformations in Pain by Matthew LeDrew
When two girls are assaulted and one is hospitalized, the residents of Coral Beach must put their shared tragedies behind them and stop the man responsible, as well as unlock the secrets behind the true nature of the Womb…

Year One: October

Variety Show by Ali House
Local performer Wendy is introduced to the drama and mystique of The Quaint Little Theatre of Jacobi Street. But backstabbing aren't the only dangers at play in this venue...

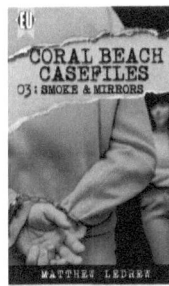

Smoke and Mirrors by Matthew LeDrew
The approaching trial of Genblade brings closure to the people of Coral Beach, until people start showing up dead in the same manner they did when he was at large.

"Scarlett" by Andrea Hackett
published in *light | dark*.
Introducing Scarlett, the slightly damaged hunter on a mission to save others from the monsters from her past.

"The Inevitable" by Ali House
published in *The Lightbulb Forest*
A young woman must contend with the emergence of a frightening new power alongside the emotional high of a first date.

The Tourniquet Reprisal by Curtis & LeDrew
A man lives in Atlanta, Georgia that people don't talk about, but everyone knows he's there. He arrived a year ago and turned a gaggle of uneducated youth into something new, something to fear.

Roulette by Matthew LeDrew
As the teen suicide rate in Coral Beach starts to climb astronomically fast, Xander travels to Los Angeles to fight his most terrifying adversary yet... and learns that the only thing worse than looking for release... is finding it.

Year One: November

Exodus of Angels by Curtis & LeDrew
Victor's enigmatic past is illuminated when Jaycee accompanies him to visit a new friend in the paliative care ward of the Black Springs hospital, where Theo also happens to be searching for a cure for Leigh.

Ghosts of the Past by Matthew LeDrew
Coral Beach faces its most awesome threat when one of Engen's past mistakes is unleashed upon the unsuspecting populous. Friends and enemies unite to fight a common enemy... but will even that be enough?

Touch Your Nose by Matthew LeDrew
Simon Monk must infiltrate the San Fransico branch of Shane Industries, a massive company with deep ties to the Engen Universe. Where do his true loyalties lie? And can he get out without causing harm?

Ignorance is Bliss by Matthew LeDrew
After being set through the ringer one too many times, Xander decides that his life with Julie needs a little more attention… which is bad news because a new villain has come to town with his sights set on Adam Genblade.

"Gristle While You Work" by Jay Paulin published in *light | dark*.
A short story centering around the rise of a new, and possibly cannibalistic, serial killer in the Engen Universe.

Becoming by Matthew LeDrew
For months Xander Drew has been doing his level best to keep the streets of Coral Beach clean, which means it's time for the forces of darkness to strike back… all at once.

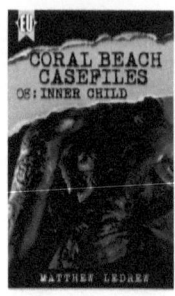

Inner Child by Matthew LeDrew
Julie is hospitalized with life-threatening wounds to both body and soul. But the real threat comes from the hospital walls themselves, as a demonic presence makes itself known to Xander and his friends.

End of Year One

Gang War by Matthew LeDrew
The Tees, a homicidal gang of evil men, has finally been taken down by Xander Drew. But his victory is short lived, as retired Tees are mysteriously killed. With a town of suspects, anyone can be the culprit... including one of their own.

Chains by Matthew LeDrew
Sociopath Derek Smith has been freed from prison and is praying on the weak; and none are weaker than August Styles: a pregnant girl with Down Syndrome who has run away from home.

"Omega" by Ellen Curtis
published in *light | dark*.
A sinister division of Engen begins a series of experiments on pregnant women in a fashion eerily similar to those that created the original Black Womb project.

The Long Road by Matthew LeDrew
Xander meets the American people — and realizes that the world is harsh and wicked, but can also be soft and gentle, even loving. Xander Drew comes of age on the road, and sets his new direction.

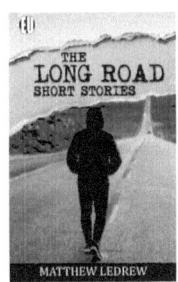

Year Two

Cinders by Matthew LeDrew
Detective Horton enters a violent and dangerous world he didn't know existed beneath the veneer of order and structure that he has based his entire deductive method around.

Sinister Intent by Matthew LeDrew
One of the killers Detective Horton could not catch has resurfaced: a serial killer who flaunts his sinister intent in front of the Los Angeles Police Department, making it so that no one is safe.

Faith by Matthew LeDrew
Xander's mysterious and troublesome past returns to haunt him on the streets of Los Angeles; a place where even more people can get caught in the crossfire of the games of death and deceit that makes up his life.

Flickers in the Night by Matthew LeDrew
Lisa Rowdan is hunted by her haunting --
and powerful -- ex-boyfriend Ryan through a
lonely city street. Can she escape him?
One of over twenty great sprine-tingling short
stories!

Diary of Knives by Matthew Daniels
While trying to help her team decompress
after the explosive events of *The Tourniquet
Reprisal*, Tash accidentally involves the teens
in a dangerous plot that holds the keys to the
Engen Universe.

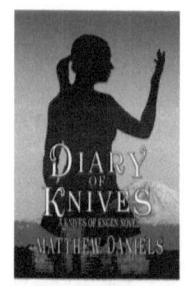

Garden of the 8th Circle by Curtis & LeDrew
Victor brings Chad, Abby, and Alice into a
dangerous conflict a decade in the making,
fighting an out of control cult for the fate of a
young soul. Meanwhile, Theo investigates a
mysterious event in Los Angeles.

Family Values by Matthew LeDrew
Xander and his new friends Crowley, Lisa, and
Tim investigate a series of kidnappings and
murders that stretch back decades, all of which
have the same similar twist: victims being
found after years of being missing.

Fate's Shadow by Matthew LeDrew
When one of Xander's old cases comes up for trial, Megan Greene returns with it. The former friends are led into conflict regarding her client's innocence. However, they put their difference aside when they both become targets of the vigilante known as Shiro Gilbert.

First Aid by Matthew LeDrew
Xander takes his feud with mob boss Stephen Fields to the streets, and his attracts the attention of the *Infinity* team. Before the arrive, he'll have pushed the mob boss into an all out gang war, the likes of which the city will never recover from.

Exposure by Erin Vance
Joshua Deering just wanted was to pass his final photography project. But that's not what happened. But hindsight is 20/20, and now creepy cemetery guy Adrian, Josh, and Josh's two friends are being stalked by nameless, violent strangers.

The Future

"Remers" by Sarah Thompson
published in *light | dark*.
In the not-too-distant future of the Engen Universe, young athletes are the targets of a scouting program to create the next stage of super soldier with cybernetic enhancements.

DARK STORIES FROM ENGEN BOOKS

THE HOWL BECONS

Werewolves and a dark family secret in Northern Labrador! Growing up without his father, Tyler had no way of knowing the horrible secret that has plagued his family for generations. To free himself and find the cure, he will have to look beyond himself and into his dark history.

"The perfect mix of suspense and literary storytelling, Werewolves as metaphor for the original sins of Newfoundland & Labrador make this book the best in its class ,"
— Matthew LeDrew, author of *Infinity* and *Xander Drew*.

WESTON'S WAR

Something evil grows in the heart of Colorado. Bill Weston was a man of the West. He knew it – its land, its people, its stories. It was where he plied his trade, hunting men for money. His life wasn't easy, but it was predictable. That all changed when he captured Faraway Sue and he was led on a trip through the Colorado forests

"Take a little Zane Grey. Add a little Penny Dreadful. Read with Sam Elliot's voice. Discover Jon Dobbin's masterful The Starving." — Darrell Power, Great Big Sea

FANTASY FROM ENGEN BOOKS

HEED THE CALL

After a heated fight at sea between twins Ben and Alex, Ben vanishes from their boat without a sound or even a ripple in the water. Unwavering in his dedication to find his brother, Alex begins the adventure of a lifetime armed only with the help of a local girl named Meg and his own mysterious musical abilities… the key to which, and to the mysteries that surround him, may be tied to the alluring song of the dangerous girl he finds among the ocean's frothing waves.

"A mysterious figure in the ocean, a suspicious loss in the waves, a riveting treasure hunt, and surprise after surprise, how could anyone not want to read this novel?"

~Alice Kuipers
author of Life on the Refrigerator Door

"Loved this book and can't wait for the next one."

~Helen Escott
bestselling author of Operation: Wormwood

"It's been a while since I've read an entire book in one day, but…Whenever I tried to put it down, it would call out to me, luring me back like a siren's song."

~Ali House
author of The Six Elemental & The Fifth Queen

"Call of the Sea seamlessly weaves together the hardships and humour of rural Newfoundland life with a fantastical storyline that will leave you wanting more. This book will not disappoint."

~Lauralana Dunne
author of Ashes

The early years of **Xander Drew** as he struggles with the evils of his small rural hometown of Coral Beach, Maine. Cursed with the heart of the Womb and the gift of seeing the world around him for what it really is, Xander must learn the hard lessons about the nature of humanity to traverse the minefield of criminals, gangs, and abusers that stand between him and ultimate happiness -- but most of all that **sometimes it takes a monster, to catch a monster.**

"THE WRITING OF ITS GENERATION- - VISUAL, TO-THE-POINT AND IN-THE-MOMENT."
- The Northeast Avalon Times

The Coral Beach Casefiles series by Matthew LeDrew:

For more information, please visit

www.engenbooks.com

Infinity

The world is changing, and we have to change with it. That was the one thing that Victor was really sure of when he started looking for special people: people who could change the possibilities of the future from something certainly grim... to something *infinitely* positive.

Now four unsuspecting people from different backgrounds and walks of life have been thrown into the mix together, and nothing will ever be the same. But there's a difference between hoping for a better world and actually having one, and there will always be resistance to change.

Book One: Infinity (October 2010)
Book Two: The Tourniquet Reprisal (October 2012)
Book Three: Exodus of Angels (April 2016)
Book Four: Garden of the 8th Circle (August 2020)

Related Books:
　　　　　　light|dark (April 2012)
　　　　　　Roulette (October 2009)
　　　　　　The Long Road (May 2014)
　　　　　　Touch Your Nose (May 2018)

Written by the superstar team of Ellen Curtis (*Compendium*) and Matthew LeDrew (the *Xander Drew* series).

Destiny doesn't wait for anyone.

ABOUT THE
AUTHOR

Matthew Daniels is an author currently living in St. John's, Newfoundland.

He has over a dozen writing credits both locally and internationally, and his work had been featured in best-selling anthologies on five separate occasions. Stories include 'Grey Anatomy' in *Paragon*, 'Where With All' in *All Borders are Temporary*, and too many stories to count in the *From the Rock* series.

In December 2019 he was named a member of the Engen Books Board of Directors.

His first novel, *Diary of Knives*, was released in January 2021.